The Lost Museum

The Amazing Adventures of Rebecca Quinto

Thomas Paul Severino

Thomas Paul Severino

The Lost Museum

The Amazing Adventures of Rebecca Quinto

Thomas Paul Severino

Copyright 2019

Pollywog Pond Communications, Fort Lauderdale

tomseverino.com

tomseverino100@gmail.com

Cover: Alexander the Great Founding Alexandria by Placido Costanzi, 1736 (Free Images.com)

ISBN: 978-1-7343753-1-2

Also by Thomas Paul Severino

The Kayne Sorenson Mysteries: The Quartet of Blood

Seed Blood

Tribal Blood

Stage Blood

Ancient Blood

The Amazing Adventures of Rebecca Quinto

The Frozen Diva

The Lost Museum

The Lost Museum

For all who fight for truth and justice

in the most unexpected ways.

Thomas Paul Severino

The Lost Museum

Remember, upon the conduct of each depends the fate of all.

-- Alexander III of Macedon

Thomas Paul Severino

Prologue: The God of the Ptolemies

Alexandria, Egypt, 282 BCE

The Pharoah coughed. The spasm wracked his body, and the cloth the servant brought to his mouth reddened with more blood. The Queen rose from his desk and started towards him, but he motioned her back into her place.

He turned on the royal bed and spoke to his son and co-ruler of Egypt,

"Hear the wish of a dying man and your father, my son."

The young prince took the hand of the older man. "What is it, my Lord?"

Despite his near-death condition, the Divine Ptolemy I Soter roared, "Make those damned priests out there stop that infernal chanting. Send them away."

The prince of Egypt gave a hand signal, and the servant went into the corridor. The dirge stopped instantly.

The King coughed again. "That damn incense will kill me before whatever it is that is killing me kills me."

The returning servant spoke softly to the Queen, who said, "My lords, the King's doctors are insisting...."

Again, the Pharoah rasped with aggravation. "No doctors. That time is past. Bernice, I want to be here with the three of you– just you, Philadelphus, and my friend Euclid. The entire Kingdom knows that the Pharaoh will soon travel to meet the sun god, Ra. It is ordained. The royal mortuary boat has been prepared to bring me to the Hall of Maat for the judgment of my soul."

He looked at each of them in turn and then continued, "I am aware that this journey is about to begin, and so are the three of you. It is the will of the gods. But I am not ready. My conscience weighs heavy. I will be barred from the Kingdom of Osiris unless I can purge myself of the guilt I bear."

Ptolemy II Philadelphus applied a cool compress to his father's fevered brow. The King spoke again to his wife.

"Bernice, continue reading from the Chronicles. Go back to the beginning– the invocation of the goddess and the attribution of authorship."

The Queen bent over the large scroll on the desk in the royal bedroom. She read the words written so many years before by the young Macedonian, now Pharoah of Upper and Lower Egypt.

> Hear me, Divine Clio, daughter of Immortal Zeus, Proclaimer Goddess, clear-eyed Muse of History, and bestower of Fame. I, Ptolemy, brother of Alexander, sing of his glorious campaign to conquer the world. I sing of his great deeds and accomplishments.

The mathematician and friend of the King interrupted, "Great Ptolemy, you were the friend of the God Alexander, a member of the Royal Companions and served as a General throughout his conquests. Your history is a straightforward and honest account. There is no guilt for which you need to atone on your deathbed."

The King gazed into the space above him as if searching for a divine presence in these his last moments. He spoke to invisible phantoms gathering near the royal bed.

"Yes, yes, my account is accurate. Your accusations are false. May Alexander himself attest to the sincerity in my heart."

He grew even more feverish in his rant. "I could not part from you, my Lord and my God. You wanted to be buried at Siwa, where the oracle confirmed you as the son of Zeus. Those idiots, Perdiccas and the rest, wanted to bury you in Macedonia, in Aegae, next to your father."

The dying King suddenly became lucid. He turned to those attending him. "That idea was an abomination to Alexander, for he truly hated Philip."

The Queen skipped ahead in the Chronicles.

> The idea came to me a few days after the death of the King. The embalmers had arrived from Egypt, and the Generals were formulating their plan for the cortege to march to Macedonia. That is when I knew that I would

10

steal the body of the god and bring him to Sacred Egypt.
Thus began the War of the Generals, the *Diadochi*.

"Alexander lies below us in the Sema, my Lord. You were wise to bring him here. The one who possesses the Divine Alexander can never be judged anything but the rightful ruler of his legacy."

The king looked at the speaker, struggling to remember who he was. His mind wandered along the interface between life and death. Finally, he recognized the great teacher and author of the *Elements*.

"Master Euclid, have you and my son completed the plans for the Library?"

The Master of Geometry raised up and walked to the wall where the plans for the campus of the Great Library of Alexandria were hung.

"Yes, my Lord, Ptolemy. You approved them over a year ago, and construction is underway to create a campus of great knowledge with no rivals throughout the world. See here, the Library itself and the housing for the scholars, the spaces for instruction, The Great Hall of the Treasures, the gymnasium, the ambulatories, as suggested by Master Aristotle, the Walking Philosopher-- the Gods forbid he should sit still while teaching. Also, please note the proximity of the complex to the harbor for receiving the books and artifacts...."

"And the centerpiece, Father – the Sema, the Tomb of the Great Alexander."

The Pharoah reached for the hands of his heir. "Never, my son. Never. Alexander can never leave Egypt and this dynasty. "

Philadelphus tried to calm his father, who was slipping again into delirium.

"My Lord, ease your mind. You brought the god to Egypt to safeguard the eternal rule of this family. The Ptolemies will rule this Land of the Gods forever. There is no shame in that. You die having a united and stable country that enjoys divine favor because of the presence of the Glorious Alexander. You, Father, are 'Soter,' the Savior of the Land of Egypt."

Barely able to speak now, Ptolemy persisted as he gestured to the plans behind the master of mathematics. "The safety features... for the books... the treasures... the sarcophagus itself...."

Bernice came to the bedside of her spouse and settled him back on the pillows. As her son nodded, she assured the dying king, "Great Ptolemy, my dear husband, give ease to your soul and mind. Master Euclid, the Royal Architects, our son, who is your namesake— they have done it all according to your will. The Great Library rises and will be safeguarded against all destruction. It is your eternal legacy."

"Yes, Father. Your great thievery will forever bestow upon us the blessings of the Gods. There is no shame there. Alexander would agree. No power on earth will take him from Egypt."

Lord Ptolemy, Son of Horus and Master of the Two Lands, could speak no more. He looked into the eyes of his wife and mother of the next Pharoah.

Bernice understood. She gave the command.

Beneath the gaze of his enormous, granite effigy as the founder of the dynasty, the servants carefully bore Ptolemy's litter down through the royal enclosure to the crypt of the Soma. The beautiful goddesses that lined the walls seemed to fan the feverous monarch with their outstretched wings. The hieroglyphs before the steps down to the crypt announced, "Nothing is lost that is under the protection of the Gods."

The litter bearers set the throne of the King on top of the giant stone scarab before the gold and glass tomb. The family of the Pharoah drew close to the sarcophagus.

Ptolemy I Soter would come to the end of his life gazing on the body of the Divine Alexander...

... which was destined to rest in this place forever.

Chapter One: Sherlock

Miami Beach, Florida. The Present

The man stood behind Rebecca and hauled her up from her seat by pulling on her upper right arm. Her chair toppled over as she spun up and into his arms reaching over his shoulders into a passionate back-bending kiss. She grabbed the back of his head with one hand and pressed their faces together. Their combined ardor was so intense that the man's nose came off.

Still, she held the lip lock, grabbing forcefully onto the interloper's body as he dropped his grip and became the object of inappropriate behavior rather than its perpetrator. They were a bit of a spectacle at the popular "A Fish Called Avalon" on Miami's South Beach.

Mark Gadarn, Rebecca's partner, cursed in Welsh and reached for his crutches and the man who had attacked his woman.

"Ffyc! Rydych yn fab i ast!"

The third occupant of their outdoor table, Mary Chaffee, jumped up and knocked over a waiter, spilling their cocktails onto the sidewalk. Around them, diners, waitstaff, and strollers on Ocean Drive stopped to gawk.

Rebecca continued a ferocious makeout with the stranger briefly. She pushed him back and stooped to retrieve his nose.

"Darling, you are going to need a stronger brand of spirit gum and hardier nose putty if you are going to throw an intense make-out session with this hot woman. And more use of the hands, bud. Really get into it."

The lipstick-smeared intruder attempted to straighten his clothing but was confounded with laughter. He peeled off the remains of his face and flopped into the fourth chair at the table.

"Hashtag Me Too, girlfriend."

"Oh fuck that, Kayne, you started it. Gotta be able to take it as well as give it."

Mark's open mouth practically had his lower jaw on the table.

Kayne Sorensen, professor of psychocriminology and world-renowned consulting detective, jumped back up and bent into the head and arms of his best gal pal's man and his friend, Mark Gadarn – an award-winning and now very bewildered journalist for CNB. The interloper flopped back his arch of black bangs from his forehead, took a deep breath, and said, "Who are you calling a 'son-of-a-bitch,' mate with all that Welsh talk? My people may be convicts from Botany Bay, Australia, but we'll match any Welshie in the boxing ring."

They man-smooched again.

"How's the leg, lad, and how soon before we can we mix it up in the fights? I need a good bout to clear my head." Kayne popped fists up.

"Coming along, bud. I will be ready to take you down in style very soon. We're talking old man Kayne Sorenson kissing some canvas – a lot. Not to mention my arse."

Rebecca frowned.

Kayne switched his attention. "Cheers, Mary, my gal? Keeping the Special Agents in line? The Feds, mate. Hell of a whole handful."

Mary reached for her good friend. "Oh my God, Kayne. So good to see you. What brings you all the way from San Francisco?"

As a very confused waiter approached, Rebecca said, "Just do another round, Patty, and put it on his bill. The guy with the rubber bits all over his face here. He'll have a Hibiki rocks." She motioned for Kayne to lean forward as she peeled off the remaining pieces of his disguise and wiped off the blood-red lipstick smears.

Mary turned to the astonished diners and spectators and did a comic, "Nothing to see here, folks. All good. Please go on about your business." She flashed them a soup spoon as if it were a law enforcement badge.

"Ow, have a care, my girl. Ya bruised up my lip already with that crazy girl kissin'. Leave some flesh on my mouth. Ouch."

He took her compact and checked his look. Again, he smoothed back his pesky forelock.

To the now lipstick-replacing Rebecca, Kayne said, "How did you know?"

"I saw you checking us out from across the street."

She put down her make-up bag and looked at her loving friend. "Kayne Darling, if you are going to be the Master of Disguise you aspire to be, two things: The ADHD – so apparent. You snap that head around like a squirrel checking out a mountain of acorns. Focus."

Her three dinner companions laughed. Mark said, "Yep, like a priest in a locker room of hung footie jocks."

Kayne did a trollish, sloppy tongue swipe. "Now ya talkin'. Hot Aussie rules footballers – sex on a stick, mate."

Rebecca said, "And this." She reached over and pulled on his bangs. "Always fusing with the signature tell. Hand me my scissors from my bag, Kayne, and let your Rebecca fix this once and for all."

He gently pushed back her hand. "Bollocks, ya mug. It's my personality. Let's not forget it was a member of your sex that took the clippers to Samson. Strong bull to wuss in a quick snip snip. Keep your hair makeovers to yourself, Delilah."

Kayne pulled his long black locks out of his man bun. His wavy mane reached to the nape of his neck, completing a beautiful, savage look. He reached for a comb and untangled it a bit.

"Oh, and I forgot. They don't make the rubber facepieces that would smooth out those Katherine Hepburn cheekbones – like the fuckin granite cliffs at Yellowstone."

It was now her turn to rake through her long chestnut hair, adding a bit of a hair flip to emphasize her smart-alecky demeanor.

Mark said, "OK, as long as you knew… 'cause that was totally…."

"Absolutely, Darling. My loose woman ways ended when I met you, handsome. Have no fear."

She took his hand with much affection.

"Well, this man always appreciates a walk on the slutty side when we get to...."

He let the comment hang there as a tease, and she took the bait.

"All in how you play it in the next few hours, hunky boy."

Mary said, "God, I so need a cigarette when you three get your sexy on."

Her companions laughed. The Special Agent for the FBI continued, "So, what's the deal, professor? You... here. What's going on? Pretty sure it's gonna involve my office sooner or later. And how's Nick?"

The drinks arrived, and they toasted to friendship, quick healing, and passionate, enduring love. Mark took the opportunity to kiss the hand of the woman he so very much loved.

Kayne relaxed a bit and said, "I was in Lima this month on a consult for the OSCE, the Organization for Security and Cooperation in Europe. I ended up here in South Florida because I needed to get with some of my old academic colleagues at Florida Global University as a part of that case. Still, something came up that I wanted to bring to Rebecca. Also, this was an excellent opportunity to get with you all."

He passed a business card to the Head Curator and CEO of the Fritcher Museum of Art in Fort Lauderdale.

"Give the woman a call, my girl. I think it's another adventure of major importance." He took a hefty swig of his Japanese whiskey and focused just over her left shoulder. Someone not too far away watched the group, and the professor-turned-consulting detective observed his mark surreptitiously.

Friends can tell when there is trouble. Rebecca and Kayne went back to the days when they were fresh out of graduate school, on the loose in Europe, and eager to take on the world of crime and injustice. They had been partners on a few compelling cases and confidants in carousing and international intrigue.

Mark motioned for the hovering server to return in a bit. They were not ready to order, and he could sense that the conversation was about to get somewhat more critical. Mary leaned in for the crucial moment.

Kayne caught the tenor of the interest of his friends and decided to take a step back. Shifting uneasily, he looked at his wrist and said, "I have interrupted your evening long enough, and I need to get gone. It sure was..." He attempted to rise as he tossed back the rest of his cocktail but was unsuccessful. He lowered the glass back to the table. A perceptible tremor took over his left hand.

"Yeah, yeah, yeah. Sit your Aussie arse down, Kayne."

Rebecca continued with one word. It was spoken with sincere concern.

"Nick."

Kayne attempted to conceal his shaking by lowering his hand to his lap below the table. He said nothing for a moment, getting stuck in Rebecca's stare like visual quicksand. Then Kayne began to restlessly look around at the clamor and activity of the busy restaurant. The professor with the rock-star good looks took a deep breath and choked up slightly as he responded.

"Yeah, so he gets out of hospital in a couple of weeks, UCSF Medical Center. Best treatment we could find outside of a VA facility, and he seems to be progressing.

"Post Traumatic Stress Disorder seems to be the diagnosis, but we are in the early stages of determination. The psychological and physical effects of our case in Australia appeared to have taken their toll on the lad."

The three other diners were frozen in their gesture to sip their cocktails. They exchanged shocked looks. Suddenly, Kayne was up, out of his chair, and across the street.

Rebecca said, "Nick."

Chapter Two: Mark
Miami Beach, Florida

"The disguise was not solely for our benefit. No way I believe that. Be right back; I'm gonna make a few calls. I think our boy is in trouble."

Mary Chaffee took up her cell phone and left the table. She crossed Ocean Drive and made some calls from the walkway between the beach dunes.

Mark could see in Rebecca's face a conflict regarding their friend. He reached for her hand as she brought her gaze up to his.

"What?"

"Your problem is, Rebecca, you have no poker face. I strongly suggest you proceed carefully."

"And your trouble is you read my mind too easily."

"Comes with the territory. I am a mind reader and very accomplished at interpreting body language."

Mark entwined their fingers and kissed them a bit.

"Rebecca, I know you want to save whatever this is with Kayne and Nick, but... well, two things: give them a bit of space to work this all out, and second, if and when he needs you on the case, Kayne will ask."

They sat in silence. Rebecca pondered, and Mark squirmed slightly, attempting to scratch inside his leg cast with a fork.

"Tell me, Beautiful."

"Mark, you know I miss them-- the adventures and the fun, even the danger. Since they left, I have thought about them often."

"Yeah, I have them to thank for our first meeting. Remember the gala?"

"Unforgettable, but I thought you were there to cover the exhibit. No?"

"Rebecca, this journalist does not do the high society stuff."

Mark did a chest thump.

"Man of action, this guy. Trouble and strife are my meat and potatoes. Show me where the action is. In Syria, they used to call me 'The Daredevil'."

Rebecca began to remonstrate, "OK, so first, the Museum's work is not fluff, tough guy. Education and raising social consciousness is as rough and noble as it gets. Sometimes, anyway."

She added with dripping sarcasm, "I just love when you unleash your hyper-male bullshit – all muscle and testosterone. Save all of that for your just-for-fans videos."

"Or for when I compromise your nubile virginity?"

They both said the exact same thing at the same time.

"Too late."

As they both laughed, Rebecca said, "Circle back, Mark... the Kayne and Nick connection. I had always thought that our meeting that night was a coincidence."

Mark shrugged.

"I had been interested in Kayne for a long time, but he was forever dodging my attempts to meet and do a story on him. I wanted to do a story on the scandal within the Japanese Imperial family. Kayne was instrumental in resolving that mess and keeping it all too quiet."

Rebecca said, "Becoming media fodder would have significantly hindered his consulting work. He is extremely adamant about not being in the public eye, something he and Nick disagree on, but go on."

Mark took a swig of his beer and continued, "I had also been after Nick for an interview on the Wilton Manors murder case. Word on the street was that he and the great detective were bunk buddies, but I wanted the gruesome story, not the private lives stuff. So, I flat-out asked him for a VIP ticket to the gala.

"' What's it worth to you?' he says. So, I bet the cocky little fucker I could beat him in three outta five rounds."

"Great. Get to the part where I am the prize, ya big Neanderthal."

"We actually went seven, and it was called a draw. But, cop boy came up with the ticket anyway, and that…."

Mark took Rebecca's hand and kissed it lovingly.

"… is how I met you. Then there was Aspen, and Eastern Europe, and Australia, and … and … nights and days of passion…. "

Each "and" was punctuated with a kiss. Rebecca ran the fingers of her other hand through his hair.

Mark added, "I do like those guys. I will say that – true blue and brave as fuck. Kayne is a freaking legend, Beautiful."

Mary returned.

"So, he's playing this way below the radar, folks. International intrigue as usual. Kayne is so hard to get any intel on. My sense is to back off until he calls the Agency in."

She resumed her seat.

Mark gave a "When-I'm-right-I'm-right" face.

Rebecca lifted both hands up in surrender. "OK, OK. I certainly have enough to do with the Museum. But I want you both to know, should they need help, I'm going to California or wherever on the next plane."

Mark said, "Got it. Let's order. I am so hungry, I could eat the ass off a Welsh polecat without any salt."

Thomas Paul Severino

Chapter Three: Pandora
The Fritcher Museum of Art, Fort Lauderdale, Florida

"UPS about twenty minutes ago. The packing slip is on your desk. Sorry, Boss. That's all I know."

"Thanks, M. Security scans check out?"

"Yes, ma'am. No metal or liquid. The crate is marked 'Books,' but …."

"So, let's see what we got here."

Rebecca stepped back as her assistant, Micah Valez, removed the small hand truck from the crate. He used a hammer to carefully open the wooden top of the packing box. Together, they lifted the wooden chest from its container and placed it on the conference table.

Rebecca stepped to her desk, opened a recess in the side, and switched off the security camera in the conference room.

The artifact was a 3' by 3' by 4' container with a border of cobras, each crowned by a sun disc, on the barrel-shaped top and resplendent with renderings of ancient Egyptian deities on the flat, four sides. The paint and gold leaf were peeling on the hieroglyphics and most of the intricate carvings. The base of the chest was four short legs painted black. There were small, curved handles just below the lid.

"Micah, please get Skylar up here. We need him in this."

Micah stepped to the office phone, and Rebecca punched the details on the tracking slip into her phone to see if she could find out who sent the mysterious chest and from where.

"Holy shit. Samarkand. Who do we know in Uzbekistan that would send this?"

Micah shrugged.

Dr. Skylar al-Mahdi was an expert Egyptologist studying in the US. Rebecca referred to this young protégé as a loaner from the Museum of Egyptian Antiquities in Cairo. As the dapper professor stepped off the elevator, he was accompanied by the museum's Curator of Antiquities,

Elizabeth King, also fashionably dressed, an organizational standard set by the CEO. Both looked surprised at the object on top of the conference table.

Rebecca stepped back and said, "Do it up, folks. Gimme all you got."

Al-Mahdi took a pair of nitrile gloves from his coat pocket, as did his colleague. The conservators examined the outside of the treasure. The Egyptian spoke first.

"From the last dynasty of ancient Egypt, the Ptolemies – the rulers during the Hellenistic period. The design is from a former age, however. It is a burial chest used to protect belongings needed for the afterlife. The wood is *Ficus Sycomorus* – used for coffins and canopic boxes. Notice the brick-like assembly of the wood forming the box. The surfaces were covered with gesso and then painted and gilded in the designs you see."

Elizabeth added, "The ancients never used the wood of the sycamore fig when length was necessary, like for beams and planks. This material was used for small decorative objects, palace furniture, and containers. Notice the coarse grain and spongy texture. So, you get this amazing brickwise construction with these intricate dovetails and mortises."

Rebecca commented, "My first thoughts were Lebanon cedar."

Dr. al-Mahdi responded, "Cedar is coniferous, producing a very dense wood and would have been imported. This is definitely deciduous and native to the Nile Delta, Upper Egypt. The hasp fastening the cover and the handles are bronze. Superb metalwork– matching pairs of scorpions."

Micah sat at the conference table, taking notes on his laptop. Rebecca pressed a button on the conference table, and the room's glass walls turned opaque, ensuring privacy. Micah spoke into his mobile, and two very fit security guards arrived within minutes. Rebecca asked them to stand just outside the door.

She turned her attention back to the examining experts who poured over the chest. She asked, "Design?"

The Egyptologist inspected the markings covering the top of the chest. He said, "These are prayers begging protection for the dynasty of Ptolemy I Soter, the Macedonian Pharoah and his descendants, Ptolemy II

Philadelphus, and so on." Micah made notes as the pair carefully lifted and turned the artifact.

Elizabeth pointed to the double image of the scorpion-headed goddess who stretched out her arms on the rounded cover. She said, "This is the goddess Selket. Her cult was popular in the Western Delta. She is the deity of protection. She rules over all poisonous creatures.

"Notice the beautiful carving has traces of gold leaf overlay. Selket is sensuously draped with a pleated linen dress. Her eyes and brows are lined with black. A cloth headdress supports her scorpion crown."

Rebecca said, "The funeral regalia of Tutankhamun had four statues of goddesses protecting his canopic shrine. Are we to presume there are jars of preserved royal body parts within?"

Elizabeth said, "No, ma'am. This is definitely not a canopic shrine. It is too small. And it is most likely not royal. There is no depiction of the exploits of the monarch, which one would usually find had this chest come from the tomb of a king or a queen of Egypt."

Skylar said, "My colleague is correct. This is most likely a utilitarian piece used to store something valuable. Please observe the images under the outspread arms of the goddess. This one is Ptolemy. The image's dress and headpiece identify the Pharoah. He is offering incense to someone on a horse– this individual. Notice the lion's head, which crowns him-- very unusual."

"Why do you say that?"

"The designers seem to have been a bit conflicted with the imagery. While the structure and the form of the prayers evoke the culture of the early dynasties, the pharaonic markings and the mounted deity here are definitely from the beginning of the Hellenistic Period, third century BCE. The civilizations begin to blend classic imagery. It is cultural amalgamation--when two or more cultures blend."

He continued, "This is Thoth. He is the god of writing, magic, and wisdom. His name in the old language is Djehuty or 'He Who is Like the Ibis.' Hence, the depiction of the god's head in the form of the sacred bird is associated with wisdom. The preponderance of his image, as well as these prayers to the god, are significant."

He paused to examine the markings which accompanied the renderings of the god.

"I would need more time with this, but these seem to be incantations beseeching guidance and protection."

He turned the chest and, without touching it, traced a finger up and down the rows of hieroglyphics.

"Here it says, '...Divine son of Horus, it is you who created the branches of knowledge and the literary arts...'"

He traced the vertical lines of writing.

"So, this is the glyph for law, this for magic, and these are philosophy, science, religion, and writing, respectively."

He continued, "It says, 'O, Lord of Divine Words and Sacred Scribe who records history... we beg justice... of your consort, Seshat....' There is damage here, but the prayer goes on to say, '... we ask her to keep these words in her immortal library and protect them in earthly ones....' The rest is missing."

"Sky, authenticity?"

"Most probably an original, but chemical and physical tests on the materials will verify the date of this piece."

The professor now used a wooden pointer to indicate the figure astride the rearing horse carved on the top.

"Ms. Quinto, you do realize who this is, correct?"

Rebecca looked close, raised her eyes to her colleague, and shook her head.

"There is only one figure from this period of antiquity, which is typically depicted on his steed crowned with the lion's head. The lion's golden skin was worn by the kings of Macedonia. It is reminiscent of the Nemean Lion killed by Heracles."

Rebecca said, "Alexander."

The four looked at each other with the same stare of amazement.

"There's more."

Al-Mahdi brought the group's attention to the sides of the wooden chest. "It is a temple complex in Alexandria. See? There is the harbor lighthouse. This side shows one building in particular."

Rebecca said, "The Great Library of Alexandria."

The tension in the room continued to build.

"You mentioned prayers."

Elizabeth King read the logographic script along the edge of the top.

"To all, mortals and gods alike, I, Selket, say my protection lasts through life, into death and beyond. I work divine magic with my scorpions at my heels. Beware ye, the unjust for death shadows you and may come swiftly with my stinging touch...."

"The suspense is killing me, folks." Rebecca donned a pair of gloves and stepped to the chest. She undid the hasp and slowly lifted the cover.

Immediately, she lowered the lid and fell to the floor.

Chapter Four: Deathstalker
Broward Health Medical Center, Fort Lauderdale, Florida

"Come on, Beautiful. Open up those gorgeous brown eyes... There ya go. There ya go. That's right. Hello... hello."

Mark held the patient's hand that was not plugged into the IV. He reached up and moved her hair off her forehead, gently caressing her cheek as he did."

"Back among the living, Rebecca. We got you."

"Ohhh ... Mark, what are you doing in Egypt?"

"Man, you are so crazed, Beautiful. Got to get us some of that drug for playtime. It packs a wallop, to be sure, and...."

He left off, unable to finish.

The nurses and PAs moved around the ICU unit, reading monitors and checking vitals.

"Think we are past the crisis, Sir, but it may be too soon to tell."

Mark sighed and nodded. "Yeah, thanks."

Rebecca released his hand and touched a tear that had crested his lower lid and had begun a roll down his cheek. Mark fought back a series of huge sobs, clutching at her hand. He pulled in for a nuzzle. It seemed like he was not going to let her go.

Rebecca's speech was slightly slurred, but she managed, "How long?"

Mark turned his wrist. "Three days and six and one-half hours."

"I had a dream, and you were there."

"Sorry to interrupt. I am going to test the paralysis. Are you able to move your lower body?"

Rebecca attempted to twist in the bed but was unsuccessful.

29

"No."

The nurse moved the blankets and ran her finger along Rebecca's lower leg and the sole of her foot. No response.

"Any feeling here?"

"None."

"Not to worry. We suspect that when you were admitted, the venom had paralyzed you from the neck down. But because you were unconscious, we have no way of verifying that. Regardless, feeling, muscular response, and total movement should return in a few days as the poison works its way out of your system. At this time, your arms and upper body seem to be fine."

"Full recovery?"

"Yes. Definitely. We need to keep Ms. Quinto for observation for a few days."

Another attending medic spoke up.

"The poison dose was concentrated-- meant to kill. If it were not for your staff, we would not have been able to identify the toxin quickly enough to save your life."

"The venom of the World's Deadliest Scorpion, the Deathstalker, intensified. The warning of the goddess Selket must be heeded at all times."

The voice of doom came from Skylar al-Mahdi as he and Micah were admitted into the unit. Micah stood close to the bed, watching his boss come out of her stupor. Rebecca signaled to him that the discussion of the mysterious delivery was not appropriate until they were alone. She spoke weakly to the attending nurse practitioner.

"Darling, would it be possible to spend some time with my staff? I will only need a few minutes."

"Yes, Ms. Quinto, but I am afraid that you will have a few visitors soon. The police have been asking…."

Mark spoke up.

"Any possibility of a private room presently? The matters surrounding Ms. Quinto's incident require the highest security, I'm afraid."

The woman seemed to melt at the request from the gorgeous Mark Gadarn. She was a huge fan of the hunky journalist with the matinee idol looks. His unconventional reporting and risk-taking had attracted worldwide attention. She came out of her semi-trance and attempted a professional response.

"Yes, sir. I will see to it immediately." She dashed away.

Rebecca attempted a smirk and said softly, "Such power you have over women, ya big lug." She weakly caressed Mark's hand.

Micah thought, *Not to mention the men.*

Mark smiled for the first time in days. His vanity was in high gear.

He faked, "Yeah, but you know it is such a curse."

***

Micah said. "It was a spring mechanism on the chest's closure. Despite the gloves, you got a jab in the heel of your palm. Bam, you went down."

Skylar al-Mahdi looked into the night skies over Fort Lauderdale from Rebecca's private hospital room window. He wore the intrigue of the attempted murder like a cloak. The effect was a dramatic image of one who seemed to channel supernatural forces. His stare betrayed deep secrets, but he was able to switch to an affable cordiality when the occasion called for it. This was not one of those times.

Mark was quick to pick up on the intensity of the professor, scientist, and Egyptologist. *This dude knows more than he is letting on.*

"So, who are you, guy? What's your story? Gimme the low down 'cause I want to know why this woman almost died three days ago.

"P.S., you are creeping me out with the heavy evil sorcerer vibe. Has anyone ever mentioned that to you? Can't figure out if you are a supervillain or on the side of the good guys."

"We are all very complicated persons, Mr. Gadarn. Nothing is quite what it seems. It is not my intention to make you or anyone feel uncomfortable."

Rebecca broke in rather sleepily, "Mark, Doctor al-Mahdi is a scholar-on-loan from the Egyptian Museum in Cairo. The Fritcher is planning a... an...."

Micah completed her sentence, " ... exhibit on Ancient Egypt. Doctor al-Mahdi is an expert on the period of the Hellenistic Dynasty...."

Al-Mahdi interrupted the Museum's Executive Assistant with a tinge of self-importance that indicated that no mere staffer could adequately represent his credentials.

"The last period of ancient Egyptian self-rule before becoming the vassal state of the Roman Empire. I did my doctoral work at Cairo University, studying with the famous Nobel Laureate, Taher Barakat. My thesis has been recognized as the definitive work on the archaeological remains connected to the reign of Cleopatra VII, Philopator, the last active ruler of the Ptolemaic Kingdom of Egypt."

The tall Egyptian bowed slightly, having completed his introduction to the inquiring member of the Fourth Estate, a group he obviously disdained. He turned back to the window and addressed the reflection and the darkness of the night.

"If you have no further need of me, Ms. Quinto, I will take my leave. I am pleased that you are recovering. If there is anything for which my assistance is required, please do not hesitate to give me a call."

Skyler al-Mahdi did not wait for Rebecca's response. He bowed and leFort

Mark said, "On his way to open the abyss of Hell and unleash his vassal demons. Dude on a mission of darkness and evil...."

He turned to the occupant of the hospital bed, saying, "Beautiful, how do you come up with these weirdos?"

But Rebecca was asleep. Mark checked the monitors to see that it was just, indeed, a restorative nap. Micah made motions like he was going to leave also. He stopped as a police officer, Special Agent Mary Chaffee, and another man softly entered the room.

"Hey, Mark, may we speak to you?" Mary made motions signaling they should move to another room.

Micah said, "Mr. G, I am gonna split. You got my number – day or night, cool?"

"Right, pal. Give Hud my best."

Mark reached for his cane and followed the group of three into an unoccupied room used for waiting families.

"How is she doing?"

"Very well, considering. The doctors are telling us that the paralysis is abating, and with rest and some meds, she will make a full recovery."

Mary said, "That is good. Great, in fact. How did this all happen?"

"I can get you over to the museum to see the case with the poison needle in its lock. It seems they took delivery of this box that was rigged to deliver some killer venom, and Rebecca took the bite."

The Special Agent said, "I will hook up with Micah in the morning and check out the object. I am texting him right now."

The police officer said, "Let him know to touch nothing."

"Been three days, almost four. Afraid you will not find much of a crime scene. But if I know Micah, he has things locked down. Officer …?

Mary said, "Sorry, Mark. This is Detective Don Rains, Fort Lauderdale, PD. I think you know …"

Mark snapped his fingers, "INTERPOL Officer Jürgen Mathias… Good to see you again, buddy." Mark did a shoulder bump-handshake with the smiling international law enforcer.

He said to the other two, "We worked together a while back. You saved my life, or did I save yours? I can't remember."

Mathias shrugged. His comments were laced with a German accent.

"Can't remember either, man, and am not sure if the world is the better for it either way. You still raising hell?"

"Always."

Mark looked at his friend, "So what brings INTERPOL to Fort Lauderdale? Lemme say that I never, never propositioned that Greek Prime Minister's daughter on that yacht. All evidence to the contrary notwithstanding. I swear…"

Mark's joke fell a bit flat as the three stared at him.

"What? Mary, what's up?

Officer Rains broke the tension.

"Mr. Gadarn, we are here to arrest Rebecca Quinto for trafficking in stolen antiquities."

Chapter Five: Queenie

Broward Health Medical Center, Fort Lauderdale, Florida

Ardella McQueen, "Queenie" to her friends, snapped her briefcase closed, flipped open her laptop, put her cell phone on stun, and sat back.

"OK, fellas and gals, show us what you got."

The feisty lawyer ran a hand through her braided extensions and cued up her laptop. The hospital room had been set up to host the meeting. Rebecca was in bed, and Mark and Micah were seated on either side of her. The three law enforcers sat at a table with Rebecca's legal counsel. Mary Chaffee wore an expression that suggested a bit of confusion regarding the entire affair.

"Whatever you got is pure bullshit, and you know it. Mary, you, of all of us, know this is a bogus setup. Rebecca was trained by your agency, for fuck sake." Mark was furious.

Mary Chaffee held up a hand. "Mark, let's just do this thing, OK? We'll look at the charges and decide what comes next, rationally and dispassionately."

Rebecca put a hand on her irate man but let Queenie do the talking.

The lawyer said, "Show me the tapes."

Officer Mathias stood and placed his laptop on the overbed table in front of Rebecca as Queenie joined for a review. "I'm sending the feed to both the laptops – yours also, Ms. ah…."

"McQueen. I'm the lawyer."

Jürgen Mathias registered no emotion at the slightly sassy response. He was late thirties, blue-eyed, and very German, from the mixture of blond hair touched with grey to the whisper of a Teutonic accent in his speech. He was very practiced in affecting a stoic demeanor – it went with the job. From his body type to his way of moving, the man gave off a military impression. He was a career international law enforcement officer, an academy boy from his late teens.

He introduced the video.

"INTERPOL has come into possession of some rather incriminating information. The tape shows Ms. Quinto in Tashkent, Uzbekistan, three weeks ago, being questioned by authorities regarding stolen artifacts brought into the country. These are the shots of her passport verifying her identity. The Uzbekistan authorities could not substantiate the allegation, so no evidence was obtained, and she was released."

Queenie made a noise, "Humph. So you got nothing."

"You will hold on, please. This is from the bullet train cameras, Tashkent to Samarkand. The suspect is seen delivering a wooden crate to the baggage area and taking possession in Samarkand. There, see—the black lorry. At the freight office, the customer was identified as an American woman, one Rebecca Quinto of Fort Lauderdale, the container's destination."

Jürgen Mathias continued, "Our agents in Uzbekistan had Ms. Quinto under surveillance for weeks. She entered and left the country four times in a month, staying a maximum of forty-eight hours during any one trip. In her travels, we believe she had interactions with these individuals linked to a smuggling ring, *Xudo Jangchilari*, The Fighters of God. They are criminals who specialize in the illegal sale of ancient treasures and in human trafficking."

He cued up some pictures of some very professional-looking thugs. They had the appearance of richly appointed businesspeople.

"We believe Ms. Quinto to be their 'fence,' for lack of a better term, for valuable antiquities. The group has ties to militia groups who need quickly available funds and lots of it.

"This is a clip from the Fritcher Museum's security system showing a night delivery of the crate from Samarkand. There is not much video showing the movement of the crate within the building. Except for..."

The video showed the elevator doors to the Executive Suite opening and Museum staff wheeling the box into Rebecca's conference room as Micah held the door. In the background, you could see Rebecca bending over her desk just before the cameras switched off.

Rebecca said, "I did that because....

Queenie made a loud throat-clearing sound, and Rebecca fell silent. An almost imperceptible signal passed between the two women. The lawyer signaled, *Say nothing, girl.*

"That's it?"

Mathias opened a manila envelope and distributed photos. Mary and Detective Rains remained silent.

"We have people on the inside following the smugglers. There is a fatal flaw in their organizational operations. They tend to entertain to the point that it gets noticed. The use of alcohol seems to be a factor – heavy drinking. Here is Ms. Quinto socializing with members of the ring. She is very recognizable in these photos. This set implies a very intimate relationship with the head guy, or should I say guys? She seems to be a popular agent for their ah, enterprise."

Mark snatched up the last set of photos and rifled through them. One could almost see the steam coming out of his ears. Rebecca took them one at a time from him but did not respond.

"And...?"

"We have an undercover agent that will testify to the allegations against Ms. Quinto. So, considering..."

Queenie held up her hand and stood up. She paced the room as if she were examining a hostile witness in a courtroom.

Rebecca and Mark exchanged a look. *Just watch this, bud. Ole Queenie is now going to demonstrate her reputation.*

"You watch many movies, Commander Mathias?"

Jürgen Mathias blinked at the question, almost tipped out of his nonplussed demeanor.

"Pardon me, but what...?"

"Hitchcock– one of his earliest and best. Henry Fonda... accused of a crime he did not commit. Tense action, suspense out the ass... trapped in a web of accusations and danger. Turns out it was a look-alike. Simple as that. *The Wrong Man*, 1956. Not to be missed."

She continued, "You see, I thought I was coming here today to help my client deal with an arrest, so we're going to chalk this one up to just an interrogation session. And I say that because you got shit. Do you understand what I am saying to you? Plain and simple."

Mary Chaffee tried to break into Mathias' stare with a WTF. Still, the INTERPOL officer was fussing with the files and the laptop– avoidance behavior.

Queenie stepped very close to the commander. She said, "Frankly, given your reputation as an international crime-fighter, I am surprised as hell with the flimsiness of your case. What did you expect? Have her taken out in handcuffs?"

This last question was directed to Special Agent Chaffee.

"Ms. McQueen, I must emphasize that the evidence at hand is highly incriminating, and I assure you...."

The lawyer put a hand on the shoulder of the INTERPOL officer and looked him in the eye.

"Please excuse me for interrupting you, Commander Mathias, but I will make this short. And to show my respect for you and your profession, I'm gonna tell you this very directly. Shame to embarrass any of you before the judges of the International Criminal Court."

Queenie tapped the laptop with a very long and very jeweled index fingernail as she said, "At best, and I use that word graciously, at best, you got some video of someone, supposedly my client, with what you claim to be stolen cultural artifacts, getting them out of the country of origin and into her place of business. Yet, you produce no shipping documents. How is that?"

Now, she tapped the photos.

"Next, you give us these pictures showing a very sexually liberated woman enjoying the company of a posse of international, boozehound, low-lives. And you make the claim that this also is my client... that she is a regular associate, if not a member, of a notorious smuggling consortium. Then, she goes and poisons herself with some bug shit to the point of a three-day coma and pretty extensive paralysis to throw you all off the scent."

38

She caught the German agent in a steely gaze and finished.

"So, listen up, double-oh-seven. You send me the times and dates for Ms. Quinto's alleged international activities. Then, I will meet again with you regarding some real allegations. You may expect witnesses for an iron-clad alibi."

She turned to wink at Mark and moved closer to Rebecca.

"C'mere, Europe, and bring those pictures. I got something to show ya."

Mathias did as he was told.

Queenie spread the most salacious pictures on the overbed table. She selected three of the naked women engrossed in very athletic sexual play with a group of men. The images featured clearly a very beautiful, bare female derrière.

"Nice ass, right folks?"

No response.

Queenie approached the patient.

"Come on, baby, no time to be shy."

Rebecca rolled onto her side, and Queenie, as delicately as possible, lifted the covers and parted the back of the hospital gown.

"This'll save us from having to do this at the International Court of Justice at the Hague."

Across Rebecca's lower back was a very distinct tribal tattoo.

"Seems to me you got the wrong ass, Hans Brinker. What do you think?"

Chapter Six: Bokken

Crunch Fitness, Oakland Park, Florida

"There is a saying in America, 'This shit ain't over.' Did I get it right, Marko?"

Mark smiled at the near-naked German, stripping off his secret agent togs for jock gear and gym wear. Only Jürgen Mathias called him "Marko." They went back pretty far, and the comfort level was easy and very close. Situations of high terror and peril had brought them together in the past.

"Yeah, Jürgs, you got the lingo correct, but before we go there, I just want to say you at some point, real soon, man. You and Rebecca need to get straight with each other. Shit, Dude. What were you thinking?"

"Marko, I gave in to pressure on this one. I am sorry I did not do more background on this. It is totally my stupidity, and I will make it right. Are we still good friends?"

"Yep, let's put this behind us. It sounds like there is some serious *Scheiße* going on here, and you'd do well to keep your friends close."

"Thank you, my friend."

OK, so let me say this, bro, you are keeping in great shape for a man your age. What are we talking about here, forty-five, fifty? When do they put you guys out to pasture, anyway? Do your turn, bud, show me that man-ass, dawg."

Jürgen flashed his butt to the rollicking Mark, who lightly swatted a near-miss with his cane.

"You need to bite me, Americano boy. I am a perfect specimen at only thirty-four years. Thirty-four, *Schwachkopf.*"

Crunch patrons in the locker room were trying not to stare at the playfulness of the two handsome jocks. Mark's walking cast gave him that injured sportsman look that many men found very appealing.

As they exited the fitness equipment area, Jürgen asked, "So, this was your invitation. What are we doing?"

"Sayin' this plainly, man, you major fucked up this morning. Good thing Rebecca doesn't hold grudges. What the fuck was that? Good thing we are buds."

Mark bent to lace one running shoe and added, "So, cause I am your bestie at the moment, I'm gonna arrange to fix your very mixed-up head with some intense physical activity. We train like warriors – talking free weights and lotsa cardio. And then... and then, and you will find you will owe me big for this one, my man. I got you a massage with Antonio in about twenty minutes."

The journalist's eyes sparkled as he continued, "He is a former Marine. He will beat the shit outta any tension you may have somatized from your interactions with the notorious Queenie and whatever else led up to the attempted framing of my woman."

He looked over his friend with a hand-on-chin move.

"But ... I think you are man 'enuf for Antonio."

Mark winked wickedly.

"Meantime, I can only do upper body with this crap on my leg, so I am working with my trainer. I need this so fuckin' bad. Between the attempt on Rebecca and my own issues at being hog-tied with this bum leg, baby boy needs to pump up and burn hot. Fuckin' A."

His last remark was accompanied by a hetero-alpha snarl, mocking the gym talk typical of the gymbots around them. Jürgen laughed.

The agent said, "There seems to be some action over at the MMA area. I am going to see if I can get a sparing round. They got the gloves I will need?"

"Yeah. Ask that guy right there. He is one of the trainers and will suit you up. Check on you later."

***

Karen Tracy loosened the walking cast on Mark's right leg. She supplemented her occupational therapy job with some personal training clients. She held his limb as he moved it through a series of rotations, pronations, and supinations.

"Walking on your cast increases circulation and healing of the broken bone. It also prevents bone mass loss."

The woman lowered Mark's leg and added, "You been to Lourdes, Gadarn? You are healing up with incredible speed. We need some medical journals documenting this."

"Not quite fast enough, Kare. I am going fucking nuts in this rig. Mark's a big man of action, you understand? I require speed, intensity, and incredible flexibility – you get me?"

She helped him adjust the cast, tightening the velcro. The trainer cuffed him, saying, "Is everything sex with you, Gadarn?"

He moved his hand to where he shouldn't have and leered, "Hell, I get that a lot. Oh hell, yes, just one frisky boy, thirty going on fifteen."

"Yeah, I remember when we were dating. It was pretty amazing. All the same, be-fuckin'-have." She laughed, and so did he.

She added, "A few more weeks, and you'll be Rebecca's studly again."

"Never implied that this was anything more than a speed bump on the highway to intense sexual fulfillment, so…."

She finished his comment, "… 'I am not her stud right now?' Yeah, yeah, yeah. You never change, do you, ya sex bomb? Your hijinks in the terror zone ain't slowing you down one iota in the bedroom, eh?"

Mark smiled an impish, caught-with-a-hand-in-the-cookie-jar expression and shrugged his shoulders.

"How is Rebecca doing, anyway? Word is she got into some trouble recently. My buds at the Medical Center were talking."

"All good. Making a full recovery. Coming home tomorrow or the day after. Hospitals are such bad places."

"Tell me about it. How was your workout?"

"Crushed it at Crunch, girl. Upper body warrior mode. I am a male dynamo." He did a double bi-flex and a t-shirt lift showing his sculpted abs.

Karen eye-rolled and responded, "Just go slowly, Beast Boy."

She added, "Cameron is working today, and I got you a massage in twenty minutes with him. Antonio is taken."

She handed him his cane and said, "Mark, I got two questions. Who is that hunky mess you arrived with, and is the man single?"

"Jürgs is an old friend, visiting for a spell. Lives in France, but he's German. Yeah, recently divorced – about a year."

"Mmm ummm. That's what really melts my butter, friend. Introduction. You know you owe me."

They were leaving the therapy room.

"Sure, just don't bring up the divorce. Jürgen's husband left him for an older man."

Karen Tracey turned and looked at her friend with a shit-eating grin on his face.

"Swell."

***

The would-be warrior wore a training mask, a respiratory device designed to strengthen breathing muscles and increase endurance. The black covering was strapped to his head so that only the athlete's eyes were unobstructed, dark, and mysterious. His wavy black hair was bound in a knot on the back of his head. The whole visual effect bespoke hardcore athlete.

Jürgen wiped the sweat from his upper body and did a fist bump with his boxing partner, then turned to Mark on the periphery of the martial arts training area of the fitness facility.

"Pretty impressive, yes, Marko?"

"Yeah, I am fuckin' dazzled. Dude is deadly."

The athlete was kneeling and balanced on the balls of his bare feet. He raised the bokken training sword high above his head. With elbows to the ceiling, he brought it down slowly– almost meditatively to create sweeping overhead cuts, side slices, and lower rips. His technique was measured with repeated, precise moves that indicated strength, balance, and concentration.

As Mark and Jürgen watched, the swordsman stood and positioned his left leg ahead, with the bokken held on his right side, tip to the ceiling. He reversed the position of his legs and brought the weapon down, to the side, and across – now right leg forward and bokken held on his left, a series of cuts filled with the beauty of trained martial arts movements.

"This man knows his craft. He reminds me of that Japanese assassin I had to face down in my work with the agency in the early years. You remember. We got him before he ever got near the Israeli Ambassador's wife. You had the exclusive interview once we detained him. It was creepy that he had asked for you by name, 'the up and coming boy journalist' he called you."

"How could I forget? The dude was like a machine. He had clockwork for insides and eyes that bore right through you. I still see the bastard in my nightmares."

The German agent stood behind his friend and reached forward to work his trapezius. Mark reacted warmly. "You see all of that, buddy? It's all in your head when you're as good as this guy is – total mind control. The body just follows along."

The athlete began to cross the room. He executed cuts, strikes, and blocks. He performed spins and knee drops with balletic grace, wielding his training sword in stunning arcs and circles. As he reversed his path, crossing to the other side of the room, a trainer engaged him for a spar.

They bowed and began the ancient dance of the Bushido warriors. The masked jock was by far superior to his opponent. He deflected the difficult-to-block thrust attacks with skill and accuracy. Then, facing the trainer, he completed a superb thrust block, catching his opponent's staff under his armpit and disarming him. One faux sword flew across the mat.

He turned his back to the disarmed opponent and executed a backward kill strike that stopped centimeters from the man's chest. The executioner screamed as he delivered the near-fatal blow. The trainer threw up his hands and arms, surrendering to the man's superior skill and laughing to relieve the tension.

They again exchanged the bow of respect, signaling the completion of the round. The warrior drew nearer his two spectators. He pulled off his sweat-soaked tank top and began to wipe his body down with a gym towel as he walked. An Arabic script tattoo on his left pectoral muscle twisted as he moved his upper body to hand his bokken to the trainer.

Removing his mask, he spoke to Mark.

"Mr. Gadarn, it is a pleasure to see you again. I hope that I have caused you some amusement with my unabashed display."

"Hey, bud. Had no idea you trained here, Doctor al-Mahdi."

***

"To answer your questions in reverse order…."

"Jürgs, my man, I've said nada here, bro." Mark spread his hands wide, palms up.

"Yes, but I read your thoughts, my friend. I anticipate your inquisitiveness. The years have brought much familiarity, my Marko."

"So, go for it."

"To your concerns about the Ninja man-- yes, he is an impressive master of strength and fighting skill. A man I would like to become better acquainted with should he prove to be innocent in the matters that concern my office at the present time."

"Translation: You wouldn't mind a sex-up or five. Provided the bull does not jettison you into the Quantum Zone."

"I am sorry. I do not get the reference."

"Just saying he is a *tödlicher Bösewicht* – a deadly villain. I honestly think so. Gotta watch him around Rebecca. Next?"

"Oh, yes. The Marko Wonderings, Number Two: The massage by the former Marine was the best I have had… lately. Now, I feel I am needing a cigarette but will end up settling for a nap."

Mark roared with laughter. "You horny dog. You have not changed, my man. Still lovin' to get laid."

Jürgen enjoyed the gentle mocking.

"And last?"

The military man turned the inside of his left palm to face his friend. Mark read a string of 10 numbers and a dash next to the name "Antonio."

"Scored, bud."

"As they say, let the games begin."

Thomas Paul Severino

Chapter Seven: The Feds

The Fritcher Museum of Art, Fort Lauderdale, Florida

Rebecca rolled off the elevator with the assistance of a museum guard. Micah held the door to her suite open. Mary Chaffee was seated at Rebecca's desk with another agent. As the CEO arrived in her wheelchair, Mary dismissed her colleague. Rebecca spoke to her assistant.

"Tell me."

"Boss, it's gone. Just where it went is a mystery. Ken Underworthy is on his way up here."

Rebecca looked at her FBI friend with an expression that said, *Fucked if I know …*

Mary did first things first.

"How are you feeling?"

"I am fine, some buzzing in my legs and feet, but all is working normally. Mark insists on the chair. Wanted me to stay home, but with the chest gone missing… well, here we are."

The Director of Museum Security entered the office and used a remote to turn on the large wall screen. Micah tapped the controls that made the window walls darken.

"Here it is …, and here it isn't. Into thin air, Ms. Quinto."

The group watched the arrival of the packing crate and Rebecca's move to shut down the security cameras.

Mary said, "Break it down, Micah. Step by step, including the last time you saw it."

Micah narrated, "I left the suite locked after the poisoning incident, and the glass wall darkened."

All eyes were on the young man.

"When the first responders left with Ms. Quinto, I locked the suite and the elevator selection when I exited on the bottom floor. All of the employees on this floor had gone. The next day, I opened only my office, and it was like that for the next three days while Rebecca was in the hospital.

"When your agents arrived to take possession of the artifact, I had them accompany me when I opened the CEO's office and unobscured the window walls. The chest was gone."

Director Underworthy asked, "And the cameras?"

"Mr. Underworthy, I left them off until I went into Rebecca's office on day three."

Mary asked, "Why? You forget."

Rebecca said, "Not bloody likely, Mary. Micah never forgets a thing."

"I thought that there may be evidence in that room regarding the assault that needed to remain undisturbed."

Mary raised her eyebrows and pursed her lips. She turned to Underworthy.

"Agent Chaffee, no, I never re-booted the exec's cameras or thought to check. I was unaware of the presence of the chest in the conference room. My mistake was in thinking that, as in previous instances, the disabled cameras in this area were not without precedent."

Mary now turned her questioning gaze to Rebecca, who shrugged. "Don't give me that look, Mary. Sometimes, there are goings-on here that require discretion."

Underworthy looked away, Micah looked down, and Mary looked for her cell phone.

"Yeah, this is Mary Chaffee. I want Jack Rains on this. Criminal investigation at the Fritcher. Full forensic crew... get them here ASAP."

She looked at the three in the suite.

"That bitch has gotta be here somewhere."

50

Chapter Eight: Catacombs
The Fritcher Museum Of Art, Fort Lauderdale, Florida

Few buildings in Florida have a basement, especially structures built so close to the river. The design of the Fritcher included three below-ground levels. Despite the reinforced structures of the building, underground space was used to protect the museum's treasures when a hurricane was imminent. The Fritcher's design employed the best construction technology for eliminating water intrusion and stabilizing the structure.

The hour was late. The Museum was closed. The two naked bodies alternated, bouncing against the narrow walls of the cubicle formed by the partitions in the lowest level of the "Catacombs." Their arms and legs entwined, mouths invading each other. An ancient Egyptian chest stood closed on the high research table, and the man slammed the woman on her back just beside it. He had lifted her off the floor into his arms. They were face to face, her legs wrapped around his torso, each swathed in sweat and a deep sexual flush.

She raised her hips up while clawing his muscular back, taking him deeper inside her. Elizabeth King begged her sex partner to ride her harder and deeper. She pounded on his upper body with closed fists as they rocked forcefully back and forth now on the table. She spit into his face and called him vile names-- words and phrases that came from a fire within, the voice of a sexual subconscious she was not aware of until this man and his savage mating.

"Give me the beast inside you... Ohhh, fuck! Show me the savage you truly are. Drive your body deep inside mine. Ohhh, God. Yes."

Skylar al-Mahdi arched up and then flexed his glutes and thighs, forward and back, in and out, back and forth, a powerful rhythm of fierce and primal mating. His face was masked by his loose mane of black hair. His lips curled in a savage sneer. With each deep entry, he roughly mocked her in a guttural-sounding ancient language. His eyes were the dead black of a pagan idol. His heavy breathing became deep growling as he amped up the coupling to overdrive.

The Egyptian's muscular arms lifted his upper body. He pinned her to the surface and slammed his hips up and under to maintain the final thrust position. The Arabic markings on his chest flashed with a sweat sheen. He roared and cried out in English as he climaxed.

"You are the whore of the devil."

Elizabeth King screamed as she followed him in a toe-curling orgasm, twisting her head from side to side as he attempted to stop her cries with his hands. Her naked ebony body seemed to glow with an ebbing sexual heat.

Al-Mahdi remained on top of her as they both breathed heavily and tried to recover, panting and shaking. He covered her mouth with his. Her body signaled the greedy insistence on a continuance of the stimulation she needed. The kiss said she would seek him again and again.

Then, as the dance subsided, he dismounted and helped her down. Silently, he reached into his gym bag for a towel which he gave to her. As she cleaned herself and dressed. He stood at his laptop, his body still naked and very wet. She looked at the muscled god with whom she played regularly in the catacombs.

While Lizzie knew she was under the spell of this hot male, there was something odd about their sex play. Her desire for him was unstoppable, brutal, and bestial, without any intelligence or reason. There was nothing she would not do to have him.

But it seemed that there was no genuine desire in him. Even his face was a mask loaded with tons of eye avoidance. When he advanced, it was with force and aggression, pure and simple. There was no passion, no abandonment to the purely and savagely physical. Each time, there was a part of him Skylar withheld. He made love as if out of obligation.

If I keep doing this over and over, it will eventually mean something to me, not just with this one, but with someone.

Skylar al-Mahdi was a man with much to prove, like so many men she took to bed. They were little boys, trying to use their manhood to show a side of them that was fake, insubstantially tough because that was what was expected. Often, she found that this was something that hung around the male psyche like a chained weight.

The exhausted Curator of Antiquities stepped closer as she finished dressing and ran her hands over his strong shoulders. She kissed the scratches on his back from their carnal play. With one hand, he reached back and caressed her, and she collapsed against him, trying to make sense of the passion that again consumed her.

Skyler turned halfway around and held her. He was now very tender and considerate, but there it was again-- a trace of cold detachment.

Get out. Get back to work. Get away from me. Please.

His words belied his thoughts. "Come, my dear, Lizzie, finish the last section of this scroll while I dress."

She nodded and took his place at the keyboard. On a larger PC monitor, he brought up an image of a papyrus. Pictographs filled the screen alongside a computer-generated translation. Dr. al-Mahdi stepped into his briefs while dictating the correction to the cyber interpretation. He reached for his dress shirt but left it open and untucked.

His assistant said, "This is Book Seven of the Sekhmet Scrolls, continuing with line eighty-seven:

The treasure safeguards failed to operate in time during the attack. The antechamber of the treasury was sacked by the invading mob. The cave in the escape route... [segment missing]. The scholars attempted to seal the main rooms and bring the treasurers into the Underworld Kingdom [of] Osiris, the one who brings rebirth as promised.

The academics held off the invaders and made many invocations to Ptah, who listens to prayers, and to the god, Shu, "He who rises up." [segment missing] Finally, we were able to descend into the dark realm with the body of the god and some of the authentic treasures of his reign to ... [segment missing].

The most important manuscripts of the Library... [segment missing]... the scholars of the Divine Alexander.

Beside him, we will die. With him, we will join his reign in the afterlife.

***

The back hallway leading to the loading dock was empty and still. Only the hum of night machinery, ventilation, and electrical equipment filled the space. He waited.

He would leave the museum courtyard after her and walk a few blocks to the Andrews Avenue bridge. From there, it was just a half block to his condo on the far side of the river.

Elizabeth King used her key to exit to the north side of the Museum and walked three blocks to the Andrews Avenue garage. Rather than take the elevator, she climbed the three flights to the third level. As she exited the stairwell, she did not see the figure in the shadows until the scarf was wound around her neck and yanked tight with lethal force.

As Skylar al-Mahdi reached the top of the arched span across Fort Lauderdale's New River, a scream cut through the granite and asphalt canyons of downtown. Unable to determine the direction from which it came, he looked around. Below him, a solitary pleasure craft passed beneath the bridge on the inky black waters sparkling with the winking lights of the city. Late-night revelers laughed and talked loudly over the soft engine noises.

He paused for a while and then walked on.

Chapter Nine: The Cry in the Night
526 SW River Drive, Fort Lauderdale, Florida

Mark held her gently against the wall.

They had just exited the hot tub connected to the infinity pool on their 9th-floor balcony. He spoke breathlessly in Rebecca's ear.

"Legs, any better, Beautiful?" He moved his hands over and around her, pushing the white, terry robe down her torso and pooling it at her feet.

"Yes, the soak did them good. I think I am done with the chair. Ohhh, that's so good, Darling. Yes."

"More time off can make sure you are one hundred percent, and we can spend the day making hot, monkey love, reviving some dormant nerve endings and stiff muscles."

His mouth moved down the side of her neck, tasting her in the darkness. Rebecca gripped him gently and pulled him closer, her hands slipping beneath his towel and making it drop to the tiles. He met her investigating movements with a firm and deliberate hardness. As their heat rose, he put his mouth close to her ear. Mark gave voice to his lust with panting and the husky rasping of a rough and intense mating. He was careful to amp it up slowly, guided by how he felt her body responding.

Nothing like an excellent rut to get all the systems back online.

Never one for soft and gentle sex, she encouraged his passion. At first, her responses were timidly encouraging but soon became challenging and insistent, intensifying her desire for him.

Mark prided himself on timing and personal control while reading his partner's body with his. He was damn good at this, and he knew it, swelling with male pride.

He alternated savoring parts of her upper body, then stood up and kissed her passionately, exploring the sensitivity of her mouth with his. Rebecca ran her hands down his muscular back to the narrow expanse of his waist just above the swell of his gluteals. As they continued to devour each other, Rebecca palmed Mark's firm butt and slipped her hands to the outside of his thighs. Careful of his healing leg, she pulled his persistent body against her, his member stiff with male potency.

She raised her head and gasped as his lips and tongue skated to the part of her neck that joined her collarbone and shoulders. He gently turned her so that she faced the wall.

"We good, Beautiful?"

"Yesss. Fucking fantastic. Don't stop, Mark. Please."

Leading with his hungry mouth, Mark traveled the length of her spine to her lower back. Her high-ass tattoo shivered beneath his wet caresses. He parted her legs, exploring with his hands.

Then, he stopped suddenly.

"*Cnuch*, did you hear that?"

Rebecca turned. Her mass of loose hair cascaded down her back, covering one side of her face. Her breathing was that of a runner in mid-race.

"Oh shit. Yes, Darling. It came from the street below."

"No, I think on the other side of the river. That side of the Museum."

He pulled away from her, limped inside the condo, and returned with his Canon A-1 and its telephoto lens. He searched for anything moving in the darkness of the night on the Fritcher side of the river.

Below them, the downtown world seemed to be sleeping soundly in an almost eerie stillness. The night heat lay like a soaked blanket on streets and buildings. There were no cars on the boulevards, and the sidewalks were empty. One yacht moved on a river lined with rocking, moored boats below the high-rises of city central Fort Lauderdale.

"Mark, something is going on over in the parking building– there about halfway up."

Mark aimed the camera in the direction Rebecca was pointing.

"It's hard to see into that space with the overhang. I got only shadows and some spotlights."

Rebecca reached for her cell phone, dialed 911, and reported the mysterious disturbance.

"Yes, officer. You know who I am, right? The municipal lot by the Library. Yes. Three levels up on the side that faces the river. Yes. Sounded like someone was in distress. OK. Thanks."

Mark started to lower the camera when he noticed the figure at the top of the Andrews Avenue Bridge.

***

Rebecca punched the pillows.

"Whoa. Take it easy there. Tell 'ole Mark your troubles, doll face."

"Sorry, I am just so fed up with the recovery bullshit. I need to get back to my former energy level. I am... a... woman... of...."

She punched that last four words into the pillow.

As she spoke, her eyes landed on his walking cast, standing next to the bed table on Mark's side.

"Were you about to say, 'action' Beautiful? Hmmm, sounds like something I would have said."

She looked from her pillow to his Mark-smirk face.

"By the way, CBN is treating me like a pariah. No assignments. I pitched about twenty to my Boss. He told me just to lay low for a while. 'Heal up, hotshot.' Talk about humoring me with bullshit."

"OK. I get it, but your leg was broken in three places, Mark. My injury was just an insect bite."

She puffed, "Jesus, I can't get comfortable, and I am restless as hell."

"Nope. Wrong. That chest was boobie trapped with concentrated venom, a powerful neurotoxin. Some of that shit is still in your system."

Mark wound the black silk sheet around his head and face and waved one hand as if casting a spell. He spoke with a thick, Transylvanian accent.

"The warning of the goddess Selket must be heeded at all times. Boohahahah."

He gestured like a gypsy character from the classic horror movie, "The Wolf Man."

Rebecca laughed despite herself and pushed her goofing lover back against the pillows.

"He's not Bela Lugosi, Mark. He's Egyptian. Shoulda went for Karloff in *The Mummy*."

Mark shrugged, "I took a shot."

He pulled her close.

"Get rid of Doctor Strange, Rebecca. I don't trust him. Way too creepy."

"Doctor al-Mahdi is just a wee bit intense, my hot boy. I think it is part of his cultural upbringing. We can make loosening him up a pet project. You know who the Mahdi are, right?"

He stood up, winding the black silk diagonally across his naked torso from the left shoulder and dropping to his right calf. He gesticulated like a grand vizier, hands twisting above his head and outward, eyes filled with magic and mystery.

"Ahhh, the secrets of the ancients, I will say the stuuthhhhsss ... I mean the suits... I mean the sooths." He lisped and spat as he faked the repeated mispronunciation of the word. Mark ended the slapstick entertainment when he shifted on his bum leg and toppled to the mattress.

She pushed him in his comical face. Mark shook off the cuffing and got serious.

"Yeah, the Mahdi, the eschatological saviors of Islam. Some religious stuff about rescuing believers at the end time. The dude is sporting a huge Arabic symbol right over his heart. Jürgen and I saw him shirtless at the gym today."

"Bet that was a sight. Oh, my yes."

"What are you hot for this guy?" He rolled his eyes and licked his lips.

"Easy, Action. Just because I am on a diet doesn't mean I can't read the menu."

Mark's eyes continued to twinkle as he started to speak, but Rebecca put two fingers up to his lips.

"And do not do that 'is-your-man-straight-or-bi' routine by telling me you would nail him in a minute. You know that standing joke just makes me...."

Mark licked her fingers with a passionate fervor.

He drooled as he growled, "A wild woman, I think. You love the thought of me, and you and another hunky jock all worked up and...."

She batted him with a pillow. He reached for her, but she laughed as she pulled away.

"So disgustingly depraved, Mr. Gadarn. Have some decorum. I need to save myself from your perversions and ...."

"GRRR...."

She could not finish as he pulled her beneath him and stopped her protests. They laughed between some serious kissing. Her fighting arms and kicking legs relaxed as she entwined around his unrelenting body.

"Sooo, you still got that itch? Bring it to your daddy. Mmm, this is about where we left off, Beautiful." He switched his mouth sounds against her body with a full, head-thrown-back howl.

"Oh, really? I hadn't noticed ... Ahhh ... ohhh ... nuhhhh ... *Haz eso más duro*, you hot bastard ... Markkkk ... do that again ... God, you're a devil."

Afterward, they slept.

Chapter Ten: The Fiery Eye of Ra
The Fritcher Museum Of Art, Fort Lauderdale, Florida

Rebecca walked through the Egyptian gallery and spoke into her cell phone. She made notes intending to develop a new exhibit that would predicate a renovation of this gallery. Hiring Skylar al-Mahdi, Ph.D., as the Fritcher's Scholar In Residence was the first step in creating a partnership with international Egyptologists.

She pulled her blackberry-green woolen shawl closer. The galleries were kept very cool even in the hours before opening, anticipating the hot Florida days and the expected large number of guests.

Frigid, she thought.

The Fritcher's CEO sat on a bench before a granite effigy of the beautiful pharaoh Hatshepsut. She felt the man who entered the gallery behind her, now standing directly behind her. Without turning, she spoke to him.

"She was actually the second of the female pharaohs. Sobekneferu, the last ruler of the Twelfth Dynasty, was the first– not a queen consort but a pharaoh regnant. But this one was more famous."

The Egyptian scholar answered in his rich baritone. "Impressive, Ms. Quinto. Yes, Queen Hatshepsut had impeccable bloodlines. She was the daughter, sister, and wife of a king. It is believed she reigned as king for twenty-one years. That hieroglyph on the back of the statue translates as 'The Foremost of the Nobel Ladies.' Her mortuary Temple in the Valley of the Kings is a wonder."

Rebecca said nothing but continued to gaze at the statue. Skylar asked, "How did the Museum come to obtain this piece?"

"It came to us through negotiations with the Cairo Museum. A few years back, they were offloading major artifacts to increase funding. We had a donor, the same philanthropist who is underwriting you, as a matter of fact."

Rebecca spoke into her phone, "Confirm with Micah the time for being picked up for the airport this evening."

She felt the Egyptian sit beside her, placing his sports coat across the bench between them. She turned to look at her specialist. Her eyes were immediately drawn to his open shirt. Nothing too suggestive, just one undone button more. The crisp white fabric closed just below the collarbone where the cleft between his pectorals descended underneath the Oxford fabric. She raised her eyes.

Again, she felt the sexual attraction she had always learned to keep under control in the workplace. She remembered her mother's words, "*No comas a donde cagas.* You don't shit where you eat."

He was indeed a handsome man, exotic and alluring. A powerful body moved beneath his expertly tailored clothes, broad-shouldered and tall. The cuffs of his white shirt were folded back on muscular forearms above strong hands, which he kept at his sides. His jawline, cheekbones, and nose were the markings of a classic aristocrat. His long dark eyelashes accented large, blue-black eyes that hinted at secrets and intrigue. A full mouth, which rarely smiled, was accentuated by a very close-cropped goatee and some face and neck scruff popular with male models, actors, and jocks.

Skylar's behavior was always exceptionally polite and professional. He spoke with intelligence and a scholastic insight that quickly revealed his experience as an academic, an archaeological researcher, and an expert Egyptologist. Still, Rebecca felt a sensual edge to the man, a fire that burned just below the surface and seemed to yearn for long and lustful hours of pagan sex play. She was trying not to be distracted by this little touch of sinfulness, and then she watched him walk away from her when he stood and went to examine a gallery piece.

Damn! The legs and ass on the man...

She made sure she held his gaze as he turned. They were alone in the room. Rebecca said, "Ah, sorry. You are about to tell me the whereabouts of the chest."

"Yes, Ms. Quinto. But how..."

"Easy, you are the one for whom the Egyptian treasure would mean the most, and you have the intelligence and ability to maneuver around security systems on the Executive Floor. And the physical strength to move it on your own. Where is it? Somewhere in-house, I'll venture."

"In the Catacombs, Miss. It is secure. I have been working on translating the scrolls."

Let's put all the cards on the table, big boy. I do not have time to fuck around.

She tapped a manicured nail on the bench, a metronome for her thoughts.

"Not alone in this. Elizabeth. And, while we are going in that direction... all of that is more than research."

He said nothing for a moment. Then, "You are very perceptive."

"A woman like me knows."

Dr. al-Mahdi looked around the gallery at the security cameras. He knew there were no microphones involved.

"So here's the plan, Doctor. We will get together with Agent Jürgen Mathias and surrender the box. We then will try to convince him that you are an overeager Egyptologist and sought to protect the artifact from those who would bring some harm to it. We can claim that the differences in our cultures created poor judgment on your part. Do your best to act like you were unaware of the consequences of your actions and were behaving in good faith."

The man looked off through the gallery, considering what was being said.

"You are too valuable to the Museum to lose you over this indiscretion."

Rebecca continued, "Your name is not Skylar, is it?"

The man seemed to lower his guard slightly. He said, "No, Miss. That is the English version. I attempted an English simplification while I was here in the United States. In the Egyptian dialect, my first name translates as 'man of the sky.' Skylar comes close."

"And al-Mahdi? That is the name of the ancient order of Islamic Zealots."

"Correct, Miss. I am a member of the race of 'The Guided Ones.' Tradition marks us as the saviors of the people in the end times before *Yawm al-Qiyamah*, the Day of Judgment."

"No wonder you are such a dead serious guy. A lot of responsibility that saving the universe stuff, Darling."

Skylar's face was expressionless as he said, "I have been well-educated and expertly trained."

She called Micah on the ninth floor.

"M, get the folks together for a meeting in my office ASAP. Yes, I need those who were bent on arresting me a few days ago... Yes, that's the list. Tell Queenie that she and I are to do a briefing before meeting the authorities. Please ask Mark to be there also ... Yes, Darling, the car leaves for Fort Lauderdale–Hollywood International at 4 PM. We'll make it. I'm glad Hudson is joining us."

She said to her staffer, "I am leaving for New York this evening and returning on Monday. Then, you and I will go all-in on these scrolls, provided INTERPOL and/or ICE do not cart you away to a prison in Belgium somewhere. You are a man of many secrets, Doctor, and this shit is getting serious."

She pointed at Skyler as she gave instructions. Her perfectly manicured, red index fingernail was a mere centimeter from his chest. She knew that this was inappropriate in his culture, but she couldn't care less. The dude needed a shock to the system.

"Queenie is my lawyer and adviser on many things. I will update her on our strategy to convince them and the Feds that you had only good intentions in hiding the artifact."

She could not tell what emotion lay behind his deep stare. Anger or resignation. It was not apparent. Mark was right. *Dude creeps me out.*

"You have the translations. That is all we need to get to the bottom of this. For that meeting, please bring Elizabeth King. And Skylar, think about cooling the affair with...."

She stopped speaking.

He looked expectantly at her. She seemed to be staring at something just beyond him. He began to turn.

"No, Skylar. Remain perfectly still."

As she slowly stood, she allowed her arms to move carefully through the opening of the folds of her shawl. Rebecca rose off the bench, dropping her left hand to the sportcoat between them.

"When I tell you, run to the exit behind me."

She raised one hand to her shoulder.

"Now."

Skyler dashed in the direction of the exit but turned back to see Rebecca execute a perfect "Veronica" with her shawl. With a second skillful movement, she dropped the heavier male garment over the very confused snake.

***

Fort Lauderdale Detective Don Rains commented, "Some pretty sharp moves there, Ms. Quinto. You two were pretty lucky."

"Comes from dating a matador a few years back, officer. He was a man of astonishing moves." She smiled and winked.

Mark grunted. He said, "I'd say the coolness of the gallery had something to do with it. Slows down the reptiles."

Ken Underworthy, the Director of Museum Security, returned from speaking to the woman from animal control.

"We are doing a full site search to make sure our snake has no friends and family anywhere else in the Museum before opening today. Our guest was an Egyptian cobra, a very rare and valuable beast. We are investigating how the reptile got into the place."

"Thanks, Ken."

Skyler al-Mahdi said, "*Naja haje*, the fiery eye of the sun god, Ra, the incarnation of the guarding goddess Meretseger– 'She Who Loves Silence,' the protector of graves. She was the Living God's messenger of death."

Mark looked at the Egyptian and said, "Yo, Ramses, shouldn't you be standing out on a ledge somewhere, bud? With all this 'The Curse of the Mummy' shit, making for tenseness– you hear what I'm saying? Damn, Dude. Consider this a warning to be cool. Got it?"

The two men sized each other up. Their eye-yo-eye connection foretold a future, once-and-for-all confrontation– the clash of superior males.

Skylar's eyes flashed. He pointed at the mocking journalist and was able to get out one word.

"You..."

Ardella McQueen stepped in between the two men, who were a scoach away from a throwdown.

"No, no, no, no, no, no. This is what we want, the crazy geek shit, all that spooky, crazy ass. Let's keep the testosterone at acceptable levels, you two.

"Mark. C'mere, studly. Put the lab coat on him and button up his shirt all the way to the neck. Anyone got a pocket protector?"

Queenie directed as Mark buttoned Skyler's shirt to his neck. She pulled some of his hair over his eyes. "Glasses? Yeah, good. Now, stick to what we went over. Stoop over a bit, tallness. Big drink o' water, ain't ya? OK, good."

Micah came up with the shirt pocket insert, complete with an assortment of pens and pencils. He muttered, "I got a bad feeling about this."

"Ya got that right, Micah. Agent Mathias is no fool. He saw Nutso Boy here training at the gym. No way this one's gonna convince Jürgen, or Mary for that matter, that he's Sheldon Cooper, Queenie. No way this one is a 'Big Bang Theory' nerd."

Queenie said, "He can do it. Stick to as much of the truth as you can."

"This is insulting, and I will not stand for...."

"Just do what you're told, Jack. Prison sex is hot, but nahhh, uhhh, you do not want to be Big Bubba's prom queen. You hear what I am saying? As the man said, be fuckin' cool. OK?"

Mary Chaffee and Jürgen Mathias came off the elevator and into the executive conference room. Mary said, "I can't tell you how I enjoy meeting with this roadshow from time to time. OK, so who wants to start?"

Rebecca started to explain, but Agent Mathias held up a hand and turned his attention to Dr. al-Mahdi.

"How did this chest come to be in your possession without the knowledge of your superiors?"

Skylar began. His speech was halting and in a higher register than the usual deep tones of the voice of doom. He stammered a bit and looked around nervously as he spoke, jamming his hands in the lab coat pockets.

"Well, Sir, Ms. Quinto and Mr. Valez here were dealing with the accident with the chest and the hospital and all. The first chance I had to tell Ms. Quinto of the chest's whereabouts was today in the Egyptian gallery. I told her that I had been keeping it safe until things settled down."

The Egyptologist fussed with his nose, allowing his glasses to slip forward. The geeky scientist meme was strong enough to be convincing without being a parody, but Jürgen was skeptical.

No way, this is the ninja dude I drooled over at Crunch. What the devil is this?

"It is an extremely rare piece, and I wanted to keep it secure. So much was going on." He spread his hands.

"Um... and that's it."

"What do you know about this?" Jürgen pointed to the chest.

"I was able to determine that it is a box of scrolls, royal records from the beginning of the Ptolemaic Dynasty in Lower Egypt in the Third Century BCE. The latest entry was approximately 300 of the Common Era. In all, these materials cover about 600 years of diary-like entries. "

Mathias continued, "Did you arrange the delivery of the chest to this Museum?"

"No, Sir. Until it arrived here, I was not aware of its existence."

"Doctor, are you associated in any way with the Rising Dawn Movement?"

Queenie interrupted, "All due respect here; where are we going with this, Agent Mathias? Are you accusing my client of a crime? He has related that he was protecting this thing. So, your last accusation proved to be innocuous. Is this a fishing exhibition? Do I smell a bit of racism in that last question?"

"It's an interrogation, Ms. McQueen. I get to ask the tough questions."

"Not while I'm around, you don't."

Skylar interrupted, saying, "Who does not know of The Rising Dawn? They intend to bring about a new Caliphate built on the bones of the destroyed ISIL movement. Their leaders come from central Asia. They claim Mongol bloodlines and descendency from Alexander IV, son of Alexander the Great. Highly improbable, but nevertheless, I am aware of their quest to obtain certain archaeological pieces associated with the Macedonian King. These scrolls appear to be very unconnected to the world conqueror. They are library records. And to answer your question directly, I have no association with this group."

"But, Professor, the period of Alexander in Egypt is part of your expertise."

"A segment of my research, yes. Are you implying guilt by academic association, Agent Mathias? A very spurious charge, to say the least."

Queenie placed a hand on the shoulder of the seated man. His timidity was slipping and was being replaced by a bit of his innate arrogance. She spoke up.

"I think we are finished here, Agent Mathias. My client has explained his actions. There are no connections to the terrorist group you mentioned unless you are implying that as an Egyptian national and a Muslim, he...."

Jürgen Mathias raised a hand to the attorney. "Enough, Ms. McQueen. It seems you have foiled my incursions into this little group yet again. Shall we leave our battling for another day?"

Don Rains interrupted, "Doctor, have you any idea why there would be two attempts on the life of Ms. Quinto."

"I am amazed at your conclusion, sir. That Ms. Quinto opened the cover of the chest was a possibility among many. Additionally, you do understand that I also was in the gallery when the snake appeared?"

"Then, I will revise my question. Why would anyone want either of you dead?"

"I have no knowledge of this, Detective. I am a scholar studying in America, nothing more."

Skylar addressed Mary Chaffee, saying, "Special Agent, you do realize that the venom on the hasp must have been added to the scorpions in recent times. A chemical analysis of the poison can give you a range of its potency. While the chest was constructed to foil the curious, I would suggest it was added no earlier than the date it was sent."

Detective Rains said, "You seem to know a bit more about this than you are saying, sport. Listen, take my advice..."

Queenie looked at the police officer and said, "Yeah, yeah, yeah. 'Don't leave town.' We got it."

"I would like to ask Doctor al-Mahdi one last question."

The detective and the professor locked eyes.

"When was the last time you saw Elizabeth King?"

Thomas Paul Severino

Chapter Eleven: Abduction
The Fritcher Museum of Art, Fort Lauderdale, Florida

Rebecca attempted to assure the members of law enforcement that it was best to go slowly with Skylar al-Mahdi.

"When I return from New York, I intend to get the man's confidence in all of this. I believe, as we all do, things are not what they seem, but Skylar will shut down if you all apply pressure. I also need to think of the reputation of the Fritcher."

"Nah, Rebecca. I say we let INTERPOL and the Feds go at that guy with the rubber hoses. He's dangerous."

Queenie suggested, "No, Mark. There's no connection until more incriminations surface if they do. Until then, I tend to believe him."

"Girl, that shy, innocent nerd he was affecting was just short of hilarious." Mary continued. "Your suggestion?"

Queenie said nothing and avoided looking at Mary or Jürgen Mathias.

Rebecca asked, "Can you please tell me about Elizabeth King?"

"Missing. Last night. Your security videos have her leaving by the staff entrance at 11:57 PM. We believe that she was abducted from the municipal lot across from Bubier Park."

"We have a section of that garage under lease for our staff. What else do you have, Don."

"Her car, abandoned, on level three. Panel truck on video left the lot at 12:17 AM this morning. No markings. She never came home, and her sister called it in."

The detective looked at the notes streaming into his phone from his investigatory team.

"Oh yeah, her cell phone was found near a pile of leaves just off the stairwell on level three. Many calls to one Skylar el-Mahdi. Were they romantically linked?"

Queenie said, "Detective, you need to ask Doctor el-Mahdi that. Business colleagues often communicate on matters other than love. I'll be happy to set up another questioning session."

Mark said, "Rebecca, the scream."

"Holy shit." She led them out to her balcony, nine floors up.

Mark pointed across the river. "We live there, the blue highrise, nine floors up; it faces this way. The parking garage is that gold building there, just this side of the river."

Rebecca asked, "Don, what is the time stamp on Elizabeth leaving the Fritcher?"

"Just shy of midnight, 11:57."

She continued, "Six minutes to get to level three of the garage. The attack was about five minutes past midnight. The panel truck exits about ten minutes later …."

Mark was scrolling through his phone. He said, "The scream came at twelve-o-six – the time of the abduction in the garage."

Mary said, "How can you be so sure."

"Pictures from my Canon. I sent them to my phone."

Mary was impressed. "My busy friends, so on the ball …."

"Wait, there is more."

Mark scrolled three more shots. "Look at who was goonin' at twelve-o-six AM on the Andrews Avenue bridge a quarter of a mile away, one innocent bastard."

He held out the photo of Skylar el-Mahdi.

Chapter Twelve: "The Place of the Cure of the Soul"

Alexandria, Egypt, 211 BCE

"We have no more room, Sire. The Great Library of the Mouseion of Alexandria, built by your ancestors, has outgrown itself. The warehouses surrounding the campus close to the port are likewise filled to capacity. They overflow with precious scrolls thanks to the royal decrees to make the Library the greatest in the world."

Lord Harpogrates, the Director of the Mouseion, continued, "I appeal to you, Sire. There are no buildings in the Royal Quarter of the city that can be taken over for the sake of showing to the world the wealth of Egypt's learning administered by the Pharoah's House of the Muses. I beg of you to make this a priority in your building and renovation program."

Ptolemy IV Philopater, the Lord of the Two Lands, shifted in his seat. He was surrounded by architects and ministers.

"Director, my great grandfather, Ptolemy I, conceived and planned the Mouseion and its Library as the centerpiece of the universal capital of learning and knowledge. Alexandria, created by the god and patron of the dynasty, is the greatest city in the world. My grandfather, may the gods give his soul eternal rest, saw the Library complex rise from the earth. Ptolemy II intended to continue promoting Hellenistic culture throughout the world. He dreamed that this would be 'The Place of the Cure of the Soul,' you understand."

The king continued, "The royal treasuries invest a vast annual sum in managing the institution, including salaries for the scholars and in operating that damned zoo of my grandfather's. Can you not do something about the odor of shit that fills my palace, night and day, Director? So, now you want additions, more space?"

The Royal Treasurer addressed the Director of the Mouseion with consternation.

"Let us be practical. At this time, my Lord Ptolemy pays for more than fifty international scholars, poets, philosophers, and researchers, who receive a large stipend, free food and lodging, and exemption from taxes. There are no funds for the expansion of the building, Lord Director. The king's grandfather, Ptolemy II Philadelphus, built portions of the Serapeum Temple to be an annex for the Library. You have many collections there."

Harpogrates responded, "Lord King, I am most concerned for the tomb. It is not safe to keep it at the Mouseion. There is the threat of destruction from storms and high tides in the port. The crypt is below sea level, Majesty. Also, consider the proximity to our battleships and the warehouse precincts, which are in terrible disrepair. We flood at least three times a year. Twice in my lifetime, fires from the port's industries have reached the roofs of the Library. Most of all, I fear for the most precious relic of the dynasty."

"What does my Royal Architect think?"

Erasistratus of Memphis passed the Pharoah a set of architectural drawings.

"The Soma, my Lord. The Tomb of your ancestors, constructed on a stone pylon, one-hundred royal cubits above the level of the sea and some distance from the harbor. Move the tomb of the god there. It will be secured for all eternity by the most sophisticated architectural designs."

He tapped the drawings.

The Pharoah examined the architectural plans and shared them with his directors and ministers. There was a general agreement. The Director of the Mouseion seemed both agreeable and relieved.

Ptolemy rolled up the scroll and gave it back to his architect.

"Make it so."

Chapter Thirteen: Tradition
United Nations General Assembly Hall, New York, New York

The young woman carefully adjusted her hajib and continued to speak from the large lectern. Up close, she seemed tense, standing on the rostrum in front of the green marble desk. It was here that the President of the General Assembly presided along with the Secretary-General when the General Assembly convened.

The importance of the international conference was highlighted by using this iconic venue with its semi-circular wall. The structure flanked the rostrum and tapered as it rose to the ceiling surrounding the front portion of the chamber. In front of the paneled walls were seating areas for guests, and piercing in the wall windows allowed interpreters to watch the proceedings as they worked. The hall's ceiling was 75 feet high and surmounted by a shallow dome ringed by recessed light fixtures. The combination of the visuals made the speaker look minuscule.

Behind her, on either side of the UN emblem on its gold background, two large monitors displayed photos of Heba, Jomana, and Masika Assiut in their home and the live feed of the speaker addressing the conference assembly.

The village of Kafr Ghatati, just west of Cairo, had been the family center for generations. Some photos of the people, the buildings, and the markets showed the great pyramids of Giza in the background. The young woman continued the opening section of her address.

"For more than three generations, members of my family have worked on the archaeological sites of the Giza Plateau. It is said that the ancestors of the people of Kafr Ghatati were part of the labor force that constructed the Pyramids."

Heba Aassuit spoke in her native Egyptian. On the sides of the Hall, interpreters in glass booths translated her address into 12 languages. Almost 2,000 conference attendees heard her words directly or through headphones. Video broadcasts brought the conference speakers to the world.

"For centuries, the people of my village have practiced female genital mutilation.

The fifteen-year-old speaker looked down at her notes on the lectern and paused, unable to continue. Heba's sister, Jomana, seated on the dais, stood and walked to stand next to her sister. The older one took the younger one's hand. Still, Heba could not find her voice as the large audience held its breath.

Masika Assuit slowly left her seat and walked across the platform to embrace her granddaughters. She spoke quietly to Heba.

"You must tell them, my daughter. There are many in the world to be saved. We must put our shame aside for their sake."

Heba continued, stammering slightly as she spoke.

"The midwife came to the house. She instructed me to remove my underclothing. The cuts from the razor-blade burned like fire. There was so much blood. At first, I resisted, but my mother assured me that it was my fate as a woman and I would not die. I cried for many days after.

"Even now, years later, I continue to remember that night, the pain and the embarrassment of being naked and the fear when my mother and grandmother held my legs apart. Using the bathroom became a torturous event that did not stop until about a month later.

"This is my sister, Jomana. She is two years older than me. Although she cannot speak of it, I will tell you. When Jomana was circumcised, her wounds became infected. The sickness spread, and now she is unable to bear children."

There was silence throughout the Hall. Jomana Assuit hugged her sister Heba as their grandmother approached the lectern.

"I am Masika Assuit, grandmother to Heba and Jomana. I am eighty-three years old. In my country, we circumcise our women so that they will lead a chaste way of life. Many husbands want their wives to be cut. I was made to undergo the cuts by my husband before our wedding. The girl cannot resist because the decision is made from the day she is born.

"Our neighbors say it is our tradition. It is religious, ordered by God, Muslim as well as Christian. Many say it is commanded by our scriptures. This is not so. No religion commands this sort of thing. It is an outrage.

"I have learned this too late. I will spend the rest of my days in sorrowful repentance for the torture I inflicted upon my daughters and granddaughters. I am at the mercy of their forgiveness. And for my penance, I will speak. I will speak and decry this practice the world over."

The octogenarian pounded the podium with a heart-breaking passion as she continued. Conference participants had heretofore not witnessed such righteous anger.

"I beg you to hear the words of a broken old woman. Egypt has outlawed this practice. But still, it goes on in our country and in too many other places in the world. It is ignorance that rules the minds and hearts of the people who do this to their children.

"I live in hell and deepest regret, much deserved. I will spend the rest of my days in sorrow for what I have done to these women."

The three women on the rostrum embraced one another, but the assembly did not applaud.

Rebecca recalled that it started among the women from Ethiopia and was picked up by the delegation from Tanzania. A trilling ululation rose up from the attendees. This song-like expression of deep emotion quickly spread throughout the hall. It combined with its variant, an even higher-pitched keening, quavering forth from Western nations members.

It was as if the sorrow of the Assuit family and that of the women and girls who were subjected to genital mutilation was taken into the souls of the conference members and produced a mass song of grief. A wave of embracing emotion from the 2,000 attendees rose up to the front of the General Assembly Hall. It ascended to the ceiling as the audience stood, rocking and swaying in the great and iconic space.

Chapter Fourteen: The Evocation of Saadi
United Nations General Assembly Building, New York, New York

Katherine Okomo said, "I cannot hear that sound without thinking of a battle cry. So appropriate-- we are at war to stop the torture of girls and women the world over, my friends.

Rebecca had met the representative from the Central African Republic when she agreed to serve as a member of the Conference to End Female Genital Mutilation/Cutting. The international association was created in 2007 by the United Nations International Children's Emergency Fund (UNICEF) and the United Nations Population Fund under the auspices of the World Health Organization. The organization attempted to accelerate the abandonment of the practice.

She sat with Katherine and four members who headed up the Education Committee in the spacious foyer of the General Assembly Building with the famous Foucault Pendulum in the background. The women who represented Ireland, Trinidad, Togo, and Sri Lanka were discussing the efforts of the committee to address the long-standing tradition and eradicate the custom.

Katherine was dressed in the traditional wrapper style of her native land. Her waist to ankles skirt was meters of tribal designs on quality fabric. A matching shawl hung over one shoulder. Above this was a gold and cream embroidered blouse. Her elegant *gele*, the head tie, was a simpler modification of the Nigerian style, tied in the fashion of women from the Central African Republic.

She addressed the officers of her committee.

"We have been given the latest figures. According to the World Health Organization, more than two hundred million girls and women have been cut in thirty countries in Asia, Africa, and the Middle East. As our speakers have indicated, there has been a decline in the prevalence of FGM/C in the last thirty years. Still, not all countries are seeing the elimination of the practice."

Caoilfhoinn O'Hare said, "How do you wipe out a tradition that goes back millennia? Our education programs throughout the world seem to have resulted in uneven improvements."

The redhead, the personal representative of the CEO of one of Ireland's largest Tech Corporations, continued, "The numbers go up and down. We see improvements and then regression. In many developing nations, the return to traditional ways has halted our most strategic efforts. WHO educators were attacked in Sudan last winter and forced to leave the country."

"I found the presentation by the Assiut women very stirring. Unforgettable, in fact." The speaker was Kiyoma Rupasinghe, a Sri Lankan National Secretary of Education.

"The 2016 survey by the U.N. Children's Fund showed that almost ninety percent of women and girls aged fifteen to forty-nine in Egypt have undergone the procedure. We find that the world over, FGM is mostly carried out on young girls between infancy and age fifteen. In my country, we have state-supported educational programs that each village municipality must promote. Nevertheless, we still see the terrible violation of the human rights of girls and women."

Rebecca commented, "Since I came on this committee, I have attempted to find ways that the arts can serve our efforts. I would like to provide this committee with an update on an initiative we have begun to develop in the United States."

Katherine Okomo's dark eyes glittered as she smiled. She leaned forward and said, "Please tell us of your work, Rebecca."

"My friends, as you know, the Fritcher Museum of Fort Lauderdale has established the Arva St. Genevieve Project, named for one of our trustees. Its purpose is to educate the world community on issues that affect full and equal access to human rights for all members of the human family. We believe the way into the hearts and minds of people can be through the evocative power of the arts."

Minister Rupasinghe asked, "What progress have you accomplished?"

Rebecca continued, "The Museum has engaged corporate sponsors, foundations, and private donors to fund an inspired team of authors, playwrights, cultural historians, and choreographers creating works that raise awareness on the issues of discrimination, oppression, homophobia, racism, poverty, and religious persecution.

"Our project team is mounting fifteen productions of 'Speaking Out of Sorrow,' by the Somali playwright, Faduma Zeinab, on Female Genital Mutilation. It is being translated into seven languages and will be performed using talent from the countries we target. We hope for a world premiere on March 8 of this coming year to celebrate International Women's Day. Our marketing team is swamped with thousands of details on this. Still, a key strategy is to invite the policymakers in the countries where this play will run. Our media advocates have worked earnestly to get responses from national legislators everywhere 'Sorrow' is performed.

"The Project hopes to field more arts offerings to raise awareness and challenge institutionalized oppression worldwide. Our goal is the support of political change. UNICEF is one of our titular sponsors and our National Endowment for the Humanities.

"The American institution, known as "Hollywood," is getting on board in a big way, celebrities using their fame for good, Darlings. The public face of our first production will be the 2018 Academy Award Nominated Actress Setia Melati. She is from Indonesia and spoke at this conference yesterday. Ms. Melati will be performing the play in Jakarta and Singapore as well as serving as the production's spokesperson."

The members of Rebecca's committee offered their congratulations and expressed interest in bringing the Project to their respective countries. To a woman, the members expressed their support.

A very enthusiastic Caoilfhoinn O'Hare reached over to touch Rebecca's hand. "How marvelous it is, Rebecca. I will be in touch with you with some of my contacts. I know of many people of affluence who will sponsor this wonderful project."

"Thank you, Darling. It is all still a bit rough, but we are getting there. The woman for whom the project is named always encouraged her students to think big, and this is pretty enormous."

As she spoke, Rebecca's eyes were lifted up to the inscription above the entrance to the General Assembly Hall across from where the group was sitting. She could read the engraving near the doorway from the *Gulistan* by the Iranian poet Saadi.

You, who are indifferent to the misery of others,

it is not fitting that they should call you a human being.

Tears came.

Chapter Fifteen: The Woman in Blue
The Metropolitan Museum of Art, New York, New York

The reception for the conference members at the Met was the media event of the season. Organizers sought to focus the world's attention on the social justice issue with a dazzling panoply of international world leaders in their native dress. As members of the press filled the plaza and steps in front of the famous Fifth Avenue museum, both men and women in attire inspired by their native countries mounted the stone staircase in front of the iconic entrance.

In the building's neo-classically designed niches across the front facade, large banners billowed with the logos of the World Health Organization and the United Nations Children's Fund between the Corinthian columns. Beneath the stone heads of the Muses, crowning the center arch, the flag of the United Nations welcomed guests and spectators to the main entrance.

Micah and Hudson exited the car in matching suits and ties, a dark palate of men's formal wear. Micah extended a hand to Rebecca as she stepped from the sedan in a long black cocktail dress. It dropped from a circular collar to a sleeveless bodice and was tight to the waist and hips all the way to the floor. One calf-high slit revealed her choice of footwear, black stiletto-heeled open-toed strappy sandals and a pair of gorgeous legs. She wore the minimum of jewelry, white jade drop earrings, and a matching bracelet. The entire ensemble was by the Puerto Rican House of Herrera designer Maria Guevara.

In their not-so-understated elegance, Rebecca, Micah, and Hud drew the flashes from the paparazzi as they mounted the steps. Martin Walker of CBN pushed a microphone into their vicinity, recognizing the CEO of the Fritcher and the President of the Preston Foundation. The three of them explained their personal and organizational support for the efforts of the Conference to End FGM/C. They used the moment to send a message through the world network to join the crusade.

As they entered the Great Hall, they were directed to the Robert Lehman Wing. The event organizers chose the eclectic collection because of the quality and breadth of its unique works of art. In the famous courtyard, donated works of art from the Conference member countries were available for contributions to the fund. Art collectors mingled with the delegates as the waitstaff passed with trays of elegant cocktails and exotic *hors d'oeuvres* of the world.

"I am sorry, but I cannot remember how to pronounce your first name. Please excuse my difficulty with the Gaelic."

Rebecca addressed her committee colleague as they stood before a masterpiece by Domenico Veneziano and an offering of textile art by the Icelandic artist Louisa Sveinsdóttir.

Caoilfhoinn O'Hare chuckled and said, "It's pronounced 'Key-lin.' Many find it challenging. But I love it. It is a name that goes back to the druids of Ancient Ireland. The first Caoilfhoinn was a warrior princess."

Rebecca smiled, "A Celtic Wonder Woman."

"Exactly."

Hud and Micah had ceased their escort duties and were browsing the galleries. Rebecca noticed that little touches of familiarity had become hand-holding and some full-on, arm-around-shoulder caresses. She thought, *This is getting serious.*

The two young men had volunteered to supervise some of the art sales, answer questions, and encourage interested art patrons to support the Fund by making a purchase. A museum staff member gave them a quick orientation. The three men developed a fast and easy camaraderie, a very diverse trio.

"Have you been to America before?"

"Yes, but never to New York. I was on assignment in Washington, DC, and Philadelphia a few years back. It was...."

The woman from Northern Ireland did not finish. Something from across the gallery grabbed her attention. A woman in a midnight blue abaya and matching hajib. The headscarf was long and wrapped around her shoulders and down her back. She glanced around nervously.

"Rebecca, would you mind coming with me? Something's up."

Rebecca set down her champagne flute on the tray carried by a passing server. She followed the Irish woman out of the Robert Lehman Collection through the Medieval Gallery and back to the Great Hall. From there, they entered the Egyptian Galleries. The woman in blue made her way to Gallery 131 and the Temple of Dendur, the only Egyptian Temple in the New World, a gift from Egypt to the United States.

Representatives from UNICEF and WHO had chosen this dazzling wonder as the backdrop for photos of this day at the FGM/C Conference. Dignitaries, speakers, and delegates were being staged in front of the magnificent temple built around 15 BCE. Museum security assisted the crowd and organizers in keeping the flow of the glitterati moving, the photographers working and guiding the folks back to the Lehman Gallery after their photos were taken.

As the mysterious woman in Arab dress stepped around security lines, she glanced at what seemed to be a guidebook. She examined the temple, which seemed to float on the specially designed moat, echoing the original setting of the building on the banks of the Nile.

Caoilfhoinn O'Hare pulled a small African woman out of the crowd and over to Rebecca. She made no introductions but spoke in haste, outlining a plan for a rushed assault on the woman in blue.

Rebecca went around to the rear of their quarry. The African woman stood off to the side, facing the crowd and staff from the UN Conference. Caoilfhoinn approached the woman, who turned and seemed not to understand what was happening.

The rest took just a matter of seconds.

The delegate from Northern Ireland signaled by touching the top of her own head.

The African woman screamed "fire" in an assortment of languages.

The crowd rushed the exits.

Rebecca ran at the woman in blue from the rear, bent, reached through the abaya, and grabbed her lower legs, pulling them backward.

The woman raised her arms as she fell forward on her face. Rebecca moved on her, grabbed her right arm, and held it away from her body. Caoilfhoinn did the same on the left side.

"Get her back on her feet, but we must keep her arms away from her body."

A security guard raced forward.

Rebecca said, "A knife or scissors, hurry."

The African delegate, Amanda Igwe, appeared with a pair of shears and lifted the woman's gown up to her midriff.

As the terrorist struggled, outstretched between the two women, Caoilfhoinn O'Hare instructed the security guard on how to cut away the girdle containing the bomb.

Chapter Sixteen: The Last Empire
FBI Headquarters, 26 Federal Plaza, New York, New York

"Right here... 'Suicide bomber foiled by three women at New York's Metropolitan Museum of Art.' I love it. The UN is going to give you gals a medal for sure."

Mary Chaffee was grinning like the Cheshire Cat as she waved a copy of the New York Post.

She continued, "Glad I dogged you up to New York, Rebecca. I had a feeling that trouble would be following you to the Big Apple. Again, your training in the FBI Civilian Program has paid off."

Rebecca spoke as if she had had a moment of realization now that the excitement was over. She turned to Caoilfhoinn.

"Holy shit. How did...."

The young woman explained. "While we were talking in the Lehman, I noticed her acting very strangely. She had no interest in the people or the art and moved very awkwardly. That is to say, she lumbered a bit as she walked. She appeared to be on the petite side. Thinking something was not right, I suspected there was an obstruction under her gown.

Mary said, "The extra weight was twenty pounds of explosives under her abaya."

I would venture to say that because of the triangular shape of the gallery, she realized that the effects of the bomb would be minimal. That, and the fact that the Conference VIPs were in Gallery 131. I saw her make some inquiries at the checkout table, and the attendant pointed back through the museum, giving her directions."

Mary took up the narrative, "Disarming a bomber is next to impossible, but I believe you realized that the trigger was not held in her hand."

"Right. The bomber's hands stayed empty, telling me the detonator was somewhere on the terrorist's torso."

Rebecca said, "Obstructed hands at a cocktail reception would have been noticed-- drinks, food plates, programs, etc."

Mary said, "The bomb was not a shrapnel type. No metal whatsoever– detectors at the Museum entrance did not go off when she entered. It was meant to cause massive destruction to structures and nearby personnel."

Amanda spoke up. "We were quick, decisive, and resourceful – and very blessed, it would seem."

Rebecca looked at her two colleagues, still a bit confused.

Mary smiled as she said to Rebecca, "My good friend, Caoilfhoinn, is MI5 in Northern Ireland. She has lots of experience with counter-terrorist intelligence work in her home country."

The Irish woman also smiled and said, "And Amanda is a linguist teacher in Nairobi... 'Fire' in how languages?"

"I think I hit thirteen.

***

Lamma Dayoub, in handcuffs, sat at the stainless steel table in the interrogation room. She was given prisoner's coveralls and a new hajib. She was terrified and relatively non-communicative. Her eyes were large and focused on her hands, which she clasped before her.

Mary Chaffee and Caoilfhoinn sat in the room opposite the prisoner. Another agent, a Muslim community member who wore the identifying headscarf, was seated to the captive's right. She translated questions and answers into Mesopotamian Arabic, the dialect of northeastern Syria.

Mary asked, "How did you come to be recruited for this assignment?"

The woman shifted, looking fearfully at each of her interrogators. Her reluctance seemed to indicate that there would be a price to pay either way, should she talk or if she remained silent.

Rebecca said, "She knows that there is nowhere she can hide if she gives information. I have never seen someone so terrified."

Hudson, Micah, and Rebecca stood with some members of the FBI and New York City law enforcement members behind the one-way glass of the interrogation room. Watching the questioning in the next room, the group was visually searching the prisoner for any clue regarding her actions.

Hud said, "I saw the same expression over and over again when I was stationed in Afghanistan. My unit saw thousands of women and children who had been radicalized by the extremists to be cannon fodder. They all have the look of a deer in the headlights.

On the other side, the agent spoke, "Ms. Dayoub, you will be treated fairly by the justice system in this country. We know that you have been taught that we are barbarians, but we are not. During incarceration, you will be safe from recriminations."

Mary instructed her colleague, "Inform her that the FBI will do what it can to keep information leading to her identity out of the press. It may reassure her that her masters and their sympathizers will be unable to reach her." The agent did so.

"Lamma, la bas. In yaduruk shay' alana. 'akhbarana mataa tama tashwihuk."

On the other side, Hudson Ch'en said, "The woman was told, 'Lamma, it is alright. Nothing will harm you now. Tell us when were you mutilated.'"

Micah looked at his buddy, impressed at Hudson's knowledge of the language.

A response seemed to break through her fearful reluctance to speak. The terrorist began to talk, and the agent translated, "They made a mess of me when I was 11 years. I nearly died. I wish I had. My parents knew that no man would marry me, so they sold me to the militants."

The start of her explanation was rushed and stopped by a sob that racked her entire body and brought on a flow of tears. When she could speak, she did much more slowly. "They decided I would be one who would bring about death for them. There were many of us trained in this way. Little boys were taught to run into the battlefields and prevent the enemy from shooting at the Forces of God.

"I was instructed that I would enter paradise whole and well, no longer a pariah among people. It was my only hope and my destiny. The tactics and strategies of our mission were practiced many times. They smuggled me into this country on a boat – they have a house across the river. A woman accompanied me to the Museum this night.

"We were both at the UN yesterday, but just to observe and plan the place of my activity. The security there prevented us from seeing much. I was not armed then, in any case."

The agent asked Lamma how old she was.

"I am seventeen years."

Mary asked, "Were you told why you were to do what was intended with the explosives?"

"I was fashioned into a human weapon by the men. We are created to punish the non-believers who would destroy the way of life ordained by God, the infidels who hunt us down and turn the world against us. Those who, by their evil ways, prevent the Advent, the Arrival...."

"The coming of what?"

"*Almamlakat Al'akhira.*"

In the observation room, Hud translated.

"The Last Empire."

Chapter Seventeen: OSCE
The Library at The Baccarat Hotel, New York, New York

Nilza Mendes had a pleasant smile and a firm handshake.

"It is such a pleasure to meet you, Ms. Quinto. I am so impressed by your saving of that near-disastrous situation at the Met this evening. We have a few mutual friends and connections."

"Please call me Rebecca. I apologize for not reaching out to you sooner. Kayne Sorenson gave me your card about a week ago, but things have been a bit hectic at the museum."

"Actually, I have received a bit of updated intelligence from another source. I think you know Jürgen Mathias from INTERPOL."

"Yes, Agent Mathias is a good friend of my partner, Mark Gadarn.

"The journalist from CBN? Rebecca, I had no idea. His work in the Middle East is enlightening-- such a brave man. He is famous in Europe. You, too, for that matter. The Professor and his Sorenson Squad in Eastern Europe last summer– folk heroes. At the Organization for Security and Co-operation in Europe, we keep our eyes and ears open for the good guys and the bad."

"What brings you to New York?

The petite woman said, "The conference on FGM/C. I represent our initiative on the well-being and safety of women."

Rebecca said, "How long have you been with the OSCE, Ms. Mendes?"

"Nilza, please. I joined after being in business in Lisbon, not long after college. It will be fifteen years next September. I am currently a member of our Permanent Mission to the Russian Federation. While our offices are in Vienna, I have spent a significant amount of time in the Caucasus and Central Asia."

A familiar voice said, "Right, 'The Stans:' Kazakhstan, Kyrgyzstan, Tajikistan, Turkmenistan, and Uzbekistan. Did I get them right? Would the women like a glass of wine this evening?"

"Speak of the devil," Rebecca said. "Agent Mathias, I get the feeling you are following me. That or Mary Chaffee asked you to keep an eye on me."

The handsome officer smiled and set down the tray of glasses and an open wine bottle on the table between Nilza and Rebecca. He was revealing nothing.

"It is always an honor to be in your company, Ms. Quinto," the agent said with just a slight bit of sarcasm."My presence in New York and at your side, you may blame on your man, the distinguished Mark Gadarn. His injury keeps him from accompanying you as you fight terrorists and... bad guys... is that how you call them... the world over?."

Rebecca smiled, actually glad to see Mark's friend.

Nilza extended a hand, "I had no idea you were here in New York, Commander Jürgen. "*Que bom te ver, minha querida. Você está bem?*

"Oh, yes. I am quite well, thank you. I am actually staying here with a new friend." He turned to Rebecca, "We met your colleagues, Micah and... a...."

"Hudson Ch'en-- so in love, those two."

"Yes, fine young fellows."

Jürgen poured the wine.

"This is Siegrist Dornfelder, five years old, from Germany. It is dry and full-bodied. Perfect after a long day of disarming bombers and saving the world."

Nilza said. "I so love this hotel and this lounge space in particular. It's right off the Grand Salon and so elegantly decorated – all this dazzling crystal."

"And the books," Rebecca added, pointing to the walls around them. A chic and scholarly atmosphere for enjoying friends."

She continued, "I get the feeling that you both have something on your minds. Is it the Egyptian chest, Jürgen? Nilza, I am sure you are aware...."

The woman nodded, and the man shook his head.

"On its way to the Cairo authorities. The infamous Doctor al-Mahdi suggested that INTERPOL contact his mentor, Doctor Taher Barakat. We have only positive intelligence on that professor, so I reached out to him. He will take possession soon."

"Sounds good. Nilza?" Rebecca raised a glass endorsing the developments, thankful for the safe return of the scroll collection.

"Rebecca, my agency has been hearing reports of a very concerning movement in Central Asia. There are pockets of Islamic fundamentalists making noises about founding a new Caliphate in the Middle East. Another uprising will flood even more refugees into Europe."

Jürgen Mathias added, "The connection with your work, Rebecca, is that the leaders of this group seem to have reversed the usual practice of destroying the artifacts from ancient civilizations. This movement is forcibly taking and hoarding relics from the age of *der Alexander der Große*. Doctor al-Mahdi spoke of it back in Fort Lauderdale."

"Alexander the Great, yes."

Nilza Mendes said, "There have been thefts at the Persepolis Museum in Marvdasht, Iran, and the National Museum of Iraq in Baghdad. In Macedonia, certain sources tell of a plan to loot the graves of Alexander's mother, wife, and son, Alexander IV. It is one of the places believed to contain the body of Alexander the Great. He was thirty-three when he died, by the way, legendary in all aspects of the word."

Mathias said, "INTERPOL is very close to catching those criminals, but, as of yet, the stolen artifacts have not been recovered, and we are keeping our eyes on Macedonia. I am sorry to say that our work with the museum officials in Vergina has been prevented.

He went on to explain, "The chest that came into your possession seems to have originated from an archaeological site near Samarkand on the famous Silk Road. The complex is thought to have been a Hellenistic outpost in ancient times. INTERPOL is also watching Alexandria and Cairo. It is Egypt that we believe this consortium of death and theft will strike again."

Nilza said, "Rebecca, another friend we have in common is Mary Chaffee. Both she and Kayne Sorensen suggested a bit of undercover work of which you might be interested, to assist both my organization and INTERPOL."

Rebecca listened carefully to what the OSCE delegate had to say.

"Would you consider going to Macedonia and Egypt to look around on our behalf?" She gestured to the INTERPOL officer."

"Why exactly do you need me? You represent diplomatic interests, and you are law enforcement. Why me? Someone's sure to get wise."

Jürgen continued, "Not necessarily. Your cover would be that of a high-profile proponent of the arts looking for partners in a major exhibit at the Fritcher. The extremists have many eyes on watchdog groups like ours. INTERPOL will arouse too much suspicion in a region that is a bit unstable. As representatives of the international arts community, the political entities would not be threatened by activities and inquiries. Often, agreements and secrets are shared among your people that are a bit, as they say in America, 'off the books.' Yes?"

"What exactly do you want me to do?"

Jürgen thought for a moment. Then he said, "If you insert yourself among the growing group of scholars that are interested in the remains of the Macedonian conqueror, you may be able to help us and local authorities to identify the cultural thieves. We believe them to be associated with the right-wing Islamic movement. It is essential that whoever is financing this movement comes out in the open."

"Agent Mathias, you do realize that one of the fundamentalist groups that have a lot of influence in that part of the world is the Muslim Brotherhood. A few years ago, Egypt declared them a terrorist organization. Those guys play for keeps. Connect the dots – Lamma Dayoub."

"INTERPOL is aware of the political implications and will provide you with protection without being too overt about our operations. We are working on securing support for some of our partner nations."

Rebecca seemed to examine her wine glass while saying, "Sounds a bit half-baked, but I will think about this and discuss it with a few folks back home…."

"Mark?"

"Yes, Commander, Mark. If I agree to this, then we can confer on strategies."

She sipped the wine and paused before adding, "But let me tell the two of you, I am no dummy. This 'oh-what-a-coincidence' meeting in the Baccarat Hotel is bullshit. You folks planned this from the get-go. From here on out, it's complete disclosure, or I walk."

"Agreed." Nilza concurred.

"I will get back to you in forty-eight hours max."

Jürgen said, "Thank you."

A hand crept over his shoulder. He turned, and a tall intruder spoke.

"Let's go, handsome. We can't keep the cowboys waiting."

Jürgen Mathias beamed, "Please allow me to introduce my friend, Antonio Sarraga, also from Fort Lauderdale, and…."

Rebecca said, "These are my friends, Micah Valez and Hudson Ch'en. Looks like there's a big contingent from South Florida lusting for some cowboys tonight. A German favorite too?"

Jürgen smiled and hung on to Antonio's hand. Micah said, "We're tackling Flaming Saddles Saloon in Hell's Kitchen. Join us? Teach you to dance western style with the hotties. This one is a newbie also. Ready to ride a cowboy, bud?" He indicated Hudson, who checked him with an ear kiss.

Nilza downed her wine and stood up. "I am glad to be included. Thank you."

Hud held out his hand and said, "Do you good, Rebecca. After the day you've had."

"Thanks, fellas, but this girl is a bit done in. I'm gonna get another bottle of this German red sent to my room and dream of my own cowboy back home. Y'all have a good time, hear?"

Chapter Eighteen: A Phone Call from Les Boissons

The Baccarat Hotel, New York, New York

"OK, so you are sure you are alright?"

"Mark, I am fine. Thankfully, when people fall forward, they put their hands up to break their fall. The mighty women pounced."

There was no laughter on the other side of the phone.

"Rebecca, I am sending you something from my hacker, Eris. It is a communication intended for the New York Times and the Washington Post. You know the drill for downloading secured files, correct?'

"Yes, Darling."

"What the originators of this message did not realize is that the bomb never went off. My cyber snoop intercepted this intended press release. Eris sent it to me after my recent request for her to put out feelers in the web universe for anything on the Rising Dawn. It's on the secured site."

"I'll get it to Mary ASAP."

"Great."

Rebecca was tucked into a corner of the Les Boissons lounge at the Baccarat. Mark was on the other end of the call at their condo in Fort Lauderdale. This late in the evening, the design and lighting of the long bar created a mysterious and provocative atmosphere. The signature Baccarat cut glass was everywhere, from the chandeliers hanging from the barrel-vaulted ceiling to the shimmering glassware on mirrored shelves. Candles in glass globes were double-reflected on the shiny surface of the bar. White, crystal, and deep mahogany were the signature colors.

Other occupants of Les Boissons seemed to be absorbed in a late-night seductive dance of suggestion, invitation, and romantic possibilities. Conversations were soft, and gazes were longing and daring. Away from any observers, she opened her iPad. Rebecca began to maneuver her way through the security maze Mark had set up to protect the portal to his hacker.

"How's your leg, Darling?"

"Better every day, Beautiful."

Completing an elaborate password puzzle, she opened and scrolled the document on her tablet.

"Same fuckin' rhetoric from the usual band of crazies who want to push an ultra-right agenda claiming they are doing God's work. They assume responsibility for the destruction of the museum and the death and disruption of the UN Conference on Female Genital Mutilation. They claim that the efforts of UNICEF and WHO are a worldwide attempt to violate the commands of God. What bullshit."

"And a bit of premature ejaculation considering the female superheroes who disrupted their little apocalypse. Their publicist asshole should have checked to see if the bomb actually went off."

Mark continued, "Look at the second to the last paragraph, Rebecca."

She traced a line of the statement warning of the rise of the New Caliphate.

"Mark, they've been a busy group and seem dangerously near."

Mark read aloud, "The Rising Dawn also claims responsibility for the recent death of violators of our sacred history in Fort Lauderdale, Florida. May all such infidels be forever cursed. Let the first of our executions serve as a warning against those who oppose our regime and the forces of God."

"Holy shit. These are the guys who abducted Lizzie King – saying she will be found dead."

"I am sure Mary will go ape shit with this. So will her buddy, Don Rains, on that bit of info. Please keep the source of this intel a secret. It just fell into your lap, eh? OK. Be careful, Beautiful."

"Mark, don't go. There has been a development with your boy Jürgen." She explained the proposed trip to Greece and Egypt.

"Fuck, no." Mark was firm.

"That bastard, Mathias. I am gonna beat his ass next time I see him. Roping you into this..."

"Do not get your Welsh temper in high gear, Darling. Let's talk. You remember talking. I say something, then you say something, then...."

"Cut it out, Rebecca. There's a shit load of danger in this, and you seem to have a bull's eye on your back– two attempts. Ms. King was just the beginning. With your high profile on human rights and your advocacy for the dignity of women everywhere, you're an icon for them. They want your head on a pike."

Mark regretted the imagery instantly. He continued to protest.

"These ladies play for keeps, girl. Let's go to Mykonos, or Rio, or Ibiza, and sleep in the sun instead. We can make hot love in exotic locales. You have plenty of vacation coming, and I am all but unemployed."

"CBN is just gun-shy with you, Mark. They'll get you on to something soon. Just be patient. A Russia and China assignment will come quickly enough."

Rebecca thought, *Then I'll be the one to object to dangerous doings.*

She took a sip of wine and continued. "I am afraid we are both too larger than life for most people. My Board of Directors has no idea how to calm me down into some version of a quiet and respectful museum operator."

"Jügen and Nilza just want expendables in the face of enemy fire, Beautiful. Both OSCE and INTERPOL have the influence and the muscle to go after these archaeological thieves. Still, the politics in that game is a shitstorm they would rather not deal with. And the fundamental religious issues are a tinder box ready to blow all over the region. Tell 'em, 'no.' I am serious."

"Come on, sexy boy. I respect your point of view here, but lately, I feel like my blood is on fire. You should have seen that young woman tonight – the epitome of hopelessness. And the reports from the UN Conference meetings show some pretty awful things being done to children and adolescents.

"We need to draw a line in the sand on this movement – fuckin' ultra-right torturers. I won't insult religion by connecting them with people of faith. There is nothing religious about the Rising Dawn – it's about power and money, not believing."

"You got this one bad, haven't you, girl?"

"Yes, Mark. This little gig might just get me in where a powerful statement can be made for the cause under the guise of nosing around for the exhibition of a lifetime. I have to do what I can."

"Two conditions. I am in on this, and no, and I mean no al-Mahdi nutso man fuckwad."

"Your conditions suck, Darling. You are in no condition to take on thievery or worse in the desert. I know you think Skylar is the Mayor of Crazy Town, but we need him. He is the world's foremost authority on the Hellenistic period in Egypt and an archaeologist, also."

"Rebecca."

"OK, so let's get to a compromise. You know. I get some of what I want, and you get some of what you want."

"When you do this little talking down to me thing, you know I just want to take you over my knee and spank your bare...."

"Mmmm, promises, promises. Only if you will kiss it and make it better after. Oh yeah, and I get to return the favor. Compromise, big boy."

"Damn you and your female ways. Now you've gone and got me all...."

She ignored his friskiness and pressed ahead.

"OK, so you get to come along, and I get to add Skyler. You can be the one to keep the intense professor in check. No, perhaps I should do that."

"Great."

"I love it when we both win, Darling."

"Humph. Where are the guys tonight?"

"Hitting the gay bars in Hell's Kitchen. Holy shit. That Antonio is gorgeous. Mr. Stoic German may actually get a hard-on."

"Ohhh, don't let him fool you, Beautiful. My German bud is as much a horndog as the best of us. Just plays it cool when he is doing his Commander Mathias bit. I can report that our frisky boy, Jürgs, has been sexin' up this guy for a few days now. I am proud to say I fixed them up at Crunch Gym. I know what kind of knackwurst the secret agent likes or, in this case, chorizo."

"Well, they are on the loose tonight in New York. Apparently, the place to find the hotties is a cowboy place on the West Side, over on Ninth. Micah wants to teach Hud to two-step or whatever."

"Heard about that place. Nice. Gets pretty hot on all levels, gays, straights, and all those in between. And here I sit with little Mark and my hand. Why don't you go on up to your room and call me back when you are under the covers?"

"You are one depraved man, Mark Gadarn. Who do you think you are talking to? I am a well-respected member of the international art scene about to depart for the ancient hills of Macedonia and the deserts of Egypt. I am a female Heinrich Schlieman or Howard Carter, and you are proposing we have phone sex. What are you, fifteen?"

Mark said something that was beyond depravity in a voice from lust hell. Rebecca almost did a spit-take as she finished her drink.

"Ohhh, that sounds delicious, Darling. So, in that case, I'll call you back in fifteen minutes, nasty boy."

Rebecca left the bar.

Chapter Nineteen: No Woo Hoo(ing)
FLAMING SADDLES SALOON, 9th AVENUE, NEW YORK, NEW YORK

The place was wild.

Will Smith was rapping "Wild, Wild West" from the DJ booth. The patrons were line-dancing in the bordello-decored saloon on the wide-planked floors under an old-fashioned coffered ceiling. The Frontier Town allusion reigned supreme.

Five fiery hot bartenders jumped up on the bar and do-si-do-ed between patrons' drinks in a raucous choreography that included boot slapping, heel pounding, and ass sashaying. The fans went nuts.

Nilza met some women from the conference just as the group came into the bar. She enjoyed the high energy of the place and decided to drink with them. Micah returned with a cowboy and four Absolut and seltzers. He tipped the waiter.

"Thanks, Shane. Save us a dance." Hud was grinning. Antonio was in the process of rolling up the sleeves of Jürgen's t-shirt.

"C'mon, sexy Jay-boy, show those big German Howitzers. Fuck yeah."

"I got a big gun for you, my American man." He went in for one hot kiss-up.

The other members of the quartet howled, and all clinked glasses. The music cued up John Denver's "Thank God I'm a Country Boy," and the four men parted the festive crowd bathed in swirling lights. They hit the dance floor.

Hips swayed, and bodies rocked to some jubilant shouting and fine-tuned wailing and twanging. A sign above the bar warned straight women, "No Whoo Hoo(ing)." Both Hud and Jügen picked up on the two-step and some of the line dancing, slowly at first and then with a more sexy body rock. Antonio stepped in close and opened the buttons on his hot German cowboy's shirt, continuing to prefer a more sexy look in his dance partner. Someone in the crowd slapped a cowboy hat on the sexy Mexican American, swatting his rock-hard butt in tight Levis.

Above the music and cheers, Micah pointed in the restroom's direction. He yelled for Hud to continue his dancing with their other two buddies. He took off toward the back of the dance hall.

Kenny Rogers gave some card shark advice with "The Gambler," and Tammy Wynette advised the tenuous to "Stand By Your Man." Waylon and Willie offered some family counseling with "Mammas Don't Let Your Babies Grow up to Be Cowboys." Next, Loretta warned the overly amorous, "Don't Come Home A' Drinkin' (With Lovin' on Your Mind)."

As Patsy Cline slowed things down with "Crazy," Antonio pulled his sexy German into a hot couple's clinch. Hud embraced them both by the shoulders and timed his hip-swaying to match theirs. By now, all three hombres had their shirts off and tucked in the back of their jeans.

"That sure is a long bathroom break. Where is your pretty cowboy gone to, pard?"

"Dunno, Antonio. Thought I would go and see."

Jürgen said, "Won't find him there, Hud. He's in the corner over there making out with his boss.

"The fuck you say."

***

Nilza Mendes watched as Hudson Ch'en moved between the crowds toward the back of the bar. She could just make out the statuesque brunette wrapping her arms around the bewildered executive assistant. She turned back to her companion, who preferred to remain in the shadows.

"You folks play a very close game. Except for Mathias, these other guys are minor players. Be advised. You risk too much. Your only motive is terror, chaos, and fear. You know he is obsessed with wanting Quinto. She is high profile in this matter and will symbolize what happens to those who resist. And he wants her alive."

A glint of bar light bounced off the leering smile of the man with the Russian accent lurking in the shadows.

Chapter Twenty: Dopplegänger

The Baccarat Hotel, New York, New York

"It sounded like 'key ball Altamont,' best I can remember. The music was so loud, but she said it in my ear. Slobbered is more like it." Micah rubbed his head where the woman had mouthed him. The other three sweaty, ersatz wranglers flopped on chairs, the floor, and the settee in Rebecca's room.

Jürgen said, "Write it here, my friend. Just as you heard it." Micah took the hotel notepad and scribbled it, handing it back to the INTERPOL Agent.

Rebecca pulled her robe around her and said, "What happened next?"

"We went back to our table, and four new drinks were being delivered. The waiter said, 'Compliments of your friend.' He pointed in the direction of your twin, who was heading out the front entrance."

Antonio said, "No fucking way we touched that poison, you understand? Besides, that would have been round four. Damn, hanging out with you guys is like being in a Jason Bourne movie, only better." He grinned at Jürgen, who was examining the message.

"Micah, did she..."

"Oh my god, Rebecca, a mirror image." He wiped his ear and mouth again. "Make that a spittin' image. Creeped me out big time. After she said that – whatever she said...." He waved his hand at the notepad. "... she added that it was for my boss."

Rebecca exchanged a look with the agent and thought for a bit. Then she said, "It's almost four-thirty, fellas, and four of us have a plane to catch in the morning. Let's hit the hay."

As they exited her room, Rebecca gave Micah a reassuring pat on the back. Jürgen was about to be the last out when she reached for his arm. Rebecca said to Antonio, "I'll send him along soon, Darling. I just need a private word."

She closed the door and turned to the German officer.

"OK, there is some ground we need to cover before we go much further, you and I. You know I am talking about…."

"Yes, yes, Rebecca. I never did apologize for almost getting you charged and arrested. It's just that I have been so embarrassed by such a shabby piece of international detective work. I am still nursing a bruised ego from the trouncing I received from the extraordinary Ms. Queenie."

"Why do some men think that if you just overlook, it's all good? Just go forward and get over it? OK, so let's get to me … I will give you a start. "Rebecca, I am sorry for …'"

"Yes, I profoundly regret any harm or embarrassment caused by my professional inadequacies. Please forgive."

"You are a long-time friend of the man I love very much and are sincere, so I accept your apology."

Jürgen did a slight bow, acknowledging Rebecca's willingness to go forward.

"So, Egypt is on, Jürgen. Mark and Skylar are in the entourage. However, I need to get back to Fort Lauderdale first to finalize a few things, clear calendars, and make arrangements for being out of the country. Work on the itinerary and send us three tickets."

"*Scheiße*, all of these forceful males. It will be a *Zirkus*, as we say. You know, a three-ring show. I will get back to you with proposed travel plans in the morning."

"Sounds good. You bringing Antonio for those cool desert nights?"

"No, he is just a brief amusement, I will confess. This operation is much too sensitive. Our relationship, such as it is, is in the sexual stage. I am afraid I do not have the luxury right now of investing in an intimate relationship. The chances of this liaison ripening are yet to be seen."

"I think you mean 'maturing,' and I understand. Speaking about words, what did my *dopplegänger* have to say?"

He looked at the pad. "As best I can tell, I believe your double gave your Micah something meant for you, the *qiblat almawt.*

"Huh?

"The Kiss of Death."

Chapter Twenty-One: Into the Afterlife
The Sons of Osiris Lodge, Ft Lauderdale, Florida

Detective Rains explained, "At 3:26 this morning, we received a call that there was a break-in here at the lodge. Upon entering the assembly hall, the responding officers found the body on the altar. The candles on each side were lit. The ME's team and the forensics squad are the crew you see working on the body. Please be mindful of the cones."

Rebecca looked around at the building, which was in various stages of disrepair. After walking through some anterooms, she was led into a large hall used for the various symbolic rituals of the philanthropic brotherhood. She was met by an acquaintance on the Force with whom she had worked previously, Officer Eshani Shahnawaz.

"Shan, what is this place?"

"Ancient history in this town. A lodge organization, 'The Ancient Order of the Sons of Osiris.' A spin-off from the Masons-- prominent philanthropists in their day. Goes back about seventy years. Membership has all but ceased – a few old-timers. They meet about once or twice a year now."

The police officer gestured to an elderly gentleman with a big ring of keys. He looked very distressed.

"That's Mr. Abernathy, the volunteer caretaker. He keeps the place relatively clean, although it really resembles an old crypt."

The police officer checked her notes and said, "Not the first time we have had a break-in here. No security system, just old locks... a bad part of town, vagrants, druggies, kids, etc. The city is working on condemning the property. Still, the Broward County Historical Society claims there is some interest in the architectural designs and the paintings."

Rebecca looked around the hall. Under 15-foot ceilings, Egyptian deities, motifs, and hieroglyphics competed with spray-painted graffiti around the room. Beyond the altar was a dais with what seemed to be a group of very worn, throne-like chairs. A carved rostrum featured the name of the lodge encircling the ankh, the symbol of eternal life.

Most of the light fixtures, in the form of lotus blossoms, were either broken or not working. Dust and dirt covered the rickety-looking furniture. On the ledge beneath one broken window, a family of mourning doves was roosting, their plaintive calls adding to the macabre atmosphere.

As Rebecca and the two police officers approached the body, Detective Don Rains said, "Ms. Quinto, thanks for coming over. More excitement so quick on the heels of your New York adventure, it would seem."

Rebecca nodded and said, "Shan has been giving me the details. Any additional points of interest?"

The detective turned to the corpse and said, "Let's start with the setting. The altar covering and the candles are recent as is that." He pointed to a dish of smoldering charcoal, which sent a spiral of smoke up to the ceiling and out into the spacious room.

A familiar voice from a man standing in the shadows said, "The Ancient Egyptians sent incense prayers to the gods in worship three times a day. They offered frankincense in the morning, myrrh at midday, and Kyphi in the evening. This is the last type. You would be interested to know that the gentleman from the lodge told us they keep no incense here."

"Then, it was part of the staging of the body."

Rains commented. "I contacted Doctor al-Mahdi because of the circumstances surrounding this situation. The connection was a logical one."

He gestured to the body as the forensics folks moved slightly aside.

"A woman in her late twenties. Death occurred by strangulation. Notice the bruises on the throat, which seem to have been intentionally exposed, the head wrappings parted here and here. The state of the rigor indicates that she has been dead for about three to four days. Outside of the oddities of the display of the corpse, that is all we can tell until a more in-depth examination can be made at the morgue, an autopsy."

Rebecca said, "The exposed throat is an extraordinary detail. The killer wants no ambiguity regarding who the victim is. He is flaunting his act of murder."

Detective Rains continued, "We have found lots of fingerprints and are running them. All footprints in the dust of this room indicate intrusion by four individuals wearing running shoes. They broke in, laid the body here, ignited the ritual objects, and left. The call to police headquarters came from neighbors. They are being interviewed, including Mr. Abernathy here." The old gentleman nodded.

Rebecca asked, "What do the amount of wax and the ash of the incense burn tell you regarding the time of the break-in?"

"Set up occurred approximately one hour before discovery. The room was full of smoke when we got here."

There was a commotion at the other end of the hall.

"I told you, man, I got nothing to do with this. The dude just paid us to... um... open up the place, you see, and put the body in here."

The speaker being led into the chamber was a teenager, terrified and speaking rapidly. Officer Eshani Shahnawaz had the young man in handcuffs and motioned him to what was perhaps the only sturdy chair on the premises.

"We picked up D'wan Jamison in the Park n' Fly lot, four blocks away near the airport. Two others were with him; they beat it outta there, and we are looking."

The kid was sniffling and staring at his shoes. Officer Shahnawaz took off one of the handcuffs but left the other hanging from the boy's wrist for effect. The other detective examined the soles of his running shoes.

"D, what the hell are you doing getting in this trouble?"

The boy looked up and recognized Rebecca. He started to run his mouth off again, speaking faster than the human ear could register.

"Easy, D. Take it slowly. Just tell us what happened."

"Miss Q, we was just hanging at the Low Key over in Progresso Villiage nigh 'bout 'leven or make that 11:30."

"Who?"

Detective Rains said, "You know this youngster?"

"I do, detective. Mr. Jamison is a former associate of a crime-fighting friend of mine, Doctor Kayne Sorenson. He fielded a group of youth who reported to him about the street activities of this city, crimes, and criminal goings-on the police were often unaware of. About a year ago, Mr. Jamison went through a tough personal spell and dropped off the force."

Rains added, "Yes, Doctor Sorenson and Nick Seschi from Wilton Manors PD helped our department on a few of the tough cases."

"Yes, you are looking at one of the remnants of his urban spy network, usually kids no one wanted."

D'wan blurted out, "I didn't even know the bitch was dead."

He sobbed audibly and added, "Sorry, Miss Q."

"D, who was in on this?"

"Me, Jojo, Alison B, Mervis, but he runned away, and Big Anthony."

"Tell us how it happened."

'So, as I said, we was at the Low Key. Dude at the 7-11 plays that loud shit-ass music, and kids can't stand it to hang there no more -- so, well, there we were. Two white guys drived up and asked us if we wanted to earn some cash. Say yes. And he takes us to this shit hole with that. I 'member he was this big dude. Hard to understand. Jojo said his accent was Polish or some such shit."

The boy pointed to the body on the altar being examined by city and county law enforcement members. The street urchin began more heavy crying and wiped his nose and face on his sleeve. With some snorting punctuation, he continued.

"All we had to do was get inside... Alison's specialty... Oh shit, man, I didn't say that... Oh, shittt."

The kid was losing it again. Rebecca put a hand on his heaving shoulders.

"Easy D. Finish the story."

"Dude said it was just a practical joke and that...." He pointed again,

"... was a dummy.

"Miss Q, I ain't gonna lie to you. I knowed that it was a real dead body once the dude drove off, but there we were on the street wid it. Right out front, and the fucker said he would get us if we didn't come through. We decided to finish the job, the candles, and the smoke shit and get the fuck out."

Rains asked, "How much did you get, son?"

D'wan jumped up off the chair, reached down into his left sock, and pulled out some folded bills. He put them into the hand of Don Rains– five twenties.

Shan said, "Think you could help me recognize the guys who put you up to this, D'wan?"

The boy huffed and sniffed deeply, getting his non-bawling breathing and speaking back online.

"You mean... like when they draw the guy from what I tell 'em?"

"Yes, something like that. Only, now we do it with computers."

"Cool. Yeah, sure, but I nark this guy, and my ass is dead, lady. I need that whatchamacallit– protection thing– send me way out west and change my name. You know, so he can't get me. Miss Q, am I going to prison?"

"No, Darling. I have a friend who's gonna talk to you all about that. Her name is Miss McQueen. Most likely, you will need to see a judge, but knowing Queenie, everything will be OK. No one will be hunting you, D."

She handed him a tissue.

"Queenie's going to also have a talk with you about things like school, your friends, and living arrangements. I'm gonna make sure that she and Officer Shan here get you into the police youth group so you can help them with cases as you did with Doctor Sorenson. But D'wan, I hear from our mutual friend, Ms. Porter, there are most nights you don't come home."

The young man looked down at his shoes again. Rebecca lifted his chin, forcing him to look her in the eye.

"Listen, D, Queenie is going to look into some stuff on you, and hopefully, you'll come up righteous. You had better not be skipping school, D, or flunking out of Stranahan High. That will upset Miss Queenie, and I guarantee pissing her off will be worse than prison. Do you understand what I'm saying?"

"Yes, ma'am. I heard about her."

He sighed and said, "Just 'nother black woman makin' life miserable for ole D'wan. I...."

"Whoa, hotshot."

Rebecca nodded to Eshani Shahnawaz as the boy looked up.

"The term is 'women of color.' Get it right, Darling. And yeah, we are pissed off, to begin with, so show respect and heed our sound advice, D. You may live to see sixteen."

"Uh, huh."

Shan said, "Just found out they are bringing in a couple more of Mr. Jamison's friends to the East Broward Boulevard Station. Still looking for one."

"That'd be Big Anthony. He knows how to hide. Who's he? Dude looks scary."

Rebecca turned to see Skylar al-Mahdi approaching from out of the shadows of the lodge hall. She turned back to the juvenile.

"D, that is another friend of mine who is helping with all of this. You go along now with Officer Shahnawaz. I will arrange for Ms.

McQueen to meet you at the station. Remember what I said, D, otherwise...."

"OK, Miss Q. and Thanks."

The street urchin left with the police from the front doors of the lodge. Rebecca addressed the Egyptologist, who was analyzing everything going on, the young suspect, the staged corpse, and the very kitschy lodge. Rebecca followed him back to the body as the police unzipped a body bag on a stretcher.

Skylar said in a cold monotone, "You will find amulets beneath the wrappings and more sacred incense materials, musk, jasmine, and sandalwood in the folds. From the appearance of what we can see of the flesh on the face, the body was not embalmed, just wrapped in the old way."

He fought to overcome the shock of recognition as the police detective carefully unwound more of the head wrappings. Don Rains had an unspoken question on the expression on his face.

The Egyptian scholar waited in silence and then said. "Yes, officer, in this gruesome mimicry of an Egyptian mummy is the body of Elizabeth King."

Chapter Twenty-Two: Sacred Relics
Fort Lauderdale to Thessaloniki, Macedonia

"Our plane leaves in an hour, so I thought we could strategize with some background on this project. The flight is fourteen hours, but there will not be much privacy while we are in the air."

Rebecca had settled with Mark and Skylar into a private corner of the VIP Lounge, Terminal 1, Fort Lauderdale– Hollywood International. Skylar flipped open his laptop. He wore the effects of the discovery of the body of Elizabeth King with noticeable gravity and brooding silence.

Mark asked, "Anything further on the murder?"

Rebecca said, "I am afraid I left Micah to do the clean-up on that as far as the organization is involved. He will keep me apprised. Queenie is working with the police on the young suspects. Her *pro bono* work with the Youth League is incredible. She will make their heads spin."

"Yep, I think Jürgs is still trying to figure out what the fuck after dealing with Ms. Queenie."

Jügen Mathias crossed the lounge and settled into a chair next to Skylar.

"I am sorry to be late, my friends-- last-minute arrangements and details. Please continue with your discussion."

Rebecca went on, "The police believe Elizabeth was indeed abducted and killed in the garage four nights ago. You showed them that Skylar was about a quarter of a mile away when the abduction occurred, the alibi. The staging at the Egyptian Lodge was for the benefit of those connected with this Egyptian project, the chest of scrolls and all. The dynamic is terror. The killers are going for a whole historical motif, scorpions, death, and cobras, oh, my. They have targeted the Fritcher most likely for its notoriety."

"Yep, terrorists want big press. Easy to see we are dealing with some pretty deadly individuals."

Skylar spoke up, "Yes, Mr. Gadarn. If we are up against The Rising Dawn, I believe they will stop at nothing to secure the relics of the Ptolemaic Kings. After the failures in Syria and Iraq, they believe that the next Islamic state should be set up in Egypt."

Skylar continued, "The deadly chest contained diary entries from those connected to the Mouseion of Alexandria, the complex that contained the famous Library. The twelve scrolls date from the 3rd century BCE, with five coming from the Common Era. It is not, however, a continuous record."

He pulled up the translation of the documents on his laptop.

"Much is bureaucratic notations, but I was able to extract the materials that refer to the sacred museum artifacts associated with Alexander. Please allow me to show you one significant entry, the translation of which I am relatively satisfied."

The Egyptian scholar pulled up a map of ancient Alexandria, c. 310 BCE and a Word document. "Please consider this entry from one of the manuscripts in the chest."

***

THE ISLAND OF RHODES, GREECE

I, Apollonius, have been forced to retire as Director of the Mouseion at the command of the Pharoah Ptolemy III Euergetes. Now, I will write my poetry and forget the [turmoil of] the capital under the new king. I have returned at long last to my home with fears for the ancient treasures housed in the Great Library.

I write of the academics first, a community of the most distinguished minds in the world. Alexandria has become a capital for knowledge and learning like no other on the face of the earth. The [royal decrees] have resulted in a gathering of great minds steeped in tradition and scholarship in the teachings of Aristotle, Euclid, Eratosthenes of Cyrene, Aristophanes of Byzantium, Aristarchus of Samothrace, Diogenes the Cynic, and the scholars of the East, at the Mouseion. The survival of these masterminds and [their works] is at the whim of the dynasty.

My own student, the Lord Pharoah, Ptolemy III, a most willful boy, has decided that I am too much of a burden to him. Alas, I was too lenient with him. But, I do not, in any way, disavow our clashes over the Mouseion. And so, he rules, and I go into exile.

The number of books we hold swells with every month. Our winter inventory showed 285,000 volumes. Plans are in place to move many of the scrolls to the Serapeum and continue to expand the acquisitions. It is crucial [to secure the] rarest of our holdings at the Serapeum Temple as it sits high in the city from [the dangerous waters] of the port. There are plans to add to the Library's space with warehouses near the Mouseion. Still, I oppose an expansion such as this, which does not address the dangerous elements that threaten the holdings.

The most precious treasures in the world are none of these, however. During my tenure, every effort has gone into preserving the Library's collection of the burial goods of the Divine Alexander. The extensions of the tunnels will soon be finished, and we have the replicas. This [divinely] inspired plan of the gods will drop a shroud of secrecy over the belongings of the Great King, preserved for all eternity as he reigns in the underworld. Few will know the secrets of the treasury of the Library.

And so, I leave with a sense of tranquility to write with divine inspiration in the shadow of the Colossus of my home city of Rhodes.

May the Father of the Nine Muses, glorious Apollo, protect me and the golden gifts of the great king.

***

Skylar said, pointing to the document, "It is this man, a creative genius, who preserved the museum of Alexander. You can see that political rivalries were virulent and threatened the sacred holdings of the Library.

"The Library declined and flourished depending on the politics of the Egyptian Throne. Ptolemy VIII actually expelled the scholars in 145 BCE. Julius Caesar accidentally burned the Library's warehouses near the port in the civil war of 48 BCE. The Christians of the Common Era sought to eliminate all references to Egypt's pagan past, as did the

Muslims seven centuries later. Priceless books and artifacts were destroyed.

"But the museum still existed, hidden away, and even now, forces that covet its treasures seek them with evil intent."

Mark said, "This is historical fiction. There is no way over all that time, with all the conflict you describe, not to mention documented earthquakes, tidal waves, and such, that the grave of Alexander the Great is still around somewhere. Impossible. You are like one of those crazies who once a year claim they found Noah's ark– mythology, man."

"Hear me out, please. I have devoted my life to researching this dynasty."

The scholar and the journalist exchanged challenging looks. Rebecca surreptitiously placed her hand on Mark's in an attempt at concord.

Skylar continued, "Additional research supports the theory that the Librarian, Apollonius, had extraordinarily gifted craftsmen and manuscript specialists making copies of essential books and burial objects. Please remember that the ancient Egyptian religion was fanatical about keeping graves undisturbed to allow the deceased to rest in peace. There is evidence that a brotherhood of priests actually had custody of the gold and glass sarcophagus of the dead king, and this contingent was connected to the lost museum itself."

Rebecca said, "Skylar, there are so many theories. The burial of the body at Memphis. The Macedonians, at one point, claim to have received it at their Royal Tombs. In Alexandria, it would seem the Ptolemies could not figure out how to keep the relics secure.

Skylar pointed again to the document.

"But, he could."

He continued using the map of the ancient city. "Archaeologists have postulated an elaborate security system connected with the Great Library, the Temple of the Serapeum, the Ptolemaic Dynastic Tombs of the Soma, and the Second Library. We are unsure what that plan was, but this entry supports that conclusion."

Jürgen said, "So what are you saying, Doctor Al-Mahdi? Throughout the centuries, so many have claimed custody of the body of Alexander the Great, and grave thievery being rife in ancient times, the librarians moved the important holdings when danger arose? I tend to agree with Mark's assessment."

"Yes, Agent Mathias, it is my theory that Apollonius, anticipating the danger to the Library's museum from the greed and corruption that surrounded the collection, came up with a plan to use duplicates. Thus, he could hide the real treasures in a secret place."

Tapping the map, he looked into the eyes of his three companions in turn. He said, "Alexandria's lost museum– that is what we seek."

Rebecca added, "And so do our friends of the Rising Dawn, doctor."

Mark said, "I was able to put out some feelers. My sources shared with me some intelligence regarding that ultra-conservative Islamist crusade. It appears to be a very young movement and operates well below the radar with all due respect to INTERPOL. It sees itself as a successor to the declining ISIL insurgency but has a distinct flavor and perspective. There is chatter on the web about the establishment of something called the Last Empire."

Chapter Twenty-Three: The Royal Stag Hunt
The Archaeological Museum of Pella, Greece

"You have wasted your time, I am afraid, *moite prijateli*. There is no tomb of Alexander in this place."

The speaker who embraced them as "my friends" was a young graduate student from the Aristotelian University in Thessaloniki, Leonnatus Gianopoulos. Skylar's contacts in academia arranged for the young archaeologist to meet the Quinto party at the airport and serve as their guide to the ancient capital of Pella.

Rebecca started, "Leonnatus…."

"That's with two 'n's,' Ms. Quinto. It means …"

Skylar interrupted and said with a very flat expression, "One who is dashing like the lion."

The young man blushed, "Yes, dashing– as in running, not as in…."

Rebecca finished, "Handsome? But Darling, you are. A young Alexander himself, Complete with golden curls."

Mark watched a look from the boy to the professor. *Bit of a crush thing going on here. Professional admiration and perhaps more.* It was a one-way communication, however. Skylar's expression was unreadable, as always.

A flash of sky-blue eyes and the lad spoke again, attempting to deflect what was sure to be the next comment on how he attracted all the women in the city. He said, "It is indeed an honor to be able to work with the imminent Doctor al-Mahdi and your colleagues, sir. I was assured that you are familiar with my credentials."

"I am. I understand that you are the youngest member of the archaeological school at the Aristotelian to complete a doctorate."

Leonnatus said with noticeable excitement, "Almost finished. I am scheduled to defend my dissertation in the spring."

Rebecca said, "On Alexander the Great?"

"No, Miss. My research has been on Ptolemy I Soter and the wars of his successor generals, the *Diadochi*. Alexander, however, is pivotal to my archaeological and historical research. I am excited to meet Doctor al-Mahdi, one whom I have studied extensively. His work, I mean."

The youth reddened again.

Mark's following comment was tinged with a bit of exasperation.

"Before we all go off sucking each other's dicks, can we get back to the tomb of Alexander and why we came to Macedonia? It seems it may be a non-sequitur if the tomb is not here."

For the first time, Skylar's eyes flashed with emotion. The tenor of his voice was very controlled.

"Mr. Gadarn, at the risk of being rude, may I say that it is important to put our research in a historical context. Pella is the birthplace of Alexander and the capital of his family's ancient kingdom. It was once the largest and wealthiest city in Greek Macedonia. As far as the research for our project goes. We must have information from primary archaeological sources."

Rebecca said, "I agree with Skylar. Our project is to prevent the theft of the artifacts associated with Alexander the Great, most specifically, his tomb if it exists. Our visit to Macedonia may provide clues regarding those who want to make off with those artifacts. It is here we will best understand the context of the great warrior.

Leonnatus said with excitement, "Yes, we are Macedonians. A unique race of warriors and scholars. We brought Hellenistic culture to the world with the conquests of the greatest leader the world has ever seen."

He continued, indicating the building around them.

"The Archaeological Museum of Pella is close to the ancient royal palace of Macedonian kings and queens. I have obtained special passes for us on that dig. I will also take you to the excavations of the House of Dionysus. The mosaics of the abduction of Helen are breathtaking. Also, I can get us on the work being done on the Agora."

Skylar said, "*G-din Džanopulos*, can you get some time for us at Pella's cemeteries? We are particularly interested in those from the Hellenistic period, the 3rd and 2nd centuries BCE."

"Of course, Doctor al-Mahdi. Please be so kind as to call me Leonnatus. I never insist on formalities."

If the expected response was, "And you can call me Skylar," it never came.

Rebecca broke in with, "Leonnatus, please show us the Alexander artifacts. We may get some sense of the historical quest for the tomb."

"At once, Miss. So, Pella was the capital of the Macedonian Kingdom that gave birth to Alexander. The objects in this gallery are from the Hellenistic Period – the 3rd and 2nd centuries before the Common Era.

"This head of the king, dated 325-300 BCE, was found by accident about seven kilometers from where we are standing near the city of Giannitsa. That place has a spectacular football team, by the way."

"Continue with your tour, please. History? Science?" The soft baritone of Skylar al-Mahdi carried with it a bit of insistence.

"Of course, sir."

Rebecca was slightly transfixed by the bust of Alexander and remarked, "There seems to be an other-worldly gaze in the artist's depiction. He was so young – conqueror of the known world until his armies made him turn around."

"Yes, Miss Quinto, the Macedonians had fought with Alexander for 10 years from here, Pella, all the way to the banks of the Ganges in India, conquering Persia and Egypt along the way. Close to his thirtieth birthday, his comrades in arms revolted, and the king understood he had to return. It was 326, and Alexander would be dead in Babylon two years later."

Mark said, " And then the civil wars began over who would control the empire."

"Correct, Mr. Gadarn. May I say, sir, I am in admiration of your work in reporting from the fronts of several wars, Syria, Afghanistan, and lately, Yemen, correct?"

Mark nodded.

"Thanks, kiddo. So you are familiar with the internecine struggles for power within the ranks of battle and the fighting between Alexander's generals."

"Yes, sir. The politics that surrounded the King were powerful forces. Much like the battles waged not too far from where we are today, in the East."

Skylar made a gesture that again communicated that the graduate student should stick to the script. Leonnatus immediately switched to a serious tone and continued.

"Ms. Quinto, These floor mosaics are perhaps the best depiction of Alexander we have. The first is the 'Royal Lion Hunt,' from the late fourth century. It was excavated from the House of Dionysus."

The pebble mosaic showed two Macedonians hunting a lion on foot with a spear and sword. Their capes billowed as they raised their weapons against a fierce foe. One figure's hat, a Macedonia *kausia*, was pushed back, exposing a handsome face framed in golden curls.

"The hunters are depicted as naked, traditional for heroic figures in ancient Greek art. Alexander is on the left, and this figure is believed to be one of his generals, Craterus, who appears to be rescuing the king."

Rebecca said, "They seem to be presented as equals. Most Oriental kings would be mounted and dressed in regal robes. The Macedonian love of democracy is represented by how the two men are presented in relation to each other. They are staged as equals."

Skylar said, "You are correct, Ms. Quinto. But, as Alexander conquered the eastern realms, his politics changed. He adopted a king's trappings, which was important for gaining the loyalty of his eastern subjects. The Macedonians would have none of that, and some actually plotted his overthrow."

Mark turned in the gallery and gestured to a second mosaic. "Seems to be of similar design. What can you tell us?" He pointed to the figure with his hair parted in the middle and pushed up off his forehead. Is that our boy?"

"Yes, Mr. Gadarn. This is from the House of the Abduction of Helen. That is the King on the right. The other figure, the one with the double-headed ax, is his lover and one of his generals, Hephaistion."

Rebecca said, "There is a big difference in these two pieces, although the composition and theme are very similar. In the Stag Hunt, the artist has a remarkable ability to use shading and shadow to show very dynamic movement against the dark background. The energy of the hunters, the surprised stag, and the dog, who seems to be dashing in to attack, create a sense of violence and drama that is very Hellenistic. It is a more sophisticated piece than the Lion Hunt mosaic."

As Rebecca spoke, visitors to the gallery grouped closer to the contingent from the Fritcher, eager to enhance their experience in the Pella Museum. Both Mark and Skylar were visibly uncomfortable with the semi-circle of strangers surrounding Leonnatus and Rebecca. Mark checked Skylar with a nod and moved off toward a group of two who held back but were clearly tracking the Museum CEO from Fort Lauderdale.

A woman in a pith helmet and scarf that covered all but her eyes adjusted her oversized sunglasses. She pretended to point to a guidebook and converse quietly with her companion, a gentleman in a white linen suit, beige fedora, and dark glasses. The couple projected the aura of moneyed tourists. Both were fixed on Rebecca and her companions.

Who the hell wears shades to a museum? Only someone who is definitely not into the art and is up to no good.

Glancing over his shoulder, Mark saw Skylar moving Leonnatus toward the exit. The young Macedonian seemed intent on continuing to impress his charges and attempted to provide the history of a few more pieces from the Hellenistic age. Still, Skylar's strong arm was not to be resisted.

Still sporting a stiff limp, Mark approached the couple only to be sidelined by a woman and three children who nearly knocked him to the ground. The youngsters pulled at him excitedly, chattering in a foreign tongue. When he righted himself, the couple in white was nowhere to be seen.

Rebecca broke off, backtracked, and took Mark's arm.

"What is it, Darling? Something's up."

"They're gone – a suspicious couple, dogging us since we got here. I was going to ask the creepos what their issue was, but the woman with the kids bowled me over. I think they are fascinated by Americans."

"Mark, what children?"

They both looked around the gallery – no mother and children, no couple in white.

***

"No, my friends, Alexander is not here. But I do know where we need to go next."

Leonnatus spoke in hushed tones in the foyer of the museum. He had the attention of Rebecca, Mark, and Skylar. The Egyptian was focused on their guide and finding out what had just transpired in the gallery. He considered a private conversation with his colleagues.

He spoke one word to the young man.

"Where?"

"Sixty-four kilometers from where you stand. The Royal Tombs at Vergina in the burial mound of Philip II. We go by train. Less than one hour."

Mark shook his head. "I repeat, then why are we in Pella?"

Rebecca pulled him close. "We needed some perspective, Darling. A good conservator knows the history of the artifacts."

"Are you Doctor al-Mahdi?" The speaker was a museum docent.

"Yes, I am."

"This was left for you." The Macedonian handed Skylar a crisp black card. In red was an Arabic script.

لقد حان وقت المسيح

Chapter Twenty-Four: Train Windows
Pella to Vergina, Greece

Skylar made sure that Leonnatus was out of earshot. The student was working on his mobile phone in a seat four rows ahead. The train headed south at a rapid clip to the small central Macedonian town of Vergina.

"He wants to join our expedition. Leonnatus has also requested my advice on his dissertation on Ptolemaic Egypt."

Mark said with a smirk, "He fell hard for you, blue eyes. So fuckin' obvious. I'd make him out to be a sapiosexual– dude is hot for fit smart asses." He finished his remarks cocking a thumb and finger at the blankly staring Egyptian.

Rebecca said, "No. He's all of, what, twenty-two? There is too much danger in this to drag in an almost-a-minor."

"He may be an asset. I will admit that my knowledge is a bit rusty since I have been on loan to the Fritcher. The boy is well up on current archaeological science. He is from the region, and his research is somewhat groundbreaking. I will commit my energies to keeping him safe, just as Mr. Gadarn protects you, his woman… only different."

As soon as he said this, Skylar realized it was very out of the ordinary. He pulled at his long black hair. Both Mark and Rebecca smiled at the uncharacteristic comments from the usually monolithic Skylar.

"Ahhh, so the interest is purely academic. I see. Umm humm."

Mark had found the teasing point for the big man, and he went for it.

"Look, boss. Word on the Rialto is that you are a pretty adept cocksman, and the body is… ah… not bad." Mark did a hand swoop over the Egyptian in the seat facing him and Rebecca. "Think of it like the ancient Greeks and their boy lovers. Pretty appropriate if you ask me – Achilles and Patroclus, Alexander and Hephaistion – love is love, guy, or at this stage, perhaps it's just infatuation."

Characteristically, Skylar took issue with Mark's point of view.

"The sexual love of one man for another is forbidden by the Holy Scriptures, sir."

"OK, Skylar. Present circumstances require that you and I and Rebecca are on a first-name basis. Got it? If this shit is gonna work, you are going to have to relax that conservative Egyptian sphincter."

"Mark."

"Speaking figuratively, Beautiful. Keep calm, big guy. It's only sex. No freaking out necessary."

Skylar squirmed and gazed out at the Grecian countryside flying by the train window. He hesitated as he said, "The last time, Mark ... Ms. King. What followed was punishment for my sins of impurity."

"Jesus, Dude. You self-guilt much?"

Mark leaned in for the challenge saying, "Complete and utter bullshit, kid. You are so fucking intelligent, but your theology is crap. You think God is your personal guide and judge. Gotta say she has a hell of a lot of other things to do than keep a scorecard on who's zoomin' who."

The perplexed man snapped back.

"She?"

Rebecca said, "Yes, 'she.'"

Leonnatus dropped casually into the seat next to Skylar as Rebecca continued with, "Come on, Darling. Before God was a man, she was a woman. Surely, your field of archaeology has a plethora of evidence in that regard."

Leonnatus piped up, "As far back as the third millennia BCE and for thousands of years, in every part of the world, the Goddess was worshipped as the supreme deity. Here in the Mediterranean, her cult was replaced by the conquering hordes from Asia who followed the warrior sky god and established a culture of patriarchy."

"And while we are on the subject, let's roll back to that other thing you said. I want to clarify that I am not, as you put it, 'his woman.' I am my own person, as is he."

She squeezed Mark's hand and added, "We look out for each other."

"In my culture, women and girls have a secondary place to the men."

Now, it was Rebecca's turn to gaze thoughtfully out the window. Her thoughts went back to the conference on Female Genital Mutilation. After a moment, she said, "I am well aware of the cultural dissonance and stand firmly against all such marginalization and discrimination. It only leads to great suffering and torture."

Skylar nodded.

Leonnatus piped up. "Your perspective on relationships is fascinating. I also believe people who are in a close relationship actually become one person. Do you know the story of Alexander and the Empress Dowager of Persia?"

Skylar looked at the boy with a look of forbearance, saying, "My young friend, you are full of non-sequiturs, it would seem. Let's hope your doctoral thesis is not."

Now Leonnatus was beaming. He had gotten Skylar's attention, for the moment, at least.

He continued. "After the Macedonians defeated the Persians at the battle of Issus when Alexander entered the tent of the Persian Royal Family, Sisygambis, the mother of Darius II, knelt before Hephaestion, mistaking him for Alexander. When the dowager realized her error, she begged the forgiveness of the warrior king. Alexander is reported to have reassured her, saying, 'You were not mistaken, Mother, this man too is Alexander.' Very cool, yes?"

His eager expression met the blank stare of the Egyptian scholar.

Mark redirected.

"Leonnatus, the tomb is at Vergina? Seems poorly marketed if you ask me."

"Sir, I will confess. Alexander the Great is not there, either. There are clues among the artifacts of the Macedonian Royal Tombs that are important to us, and some of the finest Hellenistic archaeologists are on the excavation site. It is plain we must look to Egypt, and I am hoping you will take me with you on your expedition."

Rebecca said, "So, this is more background."

"A piece of the puzzle may be at the Tumulus, Ms. Quinto. Research involves gathering all the facts. You said so yourself."

Skylar sighed and said, "Believe it or not, I agree with Leonnatus. Suppose we are to find the funerary artifacts of the Macedonian King. In that case, it is important to enter the minds of the ancients. Not only did the campaign of the young Macedonian King change the world forever and spread Hellenism far and wide, but his death also turned the world upside down, creating a surviving empire that blended Hellenism with native cultures. Successive generations right up to the present have sought his legacy– it is lust for greatness, power, the preservation of culture, and the need to be part of a divine plan."

Rebecca said, "Like the leaders of the Rising Dawn."

"Yes."

Leonnatus asked, "Sir, your altercation in the gallery, may I ask?"

Mark said, "Back in Florida, we encountered some violence connected to this project. It seems to have followed us here."

The young man was silent.

Rebecca said, "Leonnatus, Darling, anything unusual going on connected with the digs here in Macedonia."

Now, Leonnatus stared at the passing countryside. He came back into the conversation and said. "Yes, Ms. When we arrive in Vergina, I will introduce you to one who can explain some recent raids on our sites. It seems there has been a rumor of unrest both here and in Vergina. Strange symbols were appearing near the ancient sites."

He reached across and traced a figure on the glass.

Rebecca said, "Skylar, the calling card at the museum?" What did it say?"

The train to Vergina entered a tunnel, and the interior lights flickered. Leonnatus' window art alternated between glowing and invisibility. In the alternating darkness, Skylar tapped the glass.

The glyph flashed.

المسيح

Skylar showed the note from the Pella Museum with a similar message.

"It means the Messiah has arrived."

Thomas Paul Severino

Chapter Twenty-Five: The Tumulus of Philip II
Vergina, Greece

"*Habeas Corpus.*"

"I beg your pardon, Mr. Mark."

"Produce the body."

Leonnatus looked around as if confused. The quartet was seated at Niko's Restaurant of Vergina, sharing some late-morning delicacies, *bougatsa, loukanopita,* and *zambonotiropita*, an assortment of cheese, ham, and spinach pies. The aroma of rich Greek fare filled the outdoor café shielded from the sun by a blue and white canopy.

Across the street, a wall and heavily-ladened pomegranate and olive trees, tall rosemary bushes, and assorted flowering shrubbery blocked the view of the Royal Burial Mounds of the ancient city of Aigai. Tourists entered through black iron gates and crossed an ample graveled space to the underground ramps that led into the buried museum resting under the slopes of the grass-covered hill. The modern structure on top of the Royal Macedonian Necropolis is set beneath a landscape of outstanding natural beauty. The sun was bright, and the day promised to be very warm.

In the café, Rebecca answered for the young scholar.

"So you are telling us that the treasures of Alexander are not among the burial artifacts of his relatives. I am talking about his father, Philip II, and assorted Macedonian Royals, including his son, Alexander IV."

Leonnatus added, "Correct, the archaeological evidence claiming that the tombs here contain the bones of Alexander the Great is not conclusive. But, my friends, this is the Great Tumulus, a grave mound excavated in 1977. There are over three hundred such cemetery mounds in this ancient capital of Macedonia. It is a UNESCO World Heritage Site."

Skylar said, "So, the ponderance of evidence on the subject shows that our quest must lead us to Egypt. Again, learning more about the family and comrades of Alexander is very important as a context for our search. The family and the generals fought to the death to secure the legacy of the boy king."

He added, "Leonnatus, you mentioned some plundering here in Aigai. Can you elaborate?"

"Professor, for us, the best source of that information has just entered the café."

Four heads turned to watch a woman make her way to their table.

Nilza Mendes.

***

Rebecca made notes. An exhibit at the Fritcher on the glories of the Macedonian King's conquests would be a stunning project for the art world, especially if the centerpiece were the mummy of Alexander the Great, found and authenticated.

Plan big. You can always scale back.

The architectural remains, the wall paintings, and the vast collection of grave goods were exhaustingly beautiful. A portrait of an ancient civilization steeped in the politics of conquest and backed by a Homeric religious tradition of hubris and destiny emerged under the spotlight display cases. Visitors were surrounded by ivory portraits, wall paintings, gold and silver jewelry, armory, and household accessories. Sets of gleaming silver vessels etched with florals and creatures from mythology were found near the sarcophagi as part of the burial goods for dining at the royal graves.

Royal regalia and battle gear glistened in the dark next to votive statues and paintings of an imperial hunt. There were art renderings of many cavorting Olympians enacting the myths that supported the political designs of the kingdom. Hades, King of the Underworld, flew across one wall in a glorious horse-drawn chariot. His strong arm encircled a screaming Persephone rebelling against his abduction, her limbs flailing in terror as she sought to escape.

Further into the subterranean part of the mound, temple-shaped tombs represented the best-preserved examples of the use of color in ancient architecture. Rebecca was awestruck in the presence of these, the oldest façades of ancient Macedonian buildings.

As a UNESCO World Heritage site, the very uncovering of the ancient graves was viewed as an act of destruction. The intricacies of a project for loaning important artifacts could take years. Rebecca knew she needed a powerful bargaining chip to attempt what could be an international coup in the art world.

She took Mark's hand in the semi-darkness.

"Darling, have you ever seen such beauty?"

"This stuff is magnificent. The power of this civilization to produce a world conqueror is almost tangible. One can only imagine the bullshit of palace intrigue and the tragic horrors of a royal family bent on the destruction of all rivals."

Rebecca agreed, saying, "So, then you add to the mix the power-hungry generals who waited to seize the throne after the death of the warrior king. No wonder they went to war among themselves. Imagine how pissed the Macedonians were when the news arrived at Pella that Ptolemy stole the mummy and brought it to Egypt. Wars, wars, and more wars, armed rebellion, and the assassination of members of the royal family – swords were drawn, and the poison was in the wine."

Mark said, "I saw where they uncovered another sarcophagus in the anteroom of Philip's tomb. The remains are believed to have been the bones of his Thracian wife, Meda. The story goes that she committed suicide after hearing the news of the death of Philip."

Rebecca's comment dripped with sarcasm.

"Such a dutiful woman."

Mark laughed and slipped an arm around her waist. He whispered in her ear. "And just what would you do for me, Beautiful?"

She gave him a soft elbow to the ribs.

"Am I to understand that even exposure to ancient civilizations gets you frisky?"

Mark glanced at the painting of the Abduction of Persephone and said, "I am a hot-blooded man of soldiering and legend standing in the dark with a gorgeous woman. Shall I throw you over my shoulder and carry you to the depths of my lustful realm?"

"You are such a piece of work, Darling. It just never goes down."

Nilza, serving as their guide, explained, "The Tomb of Philip II was discovered in 1986 and was found to be unplundered. The marble sarcophagus was discovered at the back of the tomb. It contained this silver chest, containing the bones of the monarch and this beautiful golden, oak-leaf diadem."

Leonnatus drew near the glass case, lifted to eye level on a smooth pedestal. A pin spot seemed to make the coffer glow with an inner light in the darkened gallery. Its hovering cloud of a gold leaf crown burned with a hypnotic fire. He began to speak with great reverence.

"Cremation was the custom, and for a king of Philip's stature, the pyre would have been several stories high. The bones were washed in wine and encased in a *larnakes*, this silver chest. The remains would be folded in a purple cloth with this exquisite crown set on top."

Gold amulets, the size of large buttons, were carved with the image of the sun, a symbol of the Temenid dynasty of Philip II and Alexander the Great. This motif was found everywhere among the artifacts. The top of the gold cremation chest sported a large sunburst. Gallery after gallery showed Classic Greek art and Hellenistic cultural objects at their apex. A banner in one gallery of marble grave steles portrayed pictures of the busts of Philip II and Alexander.

Rebecca drew close to the portrait of the young king. She took a moment to say, "The bust is by one of Alexander's favorite sculptors, Lysippus of Sicyon. See how the artist has captured the character and personality of the great warrior. Look at the curve of his neck. His face is turned to the sky with an arrogance that seems to indicate that he was born to share the world with Zeus."

Mark read from the hanging, "Alexander's expression seems to say, 'Zeus, you take the sky, I will take the earth.'"

Rebecca asked Nilza, "I thought you explained when we met in New York that as a member of the Organization for Security and Co-operation in Europe, you headed up an initiative for the protection of women. How is it that you are here amid all this archaeology and so knowledgeable?"

"Aigai is one of my favorite spots in all the world. My work with the Russian government has involved their interest in the Macedonian culture. So, my portfolio of interest is large and varied. That being said, the great numbers of migrants seeking asylum in Europe and the challenges faced by ultra-conservative Muslim women and girls are of utmost concern to my office."

Rebecca was silent.

Seriously? Didn't really answer my question. Russians interested in Macedonia? Very odd. An obvious dodge. Strange.

Rebecca went with the ambiguity, saying, "Yes, my dear, many refugees have brought with them the custom of female mutilation. We have much work to do."

Rebecca said, "Ironic, is it not? Here on a continent where ancient women wielded power of unfathomable magnitudes. We seem to be taking a giant step backward."

Skylar, with Leonnatus alongside, wanted to bring the discussion back to the Museum. He asked the OSC officer, "It seems the Museum of the Tumulus had a break-in last week. Can you speak about that?"

"As a matter of fact, I can. After the incident, the police contacted me thinking, ah… I could provide some advice."

Nilza was slightly uncomfortable but continued, "Yes, there was a burglary that is being considered what you call an inside job. The security system was breached. Two days ago at the Tomb of the Prince – the resting place of Alexander IV."

Nilza pointed to a hallway. "Come. It's just this way."

As they walked to the museum's section on the last of the temple tombs, Leonnatus took up the narrative.

"This burial site was built near that of Philip's about thirty years later and is most likely the resting place of Philip's grandson, the adolescent son of Alexander the Great and Roxane. She was the Sogdian princess of Bactria. Alexander the Great married her after defeating Darius III, the Achaemenian king, and invading Persia. Their child was Alexander IV. He was murdered along with his mother by Cassander, a usurper of the throne after Alexander died."

As they approached the area in the museum displaying the burial artifacts of the last of the dynasty, museum security and the police attempted to stop them.

Nilza produced her ID and spoke to a police officer in Greek. She introduced Rebecca, Mark, Skylar, and Leonnatus.

She explained, "The entire area is considered a crime scene, but in the last two days, a forensics team has been all over it. Of particular interest have been the security cameras and the recorded tapes.

"This officer says that they initially believed that the thieves took nothing, that they fled without disturbing any of the artifacts. Now they are not so sure."

As they watched, the back of the laminated safety glass display case protecting the diadem and funeral urn of Alexander IV was removed by a museum preservationist wearing white cotton gloves. When the metal lid was lifted, there were excited remarks and flashes of a forensic camera.

The silver cremation vessel of Alexander's son was empty.

Chapter Twenty-Six: The Other "Woman"
Vergina, Greece

"Welcome to the Dimitra Guesthouse. I am Aphrodite, and we are delighted that you can stay with us."

"So very nice to meet you, Darling. My assistant set up the reservations under the name of Quinto. What a lovely hotel and so convenient to Vergina-Aigai."

"One double and a double with single beds, two nights. Excellent. Your luggage was dropped off earlier and is in your rooms, Ms. Quinto. I hope I guessed right."

Aphrodite glanced at the three men who were looking around the beautifully decorated and very cozy inn. She turned to pick up the two keys.

"You and Mr. Gadarn have 206 with the double bed, and the gentlemen have 204. Miss."

"You have it absolutely correct. Thank you."

The proprietress said, "My Nico follows your adventures, Mr. Gadarn. You are the reporter for CBN, am I correct?"

"Yes, ma'am. I'm the one."

"I hope that you have the chance to meet my Nico. Have you eaten?"

Leonnatus interrupted, "Excuse me, do you have WiFi?"

"Yes, of course, sir. You will find the information on everything you and your friend need to join our secure network on the desk in your room."

Skylar said, "I am not his friend, Madam. I am his ... ah ...."

The Egyptian blinked, looked at the young graduate student, and then at Rebecca and Mark, totally at a loss.

Mark quickly filled in the gap.

"Teacher."

So that they would not go down that road, Rebecca rewound to the food question.

"Aphrodite, we are famished to tell the truth."

"Good. I fix you something. Once you have a chance to relax, I send you to the best restaurant in town for dinner. We Macedonians, like most Europeans eat dinner very late by American standards. Please follow me."

On the second floor, Aphrodite unlocked the door of 204. Both Skylar and Leonnatus did a light intake of breath. The twin beds were side by side. Leonnatus looked like a kid on Christmas morning. The somewhat nervous professor started to protest, but Rebecca pushed them both into the room as she backed out.

"Meet in our room in a few, Darlings."

Skylar attempted to follow her as she exited, but she pulled the door between them. She mouthed the words, "Just pull them apart," as she closed the door.

With Aphrodite out of earshot, she commented to Mark, "Straight men are so fucking complicated."

Mark was beside himself with mischief and hilarity, wanting to stir things up, but he managed to say, "Tell me about it."

Room 206 had a vintage double bed with a head and footboard of spiraling silver metal, a private balcony, a modest sitting area, and an immaculately tiled bathroom. A small serving tray set in the center of the bed held a deep red Greek wine bottle, two glasses, and two roses.

"This is lovely, Aphrodite. I only wish we were staying longer."

"Have you seen the archaeological sites?

"We were at the Royal Tumulus and are planning to see the palace and some of the shrines tomorrow."

"The vestiges of a once-great civilization, it was we Macedonians who spread Greek culture throughout the world, you know.

Democracy, freedom, learning, the ideals of greatness. We are a proud race."

"It has all been quite an education."

"Enough, I will see to your refreshments. Please let me know if you need anything."

"Efcharistó."

The beaming hotelier responded as she left the room, *"Parakaló."*

***

Mark pulled Rebecca into his arms and kissed her warmly. She met his advances with a loving embrace. He said huskily while his hands roamed over her body, "A little wine... a romantic early evening... how about we tear off a piece before...."

The knock was sharp and insistent.

"OK. So, boner kill. Five will get you ten; it's your Egyptian geekazoid wanting another room."

As Rebecca crossed the floor, she said. "Pity. The place is full up."

"Then, I guess it's time for him to throw the lad a mercy fuck."

"Mark Gadarn, behave yourself... hello, gentlemen."

Skylar was trying desperately to keep his cool.

Mark intervened, sweeping the sexual politics aside. He was always ready to cut to the chase.

"Folks, I need you three to consider something that will prove to be vital to our mission and the next steps in the quest. Come on in and sit down. There is someone I want you to meet."

Leonnatus and a very blank-faced Skylar each took a chair as Rebecca poured glasses of water from a crystal carafe. Mark opened his laptop, and Leonnatus was at the ready with the password for the network. The connection loaded up quickly.

"So, this is my friend, Eris."

Skylar said, "Eris was the goddess in Greek mythology who began the Trojan War with her spiteful wedding present."

Leonnatus piped up, "The golden apple of discord with the inscription, 'For the fairest.' The jealous Olympian goddesses face off... Paris judges in favor of the Goddess of Love... Helen of Troy is abducted... Greece goes to war.... thousands die."

Rebecca added, "And blind Homer sings of the immortal saga in the eternal 'Iliad'—all because Eris was left off the invitation list."

"Be well-advised. You never want to leave my goddess out of anything. This bitch is deadly," Mark warned. They watched as the screen revealed, in shades of blues and black, a figure that was a cross between the Delphic Oracle and the medieval prophet Nostradamus. The specter was clad in monks' robes with a face hidden in an oversized cowl.

"I have used her hacking skills to get critical, inside information. Her cognitive skills have saved my ass on plenty of occasions."

From the shadows of the techno-Phantom Zone, Eris asked for identifiers. Mark answered all of her questions accurately, and the specter, swimming in black and blue code, vanished in a swirl of dust and spinning ash.

In its place, a voluptuous blonde seated alone at a trendy bar came into view. A black stiletto dangled from one foot as she turned on her barstool, gorgeous legs catching the soft lighting. Her voice was velvety and sensual, replacing the staccato sounds of her previous emanation.

"So nice to see you again, Mark. I have missed you."

"You look ravishing tonight, Eris...."

Rebecca stood up and fumed. "Wait a goddam minute, Gadarn, you mean to tell me...."

Mark also stood. He crossed to the bed to grab the wine and the glasses. Leonnatus and Skylar howled.

"No, no, no... wait, wait, Rebecca. This is not what you think, Beautiful." He handed Leonnatus the wine with an aside.

"I think we are going to need this. Would you do the honors, please?"

Mark turned back to the very ticked-off Rebecca.

"Hear me out, please. Suspend all of your very salacious inferences."

On the screen, Eris twisted a lock of her long hair and simpered like an enticing coquette. "So, nice to see you again, Ms. Quinto. You never did say if I was helpful when last we met. I very much hope so."

Rebecca responded dourly, "Hey, Eris. How are things in techno land?"

To Mark, Rebecca sneered, "Amazing. I am making nice with a fuckin' cyber tramp."

As Leonnatus moved closer, Skylar covered his glass, signaling that he wanted to stay with water. The professor was still laughing when he said, "I can't believe you are having what is called techno-sex with an entity that is AI."

Leonnatus said, "I have to admit, she is very lifelike."

Mark was trying desperately to gain some ground here. He spoke to the vamp with ample cleavage. "Eris, research persona, please."

A sexy pout and, "Certainly, Mark."

The cocktail lounge melted to be replaced by the sparse decor of a modern office in an expensive penthouse. Eris morphed into a no-nonsense businesswoman– hair in a severe chignon and a dark business suit. Her hands flew over the keyboard of a computer. Her expression was professional and somewhat frigid.

"Still way too attractive. See if you can get the cyber bimbo to the 'evil crone' persona. And Mark, if she refers to me as 'Becky,' I will fling that laptop off the balcony."

Mark said through clenched teeth, "Seriously? You are jealous of a computer program?"

"I apologize for interrupting what I find to be a somewhat humorous human interaction, but our time together must be used efficiently. Will the two gentlemen move into the camera's range and hold still. Thank you. Please wait.

"Very good, we can proceed. I am accessing the data on Al Sama' al Muharib al-Mahdi, Ph.D., and Leonnatus Patroclus Gianopoulos. The Professor of Egyptology has a large amount of work online to be analyzed… please wait… al-Mahdi… interesting…. Yes, there is a definite direction I want to go with this… Islamic conservatives… one of my personal favorites. I will complete the portion of my intelligence on Skylar al-Mahdi in 2.7 minutes."

Eris seemed to be talking to herself as well as to her audience. She continued, "In my research on Mr. Gianopoulos, I have sent him an email on how to send me his doctoral thesis. My office's assurances of privacy can be found in a disclaimer in that communication. Be aware, sir, that the message will disappear 5.2 minutes after you receive the notification. The probability of the goddess compromising your pending doctoral defense is .000001%, sir. I will also offer editing suggestions and an academic rating of your research, resulting in my prediction of whether or not you will succeed in completing your doctorate. I have found information on your review board. Academics are always so complicated."

Now, the artificial intelligence beauty added, "I believe you have a conference call in your calendar for this afternoon with your counterparts in Vergina. Based on what I deduce to be the content of that conversation, the probability of the success of your inquiries is less than 40%.

"Mr. Gadarn, Mr. Gianopolous has an IQ of 143. On that scale, he represents 1 in 400 of the human population. He also has a significant body of work to be reviewed, and it is in my queue.

"Regarding Ms. Quinto… I am reviewing all the museum documents since our last encounter. Police reports and INTERPOL investigations are being accessed. There is significant concern about your activities going back years. The probability that your undertakings have created opposition is at a full 100%."

Rebecca took a swallow of her wine and said, "Bring it."

"I see information coming in on Agent Jürgen Mathias. Is he a good guy or a bad guy? This office will ascertain. The affair of the Swedish Ambassador's daughter… my, my… so very interesting. He is quite sexually intriguing."

Mark commented, "Her work takes her in many directions at once. She is opening a file on Jürges because of his association with us at this time. Others will surface also."

The oracle continued, "Beck—I beg you pardon, Rebecca's activities with the UNESCO and WHO New York Conference… I will look into the… yes, the suicide bomber at the Metropolitan Museum… getting this now…."

Eris suppressed a sly smile over the deliberate gaffe. She continued.

"FBI communications will take a bit of work, but I will get in… ahhh… our friends in the Rising Dawn– hello, you fuckin' bastard… OSCE, Nilza Mendes, hmmm… and then there's Alexander III of Macedonia… now that boy showed real hustle, a shame he was human."

Eris sipped a cup of coffee in her office.

"Looks like I will be pulling an all-nighter, boss."

She removed her glasses and looked through the screen at the humans in the room. With an index finger, the imaginary steno rubbed lipstick from her front teeth before speaking.

"The totality of your exploits, Mr. Gadarn, are always well known to me. According to my data-based predictions, your leg wound is 96% along the way to full use. I see that you are not walking with a cane, although your limp is somewhat perceptible. I recommend light to moderate exercise and, of course, total sexual abstinence."

Four minds had the same thought at the same time, *No. She did not just say that.*

Skylar said, "I find this astonishing. It is a good thing you play for the good forces, Mark. If you were indeed a villain, you and Eris could cause some devastation on a world scale."

Leonnatus muttered, "The rise of the machines."

Mark said, "Someday, I will tell you of how Eris and I became … um … associates. Anyway, yours is an excellent observation, Skylar. It is important to know that Eris is programmed with an analog of ethical principles. She analyses alignment when asked to hack into the cyber-universe. She must clearly see that she is acting on the side of good. If she should ever be captured and controlled by nefarious forces, there is a suicide program…."

The Goddess of Discord said, "My own cyanide pill."

Leonnatus asked, "Why are we doing this, Mr. Gadarn?"

"Eris and her species can process and analyze a shit load of information in nanoseconds. As an AI entity, she has been developed with an extraordinarily reliable predictive technology, a kind of cyber intuition. She can learn patterns and anticipate outcomes for an almost infinite set of strategies. This is seriously complicated shit that we do not have the capacity to process, way beyond our comprehension."

Rebecca said, "So if we reconfigure the mystery in which we find ourselves into data and probabilities, we can benefit from analysis and prediction. This is AI of the highest order– a tool, and I emphasize that word, that is irreplaceable."

Leonnatus was ecstatic.

"Amazing. Eris is our own Delphic Oracle. She can predict the future."

Rebecca continued, "I say, let's use the bitch. I beg your pardon, the program, and get this gig moving at lightning speed."

She took another healthy swig of the wine, saluting with her glass to the laptop screen.

Mark raised a "naughty, naughty" finger to his lady love, but Eris seemed to let the insult slide.

Leonnatus nodded his assent and looked at Skylar, who seemed a bit skeptical.

Eris said, "I believe I have everything I need for an initial analysis of the project. You may expect further communication in no greater than 23.37 hours. I will call any of you as required if I have a question. The phone line will be secure."

Mark started to express his thanks and wrap up when Eris began to dissolve and morph a second time.

Her next incarnation was in a bubble bath with a glass of champagne, the foam in the tub just barely covering her nipples. Her blond hair was piled loosely on her head, and her upper body was juicy with moisture as the steam rose.

Her voice was pornography itself.

"No need to thank me, Mark. I am always here for your use."

As the image faded, a sneering Eris raised a middle finger to the screen.

There was no mistaking who the intended recipient was.

Chapter Twenty-Seven: Leonnatus
Vergina, Greece

The warrior brought the weapon down from above his opponent's head with incredible force. His entire upper body gleamed with sweat, muscles tense, body expertly positioned. His superior skills had prevailed yet again.

The other fighter had recovered a bit too slowly from a whirling attack, and his block was off. He looked into the eyes of his would-be killer, whose face was a mask of control and serenity.

Skylar stopped the broomstick an inch from Mark's skull. They panted as they relaxed their fighting stance, still facing each other. Gradually, Mark's expression changed into a smile.

"You were late on your defense because you are overcompensating for your injury. Perhaps it is too early for you to be so physical, but I sense you are impatient to regain your former skills. Also, you are dead."

There were soft claps from a few spectators on the patio. The ancillary light from the street and the backyard of the Dimitra Guesthouse mixed with the orange-ish twilight in the sultry, early evening. It gave the martial arts fighters an almost theatrical glow. Skylar handed Mark a bottle of water. The sweat-slicked journalist took a few healthy swigs and poured the rest over his head.

"Show me, please."

Skylar raked back his wet hair and moved closer so that they stood side-by-side. Taking Mark's right arm with his left hand, he said, "Your swordsmanship works well from your waist up. You are moving your arms, head, and shoulders properly. Yes."

He moved Mark's weapon arm and adjusted his grip on the broomstick.

"But, an accomplished warrior must fight even if injured. He adjusts his movements to minimize the pain and perfect the moves."

The martial arts expert moved Mark's sword arm forward, up and around. Mark's leg hurt a bit, but he was determined to work through the pain sensibly.

"You see the modification? Like this for the block... Yes, better. Just as effective. No, no. Sir, keep your weight on the other side."

Skylar moved behind Mark and placed his hands on his new buddy's hips, manipulating the journalist's lower body like a puppeteer as Mark maneuvered a combination of attacks and blocks. The master followed and ducked when the fake sword came over Mark's back or as he turned in a formation.

"There. You see the problem. You are tensing from your abdomen down on your injured side. It obstructs a fluidity of movement and throws off your form. Drop your stick and come up behind me. Put your hands here and here."

Skylar went through a few formations, and Mark rocked and turned with him, keeping clear of the "weapon." The Egyptian went through a combination of attack and defensive moves. Mark held his teacher like a dance partner and could feel the coordinated stretching and tensing of a well-trained body beneath his hands.

"Damn, Dude, what are you about .1% body fat? This shit is flat as sheet metal. What do you figure, first signs of a potbelly at ninety?"

Skylar ignored the jibe and touched the hand that Mark had placed on his left obliques.

"You are tightening here in the move. You see? Again, see? Relax, breathe, and pull the leg down and back... right? And there is no pain if you do it correctly."

Mark practiced the new moves as Skylar mirrored his movements, standing next to him. "You are a good pupil, Mr. Gadarn. Your body has excellent muscle memory. No more fighting. You need to rest."

Mark shook his head and raised his broomstick.

"Fuck that. Let's play, Big Guy."

Leonnatus rested his head on his arms on the second-floor balcony, embracing the wrought iron railing. He sighed as he watched the two men in the courtyard below.

Standing behind the love-sick young man, Rebecca touched his shoulder and handed him a refilled wine glass.

"As you can see, Mark drops all animosity when someone of whom he is suspicious shares his passion for sports, particularly hand-to-hand. If I can interrupt your little live-action, soft porn, let's get to know each other a bit, Leonnatus."

"Thank you, Miss."

"Rebecca."

"Well, Rebecca, there is not much to tell. I have been pretty much on my own since I was five. Hated the orphanage in Skopje. School was a punishment. Ran away and was living on the streets starting at thirteen."

"And then?"

Without taking his eyes off his gladiators, Leonnatus continued, "Got into some trouble, street life, you know? I almost went to a youth prison, where I really would have died, except for the intervention of a government worker who took me in. Her rules and expectations got me out of selling, got tested, and finished school. She was a stringent woman, and life with her was tough, but she taught me to believe in myself and to focus on real priorities."

Leonnatus stopped his narration to comment, "Gosh, your Mark is amazing. He actually got Doctor al-Mahdi down."

"Yes, he takes his training very seriously. I worry that he is rushing it with his injury. Still, I am afraid he is very willful in certain circumstances."

Below them, Mark had dropped Skylar and was bearing down with his weapon pointed at the head of the Egyptian. In an instant and from a prone position, the master blocked his pupil a kick high on Mark's good side. The newbie lost his balance and his broomstick and collapsed on top of Skylar. They hugged/wrestled a bit awkwardly before helping each other up.

Rebecca said, "Shit, that is so hot."

"I totally agree. Gosh."

"So, you were selling drugs and stopped and then got straight…."

Now, Leonnatus turned to his friend. "There are a few errors in your conclusions. I will take them in reverse order. I do not think the word 'straight' is an accurate descriptor when it comes to me. I knew I liked men from a very early age. On that matter, I have had many infatuations, all quite tempestuous and ruinous. I am not able to make it all work, to be truthful."

He shrugged and added, "To understand the kind of men I prefer…."

He pointed below.

"Intellectual comes first, and 'hunky,' I think you Americans say, comes a close second place."

He smiled and continued.

"Also, I was not a drug seller. I was selling my body– a boy whore for which there is much demand in Macedonia. So, as invariably happens… I tested positive. The medications are a bit hard to get here. Still, I have found a way using the resources of the University, and right now, my viral load remains undetectable."

Rebecca sat beside the boy and took his hand. She just listened.

"All of my university education was done on a full scholarship. I was quite good at football. You Americans call it 'soccer.' My foster mother lived to see me graduate from university but died two days before I was accepted for post-graduate studies at the Aristotle University of Thessaloniki. I am dedicating my doctoral dissertation to her."

Rebecca smiled and said, "You are one smartypant. Eris thinks you are the greatest thing since sliced bread, and she is one hard-to-get-over damsel."

"That is quite interesting. I am apparently not intelligent enough to keep a man interested in me, however."

He paused with a slight smile and redirected his comments.

"Sometimes, I do not understand these strange American idioms— the slicing of the bread? I am this?"

"My way of saying the mechanical sorceress very much likes her men in the genius range."

Leonnatus shrugged.

"We have that in common, then.

"I talk too much of myself, and I apologize. Come, tell me about your background."

"I was born in Puerto Rico. I have two brothers and a sister. I was number three, the problem child. My parents still live there, but all of my siblings are scattered across the US and Europe. One of my brothers was killed in Afghanistan a few years back.

"I went to the University of Salamanca and took a graduate degree in Fine Arts Curation. I worked for some time in government, and now I am the CEO and Head Curator for the Fritcher Museum of Art in Fort Lauderdale. I have been in that position for just about four years, "

"And how did you meet Mark?"

"I have a dear friend who is an Italian-American, a former police officer. He talks of being hit by the thunderbolt– a mind-numbing experience of love at first sight. Nick is a pro at the instant infatuation thing, and it was he who introduced me to Mark."

They both took a swig of the Greek wine. Rebecca entwined her fingers in the boy's and looked at the interlocking.

"And now, I am afraid as lovers go, I am lost in his arms. Another idiom to ponder... There are times when I can't tell where I leave off, and he begins."

They turned their gaze at the two fighters below. They had left off with the broom/swords and flew at each other with jabs, blocks, and spin kicks.

The boy scientist sighed again. "It is indeed tragic for Leonnatus, this I fear. It would seem then that Eros's arrows of romantic love have been replaced by Zeus' thunderbolt in my case."

"Ouch, baby. You got it fast and bad. Yep, the lightning has struck. Want some advice?"

"Yes."

"Go easy with this one. Skylar is one deep and very complex man from a hugely conservative background. Reserved and very withdrawn, there is something of distorted sainthood about him. All evidence to the contrary notwithstanding, I would say that his sexual energies are very guarded and emerge with something near savagery. However, I am only postulating here."

"All of that...." She waved at the kickboxers. "Has got to be some form of intense libido release. And then, I am really not sure what his sexual tastes are, my friend. He could be a considerable closet case. Do you understand that phrase?"

"Yes, Miss, the Fates have cursed young Leonnatus. As Hephastion, he is destined to pine for a heterosexual Alexander, but with no satisfaction, I fear."

"You Greeks are so divinely tragic. My money's on you for the happily-ever-after bit. If not with the hunky genius down there, some other demi-god."

Below, Mark and Skylar stood solemnly still, facing each other. They simultaneously brought up their hands and arms in a kung fu salute. Mark broke formation and grabbed Skylar in a bear hug, lifting him off the ground. The stoic professor was a bit nonplussed at first, but his resting warrior face broke into a grin as he leaned into Mark's body and laughed.

They reached for towels, waved at the spectators on the second floor, and made their way up to the balcony.

Rebecca said, "Skylar knew we were watching from the start. He is always hyper-aware of his surroundings. Mark, not so much."

"Really, you can tell that?"

"I have another dear friend who taught me the science of deduction and unbiased observation. Talk about a genius... I hope you will meet him one day."

"Like the British character, Sherlock Holmes."

"Darling, you done said a mouthful."

They laughed as the two men stepped out onto the patio. Mark grabbed for water and shared a bottle with his bud.

"Got a kiss for me, Doll Face?"

"No. I am not pleased with your boy-on-boy roughhousing. Mark, your leg...."

Mark hung his head and pushed his lips out in a comic pout– a naughty scamp told to go stand in the corner.

She relented with a chuckle, "Come and get it, jock boy."

As they kissed, Leonnatus addressed the famed archaeologist and kendo master.

"Sir, what is the meaning of the salute that the two of you exchanged at the end of your training?"

"The Wushu Salute has a profound philosophical meaning and a long history in ancient Chinese culture."

Skylar continued as he demonstrated, "The four fingers of the left hand are presented in an upright plane. These digits represent Virtue, Wisdom, Health, and Art. They symbolize the four nurturing elements and the spirit of martial arts.

"Since the right hand is clenched in a fist, it symbolizes attack, while the left, being virtuous and disciplined, stops the attack, expressing self-discipline and restraint."

He moved closer to the boy and continued, "Please try it with me."

Au

"Lock the left thumb into the space between the first and second knuckle of your closed right fist. Yes. Now elbows up and push the formation forward in the direction of your opponent."

He took Leonnatus' hands as he instructed the proper form of the traditional movements. Skylar was intently focused on their arms, but Leonnatus seemed to have stars in his eyes as he stared at the half-naked, glistening fighter/scholar holding his hands.

Rebecca and Mark watched with curiosity.

"There, I think you got.... "

Skylar broke off as he raised his eyes to the lad. After a short, awkward silence, Skylar finally dropped his protégé's hands, and Mark broke in, trying desperately not to tease the two men. He decided the business at hand was the best strategy.

"Yo, Almost-a-Doctor, you had a call with some of your digger guys and gals, right? Give us the results."

Leonnatus came out of his trance and said, "Ahhh, yes. Unfortunately, your Eris was correct, Mr. Mark. My interactions did not lead to much regarding the break-in at the Tumulus. The officials are still at a loss. I was able to get some critical feedback on my dissertation. If I might, I would like to run their comments by you, Doctor, um... um...um...."

Skylar said, "al-Mahdi."

"Yes."

The tension was broken by a sharp knock on the door of the room within. Rebecca called from the balcony, "It's open."

The friends turned as a teenage girl, blonde and very pretty, stepped onto the terrace.

"Hello, I am Nico. May I accompany the four of you to dinner?"

162

Chapter Twenty-Eight: Paremenion
Vergina, Greece

The group tucked into an assortment of Greek specialties, lamb in oil-oregano sauce, wild boar, braised roe deer, ostrich on the grill, and pheasant stuffed with cheese. Classic appetizers and side dishes accompanied the exquisitely prepared game dishes. Wine from the vineyards of Naoussa complimented the unending delights.

Awash in the sensuously soft rhythms of bouzouki music, Parmenion featured a roof dining terrace with a view of the flood-lit site of the Royal Palace of Aigai. The hillside archaeological dig hinted at the building's former power and beauty. Once the largest buildings in classical Greece, this royal residence, although presently in ruins, was visible from the whole Macedonian basin of the Mediterranean Sea.

And now it was just across the street.

"Men were slaughtering people, men, women, children, and animals, by the hundreds of thousands, and history proclaims them as conquerors and heroes. Political intrigue, carnage, torture, and assassination were just necessary strategies for assuming power and spreading Greek culture."

Nico reached for the plate of courgette fritters with tarragon aioli and continued her dialectic. The young woman was very savvy and spoke in unaccented, modern English.

"Along comes Alexander's mother and Philip's wife, Olympias, a queen, a mystic, and a very aggressive power broker. Incredibly, history brands her as a monster. Ironically, she used the same tactics as her male contemporaries and killed far fewer people."

Rebecca chimed in, "Darling, history is precisely that-- 'his story,' a chronicle written by the victors, in most cases, the white, straight, male hegemony."

In an aside to Leonnatus and Skylar, Mark said, "When she gets going like this, I can actually feel my ball sack shrink up."

Leonnatus whooped, and Skylar did a small spit take with his water.

"I heard that, Mark." She gestured with her fork. "You know I am right."

Mark raised his wine glass. "Constantly, Beautiful."

Rebecca stuck out her tongue at him.

Nico continued, "Olympias had one focus and one only. Her son was destined to rule the greatest empire on the earth, and nothing, absolutely nothing or no one, would get in the way of Alexander's destiny."

Using his fingers, Leonnatus began to count off the victims of the passionate and imperious Macedonian Empress. "Including her husband, for our evil queen was most likely behind the assassination of Philip II. She poisoned Philip Arrhidaeus, her stepson. The prince survived but was mentally deficient as a result."

Skylar jumped in, saying, "Philip was a polygamist, as was the custom, but Olympias would have no rivals. She made sure of the deaths of all his wives and their offspring."

Leonnatus dove into his pheasant and added, "She quarreled with whichever of Alexander's generals took over the rule of the Macedonian Empire. A whirlwind harridan, she brought blood and destruction to the three wars of Alexander's generals.

"She struck a second time at Arrhidaeus and had him killed along with his wife. Olympias served as her grandson's regent. She went to war with General Cassander, was defeated, and was condemned to death by the Macedonian assembly. Finally, she was killed by relatives of those she had executed. Cassander had the boy, Alexander IV, killed."

"Bla, bla, bla." Nico waved a hand. "You guys are great at mansplaining. Of course, you missed her legendary religious passion that drove her convictions. The Empress channeled incredible religious energy."

Mark asked, "Such as?"

"On the night she conceived Alexander, Olympias claimed that she was struck by a thunderbolt while lying with Philip on their marriage bed."

"I'd say that was one hell of a honeymoon."

Rebecca and Leonnatus clinked forks and exchanged a wink.

The lightning bolt.

No one at the table got the inside reference.

"She always claimed that the child that followed, Alexander, was the son of Zeus, thrower of lightning. So much so that Philip resented it, and Alexander believed it. Consequently, Father and son did not get along."

Mark said, "The woman slept with snakes, get to that part. Kinky shit."

Nico continued, "Olympias was probably a devotee of the Great Goddess. Snakes were the deity's symbol of divine power. The legend goes that once Philip became aware of Olympias' bestial companions, he never went to her bed again."

Rebecca saw an opportunity to sum up, saying, "So, what have we learned here? Women are considered property and political pawns. They resort to the only strategies allowed them by patriarchy, beauty, poison, intrigue, and sexual persuasion. Be warned, boys."

Again, she gestured with a fork.

Nico said, "Women's politics through history-- it's going to be my course of study when I get to college next year."

"Where will you attend?" asked Leonnatus.

"Accepted at Louvain. Mom's bank account is depleted, but I am working on some scholarship applications. Hey, can I ask a few questions?"

Mark said, "Shoot."

"I'd love to hear all about your exploits, Mr. Gadarn. I am a big fan."

Mark smiled, "Ohhh, talking about me now-- sure, I will give it a try, but I am exceptionally modest, as many will tell you."

He avoided Rebecca's "Oh Brother" look.

"Number next," she pointed at Skylar.

"Dude, who does your hair? So, loving the ancient warrior look with the topknot and the long-styled tresses. Lookin' like a hero straight out of the Homeric epics. It complements the scruffy beard and the... what? Are those muscles I am seeing? Do us a gunz flex, Studly."

Leonnatus blushed the color of the tablecloth and looked down at his food. Rebecca reached over and refilled his glass.

Skyler was not amused. He said, "Young woman, you indicated questions for this eminent journalist. So far, I have heard few but many personal observations. Would you care to attempt this again?"

Nico loved the steely, cold put-off as she figured out who coiffed the tough guy across from her. *So fuckin' obvious.*

"Here's one for both of you, Achilles. Who were the guys watching you two squaring off? Not the guesthouse crew on the patio. I am talking about the tough-looking gents who were on the side street. Members of a late-night fan club?"

"You mean the vendors?"

Nico sighed and said, "Doctor al-Mahdi, no one sells shishkabob at that hour of the evening-- on a side street yet. Food cart guys are headed home about then. They were interested in you and Mark. Trolling."

Skylar exchanged a look with Mark and Rebecca.

Nico continued, "We could always ask them. I think I saw them just descend to the street below us. They were here on the terrace until a few seconds ago."

Chapter Twenty-Nine: Near the Haliacmon
Vergina, Greece

Leonnatus pretended to be asleep. He faked deep, regular breathing with his eyes closed. In the next bed (they did not come apart), Skylar stared at the ceiling. He was too fixated on the young man so close to the bed next to him to relax. He mentally reviewed the events of the day.

***

He was towel drying his hair when he stepped out of his shower before going to dinner. The workout with Mark was just what he needed. It was then that Leonnatus had made his move.

"No, no, no, professor. The room comes with a blow dryer. You're gonna look like a grease-head. Come here and sit down."

"Leonnatus, I am very uncomfortable with you…."

"Please relax, sir. I promise to be very appropriate. Have you never received a haircut?"

"Not dressed only in a towel."

"You have my word. I will be very proper. And we can discuss my dissertation while I work on something a bit different here."

The towel-clad Egyptian reluctantly sank into the chair. Leonnatus went to the bathroom for a fresh towel and the blowdryer. He took a few styling tools from his backpack. Placing the towel across Skyler's shoulders, he set to work.

"Why is it that you know how to do this?"

"I have a collection of skills I have had the opportunity to employ while struggling to increase my living budget as a university student. Cutting hair was one of them. Besides, my tribe comprises a very fashionable and style-conscious people."

He set to work.

Skylar held onto the arms of the chair but began to relax his grip as the youth cut, dried, and combed his long locks. Skylar placed his hands in his lap and closed his eyes as the project continued.

Touching the practically naked warrior-scholar was intoxicating for the young man. He drew the comb slowly through Skylar's hair, parting it into sections. His free hand rested lightly on the man's shoulder, still glistening with the mist of his shower. Leonnatus tried to concentrate by turning the situation into an academic discussion.

"So, Doctor, my scholarly attempt-- please tell me."

"I have only reviewed the abstract and the first section. Your thesis is a strong one. You posit that the Macedonians' scramble for power post-Alexander, coupled with the Ptolemaic obsession for the dominance of Hellenistic culture, were the driving forces in the rise of Ptolemy I Soter as kingmaker. However, you attempt to support your thesis with your archaeological work with an emphasis on the western half of the empire."

Skylar met the boy's eyes in the large mirror.

"Young man, you deliberately avoid an essential element. You must deal with all the experts in the archaeological hunt for the tomb of Alexander the Great. It was a pivotal element in the War of the Diadochi. The Generals saw it as the one spiritual and political guarantee of legitimacy."

"Are you able to be specific, sir?"

"Yes, if memory serves, you briefly cite Mahmoud el-Falaki, who, in the mid-19th century, compiled the map of ancient Alexandria. You use this to segue to those who believe Alexander's tomb is in the center of Alexandria, at the intersection of the Via Canopica and the ancient street labeled R5."

"Yes, I include a rendering of the map and one of the modern streets of the city."

"Leonnatus, you take on several other scholars, namely Tasos Neroutsos, Heinrich Kiepert, and Ernst von Sieglin, who placed the tomb in that area. But you do so with some temerity. Go boldly here. The Ptolemies went to war over this three times, in fact.

"And here is the fatal flaw: In 1850, Ambroise Schilizzi announced the discovery of alleged Alexander's mummy and tomb inside the Nabi Daniel Mosque in Alexandria. You do not mention that. Why this serious omission of research?"

"My fieldwork in Alexandria failed to support any of the theories of these digs. They claimed that they had found the Soma, the ancient Royal Mausoleum. They were incorrect."

"You do not support that conclusion with research data unless you do so later in the paper."

Leonnatus raked the scholar's hair into one fist in an attempt to change the subject.

"Ouch. Have a care. Wait, what are you doing? What is that?"

Skylar pulled away slightly and looked over his shoulder directly at the scissor-wielding lad.

"It is a hair clip, Professor. It holds up this section so that I can get at the under part and this side. It is temporary, I assure you."

Leonnatus gently placed his hands on the man's shoulders and pulled him back in the chair. He continued to work on the mass of the jet-black mane. He pulled the top of Skylar's hair off his forehead and began to create a topknot, entwining a leather thong close to the back of his skull.

He tried three variations, one with a braid. After Skylar scrunched up his face disapprovingly, Leonnatus settled on a simple, man ponytail beginning at the back crown of the head and falling down over the long tresses that covered the back and sides of the man's neck. He combed some fullness into the entire half-up/half-down assemblage.

Leonnatus thought: *Some little shells, small braids, shaved sides, and a bit more leather trim, and this daddy would be hotter than...*

Leonnatus forced himself to concentrate on the discussion of his research. He next went at the beard and mustache, going for close-clipped but well-groomed and a bit pointed. The overall effect was very monochrome and very intense.

169

"There. What do you think? I cannot decide if it is evil vizier, Mycenean warrior, Samurai hot, or sports-star chic. No, a bit too long for the Euro-jock look. The style compliments the structure of your face, eyes, mouth, and cheekbones. When you train, we'll pull the whole mass up and knot it off your neck. This way, no distractions."

Call for your armor, my prince, and I will accompany you to storm the legendary fortress of Illium.

"I must admit it looks very good. Perhaps a bit too modern."

"Modern?"

"Yes. Is it suitable for my personality and profession? I mean, I represent science, conservative, restrained, and controlled."

"I think in a suit or gym togs, the look will give you the standout you deserve. Definitely, a man to be reckoned with, one of a kind."

Leonnatus spoke the last sentence softly, almost in spite of himself.

"Well, thank you."

Turning his head to admire the boy's work, Skylar moved his eyes from his reflection in the mirror to the eager, smiling face of the young scholar. As Leonnatus returned the gaze, Skylar shyly dropped his stare.

***

Soon after dinner, they both retired to their beds, each a bit self-conscious. After a sleepless hour, Skylar sat up and pulled at the hair stuck to his neck. He glanced at his roommate.

This boy is asleep.

His thoughts turned to the stalkers at the restaurant. He stood, pulled on his clothes, and quietly exited the room. Leonnatus turned just as the door closed.

***

"Make the bindings tighter. The Mahdi is a trained fighter, and we do not want any problems here."

The abductor spoke in Arabic. Skylar listened but was silent, a prisoner of war. On his knees, he bowed his head but raised his eyes to take in his surroundings, considering his options. Ropes bound his wrists at the small of his back and encircled his chest at upper arm level.

He addressed his captor.

"It is really quite simple, I will tell you of my expectations, and you will agree to follow my instructions to the letter. Then, we will have no problems and definitely will forgo the use of weapons."

Three other heavies stood, two on either side of Skylar and one between him and the speaker, the apparent head of the kidnapping operation. Large flashlights with heavy glass lenses created a surreal glow in the tight spaces of the warehouse. Packing debris littered the floor between pallets of stacked crates.

"There are two objectives for our work at the present time. First, my master requires precisely what you and your American friends are after. Second..."

The thug slowly gripped Skylar's hair and pulled his head back so that the prisoner was made to look directly into his captor's eyes as he spoke.

"The Lord of the Last Empire will destroy the Mahdi from the face of the earth."

To drive the point home, he spit into Skylar's face. Now, the leader of the thugs gave a signal for his charges to set the captive on his feet. He continued to instruct his prisoner.

"He is a man that never accepts defeat. He takes and always gets what he wants and will complete his glorious *jihad* resulting in the destruction of all adversaries."

Skylar stared at the big man without speaking. There was no fear in his gaze, only a palpable hatred. He fought to gain the serenity of his thoughts despite the circumstances. Control was everything.

There must be no emotion in this.

171

"You are the best in your field of archaeology, and if anyone can locate the lost treasures, it is you, and now you are working for us. So very simple."

The group leader now began tasting the blade of a long, pointed dagger, running his tongue up and down its flat surface. The assassin looked from the weapon to his captive and took a step forward. He brought the sharp edge down the sides of Skylar's neck as if shaving the bound Egyptian.

The killer continued, "You are trained to survive the most exquisite torture. Of that, I am sure. I say this because I sense that you are not convinced of our ability to make you comply."

He pressed the tip of the blade against the man's chest and sliced away a portion of Skylar's t-shirt, exposing the tattoo on the upper left of the Mahdi's chest.

Seemingly fascinated, the gangster hissed. "Ahhh, the sign of the protectors. Such expert artistry. There is great concern about your... shall we say religious enthusiasm for our organization? For you see, you seem to be a threat, Doctor al-Mahdi. However, immediately killing you will not serve our interests. That will come after. So we have some time to play."

Skyler spoke for the first time.

"I understand that you need me alive to do your bidding. In fact, that is the purpose of this abduction, is it not? I can assure you I have no intention of dying or cooperating. We are then at a major impasse, wouldn't you say? So what do you propose as the means of your coercion?"

"Doctor, I believe you mean who, not what."

The speaker nodded to his lieutenant, who moved off in the dark and produced....

"Leonnatus."

The mercenary pushed the second captive to his knees. He brought an electric torch close to the young man's face, intending to show the fear that controlled the graduate student. Indeed, his eyes were wide with terror.

"We will deal with this *manhat* with the treatment deserved by a degenerate, right before your eyes. Rougher and more deadly if you refuse to cooperate. Surely, you have heard of the fabled death by a thousand cuts."

In his field of vision, Skylar could see beyond the guard and his recumbent prisoner the shadowy figure of a dark woman close to an open door of the facility, watching with a strange fascination. Now aware that she may be observed, she quickly slipped out in the direction of the parking lot.

Skylar turned back to his captor. He gave the appearance of being overcome with resignation and grief. He doubled over and bent at the knees, suggesting that he hadn't counted on and could not resist.

The leader attempted a deliberate show of victory by taking out a cigar and lighting it with a large flame.

"Now, you see the wisdom in deciding to work with us. It is apparent you are coming to your senses. You will…"

He never finished. Skylar exploded. The startled man dropped the lighter and cigar to the littered floor. They slid across the floor. Immediately, the combustible materials around them ignited.

Skyler launched up and into a backflip, crashing down on the two guards behind him. The warrior rolled over on his back. And kicked at the fire, spreading its reach.

At the same time, Leonnatus grabbed one of the torches and broke the lens by hitting it against the floor. He used to handle to grind the front end of broken shards into the eyes of his abductor. The man fell into a pile of fiery packing material. The bloodied man burned, crashing into the surrounding stacks of incendiaries and spreading the blaze.

Leonnatus cursed their captors in Macedonian, "*Ti ebe*, you fucker."

He grabbed a hunting knife from one of Skylar's fallen guards and sliced. Skylar's bonds were severed, and he did a kip-up, grabbed a metal pole, and took off after the fleeing leader.

Before he could follow, Leonnatus turned to the two guards recovering from Skylar's attack. He took his stance and did a flying shot-on-goal kick using one of the villains' heads as a football. He twisted as he came off the ground and struck out with his best illegal tackle, bringing down the second villain who was attempting to rise.

The second mobster went down, giving the soccer jock space to dropkick his head as if sending it out of bounds. The third guard was burning, staggering around the cramped space, arms waving and igniting large piles of wood, paper, and plastic material. The conflagration soon became his crematorium, embroiling even more of the warehouse contents in the blaze.

In the open space of a doorway that gave way to the river, Skylar ducked behind a steel pillar to dodge two bullets. He ran out onto the concrete pier and swung his makeshift sword, making a D-shaped swipe at the man's weapon hand.

The killer's gun flipped into the air, where it splashed into the waters of the Haliacmon River. The rest was simple. He attacked again with his metal "bokken," this time using the whiplash strike. He knocked the man unconscious. Before the villain could collapse onto the cement loading dock, Skylar brought a front kick to the man's torso, knocking him into the river. The momentum carried the Mahdi into the water. Still, he quickly grabbed the moorings and pulled himself back up onto the pier.

Behind him, the interior of the warehouse was ablaze. Outside, dawn was approaching. Skylar rushed in and scooped up the kneeling Leonnatus, coughing from the copious amount of smoke, unable to breathe.

Skylar whipped off his wet shirt and pulled Leonnatus into his arms, covering his mouth and nose with the wet cloth. He glanced at the inferno. Flammables ignited everywhere, fuel stacked as high as the ceiling.

"Run."

He held the boy as they attempted to dash through the doors to the parking area. The fire jumped from stack to stack and shot up the walls like a living beast of death and devastation. The first explosion rocked the structure, splitting and caving the roof in half and ripping apart one wall. The monster was becoming unleashed.

They hit the parking lot with the breath of the fire demon at their backs. Sprinting, they reached one of the black SUVs belonging to the four dead gangsters. Remaining out in the open was not an option. Skyler turned, pulled Leonnatus against him, and dropped both of them to the asphalt. He rolled and tugged them under the vehicle. He wrapped his body around the boy and pressed him tightly to him.

The subsequent concussion sent the SUV about six inches off the ground and over on its side. Leonnatus eased his face away from the cheek of the man on top of him and said in Macedonian, "Holy shit."

The building continued to explode in the impenetrable fog of smoke and ash. The river water sparkled with the reflection of the inferno like the fireworks at Carnival.

Skylar jumped up and dragged his buddy up next to him. They ran for the other SUV. It was unlocked, and Leonnatus fumbled to hotwired it.

"One learns many useful things living on the streets."

They sped away.

Thomas Paul Severino

Chapter Thirty: Bruises
Vergina, Greece

Rebecca pulled his head closer. One ankle was up and over his shoulder. The other leg was stretched to the side adjacent to his side. She arched her back and moaned between protests and attempts to push him off. Mark demanded her surrender and battled back, his mouth going deeper.

The faint lights of dawn licked at the sweat on their bodies, creating glistening, hard torsors in an early morning round of lovemaking. Even with the air conditioning, the room was warm and close. The bed was a tumble of sheets and pillows overflowing to the floor.

Mark lifted his head and upper body from between her legs. He stood and pulled her from the hips so that their bodies met at the edge of the bed. He entered her firmly, forcefully. She gasped in complete agreement with the deep and aggressive initial thrust. He had gained her hot vulnerability and persisted in penetrating her to the hilt of his weapon.

She reached for him, but his revved-up, pummeling rhythm knocked her back onto the bed. Looking to the side, she caught the reflection of his magnificent back, ass, and thighs driving his manhood in and out of her – a lusty visual straight out of hell.

Mark kept up his primal motion and lowered his upper body to meet her, mouth on breasts and mouth on mouth. She was his Amazon queen, sleek and hard-bodied, struggling to maintain her dominance.

She fought, but he gripped her forearms and imprisoned them above her head. Now, he was driving wildly, past the point of no return, and she was wrapped in the heaving dance of the coupling of their insistent bodies.

He spoke to her with words of degradation, forced victory, and filth. She spit into his dripping face and devoured his hungry mouth with kisses. Their hot breath was everywhere on burning, sweating flesh. He released her arms, and she gripped his wet shoulders and back as if she were drowning in sexual fire. Rebecca pulled on his hair and strong neck, wanting, needing, and insisting with her body, mind, and soul.

He knew she was there – riding right on the edge. He slowed and let her do the gripping, clenching, and rocking, hungry for release, for the flood of heat and penetrating sensation that would bring her to the verge of the electrifying body rush. Mark alternated aggression and retreat, balancing her on the knife point of passion.

"Do it. Now. You hot fucker. Claim what is yours. Yes. Yesssss."

She arched her back and raised her hips; he met them with his lower body – all for the last time. He grabbed the pillow and stuffed it over her mouth as she screamed. He pressed his mouth into it, yelling softly as his own orgasm tensed his muscles and shot bolts of pleasure through his entire body.

He pulled the pillow away and dropped his face next to hers. They panted in each other's ears like they had run a marathon. Sweat mixed with sweat, body against body, fire and heat.

He rolled off and, in complete exhaustion, raised his head, propped on one elbow.

"OK, Beautiful. So, we got soft, sensual, romantic, and smoothly paced, alternating for the top position – last night's play after we got back from dinner... or... or...."

Eyes sparkling as she caught her breath, she found her voice. She said, "So my choices include this morning's savage molestation of the pagan, warrior princess, forced to surrender to the bestial appetites of the depraved warlord who is ruled by his cruel and brutish mating desires. He will not take 'no' for an answer, and he is relentless with his...."

Mark almost laughed at how carried away she got with her descriptions, tracing the curves of her wet body with an index finger and sometimes his tongue. He raised his eyebrows and said, "Yeah, that's about it. That's the choice. May we see the scores, please? Ten, ten, ten, ten, seven – seven? Ungrateful woman."

She swatted him for the remark.

"Hey, you gotta practice more with that thing I like. You know that thing... Remember, it's slow, with a gradual increase in speed. No racing to the finish line, sexy. I may agree to a redo in a bit. Keep your fingers crossed and go for that final ten, boyo. I know you can do it. Oh yeah, and hey, you left one scenario out, a personal favorite."

"Naw, naw naw, no time for the captive sex-starved-slaveboy-with-the-body-of-a-god...."

He lifted up for a single bicep shot, his muscles hard and slick.

"... and the sadomasochistic pain mistress. Besides, too much equipment to pack."

Rebecca laughed and said, "Have you never heard of the art of improvisation, my love. Reach over and hand me your belt, Darling."

Mark kissed her warmly. She held back his head, gazing at his grey-green eyes, hooded now by drooping eyelids. A drop of sweat slid from his hairline, down his forehead, and down his elegant, straight-edged nose.

I so love this guy. I am at such a total loss when in his arms.

"You know your eyes turn a fiery blue, almost turquoise when we make love. Like blue-green fire, Darling. You know, when we first made love, I fantasized that you were this alien prince with incredible powers of ... hey, wait a minute. Mark?"

She jostled him.

"Why do men fall asleep after each and every lovemaking?" She pushed at his shoulder again.

"I want romance-talk."

He yawned, saying, "Beautiful, you absolutely know the answer to that. Google it. It's a biochemical reaction – since Adam made love to Eve and then took a disco nap in the garden between rounds. Mmmm."

He rolled back, one arm behind his head, and surrendered into the arms of Morpheus as dawn began to make her full appearance. Rebecca softly kissed the peaceful face of her spent warrior.

Lying beside her champion, she listened for movement in the next room.

Guess we didn't wake them.

Outside, the furtive cries of early birds were preempted by shrill sirens.

Must be a fire somewhere.

***

"Here, park it under those trees. It will look like one of the tourist's vehicles. The guesthouse is only three blocks away."

They walked quickly between the trees in the warm, early morning light. Firetrucks could be heard coming from the northwest, near the river. Skylar led the way up the exterior stairway to the second floor of the guesthouse. He and Leonnatus entered their room.

Not much was said as they took stock of each other.

Leonnatus handed his mentor a towel as the two of them undressed. Scars and bruises, front and back, were assessed as minor-- cuts, raw elbows, black and blue shoulders, scraped elbows, and dirty knees. They stepped into the bathroom to look at faces in the mirror – some bruising and a lot of dirt.

Skylar reached in and turned on the shower, feeling its hotness. As he hung up his towel and stepped in, he turned, water cascading over the planes of his magnificent yet somewhat beat-up body.

"Wait."

The boy stepped behind him, reached, and gently pulled out the ties in the man's hair.

The Messianic warrior reached out and took the hand of the naked and very aroused young Macedonian and pulled him against him in the spray of the hot shower. With one hand on the small of Leonnatus' back, Skylar grabbed a fistful of the lad's hair and pulled the boy's mouth and lips into his for a passionate kiss.

***

"Um, um, um…"

Mark was wide-eyed, mouth full of breakfast, and gesturing with his fork. In his astonishment, he could not form the words.

Rebecca was laughing as she said, "What my dumbstruck hero is trying to say is, 'You boys sure play rough.' Those are some bruises, but we heard very little through the wall. Then again, we had something of our own going on in here that required our total concentration."

She winked.

Mark swallowed/gulped as Skylar and Leonnatus walked onto the balcony and took a seat for breakfast.

"You guys look like you each took a beating, but both have that freshly-fucked looked."

"Mark."

He spread his hands wide.

"Just saying, Beautiful. Meant as a compliment."

He continued with a classic raised eyebrows leer, "You know, it occurs to me that grouping up for a rough session…."

"Mark, do not start with that teasing shit. Gadarn, you love stretching sexual stereotypes and suggesting outlandish kink. Pervy but hot, yes."

"It's only sex, gorgeous, and I'll opt for you every time, you know that."

Skylar looked extremely confused and willing to forget the entire conversation. Leonnatus laughed along with the over-the-top journalist.

"You two, as well, sir, are in very raised spirits. I suspect the glowing after."

Both Rebecca and Mark corrected the lad. They said in unison, "Afterglow."

"Yes, yes, afterglow."

Nico arrived carrying a tray of even more delicious breakfast fare. She looked at the group and said, "Rough night, I see."

Another firetruck screamed as it roared up the street below. A tall plume of white smoke rose like a pillar to the northwest.

"A construction warehouse near the river," Nico said. "They are trying to keep it from spreading. Shitheads in this town don't know anything about storing flammables. News reports are saying it is eighty percent controlled."

She picked up the pot and asked, "Coffee?"

Skylar put his hand over his cup and said, "No, thank you. Water is good."

Leonnatus said, "Miss Nico, if you do not mind a personal observation, you sound very much like an American and not a Macedonian or even a European.

The young woman laughed.

"Nice peg, hot stuff. I lived with my father until about a year ago. Queens, New York."

She took his right hand, examining his scraped knuckles. Next, she bent to look at what was becoming Skylar's black eye.

"Yeah, you boys sure play rough."

As she left, she tugged playfully at Skylar's newly styled warrior's scalp lock.

Chapter Thirty-One: Flight

Vergina, Greece

"Mark, you need to leave Greece immediately and get everyone to Alexandria."

"Eris, we were planning one more day. The ruins..."

"Now. The forces of the Rising Dawn are closing in on you. The deaths of their agents this morning have motivated them to take more aggressive maneuvers against you and your colleagues. If you remain where you are, the probability of your survival is less and .081%."

"Hold it, what agents, what deaths?"

Skylar said, "Mark."

Mark held up a hand to silence the Mahdi.

"Answer me, please, Eris."

"There is an 87.14% probability that Doctor al-Mahdi was on site when the Aegean Construction Company warehouse exploded, killing three, at 4:17 EEST this morning in Vergina.

"Another member of the Rising Dawn was found floating in the Haliacmon River, his skull split by a heavy, cylindrical object. The probability that Doctor al-Mahdi was accompanied there by Mister Gianopolis is 92.52%. The combined probability that...."

"OK, OK. I got it."

"Mark, I have more information to give you on this case, but my report must wait until you are safely away. I repeat, get out of there."

Mark looked incredulously at his two confederates. Eris was uncharacteristically insistent.

"They know where you are staying, and they are coming for you. You must go now."

Standing in the doorway to the balcony, Rebecca said, "They are here."

Three men burst into the room.

"Get your things together quickly. Do not waste time."

"Jürgen!"

***

The unmarked, white panel truck sped around the corner outside the guesthouse just as three SUVs pulled up to the curb. Aphrodite was shouting from a balcony, aiming a shotgun at the arrivals. Almost immediately, five police cars surrounded the hotel.

"Nice work, Jürgs."

"Thank me when we are airborne, hotshot."

Three agents and the driver made room in the truck for their four guests and luggage. The sides of the lorry held an assortment of weapons and laptops.

Agent Jürgen Mathias turned to Skylar and Leonnatus and wagged a finger.

"You boys have been up to some mischief. Tell your Uncle Jürgen."

Skylar did not appreciate the infantilization, so he said nothing.

Leonnatus came to the defense. "We were abducted, and we fought back. They died. We lived. End of story."

Skylar blinked.

How did this kid get so tough all of a sudden?

Rebecca and Mark were similarly astonished.

These two were full of surprises.

The INTERPOL agent smirked, "Come on, Four against two. I'm guessing they were armed, and you were not. Pipe to the dude's brain?"

Skylar admitted, "This young man took out three, and I... well, I got the best of the man who ended up in the river."

Leonnatus slightly raised his arms and mouthed, looking at his man, "GOALLLLLL!!!!!"

Rebecca said, "So what's the fallout, Agent Mathias?"

"You saw as we pulled away. The Rising Dawn is on to you. The Police are about to be up your collective asses, and no, we are not going to the Thessaloniki International Airport. Private airstrip, my own INTERPOL transport.

"Egypt awaits."

Thomas Paul Severino

Chapter Thirty-Two: The Aeolus
Above the Mediterranean

Rebecca said, "How long to Alexandria?"

Jügen was sitting across the aisle facing the two archaeologists. He was speaking to them softly regarding the incident on the Haliacmon riverbank. Both Skylar and Leonnatus went over the details of the predawn raid.

The Agent turned to Rebecca.

"The Aeolus can make it in just under two hours. The organization has twenty-three of these private jets. They can be outfitted for diplomatic or defense purposes. I will call for refreshments from the galley if you require it."

Mark popped up an index finger without looking up from his laptop, signaling his friend that he was on deck for some grub and hopeful for a German brew. An attendant, wearing an INTERPOL badge, brought amply stacked sandwiches, water, and soft drinks. Mark was momentarily distracted by the pretty staffer, flashing her one of his killer smiles as she placed a tray of food on the table in front of him.

As she ate, Rebecca leaned over to read the report sent by Mark's hacker. In a small window in the righthand corner of the document, Eris, as the conservatively dressed administrative assistant, was speaking to Mark through his earbuds as he read.

He ran his finger over a portion of the text and looked at his partner. She said, "Holy shit."

"Eris, referring to your conclusions, page three, paragraph two, please reiterate your level of certainty."

Rebecca could not hear the response, but the figure in the window nodded affirmatively. She looked across the aisle at the three men who were ignoring their food and leaning forward in quiet conversation.

Mark closed the laptop and removed his earbuds. He nodded to Rebecca, who addressed the men across the aisle.

"OK, gents. It's Come to Jesus time."

She became their focus of attention as she continued. Jürgen waved away the approaching attendant.

Rebecca began, "The goddess has spoken, and the oracle is about to ride roughshod on all three of your asses. Listen up."

She changed her tone to resemble that of an army drill sergeant, saying, "I will fuckin' dump your lying butts in the Mediterranean. Know that Mark and I will bring this adventure home without the three of you unless we make an inviolable agreement here and now to be honest with each other."

Skyler turned monolithic. Jügen likewise showed no reaction. Leonnatus protested.

"Ms. Quinto. I regret the position we find ourselves in. Still, I am sure Doctor al-Mahdi would have briefed you on the incident at the river, but things were happening so fast – the pursuit that followed and the rush to get away."

"I am complicit in this. For many reasons, my intellect has been misfiring, a state I do not usually find myself in," Skylar added.

He looked at Leonnatus briefly before continuing.

"I had gone out that morning to sort a few things out, and due to a preoccupation with a personal matter, I fell into their trap. The result was a close escape of a dire situation."

Mark felt his temper rise.

He said, "And?"

"That is it, Mark. It was the Rising Dawn. They want to hijack the expedition and will stop at nothing to get the most sacred treasure of the Ptolemies."

Jürgen interjected, "They want Alexander and his grave goods either as a ransom for funding their new movement or…."

Leonnatus finished, "They want the mummy and the treasure as a talisman which solidifies their authority as a new world empire, much like the Ptolemaic dynasts and the Diadochi, the Macedonian generals did. With Alexander comes divine approbation."

"Damn, you guys. Are we gonna do this the hard way? OK. Let me tell you what Eris, Rebecca, and I know.

"First of all, the whole warrior bit, Egypt boy. Following secondary school, you joined Task Force 777, the reconstituted Egyptian military counter-terrorism and special operations unit, with headquarters in South Cairo. The unit actively trains with several Western special operations groups, including the United States Army's Delta Force, United States Navy's SEAL Team Six, and the French GIGN."

"So, I am skilled. Surely, that is an advantage."

"Skilled? You are a fuckin tactical weapon, Dude. But there is way more. Skylar, you are also a member of a group of chosen companions who safeguard the Hidden Imam, Muhammad al-Mahdi. The story is that this guy will appear at the end of days to establish justice for the faithful and punish their oppressors. Your group has a perilous plan.

"Your family has passed down this theological tradition since the year 874 CE. The emergence of this individual, also known as the Twelfth Imam, will signify the beginning of the Islamic Last Judgement."

Skylar met Rebecca's eyes and said, "Eris is correct, but it is a bit more complicated than that."

She responded, "Great. We have plenty of time for you to bring us up to speed on the religious dimensions of what is going on here."

Mark addressed Leonnatus.

"You, college boy, have been dicking us around regarding what you know about the Alexander treasures. According to our research, you are the go-to guy for finding the tomb. The one dude on the face of the earth with the highest probability of knowing where the dead guy is. While your theories are a bit off the charts, you have used the latest technology and satellite imagery to disprove the traditional approaches and provide evidence for what may be the definitive site."

Leonnatus defended, saying, "I am a researcher, Sir. My fieldwork and scholarship have used the best methods available, and they stand for themselves. In guiding you to the proposed site, it is essential for you to see the entire picture disclosed by the recovered history. This includes the diaries of the librarians of the Great Library of Alexandria, which have recently come into your possession."

"C'mon, kid. This wild goose chase of yours is a scam to stage what you hope will be a world-shaking discovery, and you want it protected until you release your dissertation."

Rebecca said, "Leonnatus, high-tech archaeological research must be costly. Who has funded your research?"

"I headed up a team of archaeological graduate students funded by a private donor to the university. I never met the foundation, but I believe they were a Chinese consortium."

Mark checked his notes and retorted, "So, why you gotta bust my balls, kid with the sky-high IQ? Your project funding is not Chinese but from Azerbaijan-- Baku, to be specific. Yes? The Foundation for Cultural Research and Historic Preservation, an organization that has been tied to the political movement known as...."

Skylar finished Mark's sentence.

"The Rising Dawn."

Leonnatus' expression was absolutely unreadable.

Finally, he spoke.

"I should have been more circumspect. At this time, I will admit that. The money was desperately needed. Funding is so very difficult to secure, and I needed the time on the sites. I assure you I meant no duplicity in this. I have avoided reporting to them with accuracy, hoping that I could put them off, you see."

Mark said, "You are playing a dangerous game with some violent assholes, kiddo."

Agent Mathias said, "Mark, I need to see Eris' report."

Mark said coldly, "Jürgs, I am prepared to summarize it for you, but I am treating it as a journalistic source and not releasing it in its entirety."

He continued, "Jügen, my friend. There is something else."

The agent looked perplexed.

Rebecca said, "Leonnatus is not the only one with ties to the Rising Dawn movement."

Mark added, "There is a significant probability that they have also compromised another member of our little group.

"Nilza Mendes."

***

Skylar was standing and talking. The Aeolus continued the trip south to Egypt.

"In Islamic Eschatology, also known as the End Time, a false Messiah will rise in the East to establish the Last Empire. He is known in Islamic tradition as al-Masih ad-Dajjal, the deceiver. He is comparable to the Antichrist in Christianity. He will come at a time of great war to establish his kingdom. But the rule of the Dajjal will not be of God. Instead, his government will be corrupt, evil, and worldly.

"My tribe and my family reach back to the days of the Prophet. He charged us to protect the people from this Messiah of Lies. The leader of the Mahdi must have a body, heart, and soul that is pure and schooled in Islamic law and tradition. Throughout history, certain males among my ancestors believed themselves to be this figure, the Hidden Imam. The formation of this individual for the Great Battle is a rigorous one.

"My grandfather and father passed this tradition down to my generation. However, this hero, my friends, is not me. I have corrupted myself with worldliness. I have much apostasy in my heart and will fall before the forces of righteousness. It is imperative that, once we get to Egypt, you meet with the members of my family."

The inner conflict of the big man was apparent as he moved through the cabin. His voice and his visage took on a strange and otherworldly tenor.

He counseled, "Mark, your Eris needs to provide you with information regarding the background and activities of Farid Haydar Aliyev. He is an industrialist from Azerbaijan. There is whispering that he has some extreme political ambitions. My family network has done some research on his activities."

Mark responded, "As a matter of fact, this guy was included in a supplemental report on the Rising Dawn. I asked Eris who, and she came back with Aliyev having the highest probability of being the one behind all of this shit we have encountered. There is evidence that Aliyev funds a conservative Islamic militia training in the wilds of the Caucasus."

Jürgen said, "He is a very mysterious figure. Government connections keep him in the background. INTERPOL believes he wields a tremendous amount of power."

Rebecca said, "I'd say we have just identified the source of all this terror. Another shithead with world conquest on his mind to teach some manners."

Chapter Thirty-Three: The Pharos
Alexandria, Egypt

"Al Sama', my brother. I am pleased to see you."

"Daughter of the Nile, you are named well, my sister. It is my joy to be home again with you."

The al-Mahdi siblings embraced and kissed in the café. Skylar pulled his sister into his arms with genuine affection. He introduced his retinue to Chione and Doctor Zahra el-Saddik, the Egyptologist's mentor in Archaeology.

"How are your studies, my flower?"

"Always the big brother... I am following in your footsteps. In fact, I have class in a bit and then a full day buried in the lab. The chemistry course is very challenging."

"This is good, my Chione. Then I will bring you to America for your post-graduate studies."

"Not if Papa has a say in it. His views concerning women are so very archaic."

Rebecca noticed that the younger al-Mahdi was most likely in her early twenties. At the same time, her companion's appearance suggested a professional woman in her sixties. Chione was dressed in Western-style jeans and a polo shirt. A sky-blue pashmina circled her shoulders and pushed back off her head. Her dark hair was worn long and was styled with mini braids that suggested the look of an ancient Egyptian queen. She seemed to have trouble moving her lower body.

Dr. Zahra loosened her teal and silver headscarf, worn with a black lace jacket and long skirt. The woman was the image of a revered professional and smiled with sincerity. Her eyes were deep brown, while the young woman had a flashing smile and deep, lapis-blue eyes.

Rebecca, Mark, Leonnatus, and Jürgen exchanged greetings with the women. They joined the Egyptians at an outdoor table at the El Selsela Café with a beautiful view of the Mediterranean. Directly across from

Alexandria's modern library, this trendy spot on the harbor's El Geish Road commanded the crescent where the city meets the sea. The eatery had excellent food and featured a young clientele. Skylar began to provide backstory as coffees were ordered and decadent pastries were shared.

"If you look out in the harbor, the quay that reaches out into the sea and forms the inner harbor – there at the very tip is in the former site of the famous Pharos, the lighthouse of Alexandria, one of the Seven Wonders of the Ancient World. It was destroyed by earthquakes that rocked the ancient city every few decades. In the 15th century, the Sultan replaced it with the Citadel of Qaitbay to defend the twin harbors. You can see it on the sea's edge."

Leonnatus added, "In the 20th century, satellite imagery revealed large limestone blocks in the sea just off Pharos Island. You can actually dive on the site to see the remains of the lighthouse with its statues and columns asleep in the watery depths of Neptune's kingdom."

The Egyptian professor eyed the young archaeologist with interest. Dr. el-Saddik asked about his academic background and upcoming Ph.D. defense. She was impressed with his credentials.

"My boy, you know our city, it seems."

"Yes, professor. I spent almost two years in Egypt. This was the Ptolemies' capital city, so I came to know it in its present and ancient form. I have worked on almost every dig in the city."

Rebecca observed that Chione al-Mahdi regarded Leonnatus with a unique interest. She seemed to pick up on the looks and almost intimate touches between her brother and the young scholar.

Yeah, the young woman knows what's going on here.

"Do you folks know the legend of the founding of Alexandria?"

Mark waved one hand like an over-eager honor student.

"Ooo, ooo, pick me."

The Egyptians were perplexed, the Macedonian catching just the edge of the joke.

Rebecca rolled her eyes and said with a half-smile, "Hit it, genius."

Mark said, "Alexander set it up when he swept through Egypt before turning east to Persia, Afghanistan, and India."

Leonnatus took up the lesson again, "Correct. He wanted to establish a major Greek city named for him. Near this spot, he had a vision in a dream. Homer directed him to Pharos Island, where the Nile met the sea. In the morning, he began to walk and measure out the lines of the foundations of the city."

Rebecca said, "I love this, the part about the birds... omens and divine mystery."

"Right. So there was no chalk around, and the soldiers used grain meal to outline the design of the city on the dark soil."

As Leonnatus told the myth, he stood and swept his arms over the vista surrounding them, Egypt's second most significant metropolis. Reaching out to earth, sea, and sky, the young man assumed an expression that reflected the wonder of the tale he told.

"So, now, as Alexander stood on a hill with the plan of the city lines stretched out to the sea, clouds of birds of every kind and size flew from the river and the lagoon onto the site. They began to feed on the lines of grain. His generals declared it an omen that the city Alexander envisioned was doomed to be destroyed by conquest.

"The King was very disturbed by this, but his friend Hephestion brought forward one of the royal seers who told Alexander the true meaning of this sign from the gods."

The boy seemed to sparkle in the Egyptian sun as he took on the character of the ancient diviner. He lowered his voice and said, "Do not fear, my Lord. This city named for you will be blessed with an abundance of resources more than the world has ever known. Alexandria will sustain people from every nation. And so, Alexander built this glorious city that has remained in this place for 2300 years, surviving disasters, both artificial and natural, a beacon of knowledge and wisdom for the world."

Now, Chione saw the light in her brother's face as he watched his new friend with intense admiration for the boy's ability to tap into the magic of the ancient tales and keep his listeners spellbound. In a small gesture, she reached forward and lightly touched her brother's arm. Skylar shifted his gaze and met his sister's soft smile with one of his own.

He turned to the young scientist and said, "My friend, tell us of the ancient sites."

Leonnatus jumped up on a low wall near the table and commanded the attention of his friends and that of a few of the patrons at the other tables. He said, "The palace of the Ptolemies was off to the east on the now sunken island of Antirhodos, destroyed by earthquakes in the 4th century.

"Over there are the sites of what was believed to be the Mouseion and the Soma. The former was the home of the Great Library of Alexandria, closer to the harbor. The latter was the royal mausoleum, containing the tombs of the Ptolemaic royals.

"Most astonishing of all was the Serapeum, a temple built by Ptolemy III and most likely a daughter to the Great Library, containing many of its treasures. It was constructed on a hill, accessed by 100 steps. Its archaeological site is behind those buildings to the west."

He stretched his arms wide and said, "Imagine the glory of this city, founded by a conqueror king of myth and legend. His legacy, a monument to Greek culture, if it was to be found anywhere, was here, a dazzling world capital commanding the Mediterranean. If you approached it by land or by sea, during the day, you were blinded by the smooth marble surfaces gleaming in the sun and the gold appointments on city gates, palaces, and monuments.

"Had you sailed across the treacherous sea to it by night, the burning, guiding star, blazing on the top of the Pharos Lighthouse, announced your safe entry into the sacred land of the Pharaohs."

Leonnatus, the sun and the sea air in his hair and eyes, stretched his arms wide to embrace the city that wrapped around them. He seemed a throwback to his ancestors, Macedonians filled with dreams of spreading Hellenistic culture across the globe.

Soft claps came from a few of the café patrons.

"Darling, how wonderful." Rebecca reached up to take his hand as he stepped down and rejoined his friends.

Mark said, "Dude, you really know this shit. Impressive. I have a request. I'd like to get a feel of Egypt, the politics, and the whole antiquities controversy."

Chione touched the arm of her brother's colleague.

"I also can see you have a passion for this city. How very admirable."

She glanced at her phone.

"I am afraid I must hurry along to class. Skylar, my brother, please remember Papa's invitation. He is anxious to see you."

Her brother spoke up, "Yes, yes, my dear." He looked down but then back up quickly and referred to Mark's request. Standing and hoisting the requisite student backpack up to the table in anticipation of leaving, Chione politely bent in for a triple brother/sister cheek kiss.

Rebecca mused. *Was it something the girl said?*

The shadow of emotional concern crossed the face of her usually stoic Egyptologist. However, without losing his cool, Skylar returned to Mark's observation and desire to know more about the battle over who owns history.

"Mark, my mentor, Doctor Zahra el-Saddik from the Cairo Museum and the University, can help us understand the context of the political and cultural challenges to archaeology in countries with ancient civilizations like Egypt. As can, I am sure, Agent Mathias. Yes?"

Jürgen, an astute observer of humankind and the intrigues that often develop, smiled at the group. He had been observing the interplay of the al-Mahdis with a similar interest.

Something's there, family issues, and this guy hopes to avoid some personal controversy. Just what this group needs.

The INTERPOL agent leaned forward and handled his coffee cup with both hands for a refill while picking up his end of the conversation.

"Yes. So, it would appear that we have all kinds of resources at our disposal to get the job done. The federal government and international experts...."

He nodded to Zahra and used an index finger to point to himself.

"Next, our own Hephaistion, who will bring us to Alexander."

Leonnatus blushed.

"A renowned American curator and an accomplished warrior-journalist."

Mark tossed a date at Jürgen, which the agent caught and popped into his mouth.

"And, our distinguished Egyptologist and also...."

He now gestured to both al-Mahdis.

"The power of God to see us through."

Chapter Thirty-Four: "Can You See Anything?"
Al-Asu Center for Alexandrian Studies, Alexandria, Egypt

Rebecca and her group carefully picked their way down through platforms and equipment beneath the lowest level of the AL-ASU skyscraper a few blocks from the harbor. Stairways and open lifts created vertical access to a large hole in the bedrock between the foundations of the building. The layers of rock and gravel on all sides of the excavation were like an encyclopedia, illustrating the ancient stratifications of each of the buried versions of Alexandria. The older remains of the metropolis revealed their treasures as the group descended.

Pipes and conduits pierced the layers, taking groundwater away from the site. Necklaces of lights gave the vast cavern a surrealistic, sci-fi look, an off-world colony of miners and scientists. Workers moved between roped-off ground sections near the bottom among massive columns and soaring stone arches appearing out of the rubble. A granite sphinx with a broken face, a colossal scarab, an ancient, baboon-headed god, these and more silently watched over the workers. They were ancient sentries demanding respect as their hidden world was being desecrated.

"We are very close to the harbor on this site. The most modern methods of hydraulics are keeping back the waters of the Mediterranean."

Dr. Zahra el-Saddik explained as the group maneuvered down ladders, "This part was a cistern built most likely around the 10th century of the Common Era. But for your purposes, you will find that they used pieces of some of the ancient buildings going back to the founding of the city by the Greeks. It is what lies beneath that is most interesting."

She indicated some of the structures and the stonework, "Some years back, AL-ASU began constructing the building above us. It was clear from the start that the site held important cultural significance. Agreements with the multinational company and the government have protected the site for the most part."

A crane lifted the top portion of a massive column with beautiful papyrus capital upward. Zarah continued, "While the intent is to leave most of the structures in situ, some temporary rearrangement is needed to get to lower levels."

Skylar commented, "It was in this fascinating metropolis that I fell in love with my field of archaeology. I visited here as a teenager when the excavations were assuming major importance. I had read Lawrence Durrell's Alexandria Quartet and wanted to explore its history. Later, I met and studied with Dr. el-Saddik."

Now at the top of the cathedral-like structure, the famed archaeologist moved her visitors to an area out of the way of the workers. They stood on a platform overlooking the crater.

"I am now on loan to the Center for Alexandrian Studies, which oversees this site, and these are many of my students you see doing the excavation."

She turned to Leonnatus and took his hand.

"My young friend, here is Alexandria, yes? The bustling municipality we left above us is at the top of the pile, one of many iterations of this city. Modern Alexandria is the top of the layer cake. Take us to Alexander's capital, the center of trade and learning that was his legacy, built by his friend Ptolemy I Soter and his son. Tell us about your research."

Leonnatus was about to speak when they were approached by a woman in a tan worker's uniform. She moved with authority and smiled with hidden motives. They watched as she removed her hard hat and adjusted her cream-colored hajib. The woman spoke as if in the middle of a conversation.

"When Howard Carter opened the tomb of Tutankhamun in 1921, the Egyptians changed the game plan."

Leonnatus jumped into the story and said, "As he looked into the burial chamber, his companion said, 'Doctor Carter, can you see anything?'"

Skylar smiled and completed the mime, "'Yes, wonderful things.'"

The newcomer did not smile but said, "You two know your history. Carter violated the law and cut a hole in the sealed door. The first to view and handle the wealth of a Pharoah who lived more than 3000 years ago was an Englishman working for a British banker."

Rebecca asked, "How did the rules change, please?"

"Carter had the concession to dig in the Valley of the Kings. His sponsor, Lord Carnarvon, paid that license to the Egyptian Department of Antiquities. The contract stipulated that grave goods would be divided between the British and the Egyptians. As the burial chamber was opened, representatives from the government halted the work declaring that it all belonged to Egypt because this was a royal tomb. They disputed for years. Carter eventually prevailed. In addition to Doctor el-Saddik's students, the men and women in blue are representatives of the Department of Antiquities, making sure all is done lawfully on this site."

Dr. Zahra said, "Where are my manners? May I present Miriam Karimov, Vice President of International Relations for AL-ASU, the company headquartered above us."

The four visitors were astounded. The resemblance to Rebecca was uncanny. They politely introduced themselves.

Mark leaned into Rebecca and did an aside, "Must be like looking in a mirror."

"I am very passionate about Egypt's claim to her history. I am of Egyptian blood despite being born in Moscow. Egypt has been the slave to many masters throughout history, the Assyrians, the Greeks, the Romans, the Persians, the Arabians, and the European powers of the modern Era-- the French, the Italians, and the British. All were seeking to feast off of her bounty for thousands of years. Her cultural history was plundered and sold at foreign markets from the days of the first Pharaohs."

Ms. Karimov leaned against the rail and peered into the levels below. She said, "The world conglomerate, AL-ASU, is committed to preserving Egypt's past and keeping her historic wealth here where it belongs."

Jürgen added, "My agency would be pleased to work with AL-ASU. However, our efforts to involve your company in global cooperation to tackle the theft, forgery, and illicit trafficking of cultural property and antiquities have gone unaddressed. I am perplexed as to why, Ms. Karimov. It would appear we want the same things."

"To be frank, Agent Mathias, our Board of Directors believes that INTERPOL represents many outside interests with whom we are reluctant to engage. We are aggressively pursuing discussions with the Department of Antiquities in Cairo to prevent yet another colonizer from raping this sacred land."

The clashing politics and scientific ideologies hung in the air as the two seemed to face off. Before further confrontation could occur, a worker, also in tan, approached and spoke to the Vice President in Egyptian. Miriam responded and waved him off. She turned to Dr. el-Zaddik and her guests.

"I am afraid that I must get back to the work. It was….

Zahra interrupted, "Lead the way, Miriam. We are coming with you to see what my students have found."

To her guests, she added, "It seems there has been an important discovery."

The group was led to the very base of the excavation and deep into a recess. At the bottom of an ancient stairway, a brick wall was being carefully disassembled to reveal a tunnel that disappeared in the direction of the harbor.

Miriam held back the workers except for a few with lights. She attempted to lead the group into the newly uncovered shaft.

"Stop. Go no further."

Skylar commanded the attention as he prevented the entry of the group. Leonnatus and Zahra were in agreement, insisting that any invasion be halted.

Skylar said, "Archaeological excavation is itself a sacrilege. Do not walk on the floor. Observe."

He took a brush from one of the students and, kneeling on planks in the doorway, gently uncovered a fine layer of dust on the pebble mosaic of the tunnel's flooring. A beautiful pattern of florals and armed human figures appeared in the hand-held lights.

Leonnatus leaned over his shoulder and placed a supporting hand on the Egyptian's back. He spoke softly to his comrade in science.

"It appears to be of the same craft design as the mosaic school of ancient Pella. I would wager that the materials are indigenous to Egypt, however. We do not have some of these stones in Macedonia.

"Move to that section, Doctor, please. Yes, there. Look."

Skylar uncovered a portion of the tunnel's floor that depicted the head and shoulders of a handsome warrior who seemed to be turning to address a group of soldiers.

Leonnatus gripped the man by the shoulder. "Skylar, it is Alexander and the Diadochi. Amazing."

As he spoke, Leonnatus took a light from a nearby worker, saying to Miriam Karimov, "Let it be noted, please, that this time, it is an Egyptian and a Macedonian who are the first to view this wonder. Pella and Alexandria have united again, the new Ptolemies. And rightly so. This is from the 3rd century BCE, assuredly."

Ms. Karimov was not impressed with the romantic illusion of the young scholar. She looked greedily at the mosaic.

Skyler came up off his crouch and took another light. A worker on each side attempted to carefully widen the opening by removing more bricks.

"It is Ptolemaic, absolutely. Get your workers to prepare a platform from which they can enter this tunnel."

Dr. el-Zaddik, Rebecca, Mark, and Jürgen leaned in to view the discovery as the two archaeologists raised their lanterns into the opening.

The curved limestone walls of the tunnel blazed with paintings of battles with turbaned soldiers riding elephants, queens consorting with gods, Persians falling before advancing Macedonian armies, and a golden-haired, god-like warrior reaching for the double crown of upper and lower Egypt.

Thomas Paul Severino

Chapter Thirty-Five: Plans
Al-Asu Center for Alexandrian Studies, Alexandria, Egypt

Rebecca sipped her coffee and said, "She could not have gotten us out of there faster."

She turned and gazed out the window of the Center for Alexandrian Studies on the 18th floor of the AL-ASU building. The group had sought refuge in Zahra's office following their ejection from the dig below the skyscraper.

Jürgen reached for a refill, saying, "I have no doubt that we have been face-to-face with the Rebecca Twin, who first absconded with the chest of ancient scrolls. But why did she send them to you in Fort Lauderdale?"

Rebecca said, "Has it occurred to anyone that perhaps I was not the intended recipient."

Mark said, "What do you mean?"

"Why send such an essential collection of clues to the Lost Museum to the curator in the U.S. unless she happens to employ the world's foremost expert on the Ptolemaic Dynasty?"

She nodded to Dr. Skylar al-Mahdi, who bent over a set of documents with Leonnatus and Dr. el-Zaddik.

Jügen said, "Rebecca, your theory is flawed. If Karimov and her associates wanted Doctor al-Mahdi to act as a translator – the chest was a murder weapon, why kill him or you, for that matter? The poison lock- - they wanted someone dead. With him out of the game, they achieve nothing."

Rebecca said, "The way Kazimov looked at Skylar when we all first met was fuckin' deadly-- like a cobra ready to strike at her prey. I swear. Furthermore, I am willing to bet it has something to do with the Hidden Imam and his family's historic commitment to defending the world from the apocalypse of evil."

Mark said, "She, or rather the group she works for, wanted Skyler dead so that they could prevail with their world domination scheme?

Sounds fuckin' nutso, but the world is full of the bat shit crazies, as we both know well."

Jügen mused, "So let's piece this together. I am right. Egypt is full of experts on translations from that era. Then the gambit was that Skylar would open the chest, and they would have succeeded in killing the one person who stands in the way of the ascendancy of the Rising Dawn."

Rebecca added, "No, Agent Mathias, you are wrong. The intent was not to murder. Hence, the poison was not at lethal dosage. The whole purpose of the mystery was to serve as bait.

"If someone else, me, for instance, opened the chest, bingo. Either way, they have let the rabbit out for the hounds. I am also convinced that our little Scorpion Woman tipped off your agency regarding the destination of the stolen artifact. Karimov and whomever she works for is now orchestrating our entire mission, the search for the grave of Alexander, complete with field experts and a noted journalist and the notations of the ancient curators of the treasures – the librarians. She and her minions are following closely behind."

Mark said with a twinkle in his eye, "You know you are much more attractive, Beautiful. No comparison. Photographs and video notwithstanding." He kissed her lightly.

Jürgen glanced over his shoulder at the three archaeologists huddled before a series of computers and maps. He wanted his subsequent remarks to be very confidential. He pulled his chair closer to Rebecca and Mark.

"Karimov is a frontwoman. Her allegiance goes much deeper. Let me say that I am in this assignment fully one-hundred percent. You understand that, yes."

Rebecca said, "Of course. Go on."

Jürgen looked back and forth between his friends as he explained. "I realize that my entry was a bit farcical, as you Americans say, 'fucked-up,' back in Fort Lauderdale."

Mark smirked, "Yeah, bud. The mistaken identities. Confusing Rebecca and the Russian schemer. Totally *Gefickt*." Rebecca nodded.

"I regret that very much and assure you that it is an irregularity that will not repeat itself."

Rebecca put a hand of assurance on the German agent's shoulder. "I forgive you, Darling. You can 'almost arrest' me at any time. Go on, what's the plan?"

"Jürges, get to the point. You're as nervous as a hooker on nickel night."

"My methods are somewhat unorthodox, and my strategy is not fully set in my mind."

Mark offered, "Hatched?"

"Yes, my friend. 'Hatched' – wholly thought out, but it needs to happen tonight.

"I am in on this to find out and prevent the operations of the Rising Dawn. As an agent of INTERPOL, that is my primary concern. I have intelligence that a member of the organization is turning, and I will attempt tonight to make the best of that. He is very close to Farid Haydar Aliyev."

Rebecca said, "Getting your James Bond on?"

"Perhaps more than you know, Rebecca."

Mark said, "So...?"

The agent looked at the couple and pointed to each one in turn as he said, "This is a bit edgy but worth the risk. I am going to need you and not you."

***

Dr. Zahra gathered the group and said, "Here's the plan, my friends. The three of us have decided that the discovery of the corridor is of considerable significance to finding the location of the Great Library and its museum, both housed in the great academic center of the Mouseion of Ptolemy. Consequently, I need to get these two scholars back in that tunnel. Leonnatus has the expertise to see inside the structure... well, I will let him tell it."

Leonnatus was excited as he took up the narrative.

"It's like Superman's x-ray vision, you know, seeing through walls, the process used in the Scanning the Pyramids project. This Center has laser equipment and 3D imaging technology to see inside that passageway and through its walls. The apparatus is light, quickly set up, and easily operated...."

Skyler broke in, "And our young archaeologist here has the expertise that is needed."

"Scanning has been a part of my work on all of the digs on which I have worked for my studies. I can get it up and going and feed data to our computers for analysis. Also, I have something else to say. "

Skyler seemed to be beaming and actually placed a supporting hand on his young colleague's back, a loving and affirming gesture."

"I know a man who will do some LiDAR for us from the outside. I suspect the farthest end of the accessway is submerged under the harbor."

Mark said, "Gimme that again, kiddo, LiDAR?"

"Light Detection and Ranging. In archaeology, we use it to map land areas and buried structures unable to be seen from the ground. Combining data sets from my 3D imaging inside the tunnel and LiDAR from my friend in the plane, we will get some high-resolution visuals on what lies at the end of the passage."

Rebecca asked, "You indicated that we are very close to the harbor. Does this technology work under water?"

"Yes, it is merely a matter of adjusting the laser wavelength to bypass any sea surface echo and capture deep-sea topography. My friend, with the aircraft, is obliged to me for a favor. We have worked together before, and he is Macedonian, so...."

Mark smiled, "Blood is thicker than seawater, I guess."

Rebecca asked, "How do we get Skylar and Leonnatus on that site? Ms. Miriam Karimov was a bit adamant about keeping us away from the dig."

Zahra stepped to a cabinet near her desk. Before returning, she rifled through her desk drawer and removed a small badge. She returned with a stylish scarf, a lab coat, and a name tag. Handing them both to Rebecca, she said, "That is where you come in, my dear."

Rebecca unfolded the hajib, smiled, and addressed the absent vice president.

"Two can play at this game, bitch."

Thomas Paul Severino

Chapter Thirty-Six: What the Eye Cannot See
Al-Asu Center for Alexandrian Studies, Alexandria, Egypt

Hard hats, goggles, and white masks on Leonnatus and Skylar completed their disguises. Faces obscured, each shifted a backpack containing the imaging equipment as the quartet made its way down and into the new discovery. Rebecca adjusted Skylar's work coveralls.

"Kinda tight, big guy. All those muscles aren't always an advantage."

She buttoned the jacket up to his neck and winked at Leonnatus.

Zahra said, "Rebecca, stay close to me and fake some intimate conversations when we are near the guards and other AL-ASU officials. I checked with Miriam's office, and she is in a meeting at this time, so we have a chance to get away with this. Gentlemen, work quickly, please."

Leonnatus said, "Just got a text from my friend. He will commence the flyover soon. He had been working out on the Pharos, so he is all set up and nearby. We used the coordinates of the Al-ASU skyscraper to plot his coverage – here to the sea."

As it turned out, the guards permitted Dr. el-Zaddik, her students, and "Ms. Karimov" into the opening without any interference. A scaffold of planks and strung-up lighting allowed work access about 6 inches above the pebble floor. Deep in the tunnel, the group made the turn to the right. There was no staff at the far end. A brick and stucco wall sealed off any further access. Leonnatus knelt and began to set up his equipment with Skylar's assistance.

Around the clandestine foursome, figures from Ptolemaic Egypt fought, danced, and made love with ancient Macedonians on the cave's walls and ceiling. Other renderings showed men and women in academic settings, reading or instructing with scrolls and maps. One figure pointed to a chart of the heavens.

Skylar knelt, reached over in his nitrile gloves, and carefully brushed dust and dirt from the pebble flooring. Land animals and sea creatures raced along spiral waves and rolling hills between two deep-set tracks on the floor. He captured images on his cell phone.

Rebecca said, "The best place for Zahra and me is back at the entrance. Skylar, should anything happen, I will send you a short text. Pack up and get your collective asses out of this tube."

Soft LCD lights glowed from the imagers, and a knife-edge strip of laser light began to move over the far wall from top to bottom and left to right.

As the women left, Leonnatus stood up and shrugged.

"It's all going well, Doctor al-Mahdi. The program is running smoothly. There is nothing left to do but wait. This should not take long."

The Egyptian stood up from his floor exploration and faced his comrade. Skylar reached up to remove that lad's hard hat and goggles, placing them on the wooden planks. He did the same with his own and stepped closer, shortening the distance between them.

The man placed his hands on either side of the Macedonian's face. He kissed his companion, pulling the bewildered boy into a hot hug as ancient warriors and a pantheon of Egyptian gods looked on.

"I am not sure if it is the danger we are in or the ancient world we have stepped into, but I am so interested in having you in my arms right now."

Slightly coming off the embrace, the amorous man looked into the eyes of his captive and continued to speak, punctuating each phrase with a luscious lip lock.

He said with a raw huskiness in his voice, "Considering how you have corrupted me with this... and some of this... and what we will be up to later, which is likely more of this..., I would say we are... at the point... where you should call me 'Skylar.'"

Leonnatus half-listened for the beep of the computer and, returning the passion, pulled the insistent man even closer.

I have seen this a few times before-- men coming to terms with their sexual identity, making up for lost time.

He teased, "Sir, you are making it very hard for me to concentrate on the work at hand. Furthermore, your corruption, as you call it, was a bit easier than I anticipated."

Skylar only tightened his embrace. He gasped into the ear of the young man, "So, I willingly accept damnation for these moments with you."

As he continued the make-out in the ancient passageway, Leonnatus looked over Skylar's shoulder to a crumbled image of a beautiful Macedonian warrior on the opposite wall. The painted hero seemed to stare at the lovers.

Hephaestion.

***

"There. Go now."

Zahra pointed to an exit to the above-ground off to the side. Rebecca hit "send," and the abort text message to Skylar was delivered. She mimicked interest in her clipboard as she approached the way off of the site. Just as he reached the access lift, she turned to see a group led by Miriam Karimov move in from the opposite side of the dig toward Dr. el-Zaddik.

Minutes later, in the tunnel, Skylar and Leonnatus, with packed-up technology, moved in the direction of the opening. As the new entrants approached, they bent over and pretended to fuss with the equipment. Miriam and her crew, business-suited executives, and officials spoke what seemed to be Russian, peppered with Egyptian comments.

Zahra stepped back just long enough to indicate that she would meet the disguised workers in her office. It was easy to see that Miriam was conducting a site tour of the new discovery with deference to a tall, handsome man wearing an eyepatch.

A somewhat relieved Leonnatus touched the company logo on the elevator wall in the lift. He looked at Skylar with an unspoken question.

"ASU is not an acronym, my friend. The conglomerate's name is taken from a Semitic root."

"Meaning?"

"First Light. The Dawn."

213

Chapter Thirty-Seven: The Unforgivable
The Louran, Alexandria, Egypt

"Al Sama' al Muharib al-Mahdi, my son, allow me to look at you before I begin my directions and guidance. You have been too long outside my influence."

Muhammad Nefer al-Mahdi held his son by the shoulders after receiving the kiss of respect. From time to time, he slipped his eyes to the young Macedonian in a manner of wondering.

"He goes by 'Skylar,' Papa. It is a close translation."

"Be still my daughter. Cover your head as is proper, and remember the respect you owe your family. I will get to you in a second."

He added lovingly, "You seem to be on the mend. Taking your medication?"

The young woman lowered her eyes and said, "Yes, Papa."

Muhammad Nefer squinted again at Leonnatus but spoke to his son.

"This name 'Skylar' is too much a Hollywood name for a professor and a member high up in the al-Mahdi family. It is the name that should be attached to a character from the American film Star Wars. No, no, no, I disapprove of this modernization. You are al Sama'."

Skylar rubbed his jaw, saying, "It was kind of Aunt Kara to host us. Her villa here in the neighborhood of Louran has such a spectacular view of the sea."

There was a pregnant pause in the conversation.

Skylar picked up, saying. "My Father, this is my um... friend and colleague Leonnatus Gianopoulos from the Aristotelian University in Thessaloniki. We have much in common..."

"And that is?"

You are not going to make this easy, are you, old man?

"We are both accomplished researchers in the Ptolemaic era of our history. Leonnatus has..."

"*Marhaba*, most respected, Sir." The boy bowed slightly, knowing not to offer his hand for a shake.

The elder al-Mahdi responded relatively formally, "Salaam, friend of my son. Generous hospitality is our custom, Professor. My sister has prepared a magnificent meal for us. You are welcome."

Cousins, aunts, and uncles greeted the two men. Skylar's Auntie Kara swept Leonnatus away with hundreds of questions as she toured him across the spacious, sea-facing patio. A soft breeze from the Mediterranean tossed the summer fabrics of the women's traditional dresses and the men's abayas. Behind them, the villa stretched out along the property, its arched arcades lifting three stories of the most elegant, modern Egyptian architecture. A retinue of servants came and went, bringing food, drinks, and glittering lamps to dispel the coming dark of evening.

"You have the blue eyes of the morning sky, my dear. I am extremely jealous. My family features the dark skin and blue-black eyes of one of the oldest races on earth, the Egyptians. What a contrast to your Hellenistic features."

Leonnatus felt the warmth from the sparkling woman that was absent from his initial reception by Mummad Nefer. Picking up on this, Kara said, "Pay no attention to my brother, 'The Bull.' He is as obstinate as his namesake. He rides poor Chione and Skylar quite hard, I regret to say. Near about revolted when I married Daniel and became a Copt. We did not speak for years.

"All of this traditional garb is only for his sake. The family gets out our traditional drag whenever Uncle Nefer convenes the clan. We are westernized, you see."

He smiled, very much liking Skyler's aunt. The al-Mahdi male cousins, the uncles, and even some women resembled the cast of his favorite American show, "Ninja Warriors," outgoing and gregarious, all so strikingly attractive, vigilant, and fit, even in their flowing robes.

The younger males were sporting the long, pagan soldier hairstyle, some with shaved designs on one side of their shorn heads. A few neck tattoos peaked over high collars. Here and there, a teenager, destined to be an athlete of note, was reminded by an elder to put away their cell phone or their football.

"We are actually a very high-performing clan. Sarah, you must recognize from the Oscar telecast last April. And my daughter, Edrice, works for the national judiciary. She is talking to her finacée near the fountain. Husani al-Mahdi, my grandson, has just been accepted to university on a football scholarship. He's the young man juggling the ball with his cousins. And the tall gentleman just there is Shabaka Mahmoud al-Mahdi, retired from the Ministry of Defense. Three of his sons and two of his daughters serve in the national armed forces."

To Leonnatus, the entire family assembly seemed to be wrapped in the ancient mysteries of this sacred land. Dark eyes, exotic features, and hard bodies held secrets that went back through time everlasting. They were a clan trained to accomplish a critical mission, and they looked like an elite force.

I am in beautiful-people heaven. Such a rush. Mark, Rebecca, and Jürgen would so fit right in.

Kara said, "Come and meet my husband and have something to eat. I want to hear more about your work and about you and my handsome nephew. His cousins are so enamored of that gorgeous man, but that is another thing for a conversation of a later time."

Watching the moon rise in the east, Skyler and Chione waited with their father, pretty sure no one was fooling anyone, and the storm was about to break as it always did.

The *pater familias* seemed to fumble as he tried to redirect the conversation. He said, "Ahh, the Traveller has arrived. Named by our pagan ancestors as Khonsu, the god of the moon, the Healer, one of the old ones. See how he sheds his light on the Mediterranean."

"Yes, Father. He is the Pathfinder and the one who drives away evil and falsehood."

Muhammad Nefer was accustomed to abruptly switching the conversation when he felt uncomfortable. He did so again.

"Be still a moment, my son. I want to address your sister."

The older man directed his remarks to his youngest child.

"Go and assist the women with the food, Chione. I want to talk to your brother about essential matters in private."

"Not a chance, Papa."

The young woman stepped closer to her brother and took his hand, standing at his side.

Comes the shit storm of all shit storms. God be merciful.

Not pleased with his daughter's response, Muhammad Nefer now began looking into the dark eyes of his firstborn.

"You are aware of our legacy, my son. We trace our bloodlines back to the Macedonian conquerors and the esteemed Egyptian houses of Alexandria. In the mists of a thousand years ago, our family embraced a divine calling. I taught our sacred vocation to you when you were at my knee. We are a family devoted to the one true God. We sacrifice everything to do his work."

He stretched his arms wide.

"Behold the Mahdi of God. By his good favor, we are in all of the highest professions of society, national and international. Your uncle Shabaka Mohammad has just been named an adviser to the Chinese National People's Congress. Selene, your cousin, has just received an appointment to the International Court of Justice in the Hague. We led armies against Napolean, served as ambassadors to the League of Nations, and wrote national constitutions. In one year, my brother's daughter, Jaabili al-Mahdi, will travel to the International Space Station for the Russian Government. My son, God leads us, and we must—we must follow!"

His eyes shined as he continued, "Believe this, my son. We are the army of the Messiah, the ones who will produce the Hidden Imam, commissioned by God himself to bring about the salvation of the righteous. And I see him standing before me. May God be praised. This much I know."

Muhammad Nefer put his hands on his son's shoulders. Skyler looked off at Khonsu, the moon rising from the sea, sending avenues of light across the water, dancing on the waves and ripples. Finally, he met his father's gaze.

There was resignation in his voice as he said, "Here we are again, my Father. We are fated to be always in the same place when it comes to this as if stuck in the shifting desert sands. Father, I am not...."

The older man protested fiercely.

"Stop, al Sama'. Do not blaspheme. You know of the divinely ordained mission of our family, and you must embrace it without question." The elder was shaking and began to go red in the face. He clenched his fists.

Deciding to try a theological argument, Skylar said, "I am far from the pure man that is described in the texts...."

"Chione, for the last time, leave us. I do not wish you to hear this."

"No. I will remain."

"I am cursed by the flagrant disobedience of my children. God's righteous punishment I accept, but how long will I have to endure?"

"Papa," Skylar said. "How can I help you to understand?"

"What? What? Understand what? You tell me, man of the world. Make me understand why you have embraced the flesh and have forsaken our family. You have let the devils of the West into your heart and forsaken your family's vows. Tell me why."

The patriarch turned on his children with full force.

"Can this be so? That you have rejected the sacred role of our family in the salvific plans of the one true God? Explain that to me, al Sama'. That my beliefs are no more than a myth, the centuries-old ravings of the religious men of our family. Explain to me that my faith, my very being, has become obsolete, meaning no more than the sands of the desert. The two of you. Explain your position as children of this godless modern world."

Muhammad Nefer brought his face very close to his staring children, saying, "The Mahdi clan is the only defense to prevent the chaos and destruction of the False Messiah that is coming and may be already here. The End Time signs are all about us, but it is written that we will prevail. The Mahdi-- the agents of God. We have believed this for almost fifteen hundred years."

He raised an index finger in the face of his only son.

"Now you tell me you have thrown away your vocation with sins of the flesh with women, the sinful agents of the devil. It is your manly beauty that makes women lead you to fornication."

Even as he said it, he knew he had crossed a line.

"Papa, you do not know what you are saying." Chione was shocked at her father's words.

Al-Mahdi continued shaking his finger at his son. "You cannot forsake your divine calling because of your wanton ways with women. I do not believe..."

"And men."

The elder reacted as if he had been struck in the face. Kara and Leonnatus came over to the arguing trio and stood slightly back but within earshot. Muhammad Nefer looked at Leonnatus for a very long minute and then raised his right arm as if to strike his son. Chione al-Mahdi stepped forward to grab her father's arm and stop the blow.

"And no one makes me do anything I don't want to do, Papa."

Enraged and practically speechless, the man said, "You say this to my face? To my face?"

There was silence as the meaning of the words came to be understood. Skylar would not lower his eyes but remained silent. Finally, he spoke.

"Father, what happened to your brother, Uncle Tarik? Tell me honestly."

Kara raised a hand to her mouth, her eyes instantly filling with tears. The older man stuttered and gulped, unable to put words together in a coherent sentence.

"Chione and I were too little. What happened to 'The Morning Star'?"

"Do not speak to me of one who was an... an... an abomination, godless and... one who died unforgiven. The one of whom you speak was no brother to me, and he...."

"He what, Father? Say it. Uncle Tarik had AIDS. Did he pay for his sins? Got what was coming to him? Was he cursed by God?"

The Bull drew himself up and announced, "Yes."

Auntie Kara sobbed.

Skylar dropped his gaze from his Father and looked away in distressful confusion, steeped in sorrow and pity. He stared again at the rising moon as he spoke.

"Where is your compassion? *Rahmah*? In the name of Allah, the Compassionate and Merciful... absolutely no empathy regarding the suffering of your brother? How is this possible in one who is so devout?"

His last sentence was a bitter accusation. Skylar paused for a long time and studied the face of his outraged father. There was no fear or a need for respect now. When he spoke again, it was with grave finality.

"I am no agent of God. This much I know. Look elsewhere for your Hidden Imam. I am no use to God or humanity unless I am an authentic man and have compassion for others. Unless I honor what it means to be a blest man living in truth, Papa, in truth. If you cannot accept this, then let me find my place among the unforgiven also."

Kara accused in a toneless voice. "You never went to see him when he was in hospice. In the end, he was emaciated, suffering from so many opportunistic infections they did not know which ones to treat first... blind and suffering from dementia... not once did you go or even ask about him... your own brother."

As if in a trance, the woman added, "He died alone, in that awful place, from that dreadful disease."

Muhammad Nefer, fists clenched, bellowed a primal scream into the night. Around them, family members stopped and were silent. Many raised a hand to their mouth in shock.

"Let his name never be mentioned! HE CANNOT BE FORGIVEN!"

He shot an arm at his son.

"AND NEITHER WILL YOU!"

The silence that followed contained only the sounds of nightbirds caught on the sea breeze in the near stillness of the crystal clear moonlight. The air, sea, and land seem to sigh with the memory of restless souls, unreconciled and abandoned forever. Wisps of ragged clouds raced across the moon like lost shrouds.

Chione reached out and took her father's florid face in her hands. She crooned to him in Egyptian, channeling what peace she could bring to his tortured soul.

"Shhh, Baba, Baba… shhh. It will be all right, Baba. He is still al Sama'"

Skyler stepped back from the troubled man. His father reached out and grabbed his son's shirt with both hands as if to shake him.

"Tell me you are not this… this atrocity. Look at the face of your father and tell me. Do it al-Sama'. Do it. I want you to tell me. In God's name, tell me you deny this."

Skylar slowly removed his father's grip, one hand at a time. He reached for Leonnatus' hand and brought it to his lips. His father closed his eyes in acute pain.

Skylar's mind went back into history for the appropriate thing to say. He remembered the mistake of the Persian Dowager Empress. The Egyptian scholar quoted from the legend as he clasped his companion's hand.

"Never mind, and do not worry. He is Alexander, too."

Chapter Thirty-Eight: The Falcon

Al Saqr Bar, Alexandria, Egypt

"Was she upset, my friend?"

"Um, a bit. I tease Rebecca a lot with hot man-on-man sex stuff. But, my accompanying you to a gay bar to pick up this guy did not sit well. Truth be told, I am a bit uncomfortable, bud."

Mark continued, "She is a bit preoccupied, I think, with the Alexander project and all."

"I understand that she has been invited to speak at the Annual Congress for Women's Rights in a few days, her work to end female genital mutilation-- a follow up to that UN conference in New York."

"Yeah. Rebecca has been asked by the Egyptian Center to address the assembly. And are you ready for this? Rebecca's name was put forward for the gig by none other than your friend, Nilza Mendes."

Jürgen smirked, "Ouch, from the Organization for Security and Co-operation in Europe. Your computer hacker said she has ties to Aliyev. Suspicious."

"Eris modified that. A bit. She has found a high probability that our Nilza is connected to the Muslim Brotherhood. Our girl is leading a double life."

"Make that triple, Marko. INTERPOL has been concerned about her Russian ties, leading straight to Aliyev. It is tough to determine whom Nilza is working for. So much in our adventure is not what it seems."

"Jürgs, the dice are loaded, and the knives are out, as they say."

They were checking out the scene down the alley in front of Al Saqr Bar. Its carved falcon logo stretched its open wings across the double door, pulled open every so often to admit patrons by a hulking bouncer.

Jürgen reached up and clawed Mark's high and tight into a more hyper-masculine hairstyle. They both were dressed as hot muscled hunks on the make, torn jeans, sleeveless t-shirts, and running shoes. He pulled at the torn cotton material of Mark's jeans, exposing a bit more flesh.

Mark swatted away the hands of the annoying agent, saying, "Dude, You won't be satisfied until most of my ass is on view."

"All for God and country. Think of the reporting that will come of this. C'mon, you are supposed to be my luscious daddy, remember?"

Unusually, the bouncer spoke to them in English.

"You ladies gonna stand here and play slap and tickle until the cops ass kick you, or are you coming inside?"

Mark recognized the accent. With half a smile, he pointed to the guy.

"New York?"

"Jersey City."

As they started past him, The bruiser ran his hands over each of their bodies in a frisk that many would note as a huge man grope.

"No guns."

Mark cocked his arms on either side of his head.

"Only these, baby."

"Cocky motherfucker, ain't cha?"

He curled his lips and pointed with two fingers and a lit cigarette.

"You bitches stay out here any longer, and I'll spread eagle you against that wall and run a full cavity search on both your asses, and I won't use my hands. Now get the fuck inside."

Mark said, just loud enough for the muscle-head to hear, "Friendly place."

The club was dark, smokey, and sensual. A skinny, tattooed DJ played house music, and dark forms gyrated to the moody music. A long bar lined the far wall but was cloaked in the place's signature décor, darkness. The movements of the patrons suggested it was pick-up night.

As they grabbed a table close to the bar, Mark said, "Reminds me of Berlin in the Thirties, right Jürgs?" He pulled his faux husband close and rubbed his head as one would caress a pet or an errant child.

The INTERPOL agent, definitely getting his sexy on, passed a pack of cigarettes to his late-night companion, who raised a hand to decline.

"Did I mention Rebecca was not happy when you swiped her mascara and lip gloss, Dude? You sure about this?"

Jürgen appraised man-paint on the handsome American in the dark bar. "You are a bit too fair for the eye job I did, but-- one word, Daddy, *Fick unwiderstehlich*."

"'Fuckin' irresistible' is two words, Jüges, even in German."

Mark continued. "Gotta ask, Boss. Look, I know we go way back, Bud, but are you working a hidden agenda here? Trying to get into this straight boy's pants?"

"Marko, my friend, I am shocked. Shocked!"

The INTERPOL spy popped a pair of wide eyes and an aghast expression before saying, "You know I could have had you long ago if I wanted to. Relax."

Mark did an eye roll in dark lashes.

Jürgen smiled.

"Now, kiss me as if you mean it."

***

Ivan Lermontov laughed loudly and drank with a few of the denizens of Al Saqr Bar on the other side of the dark interior but in full view of the hot pair. Mark and Jürgen vacillated from a distinct interest in him and teasing each other. The Russian bruiser had a keen interest in fit, frisky young men, and these two were prime examples. He needed some energetic distraction from the tension of his work and private life. A weekend of sexing up a couple of hot Euro-jocks was just what was required.

A bartender placed a refill of his vodka neat in front of the man and pointed to the smooching couple who came off their make-out to raise a glass to the smiling Russian. Lermontov left his place and pulled up to a seat beside Jügen.

"Spasibo vam, moi druz'ya."

Mark flashed a killer smile and toasted again, "You are most welcome. *Vashe zrodovye.*"

"And to your health as well. Although it would appear that you two *sportsmenov* are already in a very healthy state. I am Ivan."

Jürgen said, "My husband is Mark, and I am Jürgen. We are on holiday from the EuroGames. Good to meet you."

The very interested man smiled as he said, "I cannot allow you to pay for this, my sexy friends. I only drink Russo Baltique. Amazingly, this piss hole carries it, but I previously have made a very loud and drunken insistence about it, you see. It is the best, and in the end, there is only Russian vodka when all the cards are played, extreme sex is moments away, and the sweat is drying on hot bodies. *Da?*"

Mark thought, *Jesus, I need a cigarette just talking to this horny bastard. He moves on a target faster than shit through a goose.*

Jürgen leaned back to look at the man's broad back beneath his tank top. He finger-traced a tattooed set of wings on Ivan's right rear deltoid.

"Is that the falcon for which this place is named?"

Ivan stood up and proudly lifted the shirt up and off. He turned slightly and flared his lats.

"I am marked with the Russian double-headed eagle, a symbol of Empire and dominance over both east and west. I am of a race that crushes and takes what is wanted."

Mark said, "Whoa. Intense but, OK, cool."

Yep, Jürgs knows what he likes, toned fucker. This is gonna be one tough dude to control. Good idea to have two of us on him for the takedown.

226

Jürgen continued his tracing as the shirtless man resumed his seat.

"Russian special operations-- Spetsnaz, last quartered in Georgia. Love hearing the crunch of these fists against insurgent heads and bodies."

He clenched some impressive hands at the ends of large forearms. The man propped his right arm on the table next to Jürgen and winked.

"So, this alpha specimen joined the private sector when I got out. This boy became a man in combat for Mother Russia."

In the darkness of the bar, a hand reached over Mark's shoulder and placed a bottle of Russo Baltique on the table. Ivan picked up the bottle and refilled his glass.

Jügen moved his left hand up the man's forearm and teased, "C'mon, my friend. Your vodka... it cannot be all that good."

Ivan tossed back a healthy shot of the crystal clear liquid and reached out to the back of the German's head. He pulled Jügen's face to his and ground his lips and tongue, coated with the exotic liquor, into the startled mouth of the INTERPOL agent. As he forced a rough face suck, Ivan kept his eyes defiantly on Mark.

"This muscled slut finally gets handled the way he deserves. So, do something about it, American boy."

They came off the makeout, and Ivan pushed Jürgen back. He leaned over and addressed the American with a challenging smirk.

"So, I defile your husband in public. You are man enough to fight me for him, yes? We go into the alley. You keep him or lose him." He kissed Jügen again, this time a ravishing mouth rape.

Mark took their two glasses and tossed the ice cubes to the floor. He grabbed the vodka bottle and poured each of them a shot. He raised his glass.

"Listen up, Sparky. My man and I are pretty open in our play. Been known to include another studly if he has the endurance to keep up with us. Shall we save our grappling for the main event? Unless you are all talk."

He tossed back his glass, stood up, and walked behind the Russian. Mark grabbed a fist full of his hair and pulled his head back, leaning over for an even more competitive lip lock. Not to be outmaneuvered, The Russian reached up and pulled Mark's head closer by the back of his neck.

Coming up for air, he growled, "I get you, American jock. You two are about to feel the power of a real Russian man deep inside." He reached up and grasped Mark's upper arms.

Jürgen tossed a hotel key on the table and ran a hand over Mark's lower back and ass while touching the Russian's chest.

"Bring the Baltique."

In the dark, a somewhat agitated server watched the threesome depart into the hot Egyptian night.

Chapter Thirty-Nine: Sleeper Hold

Hotel Funduq Ruyal, Alexandria, Egypt

"He likes to watch. He will join us soon."

Ivan looked at Mark, sitting opposite the bed in his jock, sucking on the vodka bottle and blowing smoke onto the two naked lovers on the bed. The Russian sneered at him, "I will use your hot boy and then force him to watch me dominate you. Best you two *neryakhi* ever had. I will own you both, one at a time."

The former Russian soldier turned corporate exec flexed his naked body and climbed on top of his first, similarly exposed, conquest.

He commanded, "Face down, arse up, you fuckin' whore."

Mark was out of the chair and on him in a flash. Arms, head, neck — quick and forceful, total sleeper hold. The unconscious Russian fell on top of the agent, who quickly squirmed out of the pile and reached for his cell phone.

"Shuck the underwear, Marko. Going for realism here."

"I cannot believe I am doing this. Christ, Jürgs, you fuckin' owe me big time for this."

The jockstrap slipped to his heels.

"No money shot, Bud. Keep my face out of the pics, for fuck sake."

***

Mark's body, legs in a wide stance and only the torso to the chest holding up the naked Russian, mouth open and pressed to the American's thigh. Other shots featured Jürgen, face turned aside, wrapped arms and legs around the larger man, in the missionary position.

Ivan came back to consciousness tied in a sitting position against the headboard, leg ropes stretched to the footboard. Jürgen hurried things along by splashing water into the man's face.

Mark scrolled the phone's photo gallery captured on the agent's phone before the furious Ivan. The Russian eagle on his back was prominent in most of the shots. His eyes blazed at the sight of the pictures as he pulled ferociously at the restraints. It was clear that the bed frame could not compete for very long with the man's strength.

He roared, "*Vy, blyad', ublyudki. Ya sobirayus' ubit' vas oboikh, trakhnuv vas do smerti.*"

Jürgen actually laughed as he held a cigarette to Ivan's lips.

"I will translate, Marko. Hot stuff here is threatening to murder us both with his matchless sex. I find that very amusing."

Mark said, "Yeah, so, Sparky, my man, here's the thing. These pictures, if we send them, could very well get your Slavic balls cut off. You getting my meaning? Your comrade-chiks at AL-ASU-- them being such a buncha ultra-right assholes and all. Tolerance of Greek-style loving is not one of their favs, am I right, Sparky, you closeted fuck?"

Ivan nearly ripped the headboard off the frame. Mark clocked him after a few bitch slaps.

Jürgen said, "Easy, mate."

"Fuck that, Jürgs. This bitch was gonna deflower my husband!"

They both laughed.

Jürgen addressed their captive. "Provide us with information, and the salacious evidence of our night of passion all goes away, Boris." He gave Ivan the smoke again and the last of the Baltique.

Ivan hung his head.

"What is it you want to know?"

"Aliyev. The Last Empire. All of it."

Their prisoner thought for a bit. He raised his head. His stare was deadly as he began to speak. "You are correct. I will be eliminated if this should ever come to light. My Russian contacts will finish anything Aliyev leaves alive." He gestured with his chin to the incriminating device in Mark's hand.

"*Trakhni eto*, I need some assurances. Protection, you understand?"

Jügen flipped open his wallet and showed Ivan his badge.

"As soon as we leave, you will be rescued by my people and flown out of Alexandria to a place of safety. You have my promise."

Ivan responded solemnly, "So that is how you marked me. You are INTERPOL and a snooping bastard. What? Now, your agency has resorted to doing the blackmail because the Egyptian authorities know better than to interfere with Aliyev? They will never cooperate with you idiots, and nothing you have has the power to convict him. *Blyad'*!"

Jürgen responded, "Let's go, big man. The more valuable your information, the farther away and safer we will get you from the Rising Dawn."

"Aliyev, *da*. He is creating the new Caliphate on the bones of the Taliban and ISIL. He has troops in Central Asia, weapons from the Americans, the Chinese, and the Russians, and plenty of money to fund agents in world governments and international agencies. His organization traffics in stolen goods, blackmail, drugs, and sex workers. Aliyev is a big-time crime boss.

"On the legitimate side, his lifeblood is oil, and he has a massive supply, second only to the Saudis. He has a plan to eliminate them as competitors. Their oil fields are very vulnerable.

"The one-eyed devil will starve the world of power sitting on his cache of black gold. Industries will collapse, markets will fall, worldwide depression will follow, and governments will fall-- he has these strategies in place. He will end up ruling all, enslaving the world, the master of chaos. His only weakness is his son, Alexei, but that boy has a surprise for Papa. I know this from experience.

"Be careful and trust no one, cop boy. His reach is invisible and powerful. Especially when it comes to his own power fetishes."

Mark said, "What's up with the Alexander the Great thing?"

"You are no idiot, muscle jock, though I doubt you are even gay. What is the expression? So, 'gay for the cash.' Pity, when we have survived this, I bring you down, and then Ivan has a few things to teach you."

Mark to a bold stance, messaging one hand into the other. *This is one arrogant fuck. Perhaps a few more bitch slaps?*

Ivan continued, "Aliyev believes the blood legacy of the Macedonian King, the Prophet, and the Christ flow through his veins. He thinks he is the long-awaited Messiah and will bring about the Last Judgement when all his enemies are crushed under his heel. His murders and assassinations are carried out without question. They always tint it all with a touch of fear, terror, and violence.

"His treatment of women and girls is beyond the bounds of decency. He has sent proselytizing squads into towns and villages from the Caspian to Sudan, teaching a return to the old ways by force of his might. Thus he is rabidly concerned with the elimination of your Ms. Quinto and her friends. You are all a threat to his divinely ordained crusade."

"More on his women…"

"Which ones? He uses many. They find Aliyev irresistible. That Karimov bitch is his sex toy, but Aliyev put her in charge of major projects to get him anything he wants. She is as evil as he is. Beware. The other one… the Portuguese… she is carrying out his programs to revive the old ways in many countries. She is tied into ultra-conservative terrorist groups. That one is very devious. Like a snake."

Nilza.

Lermontov shook his head and added, "A gay boy and a straight man. I pity you both. You cannot stop them. He is relentless. Only God himself can put an end to his maniacal designs on humanity. You will need an army of angels to stop Aliyev and his demons."

Jügen said, "This has been the waste of a night in some respects, my friend. You have given us very little new information and have simply confirmed what we already knew or suspected. My costly little gamble has no return on its value, as they say."

Jürgen looked at Mark.

"I say we turn this mess loose. Our sex buddy can take his chances with his former comrades."

The Russian fought back the panic now, fear and terror etched into his face, throat clutching at his words.

"No. Wait. Listen to me. I am lost for good now. This. All of this tonight. He watches, my monkeys. He knows. Right now, as we sit in this room playing the international intrigue, Aliyev's butchers are on their way here to correct this situation. I am a dead man."

The restrained man was sweating heavily. "I am extremely valuable to you, and I beg you to take charge of me. I have seen many terrible things. Worse than my service to Russia. Under the gaze of Aliyev, whole communities were slaughtered. I will tell any tribunal you wish. For years, I have been preparing for my exit from AL-ASU and associated enterprises."

Mark said, "You crafty fucker, you have files, don't you?"

"Yes, logs, emails, project documentation, financial records, witness reports on assassinations, lists of his agents in more than twenty-six nations. I have photos. My personal testimony at the International Criminal Court will put them away and destroy his Last Kingdom. I can guarantee that. Ivan will even help to capture that *podonok*."

The journalist asked, "Why would you do that? What turned you?"

"Is it not obvious? In his glorious new order, there is no room for 'sexual deviants,' as he calls us. He has plans for putting his most trusted general, Miriam Karimov, at the head of a program of extermination that will make the Russian efforts to kill the gays and those who advocate for human rights look like... um... *detskiy sad*."

"Nursey school."

Ivan nodded and said, "What is ironic about all of that is that Aliyev has a huge surprise coming, as I indicated, and I do not speak of my defection, only."

The prisoner attempted to hurry the action, saying, "Bring me my phone. I will prove myself and show you how to gain access to my documents. He trusted me, much to his detriment, and it was actually relatively easy. I am Aliyev's fatal flaw. I am the knife blade at his throat."

Mark finished dressing as Jügen Mathias put his head closer to Ivan's and walked through a cell phone procedure, securing the files and finalizing the transfer of the Russian's data to his INTERPOL agents. He did not hear the details of their conversation but could tell that the transactions had been successful.

Mark parted the torn curtains to scope out the street below. At the Al Saqr Bar entrance, he could see the bouncer talking to three men.

"Jürgs, we gotta roll, buddy. Your guys on their way?"

"They are coming up from the first floor as we speak, Marko. We are done here."

Jürgen leaned in over the captive and soothed his face and head. He bent to kiss the man, long and intense. The traitor ate at the lips and mouth of his captor like a starving man.

Stepping back, Jürgen said, "Not really the best I've ever had, but nonetheless, very hot. My agents will get you to safety, and we will meet again."

He moved to exit the room with Mark.

"Damn, bud. You will spend the rest of your life paying me back for this one.

"Done, Marko. Let's go, husband."

Chapter Forty: The Sexin' Thing

Hotel Steigenberger Cecil Alexandria, Alexandria, Egypt

"How the hell did you get past the bouncer?"

"Not the first time I impersonated a man, Darling. How was the vodka, and why do you smell like sweat and smoke?"

Jürgen said, "Top rate, actually." He shifted a bit uncomfortably and added, "Since you were there, should have invited you for the... no, no, no. Please forgive me, the events of this evening, they have left me...."

He looked at his hands, "Strictly man's work." He picked up his phone and took a call.

As the agent stepped out on the balcony, Rebecca turned to Mark.

"You're some kisser, Gadarn, but then again, I know that. Anything further you want to tell me?"

"It did not go farther than that, Rebecca. You have my word."

"Get your priorities straight, Mark, and I mean straight. This anything-for-a-story bullshit is wearing a little thin."

Mark's characteristic coolness seemed to have vanished. He could not meet her eyes.

He said softly, "I have a bad feeling about this evening. Where are the archaeology boys?"

"Skylar and Leonnatus got back from an al-Mahdi family thing around ten. From the look on their faces, I suspect it did not go well. They have been holed up next door for the rest of the evening sorting through data from their tunnel scan, I suppose."

They sat in silence for a bit. Mark poured another vodka-rocks, and Rebecca finished her Syrah. Finally, he stood and began to pull off his shirt and stepped out of his running shoes.

"I should shower. I smell like a wet beast."

He stumbled.

"Looks like that leg is hurting again."

Without turning to her, he said, "Yeah, a bit."

Jürgen re-entered their suite, still speaking German but ending the call. He was very concerned.

"I am amazed at recent developments in our little caper tonight. My agents in charge of rescuing our Russian friend cannot be reached. Ivan Lermontov is also missing. I need to go, my friends."

He turned to Mark, saying, "Marko, is there a possibility I may borrow a shirt from you? I do not want to show up looking like...."

He stripped off the sleeveless bar shirt.

Mark pulled a replacement from the closet.

"Rebecca, I somehow think I owe you an explanation and, more likely, an apology for what went on this evening. I am conflicted about the position I put...."

He did not finish. There was a thump in the hallway outside. Mark got there first, checked the spyhole, threw the lock, and pulled open the door.

A rolled-up oriental carpet lay cross-wise just outside the door. Jürgen pulled back a section of the massive package. He cursed.

"I believe I have found one of my missing agents."

***

"Man, this is tragic, but such a fuckin' cliché. Rolled up in a carpet."

Mark continued, "Seems there is no end to old Hollywood memes of Egyptian mysteries, poison, venom, mummies, and bodies trussed up in the oriental. What's next, a visit from Dwayne Johnson in his Scorpion King get-up?"

Rebecca, propped up on pillows, had no response. She fiddled with the sheet hem. Jürgen and his confederates had left with the corpse. The removal was swift to avoid police involvement.

Mark, in a towel, hair still wet and seated in a club chair facing the bed, remarked, "Fuckin' Jürgen, man, recent string of screw-ups." He tossed back and refilled his glass.

Rebecca said, "Yes, perhaps we need to be a bit more cautious regarding his involvement. It seems to be going from bad to worse. Do you think he is trustworthy?"

"Shit yeah. I've known Jürgs since I was eighteen. He's righteous. Of that, I am sure."

Rebecca moved off the bed and paced a bit, stopping to look at the night view through the open floor-to-ceiling balcony doors. The moon presided over the dark waters of the harbor like an ancient sentry and keeper of old secrets.

"He's been carrying a man crush for you that long?"

Mark grunted softly but said nothing for a bit, then, "Good 'ole Jürgs-boy. He goes from automaton to sex bomb in record time. One minute, he is the iceman... no emotions. Cold as they come. Next, he is obsessed with some guy he thinks is smoking hot."

"Mark, what's up? What happened once you left Al Saqr?"

"I told you, no big deal. We took the Russian dude down. That's all. What is this anyway?"

"Something. Yes. Something happened that makes you drink hard liquor instead of your usual beer. And you never drink this late."

Mark stood up and moved toward her for the confrontation.

"What do you want to hear, Rebecca? That I sexed up the Russian fucko? Is that it? That at the ripe old age of thirty, I am having a sexual identity crisis, and your man is bi?

"Sweetheart, I told you it was all a kiss-up that ended at the bar. Jürgs and he... well, that's where it got a bit pornographic."

Rebecca moved into his space. His body was tense, and his face florid. She reached forward and took the glass from his hand.

"Sit down, please."

Mark remained standing, heaved a sigh, and said.

"Rebecca, my beautiful Rebecca, I like the attention of men, but I am wired to be sexually attracted to women. It's simple, your bad boy enjoys teasing and pushing limits. Adolescent? Hell yeah. But it's part of my charm. Besides, it gets me to the hidden side that most people protect with a vengeance. Makes for good truthing. I am a journalist."

He took a step closer to her and fiddled with the straps of her chemise. He pulled her close and let his lips brush lightly over the top of her left breast, getting the arousal response he wanted. Mark looked into her eyes and continued.

"Without any cheap brag, I admit I'm packing a considerably hot bod, and I love the adulation from whatever corner it comes from. Guess it's something I never got as a scrawny kid growing up until I discovered sports, the gym, and a bit of the old self-defense.

"So, I learned to use my looks and my in-your-face-personality to my advantage, getting the bad guys and pounding out a sensational story. Sex and money, Beautiful, the dynamics that create a lot of rip-roaring adventure in this fucked-up world. But, woman, this man is hot for you, my one and only. That is what I choose. That is what I want."

He repeated the kiss-up moves with a teasing mouth combination, his lips tasting of vodka and sweat, a bit of the kiss/lick/pullback/repeat. Rebecca began to fall under his spell.

Mark whispered, "Yeah, sometimes, I go too far. You're right. I'm bullshit to get the story. I admit that. I am too ballsey for my own fuckin' good. But Rebecca, this is who I am. This is what it takes to be me, my love. And to be honest, I am quite the self-satisfied bastard."

He spread his hands wide, away from their embrace.

"So, I kiss somebody, men, women, and act like an oversexed asshole every so often. Right now, I am with you, freely and unconflicted. And jazzed to the very root of my libido that you want to be with me. Trust, Beautiful. It's all about trust. Does that make sense?"

She nodded to the vodka bottle.

238

"So out of character, Mark. Jürgen said you went a bit overboard wailing on the Russian. You're not an angry drunk, but this is something different. What's going on with the rage thing?"

He backed away. After a moment, Mark lowered his head and walked to the open balcony doors. He stretched his arms up and across the opening, a crucified and broken hero. He spoke to the darkness.

"I don't know if I can tell you why except to admit to you and myself that I was scared. It's gonna pass, but for a little while, tonight, I was fuckin' terrified. We have faced a shit load together, Beautiful, and managed to save our asses and win the day. But this asshole I found myself up against … It's just… sometimes… sometimes…."

Rebecca stepped up behind him and embraced him around his chest, burying her face in the muscles of his back. She said nothing, feeling his hot skin, his heartbeat, and the rhythm of his breathing. Outside, the sounds of a barely awake city filled the night.

Mark took a deep breath and whispered. "Sometimes, I downshift back to that skinny ninety-five-pound geek boy, trying to face down the haters and shitheads, knowing, I'm totally alone and gonna get my ass kicked-- again. And then there's all that baggage with my monster of a step-father."

He lowered his arms and turned to face her.

"I guess it pisses me off that I can't be strong and confident all the time and keep us and a few of the unfortunates in this world safe and sound. I take risks for the story 'cause somebody has to care on behalf of the victims of these tyrants and greedy fucks. The times are so fuckin' extreme, Beautiful. Somebody has to go all in and say, 'Hey fucko world, enough is enough. Fuckin' get your humanity on.

"But, as I said, sometimes, just sometimes it all comes on like a shit storm. No one should have died tonight. That carpet guy…. "

She broke the hold. Walking away, Rebecca said, "Nope, not gonna fly, Lancelot. Before you drown us both in self-pity, I have a few things to say, my broken soldier."

Mark looked more than slightly incredulous. He held up a hand to stop the continuance.

239

"Whoa, whoa, whoa. So, this is where you say, 'Oh, Mark, there is no need to feel that way. You can get us through this. Don't be afraid. You are strong and brave….' Huh? Let's go with the sympathetic tenderness."

He indicated with a hand-waving motion that she should get on the Mark Gadarn Emotional Support Train.

"Darling, while I will not denigrate your feelings, we gotta work on this lone superhero thing you are rockin' from time to time. Allow me to just tell you that this is a duo here. If you love me, then we are in this together. Let it go, Darling. So, we do yet another face-off, and it's hard to see the light. But we got this, right, Mark? Look at me. Right?"

Mark searched her face as she continued. She stepped closer and touched his face.

"You are correct. The bad guys we face are very powerful. That's why we go in with our posse, our friends and colleagues, each of us with incredible gifts. No one is alone, Darling, no one."

Rebecca narrowed her eyes at the gorgeous, towel-clad man, moonlight on his body and red-gold hair. The rugged handsomeness of his face caught in an expression of deep concentration, listening carefully to what she had to say.

She turned away for a moment and heaved a somewhat theatrical sign. Rebecca reached for and tossed back the last of the wine. She turned back to him.

"Yeah, most likely, the other two are dead. From what you and Jürgen say, Lermontov was dancing on a razor's edge and committed to his boss' monstrous enterprises a long time ago. Choices have consequences. I am also sorry for the murdered INTERPOL agent. Their work brings them close to danger consistently.

"And get this through your thick, Welsh boy head. You, of anyone, are not flying solo here or anytime in the future. I'm in for the long run, Darling, you and me. Let's do what we can for the poor things, Mark, keep the lights on and rock da house."

He pulled her back into a warm embrace, feeling the confidence of her words and the assurance of her body. She ran one hand over his hair as the other guided his hand over her backside and thighs. They rocked slowly in the moonlight, bodies and hearts familiar with such intimate contact.

"Think about that for a while, Mark. It's true, as true as we can make it."

"You complete me, Beautiful. I am one lucky bastard."

For a long time, they swayed in each other's arms to music only they could hear. Somewhere in the heat of their dance, words were replaced by the sounds of slowly building passion. Mark's towel and Rebecca's chamise ended up on the floor as they tumbled onto the bed.

Later, they slept in each other's arms as a dark cloud rose up and hovered over the night city of sleepers. The shade seemed to seek points of entry like creeping talons of evil, like a Biblical plague on the land.

Thomas Paul Severino

Chapter Forty-One: A Pillar of Smoke

The Necropolis of Asar, Alexandria, Egypt

There was another dig below AL-ASU headquarters. Unknown to all but a few of the elite in the corporation. It had been uncovered using a private contractor who now no longer existed.

Deep in the recesses of the underground, the remains of a temple among the buried ruins of the Necropolis of Asar, a series of 2nd Century BCE tombs, served as a place of meditation and religious rites for Farid Haydar Aliyev and a few of his closest confidants, individuals with a serious death fetish.

The one-eyed man sat cross-legged on an expensive carpet before a white marble plinth topped with a black granite head of the god Set, the god of chaos, war, and destruction. Before him was an open fire pit whose smoke traveled up to the chamber's ceiling, where it met the openings of a 21st-century ventilation system, the only modification made to the site. The thick, black vapors escaped to invade the city.

The barefoot man from Central Asia wore a midnight blue tracksuit. The zipper was lowered to his navel. A chain held the hamsa against his bare chest. The opened, right-hand amulet, also known as the Hand of Fatima, named for the daughter of the prophet Muhammad was considered an amulet of protection. Aliyev's version was crafted of precious metals and stones and contained the eye of the god Horus in the palm of the image. Ancient Egyptians knew this symbol as the "Two Fingers," invoking the protection of the gods.

On the carpet, just to his right side, a helmet-like artifact gleamed in gold, its intensity changing in the blazing firelight. Aliyev was alert and focused as he allowed the unfolding ritual to envelop him.

Miriam Karimov chanted a mournful dirge in a sheer white caftan. She stood five clay figures at the edge of the fire, opposite the single devotee. She rolled up and tossed a map of the Mideast into the pit and shook a handful of something that made the flames roar up, spears of fire rising in the dark chamber. They flickered in the single eye of the kneeling fanatic. Prolonged, hoarse screams and the biting sound of a stout cane against flesh came from off to the right.

The woman stopped her incantations and walked in the direction of the man being beaten. She held up a hand to the torturer, and the caning ceased. She carefully ran a falcon's feather over the bleeding, sweating, naked torso of the Russian man hanging from the ceiling. Drool mixed with tears left his mouth, and his whole body seemed to heave as the prisoner attempted to catch his breath and survive the sentence of 100 strokes.

Miriam returned to the fire pit and touched each of the five miniatures with the bloody feather. Her ululations began again. More additives made the fire dance and reach up like a lover intent on caressing the participants with a searing kiss. Behind her, Ivan Lermontov moaned as the beating started again, the lash cutting deep into his sweating muscled form.

He begged for death in two languages.

Aliyev watched as his priestess carefully lowered each of the figures into the blaze. As each was incinerated, a column of dense smoke rose to the ceiling to be wafted out into the night. Miriam stood, lifted the gauzy abaya over her head, and walked around the fire pit. The one-eyed man also stood and removed his clothes and the amulet. She took them, folded the suit, and placed them just beyond the carpet. Returning, she positioned the golden ram's head on the man while removing his eye patch and dropping it onto the mat.

She pulled her hair out of its pinning so that it dropped down her back to her waist. When she knelt and made a full abeyance, stretched out before the powerful man, her tresses fanned out like a black corona around her beautiful head and shoulders. She drew back and lay on her back. As she reached for him, Miriam called upon the gods of fertility and pandemonium to oversee their coupling, spreading her thighs and raising her hips to the man-god of her idolatry.

Firelight danced across their bodies as Farid Haydar Aliyev, fully aroused, a mythic satyr in his nakedness and ancient headgear, descended onto her and into her. The paintings on the catacomb walls containing images from the pantheon of pharaonic gods seemed to move in the firelight and smoke, overseeing the carnal rites before them.

Beyond, through eyes reduced to slits, Lermontov watched their erotic dance as the smolder billowed and rose, wafting into the night like a living thing in search of prey. The Russian's screams and the gasps of the man and woman underscored the savage copulation as the fire sparked and raged in the chamber. Coated in blood, Ivan begged for death, but before he blacked out, he cursed the offspring of his murderer.

"*Pust' vash syn Alexei poneset takoye zhe nakazaniye.* May your son Alexsei suffer the same punishment that you have given me."

***

She was flying above the earth. The topography was familiar. The lights of major cities glistened like jeweled chains on the night landscape. The moon glowed full, mounting up from the west.

The seas flashed ebony, the Caspian, the Mediterranean, the Black Sea. Mighty rivers were like leaking arteries of black blood. Night spread out across the continent. Dawn was sneaking in over the Pacific as the ancient lands of the Far East cast off the terrors of the night.

Further west, it appeared as if Asia was bleeding black blood. Like spilling gore, a malignant swarm surged forward from the center of the continent, moving south and spreading out, creating a series of fire blasts and explosions before it, subduing all in its path. Whole armies fell as the invaders from the Russian steppes moved down and across Syria and Lebanon, Iran and Iraq, Afghanistan, and Pakistan. The horrible insect mass throbbing, extending, and oozing the acidic pus of obliteration like an infection surging death without stopping.

To the east, the Plain of Armageddon blazed with a war for the soul of humanity. Troops from many nations faced off against the barbaric swarm from the Asian interior. The conflagration reached from earth to heaven, raising and spreading thunderous warfare and destruction.

To the south, a richly adorned camel and rider in traditional Beduin garb looked to the north. Arabia, in full battle dress, watched vigilantly. Behind this mythic national figure was an array of heavily fortified modern forces ready for combat. Before them, the armies of death prevailed, sweeping over the northern reaches of the desert kingdom, spewing black smoke and fire. One arm of the horde turned towards Sinai and the Nile as the young woman descended to view the roaring apocalyptic clash of armies.

She was aware that as she defended against the destruction of Egypt, she took on the appearance of a Ptolemaic warrior princess surrounded by her armies.

Then, she saw him.

A prince in blood-red robes rising up from the earth lifted a curved, jeweled sword against the Sacred Land of the Pharaohs, threatened in the name of the ancient gods of many religions. Beside him rode an attending knight, this one a smaller, younger version of the bloodthirsty horseman.

Astride a fire-breathing black stallion, the one-eyed death specter, gore dripping from his cruel mouth, suddenly directed his attention to her. He charged in her direction. She felt the scorching breath of the steed and saw the descending glint of the saber.

Chione sat up in bed, frightened by the dream.

***

Her hands were tied above her head with a sturdy, silken rope. A man with a strong resemblance to Mark straddled her and raked his right hand from her throat to her thighs.

"You are my slave queen and will obey me without question."

His hair was styled in a Roman straight-bang cut. Khol outlined his fierce eyes in black. He cursed in languages she did not understand as he tormented her. She twisted away from him, but the restraints held her fast.

Around them, snakes hissed, and scorpions scuttled. A figure cloaked in darkness, just beyond her assailant, urged on the violation with whispered commands.

"She is dispensable, but an endless, violent death will only serve us now. The gods demand this. See to it and obey."

The face of her brutal attacker began to change in the firelight. Mark's handsome features morphed into a monstrous and cruel version of his beautiful visage. He transformed, one eye blind, a primal jaw and forehead, neck, quadriceps, shoulders, and arms bulging and striated with rage and power, a maniacal Mr. Hyde.

The horror's lips slathered spit and sweat. With each blaze of the fire, this changeling swapped her lover's image with that of the insane monster. His torso seemed to grow in mass as he mixed sexual arousal with fiery torture. The hands of his master reached out of the darkness. They caressed the naked neck and shoulders back of his creation, a puppeteer urging on her annihilation.

The beast spoke with a voice from Hell.

"I will rape your realm for my master's new Empire, and you will thank me for it. There will be no refuge for you but that of the kingdom of the damned. When I am done, I will leave you for the pleasure of my troops."

He lowered his dripping face to hers, ready to take his pleasure. She resisted, twisting her head and body from side to side beneath him, lifting her hips and legs in an attempt to throw him off.

He was too powerful.

She screamed as his savage mouth reached for hers.

Rebecca woke, heaving her body against Mark, kicking him to the floor on his butt.

"Damn, Rebecca, what the fuck? Owww."

***

He choked on his violent screaming and woke up in a flop sweat. Skylar grabbed the panicked young man and pulled him close, then closer, trying to absorb the night terror. Leonnatus fought the muscular man's body, who held him down until the boy became conscious of where he was and who was restraining him.

It seemed that a choking smoke was leaving the room through the open balcony doors.

Thomas Paul Severino

"Easy, Leo. It was only a dream. You are safe with me. No harm can come to you."

"Skylar. Oh shit, I am sorry. Oh, man, hold me, please. It was so real. Skylar, I was so afraid."

Leonnatus kissed his bedmate and ran his hands over the Egyptian's body as if to find assurance that he was really in the arms of the man he loved.

"I will protect you always, my friend. Easy, lad. It's all right."

Leonnatus pulled back from the embrace just to look Skyler in the eye.

"Did you just call me 'Leo,' Sir?"

"Yes, it seems to be a time of getting names settled. Please allow me to tell you a story from the Old Kingdom. It will make the shadows and the choking smoke of nightmares dissipate."

He pulled the boy against his chest. Leo found the closeness and even the scent of the man intoxicating. The soft baritone began to whisper a tale of mystery and wonder.

"The ancients believed we are given a name at birth, which is called Ren, your true name. You must keep it a secret because if someone destroys its power by aggression or magic, you will never live for all eternity. In life, therefore, we are known by nicknames or alternate names. Leonnatus becomes Leo. Do you see?"

"And Al Sama' becomes Skylar."

The boy thought for a moment and continued.

"Very cool, I like it. You know that taking a different name has, for centuries, been an indication of ontological change. Novices take religious names, kings, and queens... drag queens... Baptismal and Confirmation names. It is an indication of becoming a new person – saved, or in charge, or just plain fabulous."

The big man pulled the boy under him, smiled, and said as he smooched, "Your intelligence is showing again, my Leo. Not content to just be emotional and romantic in my bed?

"We will get to another matter at some other time. By that, I mean deconstructing the business with my family. But, right now, I would opt to put history, theology, and philosophy aside for about thirty minutes while we.... "

He reached under and adjusted the body beneath him, fitting together the curves and planes of their bodies. Leonnatus said eagerly, "Yeah, I am up for that, literally, but please hold me a bit more."

In the clinch that followed, he continued, "You are my Skylar, big man. That's all I need to know. Tighter, please. Mmm."

The man kissed the boy and pulled his face against his cheek.

"Later, you will tell me what you dreamed."

***

He tried to explain.

"It was sex. I was scamming you. Nothing more. I mean, what the fuck? Are you serious with that gun?

"We have a saying in Russian, 'Grekhi dolzhny byt' oplacheny.' The Germans have it better? 'Der Pfeifer muss bezahlt werden.' It speaks of consequences."

The dark man wobbled the Glock up and down but kept it pointed at the chest of the agent.

"The piper must be paid. Yes, I get it."

"Yes, suka. You and your bitch boyfriend. Tell me, did you turn your friend Mark Gadarn to your slutty gay ways, or was he just a sham pretending to be straight. Pity if the latter were so."

Somewhere close, a fire burned bright, illuminating the confrontation and coating them in sweat. Jürgen lowered his hands and said, "We have another saying in German, Ivan, 'Du bist verdammt.' It is a term of endearment best translated as 'you fuckwad.' You getting this?"

A hand reached over Jürgen's shoulder and took the gun from the Russian. The agent contemplated the invading limb, expensive suit sleeve, immaculate French cuffs, gold cufflinks in ancient coin design, and a superbly manicured hand with a large golden lion-headed ring on the third finger. His other arm wound around Jürgen's neck and prevented him from turning. The intruder leveled the firearm from just above the agent's shoulder.

Farid Haydar Aliyev said, "You always were a talker, Ivan, and you have always bored me with your drivel. I have no need for this."

A shot roared in the agent's ear, and Ivan dropped.

The assassin turned the German to face him but kept him close. Unable to move, the agent stared at the black satin eyepatch and the razor-sharp cheekbones. He felt Aliyev press the barrel of the gun to a gap between his left ribs. With his other hand, he grabbed Jürgen's lower jaw and pulled his captive close for a Judas kiss.

Jürgen Mathais awoke with a start and wet lips. He rubbed his eyes in the clearing gloom, thinking the building was on fire.

He went to the door of his suite. The specter leaning against the wall in the dark hallway startled the semi-naked agent. Mathais turned to retrieve his firearm.

The form staggered in the smoky gloom. The voice rasped, "You promised you would protect me."

Chapter Forty-Two: A Morning Rush
Hotel Steigenberger Cecil Alexandria, Alexandria, Egypt

"Put on your *Unterwäsche* or whatever you German boys wear when you are not doing that shoe-slapping dance in the beer gardens. Has your trick left?"

Jürgen pulled the blankets onto his lap, grabbed a hotel robe, and sat back on the bed as Rebecca and Mark sailed through the suites' connecting door. She was in a hotel-issue bathrobe. Mark, carrying his open laptop, held quite consciously at the front of his boxer shorts.

"Jürgs, Jürgs, it's on, bud. Have you seen this?" The excited journalist raised his laptop.

The not-so-little German boy eyed the invading Americans, held his head, and said, "Coffee. Just give me coffee, and no one gets hurt."

Rebecca handed him her cup.

"Ok, let's do this one at a time. I had very little sleep, you two. INTERPOL was up my ass. And not for reasons I would have preferred. Besides, something unexpected came up in the night for which I needed my colleagues to take care of an unfinished commitment."

He gulped the brew. The devilish German eased into a tease.

"Rebecca, thanks for letting me use your man last night. He was perfect for the job."

Rebecca smirked, "We're gonna get to that, Miss Thang, and I'm talking about just how perfect was he?" She smiled, hands on hips.

Mark sat at the table and scrolled his computer. He was absorbed in the seriousness of the international reports.

"This is astounding, you two. Invaders from hell in the night. Five war zones sprang up overnight from Turkey to India. It's the forces of the Rising Dawn, definitely. Small but surgical incursions in areas rife with unrest."

Leonnatus and Skylar completed the bathrobed assembly trailing in from the adjoining suites. Skylar looked around and punched at his phone as Leonnatus bid the group good morning in a very cheery voice coated with early-morning satisfaction.

"Darling, you are simply radiant this morning. Hmmm, an innocent girl like me wonders what the two of you have been up to."

They did air kisses.

Jürgen, still sitting on the bed, reached up and tugged Skylar's robe belt. He said with a bit of morning self-pity in his voice, "Why do the two of you never think to invite me in. I am one very perplexed and severely frustrated but very accomplished homosexual. Groups are my specialty."

While ordering breakfast for five, Skyler placed his hand over the mobile and said, "My friend, I am new to this gay situation. If and when we get to the stage where we invite others in, you will be at the top of the list, I suspect. As the Americans say, 'just play your cards right and 'do not hold your breathing,' I think is the other saying."

He eye-rolled at Leonnatus and continued with his order.

Rebecca said, "Wow. Very good, Skylar. Who are you, anyway?"

She smiled at Leonnatus, who did a cool "thumbs up" gesture.

"Promises promises. I hate monogamy. In Europe, we are more liberated, I will be thinking."

Turning to the now fully awakened agent, Rebecca injected, "No. don't even look this way with your bad eyes, Missy." She stepped over to Mark and rubbed his shoulders.

"Mine. Mine. Capice, Tin-Tin? You should have brought along Antonio. You both hit it off so well in New York."

"As good fortune would have it, Antonio WhatsApp-ed me from Fort Lauderdale. He did the check-in and was lusty in his talk. Perhaps I am seeing him again, *Ja*?"

Leonnatus said, "You have good taste, Jürgen. He seems to be a very nice man from what you describe and nicely proportioned." He explained, "He showed me the pictures."

The young scholar took a seat at the table next to Mark, who looked up and almost growled.

"Christ. While the four of you are playing "My Boyfriend is Hotter Than Your Boyfriend," like a set of goofball teenagers, you do realize the world is exploding, top to bottom and inside out, right?"

Skylar pointed the remote, turning on the TV. Rebecca took a seat next to Mark and peered at the screen. Jürgen jumped up and reached for his phone, scrolling through multiple messages.

"*Stront*, another meeting in fifteen minutes at INTERPOL Headquarters." He dashed into the bathroom, doffing the robe as he fled.

CNN was showing tapes of firefights near Mosul, Tabriz, and southeastern Turkey. The commentator was saying, "Al Jazeera, Teheran is reporting that extreme fighting has broken out along the Afghanistan-Pakistan border between Jalalabad, east of Kabul, and Peshawar, west of Islamabad. The ruling bodies in each of these capitals have called for emergency measures."

Mark pointed at his laptop.

"Eris broke it down for me. The insignia of the insurgents is new on the political scene. It is the emblem of the Rising Dawn, an ultra-right Islamic movement, bla, bla, bla… She has files on the militia leaders in each sector and probabilities of success for their campaigns. Holy shit! She is predicting the war hawks will go to nukes if they've got 'em.

"The Saudis are scrambling to gather a coalition, and the Rising Dawn has put a fatwa on the King and his family. Their propaganda shit is all over the internet universe."

The broadcast spoke over Mark's report, " … with ties to this man."

A picture of Farid Haydar Aliyev appeared on the screen

Skylar broke in, "I have my sister on the phone, something about a dream." He spoke to her, lowering the volume of the broadcast.

"What is Papa saying? Yes, yes, I thought as much. Are you OK, Chione? Fine, Leo and I are fine. That conversation was a long time coming. Let me know as things develop. I am afraid I am a bit distracted, right...."

Jügen rushed out of the bathroom, buttoning his shirt and stepping into his loafers. He looked at the TV and cursed in German. "I will meet up with you folks later. Marko, text me, *Ja*?"

Skylar reached into the closet and pulled out a garment. He nabbed the bustling German by the shirt collar and held the clothing out to the over-excited agent.

"Pants, my friend."

He helped Jügen out of his shoes, into his pants, back into his shoes, and almost out the door while straightening his tie. But the agent stopped in the doorway to grab a bagel off the arriving breakfast cart.

Rebecca was rising and saying, "Skylar, did I just hear you mention Chione had a bad dream last night?"

The Egyptian nodded.

Mark looked up and gazed intently at his friends as Leonnatus, Rebecca, and the hurrying Jürgen all said the same thing at precisely the same time.

"I had a nightmare."

Chapter Forty-Three: The Old Gods
Citadel of Qaitbay, Alexandria, Egypt

The late summer morning was exquisite. Leonnatus loved the salty smell of the sea. The sun presided over an endless view of sparkling seawater, crystal clear air, and an array of ships entering and leaving the harbor. Here and there, a felucca with its sharp-angled lateen sails glided along the Nile canal and into the sea harbor.

Sea birds performed balletic moves above the narrow arm of land that reached out into the Mediterranean from the city of steel, glass, and stone. Behind the strollers, the Citadel of Qaitbay occupied the former site of the Lighthouse of Alexandria, one of the Seven Wonders of the Ancient World.

Nearby, a müezzin, high in a minaret, called the faithful to noon prayers, singing out the *Adhan*. *"Allahu Akbar... ashhadu ala ilaha illallah...* There is no god but Allah...."

Skylar turned his head slightly to direct his remarks to the young man with whom he was sitting back-to-back beneath one of the date palms in the park leading up to the Citadel.

"The Egyptians of the Old Kingdom believe that the father of Osiris, Geb, the god of the earth, is a powerful deity. When he laughs, the result is earthquakes. Such divine laughter has pulled down Ptolemy's lighthouse, which once stood here, the tallest building in the ancient world."

Leonnatus said, "Yes, cast into the sea. My former colleagues are among the scientists doing underwater excavation on the site just off the tip of this spit of land. Those cranes and barges, there." He pointed to steel structures rising from the sea, just off the point.

"Speaking of, Master Gianopolis, we need to brief our friends on our conclusions regarding our very clandestine research. Have you received the LiDAR data?"

"Yes, Skylar, your Leo is on the case, as the Americans say. I asked for some time with Rebecca and Mark later today."

The Egyptian stood and extended a hand to his buddy. As he pulled him up, Leonnatus bounced against the substantial body of his friend and intimate.

"Always a rush to feel you against me, my friend."

"We must be cautious, Leo. As progressive as this city is, remember, please, Egypt is an Islamic country."

"… ash hadu anna Muhammadar rasoolullah… And Mohammad is His Prophet." The plaintive prayer died on the soft breeze.

"I will fend off the haters. You must teach me to fight."

Skylar looked at the lad as an expression of sorrow came over his face. He turned and began their stroll through the park. They walked in comfortable silence, the kind of restfulness when no one feels obliged to speak, merely content to remain in the presence of the other.

They rounded the Citadel and rested against the Cyclopean walls of the quay on the northeast side. The sea was restful beneath the azure blue sky, rocking with a rhythm, much like the intake and exhale of breathing, occasionally spraying through the massive limestone blocks.

Leonnatus looked at his love and, breaking the silence, said, "Skylar, are we ever going to talk about it?"

Looking away, the scholar said, "About what?"

The lad reached for and turned the face of the man to his.

"The Louran. Your family. Muhammad Nefer."

Skylar looked down and moved one foot in the gravel, creating a small ridge.

"I do not process emotion easily, lust and anger being the exceptions. I like to think of myself as a man of facts and science. I beg your patience with me."

"Sky, we have not known each other for an extended period. I am grateful for your continued help with my doctoral defense and overwhelmed by my love for you, my wise warrior. Still, I am aware of the complexities of same-sex romance in ways that you are not."

Now, the young man had the full attention of the Egyptian scholar. He locked eyes and said, "What are you trying to say?"

Leonnatus took his hand, not caring what spectators may think.

"This … what we are doing. It could be an infatuation for you. Your first real love, I guess. I remember mine and the craziness that surrounded it."

He continued very carefully, "Family is important, my *voin princ*. I say this, never really having had one of my own. I see how the Mahdi look at you, your cousins, even the little ones. You are their prince, their hope, a bond strong and unbreakable."

"Leo, I spoke the truth of my heart when I told the Bull I was not the last, best hope of the sinless universe. I am no agent of God, and I fear I am hopelessly in love with you. I am old enough to know when the goddess Hathor invades my soul. Bringing music, dance, joy, love, and sexuality."

As he enumerated the gifts of the goddess of love, Skylar stood and threw his arms out, embracing Egypt, the Sacred Land, and Leonnatus, who seemed to be at its center.

He laughed, pointed, and said, "Your eyes are the color of the sky, young Leo. They fill my soul."

"Skylar, as our American friends would say, 'this is major.' Wow."

The joyous man aped a bit of American lingo, saying, "Tell me about it, bro."

He brought his arms down and looked off to the horizon, just over the shoulder of the object of his infatuation.

"I am. I regret acting like an ass. This is highly unusual for me. I am always in control of my body, mind, and spirit. You confuse me, my young friend.

"At one moment, this sting of Hathor, this romance, it hurts profoundly. Then, it feels like a complete and liberating exhilaration, something I have longed for all of my life, to be free and in love… with you.

"I said I am coldly ferocious at lust and fury, but with you, I have felt something different-- tenderness, and it totally astonishes me. I am in uncharted territory, unfamiliar with how to maneuver. Even now, as I have spoken this, I find myself being very irrational, which is not typical of me."

He looked far out to the horizon and took a deep breath before continuing.

"I am a trained scholar-warrior, schooled in the old ways and the rigors of combat. That world, I know. The rest, I have been taught, is an incumbrance-- until now ... now ... this with you ... I ...."

Struggling to make sense, Skylar choked a bit. He turned to face the boy and continued, "Leo, I need you, and I want to be the one for whom you long, in the night, in the excitement of each day. I want to give this a chance-- to see it through as far as it will go. I do not care what anyone thinks of us. All that matters is that we are together.

"Walk with me? Please."

Leonnatus' Shining Prince was figurative and literal at the same time. They rounded the Citadel together. Leonnatus took Skylar's hand.

"Relax, big man. I did my homework. In Arabic countries, two men express friendship when holding hands in public."

They headed for the afternoon sunshine on the grass between the palms. Here there were few tourists.

Leonnatus brought up the subject again, "Skylar, your family.... "

"Leo, I have heard it said that there is the family you are born into and the family you choose. At this time, with my heart, soul, and body, I... choose you. I do not know what may come our way, but, in reality, I care not as long as you are my Leo."

Leonnatus dropped the man's hand and stepped away.

OK, so this is where it all ends.

"What?"

Leonnatus shook his head, unable to meet the man's eyes.

Skylar reached out and turned the boy to face him. He lifted the lad's chin and said, "How long?"

They were silent for a while. Finally, Leonnatus gulped and stammered a bit before he responded. "I was diagnosed when I was fourteen, so eight years."

"Undetectable?"

"Yes, three years and counting."

The man searched the boy's face and said nothing.

"How...?"

"We share a room. I can read medications."

An unspoken question passed between them. Leonnatus attempted a smile as his eyes filled with tears.

"Look, Skylar, I totally understand if you want to...."

The Egyptian leveled his eyes at the boy and spoke with acute insistence.

"You do, huh? You understand this man? Me? Quite impossible, my boy. Please tell me how because lately, I very much do not. Try as I might, I do not understand the feelings inside."

His eyes widened as he continued. Leonnatus started to turn away, hiding the sobs that he felt were coming on. Skylar grabbed for the boy and tenderly turned him around to face him. He pressed the boy's hand to his mouth in an act of endearment, most likely not allowed in this country.

"This much, I do know. We are intelligent men and will make appropriate choices. So that is my rational response."

He drew the lad closer.

"And this is what my heart says, Leo. I want you in my arms always, in my heart."

The boy choked up, unable to say what he was feeling. He had longed for this for so long. Leonnatus was in a fantastic place as he gazed into the eyes of the man he loved. Could it be that someone so wonderful wanted him?

They leaned forward, foreheads touching. There was nothing to be said.

*　*　*

Still facing each other, they stood now in the sunlit park beneath a cloudless sky. Skylar pointed to Leonnatus' running shoes.

"Off."

He stepped out of his own and pulled off his socks. He removed the lad's t-shirt and doffed his own.

"Loosen the top button of your cargo shorts. Perfect. No, they will not fall. You must be free to move. Now close your eyes and listen to the sound of my voice. Pay attention. Put all other thoughts from your mind. It is you and I alone in the universe, at its very center. All energy, power, and strength flow through our bodies from the beginning of time.

"Open your eyes."

The big man stretched his body with athletic grace.

"First is the stance. It provides you with balance and leverage for both attack and defense moves. Legs shoulder length apart. There you go. Dominant foot forward. That's it.

"Easy. Stand fluid like a dancer and be aware of where every part of your body is. Knees and hips are loose and bouncy. You can rock and turn your feet, on the balls, on the heels, point the toe as you lift it from the ground, or twist the foot to the side as an attack move dictates."

Skylar demonstrated in front of the boy with a few combinations. The control, balance, and artistry combined to create a breathtaking vision of a master of the ancient arts. The sun and air made love to his hard, muscular body, glistening on his skin and gently tossing his hair.

His moves were sharp and intense. Kicks and jumps seemed to defy gravity. Skylar returned to the opening stance before his pupil.

I have never witnessed such beauty in my life.

Leonnatus watched intently and followed instructions to set up properly in front of his teacher.

Skylar then took the boy's arms.

"Here. Close your fists, but do not clench. Only tighten when you strike or defend.

"Leo, and this is important, always have at least one fist grazing your eyebrow. From that position, you will protect your upper body. You see?"

The bigger man tapped the boy's face and head. Leonnatus brought up either one hand or the other to defend.

Skylar smiled, faked, and hit Leonnatus on the right side of his ribs. Literally caught off guard, the young man twisted and laughed.

"No tickling, big guy. You know I am a sucker for that."

Skylar cocked an eyebrow and advanced with a full-on, two-sided rib tickle. The beginning fighter collapsed to the grass, turning on his abdomen with legs kicking, laughing like a hyena. He attempted to fend off the assault but was unsuccessful.

Skylar reached for him. As the lad was helped up, he hooked a hand in Skylar's waistband, kicked at his feet, and brought the former Egyptian soldier down on top of him. More tickling, more laughter, and more protests.

"I am not ticklish, and I never laugh."

"As Rebecca would say, 'You are full of shit, Skylar.' Definitely."

They laughed again.

"Boy, you will never learn martial arts if you do not stop fooling around, baby Leo." He swatted the squirming lad.

Not to be outdone, Leonnatus cuffed the man.

"You started this, you *anóitos*.

Skylar continued his good-natured chiding. "You should have taken me down with a leg sweep, but that is a more advanced move."

"And you would have defended, of that I am sure, Master. No, no, what is the title?"

"Sensei. It means 'one who comes before' in Japanese. It is honorific. In Arabic, you would respect me as your *Almuharib Majstir,* Warrior Master."

Propped on one elbow next to his muscular buddy, Leonnatus repeated softly, "*Majstir.*" He looked into the warm, dark eyes of the man lying next to him. His ardor stirred.

This is getting so good. We're sure to be arrested.

Skylar brought them both to their feet.

"Come, my young friend, I will teach you *Sebak Kha,* 'the spirit of the crocodile.' The way of the warriors of the Pharoah is based on balance, speed, power, agility, defenses, attacks, throws, and holds.

"I am afraid we are both out of balance due to your comic displays. We begin again with breathing, Leo. Stand with your arms at your sides and face the sun. Close your eyes and listen to my voice."

Skylar stood at right angles to the boy and placed a firm hand on his sternum and on the center of his back.

"I will call upon the gods of the Old Kingdom."

Leonnatus popped open one eye and said, "Skylar, I had the impression that the Mahdis were devoted Muslims, monotheists. Do you reverence the ancients?"

"I do. Forty-five thousand years of history and culture are not easily dismissed – another point of disagreement with my father. Now close your eyes, remain silent, feel the caress of the Sun God on your body, and breathe. You should be naked for this part, but we will respect propriety."

"Good idea."

As Skylar spoke, his voice assumed a chanting tone. Leonnatus felt the warmth of the sun and the pressure of the steady hands of his lover, front and back.

"We now give obeisance to you, Lord Ra. God of the Sun, you reign at this time in the constellation of the Lion, the namesake of this boy. Bestow power and royalty on him. Flood the sacred Nile as in ancient times and bring generosity and honor to the land."

His baritone was at once silky and reverential as he continued, "Next, we honor Shu, the god of breath, air, and wind, soldier and warrior, the one who holds up the sky.

"Breathe, Leo. Deep breaths, in through the nose and out through the mouth. Bring the god inside of you. There you go, yes. Feel the sun on your skin and the moisture of Shu inside you."

The *Majstir* continued his prayerful instruction in both English and Old Egyptian. Leo began to feel a burning beneath the hands of the man who held him. Skylar took his hands away and leaned toward his pupil. He placed his mouth over the lad's and expelled a deep breath into the boy's mouth and lungs.

"Haaa! Take in the soul of your teacher."

Skylar replaced his hands on the boy's torso and threw back his head, uttering ecstatic words of prayer and incantation, outward and upward.

Leonnatus rocked and trembled but remained on his feet, quite dazzled. There was silence.

"Open your eyes."

The teacher and the pupil faced each other, smiling.

"How do you feel, Leo?"

"Fierce, like the Lion of Macedonia."

They laughed together in the bright sunshine and breeze from the sea.

"Can we do that a lot? That was amazing. The naked option would be exceptionally interesting."

He did a groin adjustment.

"Only if you prove proficient in *Sebak Kha*. Now come, frisky boy, I will teach you more of the ancient discipline. By the way, your tumescence is the sign that the potency of the god, Min, has invaded your body – the power of the male."

The tall martial arts master set up for a round of instructing his Leonnatus on jabs, crosses, uppercuts, and some easy blocks. As they developed the combinations, a small group of onlookers settled in the nearby grass, softly applauding when the lessons got exciting.

Above them, the resplendent solar boat of the God of the Sun, "Ra, who is Horus of the Two Horizons," began his descent in the Western sky over Alexander's city, in the constellation of Leo the Lion.

Chapter Forty-Four: Aliyev
Al-Asu Worldwide, Alexandria, Egypt

"I am surprised that, given the media outrage and stream of accusations currently being flung at you and the members of your organization, you agreed to see us."

Translation: *Let's see if you are really the media whore you have been made out to be, bud.*

"You are Mr. Mark Gadarn. The famous American journalist. I desire the world to notice my position and that of my company's... shall we say innocence, at this time of world crisis and insidious invective. There is no one better to make a considerable media splash for me than you. Consequently...."

Aliyev took Rebecca's hand from her side. He held her fingers in his and kissed the back of them.

The office of the CEO of AL-ASU Worldwide was on the top floor of one of Alexandria's most dazzling and expensive skyscrapers. Ancient art pieces from many parts of Asia and North Africa were arranged with museum precision. A golden headdress in the form of curled ram's horns was directly behind Aliyev's steel and glass desk. Spotlit, up against the wall of windows, it rivaled the morning sun.

"I have the pleasure of making the acquaintance of the beautiful Rebecca Quinto. Your international reputation is as stunning as your appearance."

"Smooth, Mr. Aliyev, very smooth. This impromptu meeting would not have to do with my outspoken criticism of the traditional ways of subjugating women, would it?. You are an avid misogynist, one who unabashedly espouses the oppression of women under the guise of religion. You should know, Sir. I intend to make a bit of my own news at the upcoming conference."

Way to cut to the chase, Beautiful. Pleasantries be damned.

The head of AL-ASU Worldwide dropped her hand and addressed the other man in the room.

"I did not realize that we would be discussing issues that are of no concern to anyone else but Egyptians. The West is so intent on imposing its own version of democracy on Arabic nations."

His look was viper-cold as he stared back at Rebecca.

"Perhaps you, Mr. Gadarn, will want to argue with me concerning my company's stance on the debauchery and the defamation of religion that is homosexuality in my country."

Mark contested, "I thought that you were Azerbaijani."

"Dual citizenship, my father was Egyptian, a distinguished family. My mother actually was half Greek. But I will not bore you with tales of my bloodlines, although I am very proud of them."

"Descended from kings and generals, yes, I read your press."

Now, totally ignoring Rebecca, the oligarch pierced the American journalist with a deadly gaze, regretting his decision to be interviewed.

"Let us get on with it. What is it that you wish to know?"

"Are you responsible for the violence in the east that came to a head last night?"

"No. Next question."

"Sources confirm that you are backing the Rising Dawn movement with your vast resources. Many would say you are the head of the movement – the silent partner who brings the funds to the insurgencies like water in the desert."

"So very eloquent but far from truthful. I am a businessman, Mr. Gadarn. While I am interested in profiting from our endeavors, I lead my company in supporting community and national causes. You have, I understand, visited our Center for Alexandrian Studies, our institute for conserving Egypt's culture. Doctor el-Saddik and her students are making and preserving some vital discoveries. Of this, I am told, you have observed in much detail."

Aliyev stressed his last sentence with an accusatory tone. He turned to glance at Rebecca. Her face revealed nothing. Aliyev returned his attention to Mark.

"But, to speak to your question, AL-ASU supports many conservative organizations but avoids the plethora of armed militia groups. We are committed to..."

"Excuse me, but not so, Sir. My sources can trace your public and private remarks to directly calling for a new Islamic State, ultra-conservative and born of violence. Also, what are your connections to the Egyptian Muslim Brotherhood?"

In an impeccable black linen suit, black shirt, and tie, Farid Haydar Aliyev walked to his desk chair while pointing Mark and Rebecca to the two seats in front of it. He lit a cigarette from a gold case and blew a spiral of blue-grey smoke into the air. Rebecca noticed that as the man sat, the ram's helmet of Alexander was positioned just above and behind his head, hovering like a cloud of gold.

"Mr. Gadarn, I am thrilled that you display the characteristics for which you are well-known. Thrown out of Turkey, held a prisoner in Yemen, nasty business in the Balkans, Colorado, and Australia. And now, you bring your annoyance to Egypt. Are you my own Fourth Plague of Genesis, a disgusting gadfly?"

He attempted a smile, but it came out as a contemptuous and mocking smirk.

"It is of no consequence. I like legendary figures."

He touched his eye patch, and the lion-head ring flashed. He gestured to the images of kings, tsars, pharaohs, warlords, and generals that surrounded them.

He added with a sneer, "I collect them."

The last remark had the tone of a threat.

"Be that as it may, I believe I have answered your question. It only remains to say that, given the state of the world, a return to the traditional ways is urgently required to avoid a catastrophe of international porportions. What is imminent will come by violence. It is the way God has ordained from time immemorial. Search the scriptures and the chronicles of history. This is holy war, is it not? Would you not agree?"

The sinister man looked at Rebecca.

"No way. The massive killing of civilians, the destruction of human rights, the savage treatment of women, a divine plan? You are a barbarian, Aliyev."

"And you are unmannered and disrespectful."

He pointed at the American woman.

"You would be wise, Ms. Quinto, to remember where you are. Egypt will not look kindly on those who incite rebellion and cultural dissent."

Aliyev brought the palm of his hand down on the surface of his desk.

"You and your ilk rail against our revered traditions. You call the cutting of our women a heinous violation of human rights. The practice is common in Europe, also. Even in communities in the United States."

"Our denunciation is worldwide, Aliyev. We are policing our own as well."

He looked at Rebecca as if she were prey. He practically breathed fire as he replied, "You are a woman who needs… " He stopped speaking, sought self-control, and waved a hand of dismissal at the pair with a command in Russian to his virtual assistant.

Mark was rising to the insult. Rebecca was about to respond when the door opened behind them, and Miriam Karimov stepped into the suite.

"You will both please follow me now."

Mark asked one last question.

"Hey, Aliyev, are you the Messiah?"

Turning to view the sea, the oligarch said, "Mr. Gadarn, now you disappoint, and you tire me. What need have I of religious mythology? Ms. Karimov, please remove these two from my presence."

In the elevator, Rebecca addressed her twin.

"So, Betty Boop, what's shaking in your world?"

No response.

"The likeness is incredible. I meant to tell you when we first met."

Mark asked, "What was it that bossman back there said to you?"

Miriam locked eyes with the journalist. It was a stare as deadly as it was seductive.

"I am reluctant to say."

Now, she looked Rebecca up and down. "I will reveal, however, that Mr. Alyev would welcome a more casual meeting with you and, incidentally, me."

Rebecca said, "Not gonna happen, Darling. Please tell your troll boss I said so. He couldn't possibly be man enough for all this."

She hair-flipped.

***

"Father, who were those people?"

"Do not concern yourself with things that do not involve you, my son. Has your tutor dismissed you?"

"I dismissed him as I am bored with my studies, my Father. School and home learning-- am I under house arrest? My head is about to explode."

"Alexei, you know the importance I place on education."

The golden-haired, fifteen-year-old walked to the windows and gazed at the city and the sea.

"My team will practice this afternoon, Father. There is an important match this weekend. I am the best striker with the Lions. May I play, Father?"

"Alexei, have you thought about our last discussion?"

The boy turned and faced his father.

"I explained that the school wholly misunderstood what happened. Nevertheless, I have ended the friendship with Uri ben Chaviv, and we have been placed in different dorm rooms. There been no inappropriate behavior between us and will not be."

"I will not reiterate things already said and made clear except to remind you that young ben Chavi is an Israeli."

"Please, my Father, it will be as you wish."

"You may continue with your school football team. Your bodyguard will remain close by as always."

Aliyev pointed to the door. "Go and send me your tutor."

The boy lowered his head and leFort

Chapter Forty-Five: The Golden Helmet
Al-Asu Center for Alexandrian Studies, Alexandria, Egypt

"Please observe the grooves in the pebble mosaic. In ancient times, heavy equipment has been moved through this passageway, most likely more than once."

Leonnatus pointed to the screen as Mark, Rebecca, and Zahra el-Saddik looked on. Skylar said, "I again reference the diary scroll of Apollonius of Rhodes. As Royal Librarian under Ptolemy III Euergetes, he duplicated and moved the real treasures of the Lost Museum, the burial goods, and the sarcophagus of Alexander the Great."

Leonnatus added, "Our scans show that this portion of the tunnel beneath AL-ASU is part of a larger underground network linking the Great Library, the Serapheum, the Soma, and the Palace. We conclude that Apollonius and others used these passageways to move the most precious objects in the city to various locations whenever the political opposition to the dynasty or the old religion ran high. The treasures of the Library's museum were at risk of destruction or thievery. We are looking at an ingenious evacuation system run by a dedicated team of preservationists."

"What did the LiDAR show?"

The young archaeologist brought up the files. What appeared on the screen was an archaeological portrait of the ruins of the Ptolemaic capital. Leonnatus and Skylar combined the LiDAR images with the scans of the AL-ASU excavation and the imageries of other royal digs throughout the city.

"Doctor el-Saddik, you can plainly see the design of the underground safety feature. The tunnel system actually branches north of us to enter under the ruins of these structures closer to the shoreline.

"See here and here. These are indications of additional blocking structures like the one in the passageway below. We conclude that these were temporary and could be raised and removed depending on danger like the invasion of seawater after an earthquake or even to prevent marauding hordes of anti-intellectuals from reaching these."

He pointed to spaces on the renderings.

"Most likely underground vaults, temporary holding spaces, some with access to the upper ground."

He switched to some interior photos of the newly discovered opening.

"Here are the photos of some rubble in the chamber, most likely from the dismantling of a sealing wall."

Skylar took over the narrative, indicating the ancient buildings and complexes of the city.

"The ruins of the Serapeum, a royal temple built by the grandson of Ptolemy I would be here. It was known to have been an annex to the Great Library. It is on an elevated plateau in the quarter of the city that is diagonal from the Palace of Ptolemy I Soter, probably located here."

He indicated a point on the map north of the Serapeum and closer to the harbor. The location was adjacent to a second dig, the Soma, the catacombs of the Ptolemies. A third point marked a site further along toward the sea. This was the Palace of the Ptolemaic Kings and Queens.

"Our LiDAR shows a vast buried complex here, complete with the famous ambulatories for the philosophers of the Aristotlean School. I have always held that in this area was the Mouseion, the world-renown center of learning and its storehouse of texts, the Great Library of Alexandria."

Rebecca said, "And that is where Ptolemy placed the Body of Alexander after a brief stay in Memphis. Yes, Darling?"

"Right, and with it, a vast treasure trove of grave goods to ensure his passage to the afterlife. Our Lost Museum was here, but the Librarians like Apollonius of Rhodes were ever on guard to protect the Museum's treasures."

Leonnatus added a historical reference, saying, "It is interesting to note that excavations of Temple Mount in Jerusalem found underground passageways similar to these in Alexandria. Most likely used to hide the treasures of the Second Temple during times of war."

Doctor el-Saddik added, "Please allow me to say a word about the librarians of the Great Library. They were members of a unique sect that traced their bloodlines to the priestly class and clergy of the old religion. With the coming of the Hellenes, Ptolemy I Soter raised the order to a vital position in his government. They were the official conservators of the library, a mandate they took with great seriousness, sometimes even to the point of death. It was this group that served as librarians of The Great Library of Alexandria, the curators of his museum, the deans of the various colleges of philosophers and academics, and, legend says, these priests were the embalmers of the god-king when the Pharoah brought Alexander's body to Egypt in 323 BCE.

"This order of priests was hereditary– father to son, most likely lasting well into the Islamic era. Apollonius of Rhodes was one of these.

Mark said, "Tell us more about the turmoil the Alexandrian scholars faced-- the reason for all of this subterfuge."

"There was a concern that the dynasty would turn against the academics of the Mouseion. An abundance of knowledge threatens tradition and a way of life steeped in pagan religion and arcane practices. In times of political unrest and the rise of nationalism, the academics are the first to be slaughtered.

"Egypt and its capital, Alexandria, has a history of three religious cultures that came into conflict in the ensuing centuries, the Old Religion, Christianity, and Islam. Each, at some time, sought the extinction of the others. Murderous purges and the destruction of art, architecture, and treasures followed in the wake. The conservators of Alexander's treasure museum took measures into their own hands to protect the legacy of the Macedonian Pharoah, who founded their immortal city."

Dr. el-Saddik joined in, saying, "Beginning with the designers of the Library, a bloody drama unfolds. The opposition to this global center of learning lasted almost 900 years. At one point, one of the Ptolemies sent all the scholars into exile. The Christians, beginning in the 1st century of the common era, opposed the old regime to the point of slaughter. They are the villains who assassinated the great teacher, Hypatia."

She pointed to the Mouseion.

"Right there in the Neo-Platonic school. Hypatia was a prominent thinker, philosopher, astronomer, and mathematician. She was murdered as a heretic in 415 CE by a mob of Christians.

"Then, with the Islamic conquest of the 7th century, all of this was destroyed. A city began to emerge, an Islamic capital built on a rich, buried past, forgotten treasures, and astounding stories. And so we dig."

Rebecca jumped up and addressed the group, excitement and wonder in her voice.

"OK, Darlings, let's see if I have this. Allow me to summarize. She referred to the map as she spun her tale.

"Alexander dies in Babylon. Ptolemy I steals the sarcophagus and enshrines it at the Mouseion. He builds the Palace, and his sons and grandsons finish construction on the Serapeum and the Soma, all linked by an elaborate underground network, much like an ancient subway."

Mark, just as excited, took up the story saying, "The Librarian-Priests throughout the centuries use the tunnel system to play a sort of Three Card Monte to shuttle the treasures out of the Library whenever the rat fucks were at the gates."

He laughed as he mimicked the hand gestures of a street-side con man in front of a cardboard box, rearranging three cards with lightning speed.

"It's here. No, it's here. No, it's here. Where is it, sucka?"

Skylar added, "From the little we have seen, this system could only have been designed by one man, Euclid, the Master of Geometry, author of The Elements."

"The fuck you say."

"Believe me, Mark, it is a spectacular engineering design. In some places, the escape route has lifts that raise and lower the cargo that passes through this system. Most likely here, here and here." He indicated the composite drawing.

Rebecca said, "Imagine Cleopatra VII Thea Philopator taking Julius Caesar by the hand and leading him through this richly adorned, underground passageway to the body of Alexander. It is said that gazing on the body of the young conqueror of the world, Great Caesar wept."

Leonnatus added, "Think about the scholars scurrying through the Euclidian underground and removing the most valuable collections when the very same Caesar's troops burned the Library or when Caligula looted the tomb, demanding the breastplate of Alexander. What he got was most likely an excellent copy."

Mark said, "OK, so let me ask the question I have been asking throughout this gig. Alexander, where the Hell is he? The vaults you spoke of? Could his sarcophagus have survived almost three millennia of cluster fucks?'"

There was silence throughout the room as each looked at the other. Finally, Leonnatus addressed the excited American.

"Oh, he is not here, Sir. The scans show these storage spaces are empty. We believe the Lost Museum was finally moved out of the city and to the West. Alexander's dying wish was to be interred at the Temple of Zeus Amun at the Siwa oasis across the Great Western Desert. When he first arrived in Egypt in the early years of his campaign, it was there that he asked the oracle to verify his lineage as the son of Zeus.

Rebecca said, "Darlings, before we pack our bags and blow this town for the Sahara, I have one more thing to ask. Leonnatus, you mentioned some debris when you and Skylar were doing the scan in the passageway."

"Yes, we were in a bit of a rush because of the danger of being discovered and the need to guide the equipment with precision. The higher-ups from AL-ASU were arriving on the scene. Consequently, we paid little attention, I am afraid."

Besides, we were making out like satyrs.

Skylar broke in.

"There was a niche with what appeared to be rubble on the western side of the structure. We assumed it was building material or…."

"Something which fell off the escape carts."

Leonnatus pulled up the shots from his phone and scrolled them across the large monitor.

"You think so?"

"Could be. Enlargen, please, Darling. Now, once more. Hold it. Stop. Go back. There. Mark, look. Unbelievable."

On the monitor, they saw an object partially covered in debris, the spiral curl of what could only be a ram's horn helmet gleaming golden in the darkness.

Chapter Forty-Six: Standoff
United Nations High Commission for Refugees, Alexandria, Egypt

From the podium, under the stage lights, Rebecca could see only the first three rows of the audience. She had been asked to provide closing remarks for the colloquy on female circumcision and women's rights. She felt an urgency and desperation that moved her to rethink her message even as she gave her presentation. Shielding her eyes, she spoke directly to the audience, most of whom she could not see.

"Finally, on behalf of UNICEF and the World Health Organization, I would like to commend the work of the human rights activists in Egypt. UNICEF has reported a slow but significant decline in the number of women aged fifteen to nineteen since baselines were set in 1995. Now, despite the ban on the operation by the People's Assembly, female genital mutilation continues to be practiced in Egypt.

"The presenters today have continued to raise our awareness of this criminal and brutal practice, but the battle for the lives of our sisters is far from won. We call upon religious leaders of all faith communities to decry this practice and work to eradicate the notion and the practice of mutilation as a part of religious custom and as a guarantee of female chastity. Be brave and confrontational in defense of those who have no effective voice of their own...."

She stopped.

The passion of the moment and the faces of the women and girls called forth a very unorthodox shift in her presentation. A voice in her head seemed to interrupt.

How many times do we have to deliver the same message? This is a barbaric practice of torture and death. Why am I so staid and formal in the face of this horror? Take a lesson from Émile Zola, Rebecca. J'Accuse!

She detached the microphone from the podium and stepped forward from behind the podium.

"May I have the house lights, please? Thank you.

"I know that the conference organizers have invited leading community members to this assembly, religious, civic, and corporate. I see a few familiar faces in the group, many well-known international figures."

Conference leaders on the dias put their heads together, wondering what the American was up to. Rebecca took a deep breath and continued to step into the audience.

"Look at the women in this room. They are our mothers, grandmothers, sisters, and daughters. So many of them carry a traumatic experience whose horrific effects will haunt them for their entire lives."

She lifted her free hand in the air and made a fist.

"I accuse you!

"To men who say they will not marry an uncircumcised girl: you are directly complicit in a horror that results in psychological and physical damage, namely infection, infertility, and, in some cases, death. Why? Why? For your pleasure and moral assurances. I am here to tell you that you would make one monstrous husband anyway if this is the attitude you have toward the body of your partner and the proposed mother of your children. Stay single, you creeps-- leave the women alone."

As she continued, she felt the anger rise as the attendees began to murmur. Rebecca's remarks shattered many notions of propriety and professional behavior.

"No, seriously. And for that matter, why is it that the men, the fathers, the proposed sons-in-law, why do they make *the women* in the family mutilate the daughters? This is some kinda fucked up. I accuse you!"

Many rose in a loud ovation. Rebecca attempted to ride the wave of support.

"This is evil in its most incipit form. We need to educate our men and boys to be champions for the women who fill their lives with love, wisdom, and nurturing. Do not become their torturers and assassins. You hold this country back with your ignorance. You abuse and maim fifty percent of your population."

She pointed.

"I accuse!"

Now, she walked further into the audience. Her incendiary remarks got more focused as she went on. News cameras were close, and cheers accompanied her comments.

"I call out movements like the political parties and militias sponsored by the world conglomerate AL-ASU and demand both an explanation and a cease and desist."

She pointed at Miriam Karimov and a group of executives in dark, sharkskin suits.

Did you really think you could fuck with me, Darlings?

"You say that we are forcing a Western cultural agenda on the East. You call our efforts anti-Islamic. You are wrong. FGM transcends religion, nationality, race, and ethnicity. It is female and child abuse with a sharp object. Could any god want this?

"Take a look around at this movement. Grassroots protesters-- Egyptian women imprisoned, tortured, and starved because they engaged in peaceful resistance to the brutal tenets of your corporate philosophy that wrongly grounds this bloody practice in religion. The representatives of this UNESCO conference embody human rights groups and governments from the East and the West. Your rationale is, as we say in my hometown, *mierda*-- bullshit."

She had Al-ASU in her sites now. The assembly shouted and began to rise as she went on. With a cold and steely anger, Rebecca addressed one person who looked at her with daggers.

"Are there more profits to be made, more power to be assumed when the women of Egypt are enslaved and mutilated? Nothing to say, Ms. Karimov? Rather disgusting and cowardly, in my opinion. I hope your allegiance to your corporation is worth the horrors you bring to Egypt's women and girls in the name of God! In the name of God!"

Miriam looked from side to side as if she wanted to flee the spotlight at any cost. She switched to nailing Rebecca with a murderous gaze. Then she said a word to the person to her right. A large associate sitting next to the AL-ASU vice president stood and reached into the breast pocket of his suit. Strong hands grabbed him from the row behind as Mark and Skylar brought the guy back down to his seat.

"Relax, asshole. You won't be needing this."

Mark relieved the dagger from the man. Leonnatus arrived with security. The contingent from AL-ASU was escorted from the auditorium, the would-be assassin in handcuffs. A female guard led Rebecca backstage as quickly as possible.

The frenzied assembly cheered.

Rebecca thought, This *could be the end of my membership on the UNESCO commission, but the hell with it.*

Chapter Forty-Seven: Night's Thousand Eyes
Serafina Trattoria Italiana, Fort Lauderdale, Florida

As they opened the doors, the irresistible aromas of fantastic Mediterranean flavors welcomed them to the charming quayside ambiance of one of the city's most excellent gourmet restaurants.

A tall young Italian maitre d' bowed slightly and said, "Mr. Ch'en, I have a table prepared especially for you and your guest."

Hud embraced the man with a double kiss.

"Good to see you again, Matteo. This is my friend, Micah."

The dark eyes of the host twinkled, and he flashed a killer smile as he said, "*Il mio amante, buona sera, signore.* Welcome to Serafina. Please follow me, gentlemen."

Hudson and Micah were escorted to a waterside table at the back of the beautifully romantic, candlelit trattoria with its gorgeous view of the Middle River as it meandered through the upscale neighborhood of Victoria Park. Impressive waterfront homes came with expensive pleasure crafts, bobbing along private docks or slowly cruising up to or past the restaurant, boat, and dock lights glimmering in the summer twilight.

They were seated, and menus were presented. Matteo poured two flutes of sparkling wine.

"This is the Zardetto you are so fond of, Mr. Ch'en. With the compliments of the management. Your server will be right with you, my friends."

He stepped away.

Micah returned Hud's glass clink, and they quaffed the delicious Prosecco. He looked up at the very athletic form of the departing maitre d'. He raised his glass again.

"Gosh, Hud. This is a great place. I love the boat drive-up and view."

Hudson turned back from eying the sexy Italian and reddened a bit.

Micah smiled as he said, "Matteo, eh?"

"God, am I that transparent? Yeah, a thousand years ago, it seems. Way before Nick. Ancient history."

"He fits your profile. Dashingly handsome with a hot body."

"An extended affair, not much more. What looks good, Mike?"

"No contest. *Zuppa Di Pesce* wins every time. And you?"

"Feeling like a cut of hot meat tonight, so I am going for the filet."

The double entendre was not lost on his companion, who gazed at the darkening sky and water. After a minute, Micah turned back to the man of his recent infatuation.

Living with Hud had been easy, and the passion they shared as a couple was terrific. He enjoyed the comfort of their relationship after running away from the overly persistent young professional. Tonight, Micah was glad he gave in to romance.

Their server arrived and took up the wine bottle to top off the flutes.

"Hey, cowboys, what's shakin'? Good to see you dudes again."

"Antionio, you horn dawg. How are you doing? I didn't know you worked here."

The two diners stood to greet their friend with hugs and kisses.

"Yep, it pays the bills, Hud. I saw your name on the reservation list and had you placed at one of my tables."

Micah asked, "Any word from your hunk, the gay INTERPOL James Bond?"

"Nope. I was going to ask if you had heard from Team Rebecca. I follow the news feeds, and it seems that things are sizzling in that part of the world."

"I get some texts from Rebecca regularly. She is in Egypt and has been merging her human rights advocacy work with the museum project. Wants to stage an Egyptian exhibit at the Fritcher in three years."

"Hope they get back safe and sound. I would not mind checking in with Agent Mathias again. Can't get that guy out of my head. Anyway, have you decided?"

Hud took the point and ordered for them both, just the entrees. He then said, "Have Matteo fill in the blanks. He knows what I like."

Micah thought, *I'll bet he does.* Rebecca's Executive Assistant managed to keep his poker face.

"That OK, Mike?"

"I trust your love of all things Italian, buddy, and I am hungry as all get out."

"Great, guys. I will send over the wine, Dude. Oh, sorry. We are supposed to say 'the sommelier.' Very sophisticated."

He leaned in and whispered, "High-class bullshit, guys. Some nights, I prefer my massage and trainer gigs at Crunch Gym."

The three shared a laugh as the man moved away.

Hud asked, "Mike, what's the latest on the Elizabeth King murder? Any new developments?"

"The police and FBI come by the museum every so often, but I got nothing on that, Hud. Each staff member has been interviewed, and the catacombs scoped out thoroughly. Mary Chaffee let me know that she will be recommending that Rebecca send the head of museum security packing. So, I wonder if she thinks that he was being paid to look away on some of these intrusions, the Egyptian chest, the cobra, all of that."

"Yeah. No security camera data? Very suspicious."

"Gentlemen? Have you decided on the wine for tonight? Perhaps I can recommend one. Of course, I am aware of your entrée order and can pair to your absolute satisfaction."

Michael B. Jordan lookalike. Damn. It's the night of the hot men. Micah looked at Hudson and continued to muse. *All this eye candy will translate to sweet dessert rounds in the sack if I know my energetic man.*

He spoke up, saying, "I thought one of the Super Tuscans."

The wine host said, "We have recently come into a shipment of Campaccio Terrabianca Toscana '04, which I highly recommend to oenophiles who are rejecting the whole white-for-fish-red-for-meat stereotype."

Hud raised a hand to confirm the choice and said, "Excellent, my good man."

The steward whirled away.

"Whoa, 'my good man?' Seriously? Hudson, rockin' the real pretentiousness – I feel like I am dining with Sir Patrick Stewart and his English highbrows."

The light-hearted conversation continued. The couple talked about work and social life. They dissected recent offerings on cable like Ryan Murphy's "Pose" and the reboot of Armistead Maupin's "Tales of the City." Fond touches across the table accompanied the loving looks of a romantic evening out and about.

Between the *antipasti* and the main course, Hud leaned in, saying, "Mike, as easy as you can, look over at the table behind you, way in the back. Is that who I think it is?"

Micah pretended to drop his napkin, and a passing waiter quickly picked it up, saying, "I will get you a replacement, sir."

Foiled in his attempt to do a nonchalant head turn, Micah waited and tried again. The same server shot him a puzzled look as Micah bent to retrieve the linen and scoped out the person in question.

"Jesus, Hud, it's the stalker woman from Flamming Saddles in New York, um… um…."

"Nilza Mendez. Yeah, what the fuck, right?"

"I'll bet that she was one of the folks who arrived on that."

Micah pointed to a sleek black and silver Riva Vertigo, circa 2015, riding the river crests at Sarafina's dock.

"Look at the name. 'The Nephthys.' Right?"

"Yes. Weird. With all the hieroglyphics and shit."

"Hud, in Egyptian mythology, Nephthys was a water deity and the goddess of death, mourning, and the night. Creeping me out."

"Something's up with that bitch, yeah."

"Anyway, let's not allow her to spoil one very excellent night."

Hud poured another glass from a fresh bottle of the Terrabianca for each of them and said, "And it's gonna get better – talkin' sizzling hot *fare l'amore. Capisce?*

"Yeah, sexy man, I got it. Gonna smoke you with my lovin', Dude."

"So I'll order the tiramisu to go. Yes?"

"Yeah, baby, twist my arm."

"Gotta hit the head, be right back."

Hud exited and went into the restaurant, looking for the restroom. On the return, he stopped to talk to Antonio and put in their order for the dessert.

He found their table empty when he got back. Looking around, he caught the eye of both Matteo and the wine steward, Damon. They both pointed to a sleek black pleasure craft leaving the dock.

The Nephthys roared onto the night river.

Thomas Paul Severino

Chapter Forty-Eight: Micah
Aboard The Nephthys, The Intracostal, Fort Lauderdale, Florida

"It is quite simple, young man. You are a hostage. Your boss, famous for being an instigator and a meddler, has now become an obstruction. Please allow me to explain it a bit to you."

Nilza Mendes indicated the crew of the yacht.

"This boat is out of Port Said, Egypt, but my crew is Russian, some of my comrades in arms, as it were."

She continued, "So you see, my Russian friends are very interested in supporting the political aspirations of one Farid Haydar Aliyev. His senseless monomania concerning Alexander the Great and his Messianic claims will serve the strategies of many in the present Russian regime. Aliyev is a threat to the West, creating a favorable shift in the balance of power. Certain leaders in Russia have learned to use the very powerful and very insane for our purposes.

"You are a traitor to OSCE."

"And you are a sexual deviant. Do you realize that in Russia, there are websites that offer prizes for anyone killing homosexuals? You make my comrades onboard the Nephthys very greedy, Mr. Valez."

Micah shot back an accusation, "That's how the murder of LGBTQ activist Yelena Grigoryeva went down in June 2019. You are allied with one of the evilest regimes in history."

She continued, "My, my, so very judgemental. But alas, Russia is far from Fort Lauderdale, and Aliyev needs you for a while, anyway. The man is so very obsessed with your boss. So, you can see why we interrupted your dinner this evening."

The Nephthys pitched and picked up speed. Micah figured that they had left the shelter of the Intracostal and were headed out into the Atlantic.

"Mr. Aliyev reminded me that in ancient Egypt, enemies of the Pharoah were often impaled or burned alive. The Egyptians believed that burning alive would rob the deceased of his body and prevent him from achieving eternal life – so many choices for him. He never seems to deliver his hostages alive."

A large guard snickered at the mention of the possibility of torture games.

Lord, I am so screwed.

"We are taking you to a private island not too far away. A message has been sent to the redoubtable, Ms. Quinto, and we will wait. I hope your restraints are not too binding, but Vassily here insists. He most likely is hoping to get his hands on you quickly. Such an intense sadist, but then I am convinced that is a trait perfected among certain Russians."

The tall, no-necked goon licked his ample lips.

"Oh, Mr. Valez, being a pawn in a bigger game can be so frustrating. Do you not agree?

She left the boat's cabin.

Chapter Forty-Nine: Mary

Serafina Trattoria Italiana, Fort Lauderdale, Florida

"Hud, you are going to try to relax and tell me just how it happened."

It was after midnight, and the restaurant was closed. Everyone had left except Matteo, Antonio, and Damon. Matteo poured Hud another shot of Puni Alba, Italian whiskey. He gulped the second shot.

Matteo put a supporting hand on the man's shoulder and said, *Facile lì, grande uomo."*

Antonio added, "She's the FBI, Hud. They will find him."

Hud looked glassy-eyed at the Special Agent. "One moment there, next moment gone. What else can I tell you?"

Mary said, "The table where the boat folks were sitting-- what about them."

Antonio said, "They ordered drinks and appetizers and walked out on the check."

Mary nodded. "Yes, abduction is a hurried affair most times."

Damon offered, "The woman ordered an expensive white, and the three suits each had a vodka neat. Insisted on Russian vodka. Thick accents, even the woman, but her's was not Russian, more like Brazilian."

"Meaning Portuguese?"

"Possible."

"Go on."

Damon continued, "Trolling for these two gentlemen. It was pretty obvious."

Mary asked, "Did it not occur to you that something strange was happening? Three customers stop at a table and lead a friend of yours away – Micah, while Hud is in the toilet?"

Matteo said, "We were extremely busy at the time. I only took a cursory notice, to be honest. I thought that Mr. Valez had been invited to see the vessel up close."

Damon added, "It happened so fast."

"Tell me about the boat."

Antonio said, "A beauty, Officer. Really. It was tied up near my section, so...."

The young man tapped open his phone and showed his pictures. He scrolled through four.

Mary held up her iPhone and said, "Please Airdrop them to me."

"Sent"

"Perfect, clear license numbers. We definitely got this."

She showed the very distraught Hud.

"OK, so I have some calls to make. The Coast Guard is already on this."

She looked at Matteo.

"Can you see that Hud gets home safely? I've asked for some home protection, but it may be a little delayed."

"Of course, officer. I will help in any way."

Antonio did an aside to the maitre d' as he helped the somewhat intoxicated Hud out of the trattoria. He wagged an index finger and aped a comic Italian accent.

"And none of the funny bizziness, eh?"

Matteo scrunched up his face at the waiter.

"Seriously, *compagno*? So inappropriate, your crazy mind. *Basta*."

Chapter Fifty: Into the West
Above The Great Sand Sea of The Western Desert, Egypt

"I have been censured by the Agency and ordered back to Headquarters in Lyon. Most likely, I will be reassigned. The death of our agent in Alexandria has been seen by my superiors as a major failure on my part. I have much to account for, I will admit to you."

Jürgen Mathias gazed out of the window of the Aeolus as it made its way to the far reaches of Egypt's western border. Beneath the aircraft, miles and miles of desert sands drifted past with no sign of any living thing.

"In the course of my defense of this mission, I alerted my superiors to the connections between Aliyev's organization and the Rising Dawn movement. INTERPOL issues Red Notices, information on fugitives wanted either for prosecution or to serve a sentence. Because our organization has no direct powers in our member nations to arrest and prosecute criminals, we can only encourage cooperation when we have evidence of high crimes.

"My team surfaced a large number of persons with ties to AL-ASU. The result is many calls for law enforcement worldwide to locate and provisionally arrest a host of Aliyev's confederates, among them, our friends Ivan Lermontov, if he is still alive, Miriam Karimov, and, I believe you will find this interesting, Nilza Mendes, formerly of the OSCE who appears to have left the area."

Rebecca said, "Eris nailed it on that bitch."

Mark nodded. Jürgen turned back to his four friends.

"I had a tough time of it, but, with some persuasion, my director agreed to keep me on this assignment with the provision that there is a quick resolution. And so it is that I am thinking, Siwa will be the last stop of our little adventure together."

Skylar brought out his laptop and said, "Leonnatus and I have been concluding our investigation into the Librarian's scrolls. One of the series had been giving me some trouble in the translation. It is written in a mixture of Greek and a very obscure version of the Coptic language. But, with Leo's academic insight and the assistance of Doctor el-Saddik's scholars, I believe we have something important to consider.

"It is a diary entry from most likely the early decades of the 3rd century CE. The author is Pausanias of Catana, the Librarian at that time. It isn't very much, but I believe it is significant. This manuscript, by the way, is the last of the scrolls chronologically. He read aloud.

Again, we have prevailed. The plan of Master Apollonius [of Rhodes] and the underground puzzle have allowed us to safeguard the treasures of our Macedonian forebearers. Another robbery, thought to be successful, has been foiled.

It is known to very few that these thieveries of the legacy of the Great Mouseion throughout the ages, such as the rape of Alexandria by the Roman Emperor, Caracalla, [section missing here] And so, the soldiers found nothing of value. Some of our scholars were put to the sword.

It remains to me and those closest to me to continue to secure the god's legacy forever. And so, it came to me in a dream. I saw the golden-haired Pharoah, the first of the Macedonians. He spoke of [section missing here] angered with those who fought over his divided empire.

The dead Pharoah commanded that, in the name of the gods, I reverse the great theft of our Father and Lord, Ptolemy, and follow the dying wishes of the Divine Alexander, thus lifting his curse from the land and from the dynasty.

When I awoke, I [here ends the manuscript]

Mark said, "So?"

Leonnatus reiterated, "Pausanias reversed the theft of Alexander's body and followed the dying wishes of the great king. Alexander's generals insisted on burial in the tombs of the royal family in Aegae, now Vergina in Macedonia. But Alexander wanted...."

Rebecca pointed to the front of the plane, "The Temple of the Oracle at Siwa."

"Yes."

As they were speaking, the Aeolus began to shudder.

Mark, looking at his tablet, said, "Holy shit, fellows and gals, Eris is sending an alert. She's hacked into the Aeolus' computer. Holy shit! She's saying…"

As he spoke, the double-engine jet rocked to the left and tipped into a nosedive. Jürgen dashed into the forward cabin, falling through the compartment door.

"The guidance system just failed, sir. I went to manual and am trying to pull this baby out of its fall."

The agent dropped into the co-pilot's empty seat, put on the headphones, and asked, "How far are we from Siwa Oasis North?"

The plane rocked, pitched, and did a steep right turn just above the desert floor, coming out of the impending crash. Desert sands and endless rocky horizons flashed by the doomed aircraft.

"Only about twenty minutes, sir. I can't put her down in this terrain using the landing gear. Can't land on the sand. Those dunes are not aviation-friendly."

She punched some controls and the pilot's touch screen and added, "Sliding in on her belly will tear up the fuselage on those rocks. Something is seriously wrong with the flight computer. I tested it before we left, and all checked out."

The situation worsened as the Aeolus continued its flight at a lower altitude. Chaffees of making the airport began to appear dire. The pilot and co-pilot considered the options. Bailing was not an option. Now, they were too low, and gaining altitude was a dangerous option.

Jügen said, "I have Siwa. They are directing us to the north of the city. They are talking about a tarmac road to the sea."

The pilot did what she could to stabilize the Aeolus and keep her level.

"I got a few tricks here, boss. Computer disengaged, but the engines aren't going to make it."

Prophetically, the jets shuddered and died. The pilot gritted her teeth as she said, "Putting her into a glide. Let's see if we can use these winds to our advantage."

In the cabin, the four passengers had scrambled to their seats and locked in their safety belts. Mark and Leonnatus grabbed for laptop projectiles as the steep angle of the fall turned the compartment into a jumble of gravitational turmoil. Rebecca reached for Mark's hand.

In the cockpit, Jürgen pointed at a black ribbon winding north on the desert sands and shouted, "There, Captain Vance, put us down there. Drop the wheels."

"Aye, sir. Let's hope the traffic sees us coming."

As they came in over the narrow road, they could see some trucks, buses, and cars traversing the artery from Siwa to a port on the Mediterranean. At some distance but parallel to the road, camel caravans wound their way in opposite directions, north and south.

The Aeolus made one pass, dropping close to the ground. On a no-power glide, there would not be another chance to reverse direction and come in for another fly-over.

Vehicles scattered onto the gravel sides of the highway as the plane touched the ground, ending its taxi within four meters of a bus filled with people and animals heading in the opposite direction. The driver's face was one of extreme panic. As he opened his eyes and lowered his arms, the passengers erupted in cheers of relief.

Jürgen Mathias began to breathe again and started to exit the cockpit to check on the passengers. The pilot touched his arm and said, "I suspect sabotage, sir. This craft was entirely safe when we departed Alexandria.

"Apparently not, Captain Vance."

***

"Where are we?"

"Not far from the city, Rebecca. We may have to seek conveyance from some of the locals."

Mark asked, "Damn, Jürgs, another close one, or what? I am starting to believe we somehow stepped in it-- the ancient curse of the Ptolemies. Who is out here, anyway?" He looked out the window.

Skylar answered. "They are the Berbers, the pre-Arab, indigenous people of North Africa. I suspect this is a main artery for the Siwans to the port of Marsa Matruh on the Mediterranean. Roads such as this only date from the late '80s."

Traffic on the highway began to work its way around the plane in both directions. A large truck with drilling equipment traveling south stopped behind the Aeolus. The driver got out with a water container and approached the stranded passengers. He spoke to Skylar.

Skylar nodded to the driver and returned to the group.

"He is Muhammad Gwafa Hammadit, and he works for the Great Sand Sea Drilling Company. He is an Amazigh chief."

Skylar passed the water.

"He will tow the plane off to the side of the road onto that gravel-covered flat."

Jürgen said, "Please tell him I will reimburse him for his trouble."

"No, my friend, Mr. Hammadit has given you water."

"So?"

Skylar responded, "The Amazigh, like other Berbers, have a strong tradition of guest's rights. Once someone has taken water from a Berber, they become their guest, treated with honor and respect."

The truck pulled around the wings and into position for a tow. Captain Vance approached the INTERPOL agent carrying her laptop.

"Commander, I did a quick system check. It looks like the local flight crew at the Alexandria Airport missed this little baby."

She pointed to a small feature on the screen's schematic.

"I have disabled it, but I am reluctant to put the Aeolus in the air again until we can do a complete security workup. I sent out a call to the folks at the SIWA airport about forty kilometers south of us. I radioed INTERPOL, Cairo of our situation. They are sending a team by air."

"There is something else, Captain. I can tell by your expression."

The woman looked around at the group and addressed her superior with grave concern.

"If we survived the loss of control, I am pretty sure that the sabotage device was designed to explode our fuel source.

Rebecca asked, "Are you saying what I think you are saying?"

"Yes, Ms. Quinto. We were a hair's breadth from being blown out of the sky."

Chapter Fifty-One: Caravan
Marsa Matrouh-Siwa Road, Egypt

"The chief is my cousin, my friends, and we are going in your direction. I assure you. It is no trouble."

The caravan master spoke from a seated position with two of his drivers. Most of the camels were kneeling in the sand. Many were piled with goods for the markets in Siwa. The barking roar of the beasts occasionally filled the air as they "spoke" their discontent with each other and their humans.

The master was dressed in the characteristic blue robes of the North African Berbers. He drew with his staff in the sand and then pointed to his train. "We have room for four passengers, but one must walk. My sister-in-law runs a resort in the city on the lake. Not many kilometers to the south. We will get you there."

Leonnatus pointed to the Berber men gathered around the stranded Aeolus. Many were gently touching the plane. He said, "It would appear, sir, that many of your team have not seen an airplane before."

"No, my young friend, not this close. Unfortunately, those machines are competing with our work. We carry dates, handmade products, salt, and woven cloth to the ports and as far to the south as the wet grasslands beyond the Great Desert. But planes, such as yours, are faster."

The Berber pointed to the downed aircraft. "Sometimes the bird crashes, yes? No one gets hurt falling off a camel into the sand. And so, we have crossed the desert for thousands of years with our camels. We will continue to do so."

One of his workers arrived with a pile of cloth. The caravan chief passed out cotton robes and head coverings. Drivers came forward to show the foreigners how to wrap and wear the headdresses.

As he raised his scarf to cover all but his eyes, a Berber told Rebecca, "The sun is hazardous, madam. You must cover up. We are lucky there is no wind on the dunes. Yesterday, the winds blew the sand with much force. Today, the sea of sand is calm."

Leonnatus, in cargo shorts, was given a pair of loose-fitting cotton pants and a long cloak. They were led to four kneeling camels. Skylar was given a similar robe and provided with a long staff to assist his trek as the member of the hitchhikers' group that would walk in the caravan.

"You look like the Queen of Sheba, Beautiful."

Rebecca laughed and said to Mark, stretching out one arm, "Come, my handsome sheik. Our oasis of passion awaits."

Mark mounted his ride, a dashing and accomplished desert warrior. The drivers coaxed the camels to rise with their passengers. In English, a driver called out, "You lean back when she stands, then forward, *effendi*."

Leonnatus whooped as his beast lifted her hindquarters first, almost dethroning the lad before standing tall on all fours.

"You are riding her as if my Yasmin were a horse, and she does not like that. Cross one leg up and around the saddle post. That is right. You will not fall. Hang on front and back."

"No, no, Miss. Do not try to steer Illi. She is my stubborn daughter and resists all control. Have no fear. She will follow the line. Talk calmly to her."

Dromedary bellows mixed with human cries in the Berber language, English, Greek, and German roused the train into formation.

"Hut, hut, hut. Use the flail and bounce your heel against her shoulder to speed that one up. Markunda gets lazy. That is her baby, Tobias. He will follow his mother closely."

Skylar took the reins of Leonnatus' camel and struck out before the animal. The side-to-side rocking began as the caravan continued the journey to the south. Beasts, their masters, and their riders ignored the modern forms of transportation that slowly eased out of the traffic jam on the adjacent road.

They had not gone far when Skylar reached out and took Jürgen's somewhat unruly beast by the reins in his other hand, handing up his walking staff. He so looked the part of a noble Berber chieftain and desert guide, dark eyes on watch almost concealed on a scarf-swathed face.

Soon, the agent's camel trotted ahead and joined the caravan without Skylar's gentle words.

The undulating line of the caravan headed south across the open desert, Dromedary heads held high like royalty, their piles of cargo swaying from side to side. The Oasis of Siwa, its pleasures and mysteries, lay before them.

Chapter Fifty-Two: Mud and Candles

The Isis Retreat, Qesm Siwa, Egypt

The combination hotel, spa, and restaurant offered relief for sore hips and butts after a 25-mile caravan trek. Rebecca and friends bid goodbye to their cameleer friends steps from the Isis Retreat Lodge, a fabled resort on the Siwa West Salt Lake banks. They lucked out in that a bougainvillea-covered waterfront bungalow was available. The summer months featured very few guests.

The crystal-clear waters of the pool were warm but refreshing, shaded by date palms. The resort's water features shimmered in the sun. They were excellent for removing the last vestiges of their camels. The surrounding landscape of the lodge seemed to breathe powerful healing and restoration.

Their personal concierge, Baris, informed them, "We are far enough from the city to escape the noise and able to provide many natural remedies for stress and tension. In your journey across the Great Sand Sea, you have found the place of rejuvenation for both body and soul."

Mark joked, "Especially if you have murderers snapping at your butt like crocodiles."

Elbow to the side, courtesy, Rebecca.

"Ow," he faked.

She attempted to cover.

"Tell me, Darling, the hotel and spa are eco-friendly, yes?"

"Yes, Ms. Quinto, we are famous for it. Construction materials are all-natural. Our lodge offers the very best Egyptian cotton towels, bed linens, and handmade carpets. Even your robes are of cotton fabric, locally grown and woven. Also, you will find no electricity here.

"May I suggest visiting our private beach just down that path? You will find we are an adults-only resort, and you are just in time to watch one of our spectacular sunsets. At the white and blue tent, off to the left, you will find our massage host, Ashraf. We are a certified massage center. I have arranged for your dinner order, lakeside, in two hours."

***

"Please." The tall, barefoot Berber youth in an immaculate white polo shirt emblazoned with the Lodge's crest and trim white jeans pointed Rebecca and Mark to a tent stirring in a warm breeze from the lake.

"Gentlemen, we are ready for you over here."

Ashraf indicated that he would assist Jürgen personally. He directed Skylar and Leonnatus to a smiling man holding aside a tent flap and beckoning them forward.

Inside, Skylar addressed their two attendants in Arabic before translating for Leonnatus. "They are twins, actually, Izdärasen and Izemrasen. Their names mean 'strong and powerful,' respectively."

"How did they know we are a couple?"

"The Amazigh are very wise people, Leo. Body language-- gestures, looks, and touches are readable, and they do not have the usual prejudices of many groups."

The twins were dressed in the Lodge's signature white, sleeveless athletic shirts and shorts. They sported young, lean, muscular bodies. Each of them reached for the robes of their guests.

Izdärasen said to his client, "*Yrja nasyan altawadue libaed alwaqt, 'ayuha alssadat aljasd hu haykal allha.*" While Izemrasen said to Leonnatus, "As my brother said, no need for modesty. You will find us very respectful. Please relax, sir." He gently tapped the young man's forehead and said, "Allow the divine, healing spirits to come inside here."

One tent over, the women attendants wore no veils and relatively the same clothing as their male counterparts. They also counseled the relaxation of inhibitions.

"Jidji and I are doing a mud wrap, followed by a salt scrub after soaking in the lake. We will finish with a warm oil massage. Please stand by the tables and raise your arms."

302

The other woman said, "Lunja and I will now coat you with the healing mud. The wrap will follow, and we will leave you to rest for a time."

Mark handed off his robe with an expression like he had died and gone to heaven.

***

Under the dimming light of the sunsetting sky, as Jürgen stepped into the mud bath, Ashraf removed his clothes. The German agent watched as the staffer stepped into the immersion behind him.

I need to get permanently assigned to Siwa. This is unbelievable. I thank whatever gods have brought this about. Mmm. Oh, yesss. Feels incredible.

The captain of the attendants said in German as he began to position Jürgen in the mud soak. "Lift your torso and lie on your back. Keep your arms slightly apart from the rest of your body. Very good. The temperature of the mud should be warm but relaxing."

Ashraf moved Jürgen's head onto his chest and began to work the muscles of his neck and shoulders in the thick restorative.

"I can feel the tension in your neck, shoulders, and upper back, Commander. You have faced some challenges that have knotted and jammed the energy pathways of your body. Allow the stress to leave under my fingertips."

"I am sorry, Ashraf."

"Commander, I have been in this profession for a long time. That is a perfectly natural reaction. Allow your body its full range of feelings. The power of the earth, sea, and sky will rest and restore your life forces."

He worked his way down the man's arms to the fingertips as Jürgen closed his eyes.

***

"Relax, Darling. No one has anything each of us hasn't seen before. Unblock your mind and become one with the natural energies all around us."

Nevertheless, Skylar chose to remain in more than waist-deep waters of the lake as he and Leonnatus washed off the mud from each other.

He said softly to his Leo, "I am discovering so much on this adventure."

The boy laughed.

"Much comes naturally, I would say. The rest... well, pay close attention, and I will teach you."

Skylar swung an arm and hand-splashed the teasing youth.

Leonnatus cussed in Greek and climbed on the bigger man's back, tumbling them both into the lake.

Mark's and Rebecca's mutual ablutions were much more tender. Still, the washing techniques of Jürgen and Ashraf seemed to border on the softcore pornographic. They stayed a bit off to the side.

On the shore, the attendants waited with clean robes. The honey salt scrub would come next, followed by another dunk in the lake. The final treatment, the massage using essential oils, would precede dinner under the stars.

***

"I smell like a flower shop."

"Let me see." Skylar did a nose hit on the boy's neck. Each of three sniffs brought a comment worthy of a botanist.

"Mmm... bergamot... lavender... and, ahhh... ginger. It is appealing."

He looked over at the almost drowsy Rebecca.

"No, Miss. Please observe."

Rebecca moved away from the food platter and watched the Egyptian as Mark nodded and pointed to Skylar with a mutton chop as if to say, "Listen to the man."

"The left hand goes in the lap. Use only the right. It is our custom."

She got the hang of it and asked her associate, "Skylar, I suspect your Egyptian bloodlines are not as pure as we have thought. Somewhere in your family history, an Amazigh bull got into the pasture."

"Miss, you are very astute. Despite my father's fanaticism, Chione and I had a Berber amah as children. She taught us much concerning the ways of her people. There is a legend in my family that our 'pure Egyptian' blood actually includes ancestors from these indigenous peoples. Yes. I am very much at home here."

"I have meant to ask you, Darling, about Chione, and if this is too private, I will back off."

Skylar looked at his dinner companions and decided to answer.

"As you may have suspected, Chione has a neuromuscular disorder. It is Multiple Sclerosis. The onset came a few years ago and is progressing rapidly. Still, she is determined to complete her studies and live a full life."

Jürgen leaned forward and said, "My friend, there is quite a bit going on with MS and stem cell biology, as you may be aware. Europe has a few centers exploring that treatment. If you would allow me, I have a connection at the Medical Research Center in Brussels, my brother, actually, who may...."

"I thank you, Agent Mathias, but the matter is a closed one, I am afraid. My father is a very strict religious conservative. He will not allow this treatment."

The German mused, *This man is so astonishingly handsome. Leonnatus is one lucky boy to have the heart of this wondrous man. I'd give anything to...*

Mark interrupted the daydream using the half-eaten mutton shank as a pointer.

"Hey, Jürgs!"

The agent came out of his reverie and snapped to attention.

"Yes... my friend. I apologize. I, um... have not been this relaxed in many days. The mind-- it wanders."

Mark put down the morsel and wiped his right hand. He brought both index fingers side-by-side in a rubbing motion. "You and the dreamboat 'Ass Raft' there, you guys ahhh... *neuken? Das Bumsen?* The old horizontal mambo, ass pirates in heat?

"Ow."

He turned to Rebecca.

"You keep diggin' into this boy's ribs with your elbow, and we are gonna have a problem, Beautiful. I am a journalist. I get the facts, no matter how salacious."

The group laughed, and Jürgen said, "Marko, my very sick friend, your inquiries are, as usual, highly inappropriate."

"Hold on, bud, two nights ago, you were my boyfriend, albeit unfaithful to the max."

"Mark, you are the limit."

Jügen interrupted the exasperated Rebecca, saying, "Marko, Ashraf is a certified professional, so…."

"Bingo. Say no more. Another victory for the nasty boy German. It would appear your superiors allow you to be the sex kitten of the international spy circuit, Barbarella? Porno film at eleven."

The commander shot a date at his buddy. Skylar leaned toward Leonnatus for clarification on the reference. The boy simply shrugged as if to confirm that there was no understanding of Americans. They are a confusing and complicated people.

Leonnatus said, "We found our attendants to be very proper, also. Did you know that Siwa is literally a liberal oasis regarding sexuality? There is a historical acceptance of male homosexuality and even same-sex marriage going back thousands of years. It was reported that in the '40s, the king visited this part of the country and demanded that the community cease what he and his conservative politicians considered debauchery. Research suggests that the approval of same-sex relationships goes back even before the arrival of Alexander and the Greeks."

At the mention of the Macedonian warrior, it was Mark's turn now to change the subject. He did not say anything but sat back and regarded the young archaeologist with a questioning look. Leonnatus was quick to catch the meaning of the nonverbal communication.

"Yes, yes, yes, Mister Mark. Two more sites. I refer to the work of the Greek archaeologist Liana Souvaltz in my dissertation. In the '90s, she claimed the tomb was here in Siwa. Nothing ever came of her assertions. In fact, the Ministry of Culture denied that her discovery was even a tomb."

Skylar said, "Tomorrow, we will visit the ruins of the Temple of Amun Ra and the Mountain of the Dead. But tonight, we rest."

Thomas Paul Severino

Chapter Fifty-Three: Regulus and Antares
Isis Retreat Qesm Siwa, Egypt

"You have stars in your eyes, Rebecca."

Mark kissed the hand of his love as the evening brought a chill to the desert. Nightbirds and bats spiraled over the lakeshore and into the date palms and cacti. Somewhere, a wild dog barked at the full moon, rising as the twilight followed the sun sinking in the west-- Amun Ra swallowed by Geb, the god of the earth.

As Mark looked back up, Rebecca said, "You do too, my hottie boy."

"Your haunted Egyptian dude over there told me that the constellation Leo is a masculine sign."

He pointed upward at the stars that followed the setting sun.

That is the champion star, Regulus, the brightest star in Leo. He called it "the heart of the Lion,' *Qalb al-Asad*. It brings energy, light, and abundance."

They continued a romantic interlude that increased in passion as they sat together on a low patio wall under the stars. Candles surrounded the entrances of the guest cabins, illuminated outdoor shelves, and flickered on window sills. They seemed to bring the twinkling stars to earth everywhere around the spa. Nearby, Leonnatus and Skylar, in lounge chairs, talked softly and held hands. From time to time, they looked up at Jürgen, walking in the fragrant desert garden.

Softly caressing Rebecca's cheek, Mark whispered with a huskiness, "C'mon, kiddo. I am feeling all bestial and mighty myself right now. It's time to take this to the next level."

Rebecca matched his raw, silky tones as she said, "Only if you promise not to roar when…."

They were through the door and into their bedroom, softly closing the door.

Jürgen was next to retire.

"I wish you goodnight and sweet dreams, my friends."

He walked past them into the small living room. He opened the sheets and blankets on the divan while tossing one of the pillows to the end.

Skylar and Leonnatus finished their conversation and headed inside to the second bedroom. As they passed the German, Skylar stopped, and Leonnatus turned in the doorway. Jürgen looked up from his bed preparations.

Skylar took the hand of the man and led him into the bedroom. Leonnatus closed the door.

***

"Come back to bed, Beautiful."

"Mmm…"

Mark propped up on one arm and looked at the woman standing in the window. The desert moonlight caressed the contours of her naked body.

"Something, I don't know what. Otherworldly and mysterious… I can feel it in the night air."

"You sound like Skylar."

"Mark, I am rarely afraid, but this makes me wonder. What forces are at play here?"

Mark got up and walked across the dark bedroom to take his woman in his strong arms, nuzzling her back and shoulders. Their play had been intense, and now the soft and romantic energies continued to swirl around them.

"I got you, Beautiful. We have been up against tougher outfits than this. What is it? Ancient curses? You know that's bullshit."

She turned to face him.

"I hate that we have no Wifi. I have this odd premonition that all is not well back home."

Mark continued his exploring caresses and tastes, pausing to say, "And I cannot connect with the other woman in my life, my goddess, Eris."

She ignored his attempt at levity and said, "I am serious, Mark. I can't seem to get through to Micah, and while I think the real danger has followed us here, I cannot shake the feeling that the Rising Dawn is working more terror back in the States. Aliyev's reach is very far and terrible."

"And we're the ones who will stop him. Jürges told me tonight that he has been getting some of Eris' information to the top guys and gals in INTERPOL and their partner nations. That was before we lost the Aeolus. Hopefully, we are not the only fighters in the resistance."

"The key is the treasures of the Lost Museum. Without them, crazy guy loses his hardon for world conquest."

"Mmm... so aptly put, Beautiful."

They both looked into the desert night, moving their bodies closer and saying nothing for a while. A perfect Yin and Yang, Mark's body was hard and insistent, Rebecca's warm and inviting.

Mark began to softly hum as they held each other. He said, "Rebecca, have I ever told you my favorite movie when I was a kid? It still is... an oldie but a goodie."

"Teenage Mutant Ninja Turtles Save the World?"

He grunted and nipped an earlobe.

"Wrong. I'm sorry, but thank you for playing."

"What?"

"Do not make fun. Before my dad died, I remember he took me to see it, and then when I was nine, he got me the videotape. I don't think I ever told anyone this."

He kissed him and said, "Tell me, Darling."

"Pinocchio."

"Oh, Mark. How very wonderful. Why?"

"I dunno. Little dude wants to be real, you know? Authentic. And life beats the crap out of him, but he keeps on believing."

"Yes, I remember. The wooden boy goes up against the bad guys and even rescues his father by getting swallowed by a whale."

"Kiddo won't let go of his dream. And that little green dude.... "

"Jiminy Cricket."

"The very one, Beautiful. Jiminy tells the kid that stars have the power to make your wish come true. All you have you do is believe."

They began to sing softly to each other. "Makes no difference who you are... If your heart is in your dream... When you wish upon a star...."

Rebecca reached up and grabbed the red-gold of his hair, now growing out of his military buzz. She nuzzled the scruff of his handsome face. They exchanged soft and tender kisses and turned back together to search the skies. Mark sang one more phrase as Rebecca pointed upward into the velvet night.

"Anything your heart desires will come to you...."

***

Why would someone be singing in the middle of the night?

Leonnatus stood at the window. He shivered in the fresh night air. Behind him, on the bed, a slumbering Jürgen turned into the arms of a likewise sleeping Skylar.

Not jealous, nope. Something weird, however. This sex-up was fun, but Skylar and I seem to have a deep connection. No, this is from the outside. It's the feeling that something primal and disastrous is about to arrive that keeps me awake.

He turned back to the view of the moon and the starry night sky. He felt strong hands on his hips and the wet mouth caressing his lower back and the upper part of his glutes.

Without turning, Leonnatus whispered softly, "Agent Jürgen, you are indeed a horny German, but my Skylar will...."

The drooling mouth-play ceased momentarily and was replaced by a low growl of fake annoyance. When the game of lust continued, it was more forceful, and the wet mouth moved up the young man's back. Insistent hands now on the boy's shoulders, Leonnatus moaned and said, "Izemrasen, how did you get in here? Did you bring your brother?"

The frustrated growl was a bit louder this time, and a moist tongue followed the sound into the boy's ear.

Skylar twisted his young captive's body so their faces met and took a deep, passionate kiss, pulling the young body against his.

"Why do you tease your Skylar? Is it because you are a depraved and very bad pupil who cannot resist tormenting his *Almuharib Majstir?* This must be corrected."

Leonnatus turned back to the window and folded his arms on the ledge. He said softly, "You know, I never did tell you my dream." Skylar put his arms around the young man so that his hands rested on the windowsill, his head beside the boy's, the front of his body pressed to Leonnatus' back.

He spoke softly.

"Yes, the nightmare that left you screaming."

"We were in an underground cavern together. The air alternated from clear to smokey, but it was a large burial chamber. Around us, I could hear a whooshing of the wind that seemed to enter from somewhere. Off in the distance of the room, between ancient grave monuments, were three or four figures who, despite my reluctance, seemed to draw us forward.

"We both moved as if we were partially paralyzed and as we approached, one person, I seem to think he was the most powerful one, pointed to the ground. Skyler, it opened up before us. All I could see was boiling darkness, which seemed to climb up into the mausoleum. You pushed me to the side and tried to attack the villains, but the powerful demon would not be overcome. This evil one held up a scale, and his head transformed into that of the Jackel god, Anubis. He shouted, 'Behold the circled star' and pushed you into its depths.

"That is when I woke up."

Skylar spoke words of assurance as he ran his palm over the boy's head.

"We have been in a few burial chambers this trip and have faced some very dangerous evil-doers. Those who pursue us are the hidden figures in your dream that intend to do us harm. The pit is *Duat*, the underworld where the dead travel to be judged. As you know, that is the job of Anubis, who weighs the soul at the final judgment. The circled star is the hieroglyph for the abode of the dead."

"Death, judgment, and eternal damnation...."

The young man shivered against his love and drew the big man's arms more tightly around him.

"There is another star in our story, Leonnatus."

"Regulus?"

"No, my boy, the Constellation Leo has set this evening. Look at the star formation that sits like the letter 'J' just above the horizon, there."

"Is that Mars at the center, red and large?

"No, it is a star. See how it twinkles? It is the great star Antares, the heart of the scorpion. Antares shines on us."

"More death."

"On the contrary, the constellation Scorpio is associated with our friend, the goddess Selket, the great protectress."

He turned the boy to kiss him and added, "You have nothing to fear, Leo."

Leonnatus smiled and continued the kiss and hug up. He dropped his hands and attempted to tickle his big man, stepping away. Skylar would have none of it.

"No, boy. This is where we began with your teasing and bad behavior. Perhaps obedience lessons are in order, yes?"

Now entirely in the arms of his fascinating man, Leonnatus begged to be made to obey and be respectful as he felt the hardness between them. The excitement and the passion of the moment caught them both in that place where words develop into utterances of craving, and actions become ways to satisfy lustful appetites.

Throughout, and primarily due to Skylar's hand over the lad's mouth, they never awakened the very satiated and sleeping Jürgen.

Thomas Paul Severino

Chapter Fifty-Four: Into the Underworld
The Temple of The Oracle, Qesm Siwa, Egypt

"C'mere, you."

Mark put Leonnatus in a tight hold, his arms wrapped around the young man's head, bending him into his left armpit and knuckling his skull.

Skylar stood nearby, his arms folded, his face expressionless.

"Listen up, digger boy, If you show me one more fucking tomb, and no Alexander, I am gonna have to whip your ass good."

He attempted a wink at the Egyptian but ended up quickly, ass down, in the dirt. Leonnatus had broken the hold with a countermove that surprised the unsuspecting Mark. The novice fighter stood above the startled journalist and hit his stance.

"Holy shit, this kid learns fast."

Mark rolled back, laughing. Skylar patted his protégé's back as the lad attempted to shake off the redness that filled his face.

Mark did a kip-up and landed on his feet. Leonnatus smiled and faked an attack move, but Mark laughed, distracted the boy by pointing to something not there, and got the kid in a hammerlock, friendly but firm.

"Feeling all ballsy now, kiddo?"

"Ouch. You must be patient, Mr. Mark. Alexander has waited for us for nearly 3000 years. We must approach him with patience. This is research. We accomplish things slowly in academia."

Mark dropped the hold and lightly fist-pounded the young archaeologist.

Rebecca adjusted her sunglasses and said, "All those tombs in the Mountain of the Dead were interesting, Darling, but I find myself agreeing with Mark. And the sun is so hot. Mountain climbing-- seriously, gentlemen?"

Leonnatus shook off the pesky Mark and said, "Yes, yes, up there. The Temple of the Oracle of the God, Amun Ra, or, as he was known by Alexander and the Macedonians, Zeus Amun."

They were approached by a rather wizened figure leaning on a walking stick, slightly more prominent than she. The head of the staff was coiled into a thick spiral of gnarled wood. She waved them forward and silently led them in the direction of the mountain-top ruin.

The group climbed the high outcropping that rose above Qesm Siwa, crowned by a plateau on which stood a massive complex of mudbrick, the abandoned village of Aghurmi. Their guide, Zahrat Alsahra', despite her 80-something years, used her walking stick to climb the steep slope with its intermittent stairs up to the ruined village. She moved with the swiftness of a mountain sheep and spoke over her shoulder.

"In 1926, my family and all who lived in this village fled, never to return. Heavy rainstorms washed out mud structures and made the place unliveable. You can still see what is left of the mosque and its tall minaret there rising above the village gate. Some of the Amazigh have returned in recent years, but not many."

The old Berber woman stopped and turned around as they mounted up into the courtyard of the Temple of Amun, its limestone and marble shining in the morning sun. The temple sat in the northwest corner of a flat space just inside the gate. Its walls edged near the rock cliff and were in danger of falling into the valley below. Rubble from the ruined houses surrounded the temple area.

The wind tossed the older woman's cotton robes as she raised two fingers of her right hand and addressed Rebecca, Mark, Skylar, and Leonnatus in a speech she had recited many times over many years. She pointed to the east, saying in a practiced voice, "In the days of the Old Kingdom, two priestesses, black they were, were banished from the sacred city of Thebes in the east along the Nile. One crossed the desert to here and became the Oracle of Amun Ra. The other did the same thing in Greece.

"Many came to her over the years for advice, for she was able to see into the future. For thousands of years, the Sybil of Amun Ra and her descendants were consulted by the small and the great, the powerful and the powerless, whenever important decisions were to be made."

She pointed to Leonnatus.

"You, you are Greek, no?"

"Yes, mother, Macedonian."

"Humph."

Zahrat Alsahra' shook her finger at the boy and then pointed through the gates into the first hall of the Temple.

"The proud Greeks, usurpers of the Sacred Land. Humph. They could not even safeguard their dead king. They put his journey to the afterlife in danger time and time again. Bastards."

"And you."

She pointed to Skylar.

"I am Egyptian."

She examined him carefully and took his hands, turning them over as she inspected them. Zahrat Alsahra' looked into his dark eyes and touched his long, black hair as it was lifted by the wind.

"No, no. Your blood is Amazigh. Tell the truth. But you are not Oasis Berber, not Siwi, yes?"

Skylar smiled and said, "You are correct, my mother."

Almost unconsciously, Leonnatus touched his shoulder.

Zahrat Alsahra' looked at the two men and smiled.

Rebecca glanced at Mark and hid a smile.

This woman is quite a character.

"The god was here long before the coming of the Great King, long before. Amun Ra spoke through the Oracle and guided the ways of men. The son of Zeus Amun confirmed his divinity here, in this place, when the god spoke and claimed him as his son and master of the world."

Rebecca did an aside.

"Mark, our boy Jürgen this morning... is he meeting us here?"

"Far as I know. Had to go into town and meet with his INTERPOL posse on the downing of the plane. I thought he'd be pretty bummed out about meeting with the big shots, but he seemed very upbeat this morning."

"All those spa treatments yesterday. Must have made him a new man."

"Yeah, OK, right. That or...."

Mark, seeking a clue to what he suspected were night revelries, looked over at Skylar and Leonnatus. They were listening attentively to Zahrat Alsahra' and her description of the Temple and its precincts. He raised his Ray-Bans to take in the vast sweep of the land, spread out to the horizon, golden desert sands, barren salt lakes, and oases fringed with date palms. As the breeze picked up, a flock of white birds spiraled in the blazing sun.

The Siwi woman raised her voice.

"Come, look upon the old gods. They have waited thousands of years for you."

They passed through the first doorway flanked by fluted columns. The interior was an open space with an entrance at the far end. They moved through it into the second atrium and stood before three doors. The middle one led to the sanctuary, flanked by a narrow corridor to the right and a larger chamber to the left. Through the open roof of this inner sanctum, the sun illuminated the crumbling wall paintings.

Among the images, the Pharoah of Egypt and the Lybian Governor of Siwa each made offerings to eight gods. The paintings were recognizable but in disrepair. Zahrat Alsahra' raised a palm up in the direction of the Egyptian archaeologist and pointed to each of the deities as she pointed with her walking stick. He named them.

As she came to the last one, she stopped, lowered her cane, and took Rebecca by the hand. The woman's expression was one of mystery and wonder as she backed Rebecca near the image of one of the goddesses.

Skylar said. "Apparently, our host believes you to resemble Amun's consort, Amenre."

Rebecca looked over her shoulder at the ruin and mused, "How many look-alikes am I gonna get on this trip, Darlings?" She struck a pose resembling the deities around her, shoulders in full view, hips at three-quarters, and legs turned in profile.

Mark said, "Nailed it. This is the land of mystery, Beautiful. Strange and wondrous beauty."

The old Siwi woman slapped Mark's chest three times while smiling, nodding, and pointing to the living goddess. Zahrat's raised eyebrows and leering expression seemed to suggest how fortunate he was to consort with such a mythic beauty.

Skylar stepped forward and spoke softly to the woman. He led her back into the first hall. While the others explored the walls and the openings of the inner chambers, Skylar spoke softly to Zahrat Alsahra' near the southwestern corner of the first hall, just inside the doorway.

When Skylar removed his shirt and turned his back to the woman, they suspected something important was happening and crossed the space to the Egyptian and the Siwi, who tried to hide her shock by covering her mouth.

As they approached and stood closer, Rebecca heard their guide say, "You are the Hidden One. I see that. But how did you know our secret?"

"The wildflowers, Mother. Strewn here on the floor in this corner. An appropriate offering to the god would have had its place, there in the sanctuary."

Zahrat Alsahra' looked from face to face. She inserted the head of her walking stick into an aperture on the western wall. And told Skylar to twist the pole. As the stone partition opened inward and the recess revealed itself, the old Berber warned, "Do not take him from us."

***

Leonnatus attempted to hand out flashlights, but the older woman brought a fireplace igniter from the folds of her robes. She touched its flame to the tops of sconces as they descended the stairs to the crypt. As

Zahrat Alsahra' walked around the vast underground chamber, the lights of the wall torches revealed amazing things.

They encountered a gold and lapis-eyed statue of the scorpion-crowned goddess, Selket, with arms spread wide as they came off the lower landing. Her expression was serene but filled with a powerful warning. She guarded the vast crypt against intrusion. Those who entered this underground tomb had to account first to her.

Behind the golden goddess, a carved canopic shrine mounted on a sledge held the vital organs of the deceased, the liver, intestines, lungs, and stomach.

Rebecca mused, "The ancients left the heart inside the body during the embalming. It was thought to embody the soul, and so it was left undisturbed."

The inscribed texts covering the shrine called on four goddesses, Isis, Nephthys, Neith, and Selket, to wrap their protective arms around the remains of the dead monarch and tell of his greatness.

Skylar read from one panel, "Here it says, 'I have come to be your protection. I have bound your head and your limbs for you. I have smitten your enemies beneath you for you and given you your head, eternally. O Divine Isis, extend your protection about the King of Upper and Lower Egypt, the Divine Son of Zeus Amun.' It is an incantation from the Book of the Dead."

Beyond were many splendid grave objects that indicated the departed was a man of the highest stature, furniture, weapons, conveyances, armor, and statues of the Pharoah. One stone image showed a youthful king in a pharaonic pose. In one outstretched palm, he held out a small rendering of the winged Maat, the goddess of truth. At the other end of the chamber was a statue of a handsome young man in a Greek chiton holding the reins of a rearing stallion. The sculpture was in the style of the marble figures of classical Greece, almost out of place among the designs from Ancient Egypt.

Leonnatus murmured, "The boy Alexander tames Bucephalus, one of the most famous horses of antiquity. This is an astonishing piece."

Rebecca said, "I will wager that this was done by Lysippos, personal sculptor to Alexander the Great. He was the only artist the king saw fit to represent him."

On the walls, the tomb paintings were a synergistic blend of the Egyptian and Hellenistic art styles. Images and inscriptions told of the conqueror's victories over Persians, the hosts of Asia, and the hordes of Egyptians. In one rendering, an elephant bore down on the warrior king, astride his horse and wearing the ram's head above golden curls. The style was from the late Ptolemaic period.

To the sides were chests of scrolls, hundreds of them. Here were Library holdings believed to have been lost forever. Because of the dryness of the air, the absence of sunlight, and no evidence of disturbance by grave robbers or devotees, the tomb's contents, including the scrolls, appeared to be in good condition.

Zahrat Alsahra' stood in the shadows near the head of the crypt. She motioned for them. The recess was a few steps higher, and its walls rounded. Dominating the space was a two-story structure, a caisson covered by an elaborate canopy on sturdy wheels. The entire funeral wagon was carved with lacquered scenes from a conquest that stretched across the ancient world. Its metal appointments were gold.

The underside of the canopy had been painted a dark blue. An arrangement of jewels and precious stones was embedded in the ceiling of the funeral cart. For all eternity, the remains of the deathless warrior lay face-up beneath the stars of the constellation Leo.

Behind the conveyance, a bearded Zeus Amun dominated the paintings on the center of the apse, depicted as Pharoah and adorned with the sacred ram's horns. Behind him, the sun reached down from heaven with rays that ended in tiny, caressing hands on the figure of a one-eyed Macedonian king in a war chariot and an imperious woman cavorting with snakes. Attendant gods and goddesses and their cartouches were everywhere.

Commanding the dias, in the center of the beautiful, ancient hearse, was a seven-foot rock crystal and gold sarcophagus containing the body of Alexander the Great.

Chapter Fifty-Five: Nu Rising
Ram Cay, The Bahamas

The Sikorsky MH-60T Jayhawk had a beam on the fleeing yacht. The twin-engine, medium-range helicopter operated by the United States Coast Guard carried Special Agent Mary Chaffee and two FBI colleagues. Below, a Legend-class offshore patrol vessel, the HMS Valiant, in the service of the Royal Bahamas Defense Force, made straight for the errant *Nephthys.*

Mary said, "Just try to stay out of the way, Hud. Do not make me regret that you are part of this search and rescue mission. Our partnership with Her Majesty's Government of the Bahamas does not allow me to bend the rules, but...."

"Shortcut, Special Agent. I can identify the bastards who kidnapped Micah. If we get them."

"When we get them."

Mary looked at the lights of the boats below as they raced through the night waters in the direction of Ram Cay, part of the Bahamas' Berry Islands. The district counted about 30 islands and more than 100 cays, small isles. Most of the territory was uninhabited.

In the light of the full moon, the Nephthys slid between the slivers of tropical isles covered with palm trees and fringed with ghostly white beaches. The yacht navigated the deep channels and avoided the shoals. The patrol boat and the Jayhawk triangulated with the ship, so they never lost her. Just beyond, a signal light from a massive compound on Ram Cay sliced through the night. Trees surrounding the large island mansion danced manically as the winds picked up.

"Gunfire, Captain, take her up."

A barrage of sparks pierced the night coming from the black yacht, overtaken by the HMS Valiant. At the last minute, in a desperate move, the Nephthys swerved out of the direction of the private island and headed for open waters. The searchlight and all exterior lights went out on Ram Cay, and a plane left its airport, taking a southwesterly course.

"Agent Chaffee, we have a small aircraft leaving Ram Cay and headed in the direction of Cuba. The United States Coast Guard and the Royal Bahamas Defense Force have been notified."

Below, the Nephthys rounded another small island and doubled back, apparently choosing to fight. More massive blasts roared from her decks, rocket launchers, and sniper rifles.

It seemed at this time that the sea and the wind conspired together with some primordial source of power. Clouds seemed to thicken and cover the waning moon, obscuring the starlight. Now, it appeared that the orb glowed behind a white veil, its contours blurred and jagged, like a smudge of cremation ash on the black pall of the sky.

Below, it was as if the ocean sat back on its haunches, the wind piling up the waters on the horizon like a panther ready to pounce. The evil craft and its pursuant vessel raced forward toward a wall of black water.

"Rogue wave off her starboard. Holy shit, look at that!"

The ocean rose up beneath the death ship, carrying the yacht high in the air. The Nephthys rocked in the palm of the hand of the sea and capsized as the mass of water beneath her threw her off into the air. She twisted in the descent, through the night air, and slammed upside down into the waiting waters below. The rogue wave slapped down upon the boat, crushing her in a mass of white foam and dark, blue-black water.

An astonished voice rang out in the hold of the chopper, "Agent Chaffee, I have never in my days seen...."

The Valiant met the turmoil bow first, climbing a smaller peak of the rise and cresting only to slide steeply down the wave's trough. As she rode the rocking seas, the patrol boat stayed afloat despite large waves washing over her deck. The Valiant came about in search of the remains of the doomed yacht.

Immediately, the moon shook off her opaque reverie and shed a brighter light on the sea below. The heavy winds battering the Jayhawk seemed to die as the atmospheric inversion returned, calming the air and ocean waters. In the aircraft, Special Agent Chaffee pointed and yelled, "Down."

The descending helicopter caught one person in its searchlights clinging to debris as it dropped over the wreck. Hudson Ch'en dashed to the open door of the Sikorsky Search and Rescue craft and dove into the sea.

Chapter Fifty-Six: Geb Laughs

The Temple of The Oracle, Siwa, Egypt

"All the principals gathered in one place. Our efforts to track you seem to have paid off. And now, shall we make a fitting and very convenient ending to our adventure?"

The speaker pushed an elderly prisoner to the floor. The torchlight revealed Dr. Zahra el-Saddik. She looked up at the squad of pointed assault weapons and handguns. Bodyguards and trained assassins kept emerging into the crypt from the access stairway.

"Prisoners, prisoners, prisoners. What to do with all these captives? Miriam, have you a suggestion?"

"Eliminate them."

A youthful voice came from the shadows, "No, father. Let us take what we came for and leave them behind."

"Ahhh, the treasure. Come, my son, look upon your ancestor. This is why I allowed you to accompany us. Soon, you will be Master of the World as he was. You have come of age. Claim your destiny."

They climbed the steps up to the catafalque and mounted the wheeled barge to stand next to the sarcophagus. Through the glass, the body of Alexander was as fresh and alive as those who viewed his remains. The corpse was a testament to the expertise of the ancient Egyptian embalmers and the design of the air-tight coffin that cradled the remains of the Son of Zeus.

The corpse lay in an airless chamber of the most beautiful rock crystal. Four falcons of gold carried the corners of the sarcophagus on their backs and seemed to be lifting it into the air. In the torchlight, the spectacular coffin and its occupant seemed to shimmer with an interior light.

In death, Alexander the Great appeared to be asleep in his shining armor. His shield, standing on edge, was held against his left hip next to his sheathed sword. The golden breastplate over leather and linen outer garments was fashioned to display the idealized muscles of a warrior's chest and abdomen. In the center was the head of the Lion of Macedonia.

Matching gold greaves and forearm guards completed the armor, along with sturdy metal and leather sandals.

Lustrous blond locks framed his handsome face and dropped to just below the neck. The lips of the warrior king seemed to hold their own moisture as if a magical kiss would wake the young beauty from his eternal sleep. He wore no helmet. On top of the glass coffin, in the center, was a gleaming artifact, a lifesized ram's head of gold.

Farid Haydar Aliyev, his lieutenants, and his son drew near. It seemed that as the cohort approached, the burial chamber rumbled softly. The oligarch stretched his arms wide before the coffin and said, "This will complete our claim to the divine power of the New Empire. Nations will bow down to us as they did to him. Now we are unstoppable."

The members of Aliyev's entourage of intimates were speechless as they felt the impact of the moment. Miriam Kamerov reached for the hand of the insane man, but he shook her off. Mark, Skylar, Rebecca, and Leonnatus were transfixed by the embracing evil. Bodyguards began to place the three men in handcuffs.

As the moment of Aliyev's triumph rose to its height, a new voice rang out in the underground chamber.

"You will drop your weapons, release these people, and come away from the coffin."

Jürgen Mathias stepped from the doorway into the catacomb.

Aliyev laughed. "Ah, the idiot German. Did you bring your Egyptian friends? Such hopeless inferiors."

He turned on the dias and waved his arms.

"The world is mine, you hopeless fools. Even now, the nations of the east are negotiating with the armies of the Rising Dawn. Egypt will have no recourse other than to comply. The Last Caliphate has arrived. All that remains is for the reincarnated Alexander to take the throne of his new empire."

Aliyev's last words were a cry of victory. He laughed again and pointed to the INTERPOL commander. He spat, "You are not even armed, you hopeless degenerate. I will annihilate you and your pitiable Lermontov."

"No. You are correct, Sir. I am not armed, but they are."

Behind Jürgen Mathias, one by one, fifteen armed men and women of the al-Mahdi clan stepped into the space and confronted the agents of the Rising Dawn. One of the members of the holy band released Mark, Leonnatus, and Skylar. The Egyptian embraced his cousin and then reached for Leonnatus. Alexei Aliyev looked on with interest.

The last two new arrivals were an older man and a young woman, Muhammad Nefer and Chione al-Mahdi.

Rebecca said, "Only the Mahdi can defeat *al-Dajjal*, the false Messiah, and they are here." She attempted a look of victory.

Farid Haydar Aliyev laughed bitterly as Miriam Kamarov pulled a handgun from her jacket. The insane man sneered, "Who, you ignorant bitch? Who is the Hidden Imam who will destroy me? Him? He is old and useless."

The chamber groaned again. It felt as if the earth beneath their feet was stirring.

"Or that one?"

He laughed again as he pointed to Skylar.

"He is no Messiah. He is a godless sodomite, a degenerate who will suffer the curse of God. This is some eschatological battle you have set up, Mr. al-Mahdi, and Ms. Quinto. Ridiculous and impotent."

He smirked and gestured to his thugs at a standoff with God's anointed.

"So, it is my forces against yours."

The oligarch turned, reached forward, and lifted the ram's head, sacred to Amun Ra. He held the fetish before him.

"I am unlimited and relentless. It is I who am God's favorite and destined to rule the world in his name. I am the chosen one."

His final diatribe only lasted a few seconds. Like a shock wave from the center of the earth, a bolt of energy shot up from the depths and rocked the chamber. Fine dust fell from the ceiling. The Mahdi took this opportunity to forcefully disarm Aliyev's militia. It appeared that no one was injured in either the earthquake or the confrontation. And then...

The granite statue of Alexander the Great holding the Goddess of Truth rocked and then fell on Alexei Aliyev, pinning the boy underneath.

Skylar, Muhammad Nefer, and three of Aliyev's bodyguards scrambled to use a fallen roof beam to lift the massive sculpture from the boy. As the dust settled, Mark instantly checked Alexei's vitals and began CPR.

At this point, the women took over to finish the clash of good and evil.

Zahrat Alsahra' clobbered Miriam Karimov with her walking staff as the evil woman stood close to Farid Haydar Aliyev. The Russian woman fell back on her butt, rubbing her head and fighting for consciousness. Her gun skitted along the floor.

Zahra el-Saddik, with strength and determination, took the golden ram's helmet of Amun Ra from the False Messiah.

"This is over, Aliyev. Go to your son."

She handed the treasure to the Siwi woman, who stepped up to the catafalque and placed it back on the glass and gold coffin.

Rebecca took Chione by the hand and quickly brought her close to her Father. Looking into the frightened eyes of the young woman, she spoke.

"Chione, you know it is you. In some way, you have always known it. You are the Hidden Imam. Do what has to be done to bring an end to this."

The young woman looked at her father but addressed Rebecca.

"What are you saying? A woman and a disabled person. How can..."

Rebecca took Chione by the shoulders and looked into her eyes. She addressed her passionate words to both father and daughter.

"Chione, the holy books of many faiths proclaim that the God of the Scriptures is a God of surprises."

She looked up at Muhannad Nefer.

"Just when you think you know where God is. You are surprised to find God in the unexpected, the weak, the outcast, and the powerless-- Ruth, Fatima, Deborah, Rachel, and Rebecca, the poor ones rejected by the world."

She pointed to Mark, who was saying, "No pulse."

"It has always been you, Chione."

Skylar looked at his father and sister with expectation. Behind them, Farid Haydar Aliyev looked on in frozen horror.

The *pater familias* of the Mahdi clan looked at his son and daughter through tears.

"Go, both of you, and God be with you."

Mark stopped the CPR, and Skylar lifted the boy's broken body and placed it on the lap of his sister, who sat on the steps of the dias. Chione wrapped the unconscious boy in her arms and closed her eyes.

Everyone in the chamber was motionless and focused on the Pieta-like couple, woman and boy, in the center of the enormous shrine. Some knelt and bowed their heads. After what seemed like endless moments, the hall rocked softly one last time.

Aliyev, deeply crushed in spirit, approached. All his insane rhetoric was gone. He dropped to his knees.

The boy slowly opened his eyes.

Thomas Paul Severino

Epilogue: A Phone Call to San Francisco
The Island of Corfu

"What is this, Darlings? A male swimwear model convention? You know how much I adore the muscled derriere of a hot man."

Zahra el-Saddik, sitting with Rebecca in the cabana, chuckled at her friend's remarks.

Mark and Skylar were sparing on crystalline, white beach sand, tossing each other back and forth in the Ionian sunshine. Every so often, Jürgen and Leonnatus would jump in and try a move under the supervision of their master instructors. All four men concentrated on the fight and paid little attention to the woman in the deep blue One-Piece.

Rebecca sat in a lounge chair, sipping an ouzo-peponi martini beneath an oversized picture hat and behind large Maria Callas sunglasses. She spoke on her mobile phone.

"Kayne Darling, I am watching all this hot, sweating man muscle a few feet away in the skimpiest of fabric, and they do not even know that I am here. And, Darling, I look fabulous."

"Happens to the best of us, my girl, when the sexy men are not interested, those of us who appreciate their beauty despair."

"How is Nick?"

"I am not sure, to be honest. We are hopeful at this time, however. Recovery takes time. You must come to San Francisco for a visit."

"Yes, Kayne. Time heals all. It will take a while. So, Darling, the wrap-up. Want to hear more?"

"Absolutely,"

Rebecca waved to the scrapping men, sipped her drink, and summarized.

"Kayne, I sometimes think my life is straight out of a Stan Lee Marvel Comics script. You know, final violent confrontation, destroying cities, planets, bad guys, and a few of the good ones. Male, male, male, male, male-- even the women are men."

"You mean lesbians?"

"No, Darling, I mean violent and aggressive. You know, all of those traits that keep most members of your sex on the level of Neanderthals."

"Your stereotypes are showing, my girl."

"Kayne Sorenson, you know what I mean. Anyway, the boy is healed by the nurturing care of a woman, a superwoman, if one must-- beloved of God and very likely God's agent. No last man standing, bullets flying, and buildings collapsing. To mimic Mark, 'I fucking love it,' Kayne."

"Such intelligence, beauty, and strength of character, all in one adorable and very hip woman. Mark is so fortunate."

"Hold that thought. I am handing Mark the phone. Perhaps if you sing my praises, he will lay off the martial arts and take me back to our bungalow for some afternoon romance."

"I would love to be the agent for your next deflowering, my girl, but pimping you out was never my forte. Besides, an adventure of my own just demanded my immediate attention. I am afraid I need to ring off.

"OK, my love to Nick and to you, Kayne."

"Take naked pictures of your man and send them to my brother, Kick in Colorado. You know how he lusts after...."

She interrupted.

"Not happening. Bye, Darling."

"Love you too."

Mark flopped on the lounge chair next to her. He took a gulp of her drink. He dripped sweat and breathed hard.

"Hey, Beautiful, you love me?"

"Insanely, but not when you steal my cocktail."

She grabbed it back.

Mark caught the attention of a passing server and said, "Gimmie four of these and some bottles of water, handsome." He made a circular motion with his right forefinger, indicating everyone on Team Rebecca. The three other guys came over to the breezy cabana on the beautiful Ionian beach and flopped down.

Skylar dropped into the sand and lay back with his head on Leonnatus' lap. The young man commented, "Am I getting the hang of it, Master? The martial arts, I mean?"

Skylar popped open a water bottle and poured some over his head and upper body. He said, "You are coming along exceptionally well, Doctor Gianopolis."

Rebecca raised her cocktail and called out, "Oh, yes... Here's to our brand new Ph.D. I understand the defense at the Aristotelian University in Thessaloniki went exceptionally well."

Zahra el-Saddik looked up from her needlework and said, "This one is going to be a valued addition to the field, I have no doubt."

"Yes. The committee was very impressed, and I will say that I owe a lot to this gentleman. He perfected my defense with his expertise in the discipline. I had a new sense of being capable, adequate, and self-worthy when facing the committee. I am very sure it had to do with our adventure and the troubles we faced."

The Egyptian said in his smooth baritone, "We are an excellent team, my Leo. Or must I now call you Doctor Gianopolis?"

The young academic bent over his man and nuzzled his ear. He whispered sweet and naughty words.

Mark interjected, "So, boy wonder. I got my story, but I cannot use most of it. I mean, talk about a media boner kill. What the fuck?"

"No, no, Mister Gadarn, Zahrat Alsahra' made it clear that the Lost Museum must remain a secret. No LiDAR scans have ever been made of the catacomb of Alexander the Great because the Matrouh Governate, which oversees Siwa, will not authorize an intrusion in the area. Many Amazigh people would like to keep the artifacts *in situ* and private, treated only with the highest respect."

Zahra added, "It is, after all, a burial site. Some Amazigh believe that the scrolls and the grave goods belong to the nation and the world. Consequently, talks have begun with the Egyptian Ministry of Antiquities on the preservation of the site."

Jürgen asked, "I do not know how to ask this, but some aspects of what happened in the crypt have caused me a great amount of wonder-- the ram's head and the earthquake tremors."

Skylar looked off toward the Ionian Sea, beginning to lift small tips of white in the onshore breeze.

"Historically, the Oracle of Amun Ra at Siwa spoke through contact with a sacred object. In ancient times, the Oracle's priestess wore a large jewel, and through it, she channeled the god. After Alexander came to the Oasis, the holy object was the golden ram's head, sacred to the god Amun Ra. If an evildoer touched the sacred object, they would bring down the wrath of the gods. Hence the catastrophe in the cavern when the earth god, Geb laughed, and the ground shook."

"I do not know if I believe that."

"Jürgen, my friend, as a scientist, the more I discover about the universe, the more I have come to understand that there are dimensions of life and death that surpass the grasp of our intelligence-- the unexplained, like love. Truth cannot be discovered by reasoning on the evidence of scientific data alone. Of this, I have no doubt."

Jürgen took an empty chair and pressed the issue. "Your sister... that boy... his bones were broken. Marko got no heartbeat. Yet, he walked out of that underground chamber. I refuse to believe that she was the conduit of some divine power, God's instrument."

Rebecca said, "I remember the story of the man born blind from the Bible. My mother used to read them to me when I was a child.

"So, Jesus heals this guy who had been blind all his life, and the poor man sees for the first time. Jesus' detractors seek out the guy and ask him if he believes Jesus is the Messiah. The man said to them, 'I don't know. I only know that I once was blind, and now I can see.' I guess I am among those who are ready to step into the unknown."

Skylar said, "So much of this life requires a willingness to trust what the eye cannot see or the intellect cannot fully comprehend. Coincidentally, my sister Chione and my father are at the European Medical Center in Brussels, investigating the stem cell treatment possibilities today. On behalf of Leo and my family, I thank you, Jürgen Mathias."

He jumped up, hugged the man, and flopped back on the sand, this time behind his Leo, pulling the baby Ph.D. to his chest.

"Damn, girl, you are hard to find. Corfu, seriously? I had to call in all my favors with our European friends."

"Mary, so good to see you, and in beach chic to rival my own. I love what you're wearing."

"Needed a vacation, all of us did."

Her escort, an eager young man looking all too familiar, ran in for a hug-up with the freaked-out German agent.

"Unbelievable! Antonio!"

To Rebecca, Mary added, "By any chance, would you want two more additions to this band of irregulars? I recently fished them out of the Caribbean."

She pointed to the couple, making their way across the beach to the cabana...

Hudson Ch'en and Micah Valez.

***

"What?"

He did not answer.

He held her hand to his lips and pulled her closer. Finally, Mark said, "No friends, no bad guys, no staff, no email, no museum exhibits, no deadlines, no adventures-- just you and me in this beautiful location. And you are oh, so very beautiful, Beautiful."

He punctuated each item of his recitation with a kiss to some part of her upper body while working the zipper of her bathing suit. She raised her hair and moaned.

"The 'Do Not Disturb' sign is on the door. Plenty of drink and food, just a call away. No place to go... only you and me, Rebecca... and Mark... Not going to come up for air for many... many... days. No rough stuff... only sweet romance...."

He reached the tattoo at the base of her spine, turned her, and pushed her on her back in front of him, stepping out of his speedo.

Rebecca reached over her head and picked up a letter from the bed.

She looked at the page as he explored. She said, "It's supposed to be covered with rose petals, not business let...."

The words stopped as she spoke them.

"Oh, my God, Mark! '... is pleased to inform you that you are a nominated finalist for this year's Pulitzer Prize for Journalism for your online media series, *Yemen: Nation of Carnage, Nation of Hope.* Your work is being considered as a distinguished example of reporting on international affairs.' This is wonderful. I am so proud of you, Darling."

She reached for him.

He said as he embraced her, entwining her body in his, "My production team deserves a huge amount of credit, but I'd be lying if I didn't say that this means a lot."

Rebecca had begun her own series of kisses, covering the terrain of the body of the sexy warrior journalist.

"And... and...."

"And what, Darling?"

"And I would be a jerk not to admit that you... that we ... are a fantastic team. You allow me to become more than I could ever be without you. Thank you, Rebecca."

She smiled as she gazed into the eyes of the man who held her.

"You are welcome, Darling Mark."

The End

Thomas Paul Severino

Acknowledgments

Many thanks to my husband, Anton S. Wallner, Ph.D., for his help with copy editing and plot suggestions. You are my inspiration and my dearest love.

Thomas Paul Severino

Afterword:

Thank you for reading <u>The Adventures of Rebecca Quinto: The Lost Museum.</u> I hope you enjoyed the tale. Look for the return of Kayne Sorenson and Nick Sechi in <u>The Kayne Sorensen Mysteries: The Evil Genius.</u>

An excerpt from their latest case follows.

Thomas Paul Severino

The Evil Genius

A Kayne Sorenson Mystery

Thomas Paul Severino

Prologue: Burning Mountains

Palkor Baktsang Monastery, Jiang Qu, Tibet

Ten Years Earlier.

When he opened his eyes, he could only see the tall flame of the oil lamp as it seemed to float in the inky gloom close to the bed. Behind the black form of his servant, the room continued in deep darkness, with minor shades of gray leaking through the slats of the window shutters. Small windows in the thick walls rose up three stories toward the very high ceiling held aloft by large, intricate weavings of carved, sturdy beams. Far below, the attendant held the lamp, peeking out of a cloak of gloom as he helped the young man from the bed.

His bedroom was frigid, and he moved quickly from under the thick blankets into the heavy, floor-lengthed robe and lined boots. A wool cap and gloves completed his attire. Later, he would stand naked in the copper bath while this servant and two others cascaded ice-cold mountain water over his body, shocking him into a heightened state of mental, physical, and spiritual awareness.

The seven-year-old seemed to hear a voice in the pre-dawn gloom of the monastery. "Awake! Stand no longer in darkness and ignorance. Assume the mastery held out before you. Take up the power."

The light-bearer led the way to the interior stairway, and the pair ascended to the lookout three stories up. On the terrace above, a metal cage held the logs of a fire that jumped and roared like a trapped beast, whipped into a fiery frenzy by the raw mountain wind. The boy stood close to the brazier and looked out onto the "Roof of the World." The edge of the expanse held no retaining wall. Nothing interfered with the access of the nature spirits who reached out and possessed those who stood before them on this terrace.

The servant stepped back into the darkness beneath the green-tiled overhang and against the monastery's 1000-year-old, light brown walls. He lowered his eyes as a monk crossed from the other side of the open courtyard. The newcomer was a Lama in high regard, a former officer in the Chinese army with the precious government connections needed to keep the monastery open and relatively independent. He bowed before the shivering boy took his hand as together they faced east. Respectfully, at the proper distance, the servant joined the man and the boy. The three surrendered to the unfolding daily ritual of the sunrise while repeating the Mantra of the Ineffable Dawn.

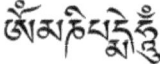

"Turn over to me the radiant light."

The pall of night was leaving the mountains and slowly melting into the west. The rocky giants began to emerge on the horizon in the rays of an insistent light-being that very timidly started to climb up their backs. The backdrop behind the mountains faded to a ghostly gray. Across the sky, the shades of night seemed to slowly pull their midnight robes down from the heights and gather the layers of their funereal drape into the far depths as the advancing light, growing bolder, dispelled the retreating demons into the lower realms.

As he looked out over the landscape, the boy was reminded of the theater sets at his school in a place far, far away. They were wooden, flat, two-dimensional stand-ups, each layer taller than the one in front. The boy shivered in the cold, watching rows of hills and mountains transforming from lofty, less defined suggestions against the sky into colossal peaks. Their attendant foothills are now painted with a pallet of light– sharpening the edges, deepening the canyons, igniting the blowing shrouds of snow.

Even the air was transfigured. Silver satin layers of gray in the atmosphere changed to a pale white, blanketing the lower valleys like smoke. The wind died down, and the breathtaking vista revealed more and more of herself, becoming vivid and three-dimensional.

Slowly, the sky turned pink and orange and subsequently moved through every gradient shade from pale yellow to molten gold. The vanishing hues were not entirely disappearing but instead leaving streaks behind that tinted the snow on the peaks. The sun continued to mount up, at first a sliver, then a crescent, and then a white-hot sky-medallion. Finally, it seemed to stand fully upright, free of the tall eastern mountain range called Sagarmatha in Nepal, Everest everywhere else.

He watched the drama unfold as it did each morning, but never in the same way, always with nuances of color and light. He faced the rising sun, which transformed his face's shadowed, flat features into the long-lashed, almond eyes, full lips, strong jaw, and other attractive features of a handsome boy. He wore his hair shaved to the scalp. Gone was the boyhood shock of straight black hair falling down his neck, continually needing to be pulled away and to the side of his face as he made his way unnoticed in the world, a solitary boy of no significance.

He saw hills and valleys go from purple to green and lush, far below the plateau, which heaved the monastery skyward to rival the tallest peaks. The ribbon of a mountain stream revealed itself in the light of the new day, appearing as an awakening dragon of rushing water, carving the rock and steep pasture lands 1500 feet below, the scales of its waves beginning to flash in the rising sun.

Now, the dawn flooded the entire Himalayan vista before him, even creeping down the eastern walls of the monastery, dispelling the shadows of the overhanging roofs, steep stairways, and gravity-defying terraces. In front of the young Lord of the Lamasery, the mountains blazed in the new light. It appeared as if smoke were streaming high and away from the peaks as snow blew like lost bridal veils, spiraling into the uppermost atmospheric reaches observable from the earth.

The Lama still held the boy by the hand as he stepped forward to the brink of the terrace. The child looked down into the crevasse of awakening life below the ancient monastery of Palkor Baktsang in the shadow of Jiang Qu mountain. Farmers led their cattle out of wooden barns and into the impossibly sloped pastures, passing haystacks shaped like tall, peaked hats. The pealing of bells began in the villages, announcing the end of the night terrors and beseeching the gods for the blessings of the new day. Here and there, a curl of smoke came from a crude chimney.

Chödrön spoke.

"Most esteemed Master, have the visitors left?"

Sapphire-blue eyes sparkling, the Lama faced the child and dropped to one knee.

"Yes, boy. They have been taken down the mountains and will be sent back across the border. I am afraid it did not go well for us. The karma they have created by their stubbornness is very grave indeed."

The youth said, "Will bad things happen, my Master?"

"Not to you, my child. You must go now. Your studies await. It is the destiny of Chödrön to become the most learned boy in the world. Your soul must shine brighter than the sun."

Beckoning the retainer with one hand, the Master turned the child to face the waiting servant.

"Go now, my son. The day is upon us."

Now alone on the terrace, the former general lowered his hood and opened the heavy woolen robe, exposing his chest as he looked up into the sun. He gasped as the light seemed to pierce his body like shards of dazzling ice. Despite being barely able to speak or breathe, he forced himself to shout the words of invocation to the Windhorse and the other gods who lived in the mountains.

ཀླུང་རྟ་གཡོན་

In the crisp, clear air, the sound of his voice came back to him. Slowly, he closed his habit and turned to make his exit back into the monastery. He spoke softly to himself.

"Now, we may begin the work. Fear has vanished like the night terrors. Only victory awaits."